Kennedy Ste
Christian Suspense
Box Set
(Books 1-3)

by Alana Terry

Unplanned

Unplanned

Cover design by Damonza.

www.alanaterry.com

CHAPTER 1

"You look really familiar. Did you go to Harvard?"

Kennedy glanced up from her reading at the red-haired stranger. "I'm there now. Are you?"

"I was." He moved to the seat next to her on the subway and furrowed his brow. "Graduated two years ago. Were we in the same class together maybe? I was a journalism major."

Kennedy had at least another hundred pages of Dostoevsky to finish by the end of the weekend, reading she couldn't get done chitchatting on the T with former journalism students. "No, this is my first year."

He situated his leather case on his lap. It looked heavy. "I swear I've seen you before. Did you grow up around here?"

She lowered her book but kept it open to the right page. "No, I've been in China for the past ten years." She thought about her dad's paranoia, how he still reminded her from a dozen time zones away to stay wary of strangers.

"China?" The journalist leaned forward. "What part?"

Kennedy had lost track of the times she had been asked that by Americans who wouldn't know where to look for Beijing on a map. Sometimes, she took pity and said she lived near the Chinese-North Korean border. Other times, she gave the actual name of the city or province and watched their eyes go blank while they nodded absently. That was usually the tactic she employed when she didn't particularly feel like talking.

"Jilin Province," she answered, picking up her book again.

The man's eyes grew wide. "Really? Were you near Longjing by any chance?"

Kennedy couldn't tell which impressed her more, the journalist's familiarity with the Chinese geography or his accent-free pronunciation. When she left Yanji at summer's end, she couldn't wait to get "home" to the States. There wasn't anything for her to miss back in China. But when she got to campus and saw how different most of her classmates were, she realized how wrong she had been. She actually carved time out of her studies last month to go to the Asian-American Students' first meeting, but she was the only white girl there and never went back.

"We actually lived in Yanji," she told him.

The man nodded in apparent recognition. "I spent a year abroad in Longjing. I'm going back in a few months." He patted the case on his lap. A camera, maybe? "Working on my first international documentary."

The T's automated announcer called out the name of Kennedy's stop. She stood and gave him a wave and a little Americanized half bow. "I've got to go, but good luck with that documentary."

"Yeah, good luck in school," he managed to reply before Kennedy stepped onto the platform and hurried to the escalators, checking the time on her cell phone.

She adjusted her book bag when she emerged from the subway station. It was one of the chilliest days she could remember since arriving back in the States. The air was crisp and invigorating, and she walked with brisk steps. What a strange coincidence to meet someone so familiar with her home region. She thought about mentioning it to her parents when they talked next. Then again, her dad would probably reprove her for divulging even that amount of personal information. Oh well. Kennedy was on her own now, and she couldn't waste her life scurrying from every shadow. Besides, Cambridge was a safe town with a public transportation system that was infinitely easier to grasp than the one back in Yanji. She didn't venture off campus much, but when she did, she never felt insecure. She pitied folks like her dad who lived their lives in constant terror. Why couldn't he be a little more trusting of people?

A burst of leaves fluttered to the pavement, and she quickened her step. She wasn't late, not yet, but she walked fast enough that it would have impressed an Olympic speed-walker. She hadn't seen her childhood pastor in years. His would be the first familiar face she saw since arriving back in the States, and she was anxious to catch up with him.

When Carl emailed her a few weeks ago, she was thrilled at the prospect of getting together. Finding the time to do so was a little more difficult. At least his new center was only a few hops away from campus on the Red Line — a convenient coincidence. *Not coincidence.* She could almost hear Carl correct her in his melodious bass voice that would make James Earl Jones drool with envy. *Providence.*

Either way, she was excited to see him. She still remembered his wife Sandy, her Sunday school teacher for years and years, and the one who let Kennedy practice time and time again on her hair until she perfected the art of French braiding.

She saw the dark green sign for the pregnancy center, felt the smile spread across her face, and swung open the door. A little bell announced her arrival. The room was empty except for the fumes of day-old paint.

"Hello?" She held her breath. Was anybody even here?

"Kennedy!" Carl Lindgren bustled out of a back office, arms extended jovially. "You made it." His voice reverberated off the walls. He grabbed both her arms to draw her in for a rib-crushing bear hug. "You sure have grown since you were little."

"It's great to see you." She didn't have to feign her enthusiasm. The past two months had been a whirlwind of college orientations, lectures, homework, and already two all-nighters. Seeing Carl's face was like stepping into a sauna in the middle of winter. The turpentine vapor intermingled with the scent of his shirt, a combination of barbecue, home-cooking, and after-shave that almost matched her father's.

"When your family left for China, you were such a little thing." He held his hand at the level of his waist. "Now look at you. All grown up, off on your own."

Kennedy laughed. *On her own* meant she lived in a dorm with a theater-major roommate from Alaska, whose entire education — from what Kennedy could tell — consisted of playing computer games, attending rehearsals, and reading an occasional play. Kennedy, on the other hand, was so busy with her pre-med studies and literature classes that she hadn't yet experienced any of the so-called "freedoms" supposed to come with college life.

Carl gave her a quick tour of the new pregnancy center, which in reality was only slightly larger than Kennedy's dorm room. There was a main waiting area still wanting furniture, a back office, and a single room tucked in the corner. "Here's where we do the counseling sessions, and that door there opens to a little bathroom stall."

"It's really nice," Kennedy stated automatically, while her head threatened to lift right off her shoulders because of the fumes.

Carl's cheeks widened into one of his chipmunk-style grins. "Well, it's something. We'll still have to send folks to the Boston campus for ultrasounds until we get a bigger place, but it's a start. Oh." His eyes lit up. "Wait until you see what Sandy rigged up for us."

"How's Sandy doing these days?" Kennedy followed Carl to his little office, the only room with any sort of décor. A golden placard marked the territory as the Executive Director's, and the desk was already cluttered with paperwork and framed pictures of fat, cherubic toddlers. A few finger-painted masterpieces were taped to the wall, along with a crayon drawing on construction paper that read *I love Grandpa.*

Carl shuffled from side to side as he bustled around behind his desk. "You know Sandy," he said with a beam. "She's been as busy as ever getting this place ready to open, doing her grandma thing three days a week, overseeing all of the children's ministry volunteers at St. Margaret's." He narrowed his eyes for a moment, but they didn't lose their playful twinkle. "You know, I haven't seen you at church, young lady."

Kennedy had anticipated the remark and was ready with her excuse. "It's just really busy with schoolwork and all, and it's hard not having a car of my own."

"I won't say anything to your father." Carl winked. "But you know my Sandy. You give her a call on Saturday night, and she'll be sure to find you a ride for Sunday morning. Be sure to get her number from me before you leave. Or if you like taking the T, we're right off the Red Line, Davis stop. Just another fifteen-minute walk from here, really." He frowned. "But maybe you shouldn't be walking that far alone."

Kennedy tried not to roll her eyes. Had he been talking to her dad? She wasn't ready to make any promises about coming to church, but she'd try finding time soon. It had been years since she had participated in an American service. She was a little nervous she might have forgotten something important. The kind of worship she was used to in China was quite different.

"By the way," Carl went on, "Sandy told me specifically to tell you she wants to take you out for coffee sometime soon." He gestured to the entrance of his office. "And if you shut the door, you can see her newest piece of art."

On the wall hung a large, poster-sized calendar. Even though it was obviously made by hand, the printing was impeccable and the lines for each date were as rigid as a surgeon's scalpel. Inside every box were color-coded sections marked *Morning Volunteer*, *Afternoon Volunteer*, and *Hotline Receptionist*. Kennedy almost remarked that Carl's wife must have a lot of extra time on her hands, but then she noticed Sandy was listed as the morning volunteer for all but two days that month and was penned in for half of the afternoon shifts as well.

Carl spread out his hands. "We definitely are asking God for more workers. But the good news is you can have first pick of whatever shift you want to volunteer."

Kennedy pursed her lips together and reminded herself that her job was to keep up her GPA, not to make everyone around her happy. "Yeah, well, I've been thinking since I got your email, and I just don't know if I can make that kind of time commitment." She didn't want to admit that adjusting to life back in the States was taking about the same amount of mental acuity as keeping up with her chem lab and its monstrous piles of work. Her mind had been reeling ever since she landed at Logan Airport. American slang she had never heard in China, fads that seemed to upgrade themselves once a week or more ... She hardly had time to keep up her grades, let alone give herself room to acculturate back to life in the States. If she jumped into volunteer work right now, she'd probably get so confused she'd start speaking to the clients in Korean or give some poor woman a lecture on chemical ionization when she was supposed to ask her to pee in a cup.

Carl's smile wilted for a short second, and his shoulders sank toward the floor while his chest deflated. "I understand. It's been a long time since my college days." His eyes twinkled once again, and he chuckled. "Compared to pastoring a church, starting up a pregnancy center satellite, and chasing around a bunch of grandkids, it sounds like a breeze." He was talking quietly, almost under his breath. "No utility bills, no board meetings ..." His head snapped up when his eyes met Kennedy's. "Never mind. I want you to know I get it. You're busy." He looked at the color-coded calendar, where his wife's was the only name on record. He smacked his lips. "Well, we'll be having our new center kick-off dinner Thursday night. That's where we're hoping to get most of our volunteers from, anyway."

Shame heated up Kennedy's core. "I didn't mean I couldn't help at all." She wouldn't have bothered taking the T all the way to the new center just to tell him that. "I'd love to be involved when I can. I was thinking as a substitute. Or maybe I could come help with paperwork or something on the weekends. I don't really know what you need."

"We need everything," Carl sighed. He stared at the calendar. When a little tinny rendition of *Brahms' Lullaby* rang out, his eyes widened, and he thrust his hands into his pants pockets. "That's the hotline phone." His face flushed and he patted his chest. "I don't have voicemail set up yet. I gotta answer it." The ringtone was almost through the first strain when he finally pulled out a small, black cell phone from his shirt pocket and promptly dropped it on the ground. His head nearly bonked Kennedy's when they both reached down to grab it. Finally, he picked it up and punched the button.

"Cambridge Community Pregnancy Center," he answered breathlessly.

Kennedy wondered if the caller could hear how flustered he was. A second later, he let out a sigh, and the vein that had threatened to pop its way out of his forehead relaxed a little.

"Oh. Hi, Sugar. I didn't know it was you. Why didn't you call me on ... Oh, I must have turned it to silent ... No, it's just that I thought it was a client. I'm here with Kennedy, you know, Roger Stern's girl. She's at Harvard now ... Of course I already told you that, but I didn't know if you would remember ... Yeah, I'll pick some up on my way home ... No, I'm not mad. I just thought we had our first call ... Ok, I love you, too, babe. ... Yup." Carl pulled his glasses down a little on his nose and squinted at the phone. He scratched his cheek. "Now how do I turn it off from my end?"

He glanced up at Kennedy, and another flush crept across his dark brown skin for a second. "This is our new hotline phone." He held up the contraption as if presenting evidence and then squinted at it one more time over his lenses. "I still haven't figured out how it works. They have these things over in China?"

Kennedy tried to keep herself from rolling her eyes. "Yeah." Why did everyone assume she was a transplant from the dark ages?

Carl weaved his way around some boxes to get behind his desk. "Well, we just started advertising for the pregnancy center on the radio yesterday. That means we could get a call on here any time, day or night. Sandy's busy, and I'm, well, I'm tied up with other things." He nearly dropped the phone again as his large hands struggled to slip it back into his pocket. "So maybe you could be our phone girl?"

He glanced up at her nervously.

Before Kennedy could say anything, Carl hurried on, "Of course, school has got to come first. Your dad told me about your program, by the way, how you're already accepted into the ..."

"You just need someone to answer calls?" Kennedy interrupted.

"That's all. The clinic itself is only open on a part-time basis — at least until we get more volunteers to keep it staffed. But we want people to be able to get in touch with us whenever they need." His eyes widened imploringly. "Would you? At least some of the time?"

Kennedy cast a glance at all the empty slots left on the wall calendar. How hard could it be to answer a cell phone every once in a while? "Sure. I can do that."

Carl's breath rushed out in a loud hiss before another smile broadened his face. "You're an angel." He took her by both shoulders and pulled her in for a quick hug. Then fiddling with his pocket, he managed to get the phone out without dropping it and pressed it in Kennedy's hand. "And if I know Sandy, she's going to want to know what kind of cookies you like most. She's convinced any college student who's not living at home must be starving." He passed her a pad of purple Post-it notes. "So you write down your address here, then just you wait if she doesn't show up at your dorm with a whole platter of them. Better write down what kind you like, too."

Kennedy jotted down her name and room number. "I'll eat anything home-baked."

Carl slammed the note onto his desk and clasped his hands together. "You have no idea how much of a burden you just lifted from me. So you'll take the phone this weekend? You don't have any plans, do you? No dates?"

Kennedy couldn't be sure, but she thought she saw him wink. "Nothing at all. Just lab reports."

"Perfect!" Carl remarked. It wasn't exactly the same reaction Kennedy had when she thought about her twelve-page write-up she'd be working on. He picked up a pink pen, squinted at the calendar, and traded it for a turquoise one. "See how proud Sandy would be of me for using her color system?" He made his way to the wall calendar and wrote Kennedy's name next to *Hotline Receptionist* for the weekend. "Oh, do you want me to teach you how to use it?"

Kennedy glanced at the model and guessed it was more ancient than the artifact her dad carried around back in Yanji. "I'm sure I can figure it out."

Carl insisted on showing her anyway, even though it was Kennedy who did most of the teaching as well as a decent amount of correcting. When they were done, she slipped the cell into the front zipper of her backpack. "So what do I do if I actually get a call?"

He adjusted his glasses once more. "Well, I think all you have to do is press that green button and ..."

"No, I mean, what am I supposed to say? What kind of calls am I going to get?"

Carl had been bustling about, apparently without aim, but now froze completely. "You've never done crisis pregnancy ministry before, have you?"

She shook her head.

He sat down with a loud sigh and gestured for Kennedy to take the miniature recliner along the wall. For a moment, he stared in silence, but then his eyes grew wide and his face brightened. "We got some training brochures just yesterday in the mail." Carl rummaged through some piles on his desk. "And if you come back next week, I can get you a few of the videos we use for training back at the Boston campus. That's where we're getting most of our materials from, you know."

Kennedy nodded. If she could get straight A's her senior year of high school while taking four AP classes, she figured she could handle answering a cell phone. She knew a passing amount of information about pregnancy centers. Her dad was quite passionate about the pro-life movement, and she had vague memories of her mother going to fancy fundraising teas when they still lived in the States. Abortion was a big problem in China with its one-child policy, and she heard her parents sometimes talk about forced abortions in North Korea as well.

Something buzzed, and Carl jumped to his feet, wincing when he banged his knee against the desk. With a focus that reminded Kennedy of her childhood schnauzer looking for his tennis ball, Carl patted himself down until he pulled out the source of buzzing from his pocket.

"Rats, I'm running late." He tapped at his phone with his beefy finger several times before he finally silenced the alarm. "I completely forgot. We have a prayer meeting for the St. Margaret's staff. I didn't even think of that when I was emailing you. I just can't seem to keep track of my schedule these days." He squinted as he stared at his screen, his brow wrinkled in consternation. "Kennedy, I'm sorry to up and leave so fast. Can I drop you off on campus on my way?"

Kennedy glanced at the clock on the wall. She was done with classes for the week and didn't have any plans except for finishing that lab report and catching up on some of her reading. "I don't mind taking the T."

"Well, since there's not time anymore for a proper training, you can give me the phone back. We can get you those brochures and have you come in and watch a few videos next week. If you're not too busy," he added hastily as he pulled a clanging ring of keys out of his top drawer.

"I don't mind taking the phone for the weekend." Kennedy saw the tight worry lines above Carl's eyes fade into his forehead, and she knew she had made the right decision.

He frowned for a second as he zipped up his windbreaker. "If you're sure you're comfortable. You can bring it back to me at church on Sunday so you won't have to carry it around during the week. Besides, that means you don't have an excuse to miss services. Oh, I forgot to give you Sandy's number in case you need a ride."

He reached down for a pen from a *#1 Grandpa* mug on his desk before Kennedy held up her hand. "That's all right. I can look up her number from caller ID."

He froze for a moment, his eyes wide. "You can do that?" He shook his head and shrugged. "All right, well, are you sure you're comfortable with the phone then? I didn't mean to spring it on you so fast and then just throw you to the wolves."

Kennedy laughed as she followed him out his office. "It's only for two days. What could be so hard about that?"

CHAPTER 2

Kennedy loved her literature courses because all that reading gave her a perfect and acceptable reason to procrastinate from math and science for a while. After she got back to campus, she hurried through a round of calculus problems to prepare for a test next Tuesday, then she took her already worn copy of *Crime and Punishment* and headed to the student union. Since it was a Friday evening, the cafeteria was pretty empty, but Kennedy wouldn't regret spending some time alone.

She picked at her vegetarian pasta while she read Dostoevsky's scene about a crazed murderer giving alms to a drunkard's destitute family. So far, she was enjoying her Russian literature class even more than she thought she would. There was something about the way the writers described the world, something that immediately engaged her emotions and her spirit. They didn't shy away from depicting human suffering in all its awful hues, but there was an underlying hope and beauty, too. After living in Yanji and walking its alleys overrun by homeless vagabonds, after spending time with the North Korean refugees her parents sheltered from the Chinese police, Kennedy appreciated the depth she found in the Russian works she read.

She turned the page, accidentally smudging a little salad dressing on the corner, when someone plopped a beige tray across from her on the table. "Hey, you."

She glanced up when she heard the familiar accent, her lips spreading in a ready smile.

"Is that all you're eating today?" her lab partner asked, eyeing her plate. Reuben sat down in front of his rice and beans, two slices of pizza, a cup of Jell-O, a bag of chips, and two cans of Coke.

Kennedy still had at least three hours' worth of reading to finish before her class next Monday, but she slipped a napkin between the pages and welcomed the intrusion. Her eyes were so scratchy she felt as though her eyelids were made of steel wool. With the late nights and excessive reading, her contacts were constantly dried out. She hadn't found the time to call her dad to ask him for a refill prescription, either. The time difference combined with her dad's long hours at his printing office made him tricky to contact. She blinked a few times and tried not to rub her eyes as she stared at Reuben's plate.

"Hungry?" she teased.

His mouth was already full with his first bites of rice and beans. He and Kennedy had been in the same small group during their first-year orientation. He was from Kenya, and they quickly discovered they faced some of the same challenges adjusting to life in the States. When they saw each other on the first day of chemistry lab, they silently agreed to stick together and make sure neither became one of Harvard's pre-med dropout statistics.

"Wichaeading?" Reuben mumbled through a mouthful of pizza. When Kennedy wrinkled her nose at him, he swallowed noisily and asked again, "What're you reading?"

"*Crime and Punishment*," she answered, showing him the cover. "It's for my Russian lit class." Reuben was already hacking at his Jell-O with a spork, and Kennedy guessed it would be her job to hold up the conversation for a while. "It's about a young man who decides to kill this old lady ..."

"Pwnvroker," he muttered.

Kennedy squinted while she tried to translate, and then she nodded. "The pawnbroker. Right. So, you've read it?"

Reuben held up two fingers. Kennedy was impressed. She enjoyed a spy or thriller novel as much as the classics she read for class, but even when she found a book she liked, she hardly re-read anything. There wasn't enough time.

Reuben's meal was half eaten in a matter of minutes, which allowed him to keep up a more regular conversation. He told Kennedy about the other books by Dostoevsky he had read, and they talked literature until both their plates were empty. After a quiet burp, Reuben leaned back in his chair with a grin.

"So, any exciting weekend plans?" Reuben sipped his Coke. He was always so easy to talk to, whether he was discussing acid-base reactions or telling her about growing up in Kenya in a family with seven sisters. He couldn't even count all his nephews and nieces on his ten fingers anymore, but he gave Kennedy detailed reports about them and their activities nearly every time he saw her.

"Not really," Kennedy answered. She wondered how he always remained so relaxed. He hadn't stressed about anything yet, at least not that she had seen. Between sips of Coke, Reuben cocked his head to the side and grinned at her until she finally had to ask what he was thinking about.

"Just wondering what my sisters would say if they met you."

She crossed her arms. "Oh, yeah?" she smirked. "And what would they say?"

Reuben kept a deadpan expression. "Stressed."

They both laughed.

"So when are you meeting me to work on our lab?" he asked.

She thought about her schedule. "Tomorrow good?"

Reuben shook his head. "No, I'll be busy."

Kennedy almost asked what he would be doing, but there was something in his closed posture that made her change her mind. That was the funny thing about Reuben. She figured it must be some kind of cultural thing she wasn't used to yet. He was gregarious and outgoing, but he could close up like a clam without any provocation and then be right back to his charming self again a few seconds later.

"What about Sunday?" she suggested after the crease in his brow eased up. She glanced at her backpack. What was she forgetting? That's right. Carl. "Oh, it would have to be in the afternoon. I told an old family friend I'd go to his church this Sunday." She glanced at Reuben, trying to gauge his present mood. "Do you want to come with me?"

Never hurts to ask, right?

She didn't know whether he would jump up and start singing like he did after they both aced their first chemistry test or if he would get sullen and silent as if she had intentionally offended him. Reuben's face turned thoughtful, but at least he wasn't scowling. "I'm not much of a church-goer," he finally remarked.

"First time for everything," she tried. "What about your family? Are they religious?"

Reuben let out a little chuckle. "Oh, we're religious all right. Christians through and through. I'm just, well, I'm not one for churches, that's all."

Brahms' Lullaby interrupted their conversation, and Kennedy held up her finger. "Sorry, I need to get that." She felt Reuben staring at her while she pulled out the hotline phone. The call came from a blocked number. She turned her body away slightly so Reuben didn't have to hear the entire conversation and pressed the green button. "Cambridge Pregnancy Center." That was the right name, wasn't it?

"Hello?" The voice was so quiet and mouse-like Kennedy could almost feel the hairs in her ear straining to grasp as much of the faint sound as they could. She stood up. Why hadn't she let Carl explain to her what she was supposed to do when she got a call?

"Hi. You've reached the Cambridge Pregnancy Center." Kennedy waited for a response. Did the caller hang up?

Nothing.

"Are you still there?" Kennedy winced and kicked herself for sounding rude. She was here to be a good listener, right? She looked at the screen to make sure the call was still connected.

"I'm here." The voice was young. Feathery, like wispy little egg whites floating in a bowl of egg drop soup. When Kennedy offered to take the hotline calls, she pictured herself talking to college co-eds or frazzled single moms. Not little girls.

"Can I help you?" What else was she supposed to say? And why in the world had she taken the job before at least reading one of Carl's silly training brochures?

"I just had a question." She wasn't exactly whispering. It sounded as if her body was so tiny and fragile she couldn't spare an ounce more breath to make herself heard.

Kennedy held up her finger to tell Reuben she'd return in a minute and hurried to the corner of the student union. "Sure. What's your name?"

There was a pause. Had Kennedy scared her away?

"Rose."

"All right, Rose. Ask me anything."

Kennedy waited for another silent eternity before the voice asked, "Do abortions hurt?"

Of course, that would be the first question. Not the clinic's hours, although Kennedy didn't even know that much. She tried to remember some of the arguments she heard her dad spout off when he went on one of his anti-abortion spiels.

"Well, the brain is fully functional very early on ..." Was it two months? Three months? She had never bothered to memorize the statistics. "And there are ultrasounds that lead us to believe that yes, babies can experience pain during an abortion." Is that what Carl would want her to say? Was she getting any of her facts right? For a minute, she thought about looking up the phone number for Carl's wife. Sandy would definitely be a better resource in this situation, but the phone model was so old she couldn't pull up the number without disconnecting the call. Hadn't Carl heard of modern technology?

The voice made a little gurgling sound that might have been a stifled cry or else a miniature cough. "No, I mean, does it hurt *you*."

"Oh." Kennedy had never thought about that before. All the pro-life arguments she heard growing up focused on the baby, not the mother. "Well, I know it's a complicated procedure. There are probably risks involved ..." If she were back in her room, she could Google the question and have an answer in a second or two. Maybe she should head back there now. The thought of Willow, her feminist roommate, listening in to the call might have been amusing if Kennedy's internal viscera weren't quivering so much. She shut her eyes. She had to take charge of the conversation. "So, are you considering an abortion? Is that why you're asking?"

Too direct.

"No. I'm calling for a friend. That's all. She was just wondering."

Nice job, Kennedy chided herself. "And how old is your friend?" She tried to make her tone sound trustworthy, inviting. She had no idea if she was succeeding or not because her pulse roared in her ear, making it nearly impossible to hear anything else.

"She's thirteen." It felt like Kennedy's whole abdominal floor dropped several feet to the ground at terminal velocity. "I mean eighteen," the voice corrected. "She's eighteen and already out of school."

Kennedy's heart accelerated so fast her pulse felt like a long, continuous flutter. *Thirteen?* "And so your friend is thinking about an abortion?"

"Well, she just wanted some information, really. Like if it hurts a lot or not."

"I see." Kennedy shot up a wordless prayer to heaven, a silent plea for help that rose from her spirit before she had time to translate it into human language. "Well, if your friend wants to stop by the pregnancy center, we're open again on Monday ..."

"I don't know if her parents will let her come in."

"Well, you certainly can't make her. But if you talk to her, let her know there are nice people there who really do want to help. They can answer all the questions she has and give her the information she needs."

"You guys are Christians, right?"

Kennedy was pacing now, because the more she moved her legs, the less her abdominal muscles quivered. "Yes, the pregnancy center is run by Christians. But you don't have to be a Christian to get help there," she added quickly.

There was silence for such a long time Kennedy wondered if there was a problem with Carl's antique cell phone. Finally, Rose asked, "And so what happens if you get pregnant, and you're too young to actually have a baby?"

Defying all laws of inertia, the acceleration of Kennedy's heart rate crashed to a halt like a car plowing into a brick wall. "What do you mean?"

"Like, what if you're too young but you still get pregnant?"

"How young?" Kennedy spoke both words clearly and slowly, as if rushing might drive the timid voice away for good.

"Like thirteen."

Kennedy paused. She was pretty sure Carl's training would have some sort of method, some sort of guidelines for a situation like this. But she had nothing to go on but intuition. Intuition that at this point was sending ripples of foreboding creeping up her spine until they wormed in and settled at the base of her neck. "Are you asking because you might be pregnant?" The question itself made her dizzy, as if speaking the words aloud could send her head into some kind of tailspin.

"Yeah."

The adrenaline that had flooded Kennedy's entire nervous system seeped out of her body in a single moment, dissipating out of each pore. She leaned against the wall and reminded herself that her job was to help and encourage the caller, not have some sort of fainting dizzy spell in the middle of the student union.

"And you're how old?" She braced herself for the answer she knew was coming.

"Thirteen."

Now what? Instinct demanded Kennedy find out where the girl lived, who her parents were. Compassion welled up in her core, urging her to find this child and ... and what? What could she do?

"Do you know about how long ago you might have gotten pregnant?" Kennedy scolded herself. Wasn't there a more discreet way to ask something like that?

"Five months."

Kennedy felt her eyes grow wide. "Does your family know?" She thought about what she had been like at thirteen. Obsessed with horses, daydreaming about NASA, content to giggle with her girlfriends about which boys at school were the cutest. But pregnant?

"I can't tell them," Rose whispered.

Kennedy wished she had written down Sandy's phone number. What did Kennedy know about pregnancy? Nothing. In fact Reuben with his seven sisters probably knew more about childbearing than she did.

Think, Kennedy. Thirteen-year-old tells you she's five months pregnant. What do you do?

"Have you been to a doctor yet?"

"No. I just took one of those tests you pee on." Rose's voice was too small to hold so much fear.

Nervous energy raced up and down Kennedy's limbs. She had to find something to do. "Maybe we should make you an appointment at the pregnancy center. Would that be ok?"

"I don't have any way to get there." Another brick wall. What would Carl do?

"All right, what about your school counselor? Could you make an appointment with them?"

"I'm homeschooled."

A roar of frustration crept up to the base of Kennedy's larynx, where she cut it off by clenching her throat muscles. "What about your boyfriend?" she finally asked. "Could his family maybe help you out? Could they give you a ride to the center? We really want to help you."

Did Rose understand? Did she guess that Kennedy's leg muscles were poised, ready to run out the door the moment she discovered something she could do, some way she could assist?

"I don't have a boyfriend."

A horrible, nagging dread nibbled the inside of Kennedy's gut. She asked her next inevitable question slowly, almost against her will. "How are you pregnant, then?"

A little sharp breath, the sound a startled animal might make when it notices its prey. A fear-drenched whisper. "I think it's my dad ... I gotta go."

"No, wait!" Kennedy nearly shouted into the phone, but Rose had already hung up.

CHAPTER 3

"No, I can't calm down." Kennedy didn't mean to snap, but after the third or fourth time Reuben made the suggestion, she was ready to gouge his eyes out. Kennedy was pacing in front of some benches outside the student union while Reuben did his best to listen. "I mean, she might not have meant her dad is the dad, right?"

"I don't know." Reuben shrugged. "I wasn't on the phone."

Kennedy replayed those last few words in her mind. She could hear Rose's voice, clear as a tiny glass beaker. Saturated with fear. *I think it's my dad ... I gotta go.* Did that mean her dad was the father of the baby? Or maybe her dad was coming, and she didn't want him to catch her on the phone. Even so, there were still troubling questions without any answers. How does a thirteen-year-old girl get pregnant if she doesn't have a boyfriend?

"Why did she hang up so quick?" Kennedy asked the air.

Reuben picked his tooth. "Maybe it was time for dinner."

She whipped her head around to face him. "I don't think it's something to joke about."

He held up his hands in a position of surrender.

Kennedy hoped he knew she wasn't really mad at him. She eyed the stupid phone. "Anyway, I better call the director." She hated running to Carl her very first night on the job, but there really wasn't anything else to do. "I'll see you later." She started walking toward her dorm, but Reuben ran up behind and reached for her shoulder.

"Wait, when are we going to work on the paper for chem lab, then?"

"I don't know." How could she think about some report while there was some traumatized little girl out there? "Let's just meet in the library Sunday afternoon."

"When? Two?"

Kennedy was hardly listening. "All right. Fine."

She turned once more, only to hear Reuben call after her, "And don't stay up all night worrying. These things work themselves out." She gave him a brief wave, discarded his last words which were about as helpful as a lobotomy, and pushed all thoughts of Reuben and lab write-ups aside. She glanced down at the phone, and her fingers trembled so much it took her three tries before the call went through. Whenever she clenched her ab muscles to keep them from quivering, the tremors relocated all the way up to her teeth and sent them chattering noisily. She took a deep breath, hoping the phone would mask the choppiness in her voice. She had been so impatient to talk to Carl she hadn't thought about what she would do if nobody answered at all. By the fifth ring, her shivering was so violent she sat down on a bench but hopped right back up again since her muscles refused to relax.

"Hello?" At the sound of Carl's voice, relief flooded Kennedy's whole body and seeped into each individual cell.

"Carl, it's Kennedy. I just got off the hotline phone."

"Oh, really? That was even faster than I expected."

She hated to squash his enthusiasm, but she had no energy left for pleasantries or small talk. She summarized the call and waited for Carl to comment.

"So, you think the father might be ..."

"She didn't say so," Kennedy hurried to explain, as if that one simple statement could negate all her horrific suspicions. "But on the other hand ..."

"A thirteen-year-old without a boyfriend ..." Carl mumbled. "It doesn't necessarily have to be her dad." His voice held the same futile optimism Kennedy had been trying to cling to.

"That's true," she agreed.

"But it does have to be somebody."

"Right."

"Do you think it'd be a good idea to call her back?" Carl suggested.

"It was a blocked number. I couldn't even if I wanted."

He let out a huge breath of air. "We better report this, just in case."

"Report to who?" Kennedy shivered. It was warm when she dressed that morning. Now she wished she had layered up. It wasn't sunset yet, but the night was freezing.

"I think you should call 911. Tell them what happened."

Kennedy hadn't expected that. The police? But then again, the idea made sense. Maybe they could trace the number. Maybe they could actually find the girl. Get her some real help.

Apparently, the matter was already certain in Carl's mind. "Tell them what you told me. And when you're done, call me back, just to let me know what they say."

Part of Kennedy wanted to ask Carl to do it. He was the director. But he hadn't talked with Rose. He couldn't give them the same details she could, details that might help the police stage a rescue. "All right," she agreed. "I'll call you back in a few."

"I'll be praying."

Kennedy's corneas were still dry and scratchy, as if somebody had blown cold air at her until each tear duct shriveled up like a parched, sandy desert. She disconnected her call with Carl and paused for a minute to calm down. Thoughts, prayers, blurred images clashed against one another discordantly in her mind. What had she gotten herself into? She was a high-achiever, but she knew when to admit she was in over her head. Nothing had equipped her for the past twenty minutes. That tiny, frightened voice kept replaying in her head until she couldn't think of anything else.

Kennedy was still staring at the hotline phone, as if Rose's last name and address might materialize on the screen if she got lucky enough. Then with a sigh, she dialed 911.

"The location of the emergency?" The operator's voice had an automatic, almost drone-like quality.

"It's not exactly an emergency. At least, I'm not sure it is."

"Your location?" he repeated, the smallest trace of annoyance creeping into his tone.

"I'm calling from Harvard."

"Square or University?"

"University. But that's not where the emergency is. I mean ..." Kennedy tripped and stumbled over her words but finally described her conversation with Rose.

The dispatcher's tone didn't change. "So you're calling us because ...?"

"The director told me to," she answered. Why had it sounded like a good idea at the time? "He thought maybe you'd have a way to trace the call or something."

"Not without special equipment. And we can't trace calls after they're placed, anyway."

They were the police. They were supposed to protect innocent people, like thirteen-year-old girls who end up pregnant and terrified, talking to strangers when there's nobody else to turn to. "So there's nothing you can do?"

"No." She wondered if he spoke in a monotone all the time or only when he was on the clock. "And even if we could, there wouldn't be enough evidence for us to take action at this point."

Frustration and rage sandwiched Kennedy's arteries, and she felt her blood pressure escalate with her pulse. "What do you mean there's no evidence?" Had he been listening to her at all?

"She didn't accuse anybody, for one thing," the operator remarked. "In fact, there's not even proof at this point that she's pregnant at all. She could have just wanted some extra attention, create some false sympathy ..."

You didn't hear her voice, Kennedy wanted to scream. Why had she thought the police would be able to do anything? The dispatcher didn't believe Rose's story. Next thing, he'd start telling Kennedy *she* was the one making things up and looking for extra attention.

"So you're basically saying I'm wasting my time trying to figure out how to help her. Is that it?" Kennedy heard the sharp edge in her own voice but didn't try to soften it.

"Without more information, there's nothing we can do."

"She said she was homeschooled," Kennedy suddenly remembered. "Can't you guys run a list or something of the families around here that homeschool their kids? See if there's a girl named Rose?"

"And then what?"

Kennedy thought she picked up a hint of sarcasm although the operator's tone didn't change from its irritating, robotic lull.

She didn't answer. So there really wasn't anything they could do? Not even trace a simple call. How hard could it really be? They did it all the time in movies, right? "What if she calls back?" Kennedy asked. "Could you trace a call then?"

The operator let out a sound that was a mix between a chuckle and a sigh. "Theoretically, maybe. But we'd need a lot more evidence before we'd set something like that up."

The last ounces of hope deflated out of Kennedy's lungs. "So there's nothing we can do."

"Well, if she calls back, you can always try to get a last name. See if you can figure out if she really is being abused or not."

Maybe the girl would call back. She could always hope. "But what if she doesn't give me her name?"

"Encourage her to call 911. Or talk to someone, a teacher or something."

"She's homeschooled," Kennedy reminded him, but the operator didn't respond. "All right," she finally sighed. "I guess that's all."

"Sorry we couldn't be more help." The words came automatically, and Kennedy doubted he meant them.

"Ok." She hung up and stared at the phone. Her first 911 call, and he had basically told her he couldn't lift a pinky finger to help. Exhaustion clung to her limbs as she made her way up the stairs to her dorm room. She'd have to call Carl back and tell him there was nothing to be done.

All right, God, she prayed. *You heard him. If you want me to help, Rose is going to have to call back.*

CHAPTER 4

Kennedy spent some time that evening looking up abortion methods online. The information she found both sickened and saddened her. Her initial search brought up several sites aimed specifically at young girls like Rose. *You don't need to feel guilty for choosing to end an unwanted pregnancy. Many girls have this procedure. It is quick, easy, and much safer than childbirth.*

As Kennedy read on, she couldn't stop thinking about those pictures in her dad's pro-life magazine showing what an aborted baby looks like. She jumped a little when her roommate threw open the door and swept into the room. Kennedy closed her browser. She had to get to work on some real studying, anyway.

"I thought you'd be out tonight," Kennedy remarked. In the past two months since they first came to Harvard, Willow hadn't spent a single night in on the weekend.

"I'm not staying." Willow sprayed some mousse into her hands and scrunched it through her hair. "I'm just waiting for Keegan."

"Who's Keegan?" At first, Kennedy had tried to keep track of Willow's dates, but when she realized her roommate hardly saw anyone more than once or twice, she gave up the habit.

"Keegan. I thought I told you about him. He's Cesario in *Twelfth Night*."

Kennedy watched Willow crumple her hair into gravity-defying curls and waves. "Isn't Cesario supposed to be played by a girl?"

Willow shrugged and studied herself in her little desk mirror. "This version is sort of a modern retelling. Drag queens, bisexuals ... Shakespeare would've loved it."

Kennedy watched Willow put on some colorful bead earrings she had made herself and wondered how her roommate found time for crafts.

Willow glanced over at Kennedy's computer. "What are you studying?"

"Oh, I just got a lab I need to get ready to turn in on Monday."

Willow, who could hardly ever sit still for more than five seconds, crossed her arms and eyed Kennedy critically. "You ok?"

Kennedy didn't think she had done such a bad job hiding her stress about Rose's phone call. She definitely didn't want to talk about it with Willow, who probably believed Carl and Sandy's pregnancy center would set back women's rights by half a century or more. "I'm fine. Just tired."

Her roommate frowned. "You don't need to talk or anything?"

What was this? Willow sounded like Kennedy's mother, who always had an uncanny way of knowing if something was bothering her. "I'm fine. I really am."

Willow raised her eyes to the ceiling as if she were trying to remember the lines for a play. Finally she lowered them to give Kennedy a penetrating stare. "I'm just asking because I saw you on an abortion site. Are you in trouble?"

Kennedy let out a nervous laugh. No wonder Willow had been so concerned. It was sort of endearing, but also a little troubling. Didn't Willow know her well enough by now to understand Kennedy's values? "I wasn't looking it up for me."

Her roommate frowned. "It's nothing to be ashamed of. You wouldn't be the first Christian girl to get knocked up on campus."

"It's really not for me." Kennedy didn't have the energy to tell Willow everything about Rose and the hotline phone. She hoped her roommate's date, Keegan, or whatever his name was, would show up soon.

Willow shrugged. "All right. Just remember, the longer you wait to deal with it, the harder it is. They even have pills now. So much easier than sitting in stirrups with a doctor and nurse gaping down at you."

Kennedy wanted to shut her ears.

"The thing with the pills is you can only take them in the first few weeks. So if you are in trouble, now's the time to do something about it. I know a good clinic I could recommend. You know me. I'm the last person to judge." Willow had stopped staring at Kennedy and was now pouting in the mirror as she applied her eye makeup. "I mean, I know you're probably all pro-life and everything, but there are obviously going to be exceptions, like when the mother's safety is threatened."

Kennedy didn't say anything. The more she insisted the research was for someone else, the more Willow would doubt her, anyway.

Willow adjusted her earrings. "Whatever you do, don't become a martyr like that Morphia lady or whatever her name was. You know who I'm talking about?"

Kennedy shook her head.

"Right, I keep forgetting you spent your teenage years overseas on some mission of mercy with your parents or something. It was huge news around here last year. Some lady denying chemotherapy since she thought it would harm her baby. Made huge headlines. Of course, the anti-abortionists had a heyday about it. When she died, you would have thought she was a war hero on the crusade to abolish the murder of little fetuses or something. Anyway, the way I see it, if she didn't want her kid getting radiation from chemo, she should have been on the pill."

Kennedy started to say something in reply, but Willow wasn't done with her monologue.

"And don't get me started when you're talking about little kids. Can you believe there are actually politicians who say that if a girl is raped by her dad, she should still be expected to carry the baby to term? I mean, even someone as conservative as you could see how ridiculous that is to make a twelve- or thirteen-year-old actually go through nine months of pregnancy and all the risks of childbirth. They'd actually rather see the girl die than take care of it right at the beginning when it's safe."

Kennedy didn't answer. The mention of thirteen-year-olds and their fathers made her full stomach spin in protest. She didn't agree with Willow. She knew abortion was wrong regardless of the circumstances. But why? She hadn't thought through it thoroughly enough to be able to enter into any sort of debate.

Willow shrugged. Her phone buzzed once and she sprang out of her seat. "That'll be Keegan. Gotta go." She flashed Kennedy the same smile that made her perfect for stage acting. "Don't wait up for me." She flounced out of the room, leaving the door open a crack behind her.

Kennedy sighed and reached down into her book bag. She had work to do, and Monday would be here before she was ready.

CHAPTER 5

Kennedy was used to being surrounded by people. The past decade in Yanji gave her quite a different definition of *crowded* than most other Americans. Still, her pulse sped up when she entered St. Margaret's Church for Sunday services. For the past ten years, church had taken place in her parents' den and consisted of her, her mom and dad, and the few North Korean refugees that lived with them.

A woman in a denim skirt welcomed her at the door, and Kennedy didn't know if she was supposed to shake the outstretched hand or just accept the bulletin it offered. "Are you a visitor here?" the greeter asked, and Kennedy wondered in a church this size how someone could possibly keep track of who was new and who wasn't. Was there some kind of glossy look in Kennedy's eyes that gave it away? She explained that the Lindgrens were old family friends and entered the main sanctuary.

In Yanji, Kennedy's Korean housemates would often arrive in the den thirty or forty minutes before services officially started. They kept the lights off and kneeled in darkness, offering a chorus of praise all at the same time. Tears, sobs, prayers, and petitions from each individual rose up to heaven simultaneously. At the time, Kennedy had found the noise chaotic and a tad frightening, but it was nothing like the din at St. Margaret's. The noise created an almost physical barrier that Kennedy struggled to pass through on her way to the pews. Children ran around haphazardly, shouting, waving, bumping into the legs of unsuspecting congregants. A whole gaggle of teen girls giggled loudly in a huddle. A mother of three snapped at her oldest to hold onto his little sister's hand. Behind her, two men bantered good-naturedly about the upcoming football game.

There was a band on the stage, with three guitars, a gleaming drum set, a keyboard, and a saxophone. Kennedy suspected there must be some sort of method in the musicians' warm-up, but it sounded like each one was vying to create the loudest, most obnoxious sound. Back in Yanji, Kennedy and the others had sung plenty of hymns, but there wasn't even a piano for accompaniment. She shut her eyes for a moment, trying to will away the noise, trying to recall the sounds of worship in her parents' den. During the ten years she spent in China, Kennedy always felt like the outsider. Now, in the second-to-back pew in the crowded auditorium, she realized she'd give about anything for a day or two back home.

The band played its first harmonious bar, and the talking and bedlam reluctantly died down as people took their seats. The ensuing music, however, was even louder than the hundreds of tiny conversations that had stopped. Kennedy clenched shut her eyes, wishing for some sort of cocoon to shield her from the volume. Was this how Americans worshipped every single Sunday?

She didn't recognize the song, and it wasn't until the tall gentleman in front of her shifted slightly to make room for his wife that Kennedy realized the words were being projected onto the wall above the stage. She glanced around, more self-conscious and out-of-place than she ever had felt on foreign soil, even though she had no logical reason to worry about her image. Nobody was paying any attention to her. The man a few seats over was busy scrolling on his phone. The woman in front of him was texting. Behind Kennedy, a preschooler kicked the back of her seat in a near approximation to the music's beat. A woman in the aisle over was having a full conversation with the mother behind her, and here and there some of the attendees raised their hands in worship.

Kennedy had never considered her house-church experience as novel or foreign or even very interesting, at least not until now. Back in Yanji, she could have isolated the voice of each individual singer. Hannah had a high, ringing soprano. Her friend Simon couldn't carry a tune to save his life, but what he lacked in musical talent he made up for in sheer loudness. Levi probably could have gone on to become a South Korean pop sensation or something if he hadn't returned to North Korea as an undercover missionary. Where were they all now? And how meaningful would it be if Kennedy had a chance to worship together with them again?

The song itself was poignant, something that probably could have grabbed her attention if she heard it on the radio. The lyrics spoke of longing, yearning. *My heart is homesick for your glory, Lord.* At that line, her throat constricted and she stopped mouthing the words. *Homesick.* She didn't know when she'd go back to Yanji. Maybe over Christmas break, maybe not until next summer. Even then, would it ever be the same?

Kennedy wrapped her arms across her chest. She wanted to hide. She wanted to run away, forget about pining for another place, forget about the homesickness that threatened to hack her heart to pieces. If she left now, would anyone around her notice? Would they care? Or were they too busy texting or worshipping to pay any attention?

The song ended, followed by another almost exactly like it. Had there really been a time when Kennedy thought the hymns they sang back in Yanji were boring and dry? Toward the front of the sanctuary, a young man with blond dreadlocks lifted both hands high over his head. His eyes were closed in rapture. Jealousy slithered its way up and around Kennedy's shoulders. Could she ever worship God that openly, that freely? She had watched the North Koreans in her parents' home sing praises with tears flowing down their cheeks, but she had never experienced anything remotely similar. Her father said that everyone relates to God in his or her own unique way, but Kennedy sometimes wondered if she really related to God at all. Or had God become such an everyday part of her life that there was no room left for awe?

After a few more songs, Pastor Carl climbed the steps to the stage. Just the sight of his face was a comfort in this rippling sea of strangers. His voice was soothing, something familiar. He gave some brief updates about small groups and then announced the opening of the new pregnancy center. When the cheers died down, he invited everyone to Thursday night's kick-off dinner. "Right here at St. Margaret's. Our special guest speaker will be State Senator Wayne Abernathy, who I've asked to come up and say the morning's blessing."

A tall, hair-sprayed man with the smile of a TV newscaster stood up to an even peppier round of applause and made his way to the platform. He shook Pastor Carl's hand, beaming the whole time, and waved to the audience with his free arm.

"Wayne is Massachusetts' most dedicated pro-life advocate," Carl declared. "He's been toiling tirelessly for the cause of the unborn child for the past eight years in the State House, and as most of you know, he's now running for governor." More applause. "Brother," Carl continued, "we'd like to thank you for being one of the pro-life movement's most devoted front-lines warriors, and we wish you God's blessings in the election next week and in all your future endeavors. Would you be so kind as to pray and bless this morning's service?"

Kennedy shut her eyes automatically when the prayer started but flung them open again at the sound of a muffled *Brahms' Lullaby*. She snatched her book bag, scurried to her feet, and tried to weave past the legs of those sitting next to her. The ringtone was starting its second refrain when she scampered out the massive double doors of the sanctuary.

"Hello?" She was so breathless that she didn't bother trying to get the name of the pregnancy center right this time.

"It's me."

Kennedy kept her breath trapped inside for fear she might blow away the quiet voice. "Rose? Are you ok?" Some teens and a few adults were loitering in the foyer, and Kennedy glanced around for someplace private.

"My uncle heard us talking."

Kennedy froze. "So he knows?" The sensation reminded her of a free-fall ride at a carnival.

"Yeah."

In one ear, Kennedy could still hear the politician's prayer from the main stage. She hurried down the hall, hoping to find a library or small study where they could talk in peace. "How did he react?"

"Says I need to get rid of it."

"The baby, you mean?" Kennedy tried a doorknob and found a tiny storage room. It definitely wasn't the coziest spot in the church, but at least she was alone.

Rose didn't respond.

"What do you want?" Kennedy prompted. "Do you want to get rid of the baby, too?"

"No." Her voice was even smaller.

"Well, nobody can make you." Kennedy hoped that was true. She didn't really know what would happen if the mother was a minor. Could her parents force an abortion on her? Kennedy needed to talk to Carl, but that couldn't happen until after his sermon.

"He already made the appointment," the girl whispered.

"Do you know when that will be? Or what clinic he's taking you to?" What was Kennedy planning? To show up and whisk Rose away before the abortion started?

"He just told me he'd take care of it."

Kennedy thought about Amy Carmichael, the missionary who literally stole girls away from temple slavery. As a child listening to the tales, Kennedy hadn't thought twice about going to such extreme lengths to save somebody. After all, her own parents sheltered North Korean refugees right under the nose of the Chinese government. But this was different. This was the United States, the alleged home of the free.

"Is there somewhere we could meet?" Kennedy asked. "I have some friends, the ones who run the pregnancy center. I know they'd find a way to help you."

Something beeped in Kennedy's ear. She looked at the phone. *You've got to be kidding.* The battery light was blinking. Carl hadn't even given her a charger. Then she noticed the number actually showed up this time on the screen. She could call Rose back. They might be able to locate her.

It was all Kennedy could do to keep her voice down as she rummaged through her book bag for her personal cell. "Listen, this phone is about to die. But I want to keep on talking to you." Where was it? Had she left it in her dorm room? She hurried out of the closet. There had to be a landline phone somewhere. "If we get disconnected, I want you to just wait. Wait there by the phone, and I'll call you right back. Ok?"

"You can't do that." It was probably the most forceful thing Rose had said, but even so her voice never grew above a hush.

"It's all right." Relief warmed Kennedy's face when she saw an open office door, and she hurried in. "I'm here to help you, remember. So if we get connected, I'm going to ..."

"Don't," the girl whispered, and then the line went dead.

Not yet. Kennedy wanted to throw the phone against the wall. Why couldn't the batteries have lasted a few more seconds? Now she wouldn't be able to bring the number up ...

Wait a minute. The battery light blinked faintly. There was still a little bit of power left. Rose must have hung up. But why? It didn't matter. Kennedy wasn't going to miss this opportunity. She checked the caller ID, settled down in the office chair, and punched the number into the desk phone with a resolute hand.

Busy.

She hung up and redialed.

Still busy.

Had Rose taken the phone off the hook, then? Was she scared of Kennedy calling?

"Can I help you?"

Kennedy jumped at the sound, and her faced reddened. It was the man with dreadlocks. He was wearing khaki shorts and a T-shirt with a picture of Jesus surfing in bare feet without any board. Kennedy guessed he had found himself on the wrong coast. New Englanders didn't dress that way. Especially not for church.

"Is everything all right?" Two stray dreads swung in his face when he cocked his head to the side.

"I'm sorry," Kennedy stammered. "Is this ... I needed to make an emergency phone call, and the door was open, so I ... Is this your desk?" She looked down and saw a picture of Mr. Dreads with his arm around a bronze, blond-haired Barbie girl. Even though her two-piece swimsuit only showed an inch or so of her belly, Kennedy immediately noted the hint of her six-pack. "I'm sorry," Kennedy repeated.

The man held up his hand. "It's no problem." He glanced at the phone. "Did you get hold of whoever you were looking for?"

"No. I ... I actually really need to talk to Carl. But I guess he's busy right now, isn't he?"

He laughed. "Well, the good news is it's a football Sunday. Which means he won't preach a minute past twelve twenty-five."

Kennedy couldn't immediately grasp how that could be considered good news. "Do you mind if I try your phone just one more time?"

He shrugged. "Have at it."

Busy again.

"Dang it."

She hadn't meant to say that out loud. She glanced at the clock. Thirty minutes until the sermon ended. She imagined Rose's uncle dragging her to his car and forcing her into an abortion clinic before Carl made it to his closing prayer.

"Is it something I can help with? I'm Nick, by the way. I'm the youth and children's pastor here." He gave a little wave but didn't offer his hand. "I actually just came down the hall because I left my Bible, but hey, if you're in trouble or something ..."

"I really need to talk to Carl."

Nick glanced at her out of the corner of his eye, and Kennedy wondered if he was trying to gauge her sanity.

"I'm one of the volunteers at the new pregnancy center," she decided to explain. "I've been getting these calls on the hotline phone ..."

A moment later, Nick was perched up on the corner of his desk, nodding empathetically. Kennedy was too emotionally drained to relive each individual detail, but she spewed out the basic premise of her two calls from Rose.

"So I tried to call her back," she concluded, "but I kept getting a busy signal."

"Well, at least you have a number now, right? I mean, now you can find out where she's calling from, get the police involved if you're really concerned."

Kennedy wasn't sure the police would be any more willing to help this time than they had been the other evening, but it was a step in the right direction. At least now, she could keep trying to re-establish communication. And if she needed to, she could probably use the phone number to get a last name or a location or something.

"Here." Nick leaned down and swiveled the screen of his computer around. He reached over for the keyboard and placed it on his lap.

"Are you sure I'm not taking up all your time? I mean, you're probably really busy on Sundays."

"Nah." Nick waved his hand in the air. "Don't tell anyone, but Pastor Carl's sermons usually put me to sleep."

Kennedy wasn't sure she believed him, but she didn't argue. She was grateful to find someone who was taking the hotline call seriously.

"Here we go." Nick had typed in a web address for a reverse phone number site. "Tell me the number, and we'll see what we get."

She read him the digits. He stopped typing halfway through.

"Read that again." His eyes narrowed, and he gave Kennedy a suspicious sideways look.

She repeated it.

He reached out his hand. "Let me see that."

She handed him the phone and watched his tanned face pale a little. Foreboding sank down in her stomach like a rock and settled there. "What's wrong?"

Nick didn't take his eyes off the cell. "This is the number for St. Margaret's. Whoever she is, she was calling from inside the church."

CHAPTER 6

"This better not be one of your silly tricks to keep me away from my football game."

Kennedy heard Carl's good-natured voice reverberate through the halls a few seconds before he entered Nick's office.

"Kennedy! So you did come!" He spread his arms out for a hug and then stopped. "Something happened." He looked to Nick. "Is this the big problem that couldn't wait?" He frowned even though his voice hadn't lost its kindly tone.

Nick nodded. "She says that ..."

"The girl call back again?" Carl interrupted.

Once they found a way to help Rose, Kennedy figured she could go a whole year without talking about the past few days and that still wouldn't be long enough. "She said her uncle found out, listened in to our last call or something. Said he's already scheduled her an abortion." She handed Carl the phone, half hoping to hear *Brahms' Lullaby*, half hoping to never see it again.

Wrinkles materialized on Carl's face the same way splotches popped up on Kennedy's skin when she got nervous.

"Wait until you hear the weirdest part," Nick said.

Kennedy took a deep breath. "She didn't call from a blocked number this time. We checked the ID. She was calling from here."

A heavy silence billowed up like a cloud of gas over a lab beaker. Carl heaved a massive sigh. "How long ago was that call?"

"About half an hour." Kennedy had been staring at the clock, counting down the seconds since Rose hung up.

"Think she's still here?"

Nick shrugged. "She could be anywhere."

"There's nobody named Rose in youth group, is there?" Carl asked.

Nick shook his head.

"But she might have made up a name," Carl mused. He made Kennedy describe both phone calls in as much detail as she could muster up. Maybe Nick could recognize Rose. After a sophisticated version of the guessing game, minus the good humor and laughter, they still hadn't made any progress.

"Did you find out anything else about her family?" Carl asked. "Something that might make them stick out from anyone else in the church?"

"She mentioned her uncle, and she mentioned her dad. That's all." Kennedy's stomach was churning.

"No brothers or sisters?" Nick prompted.

Kennedy's contacts were scratching at her eyes again. "I told you everything she told me," she huffed.

Carl stood up. "Well, you've certainly gone above and beyond the call of duty." He placed a strong hand on her shoulder. The gesture reminded her of her father, and she wished she could shut her eyes and click her heels together and end up back in Yanji. She could postpone college for a year, or maybe take classes online.

"Well, how about I'll drop you back off at school. Nick and I will keep thinking. We'll find a way to check who was in the junior high Sunday school today, things like that."

"It'll be a lot easier finding her now that we know what church she goes to," Nick added.

"But I do want to be discreet about it all," Carl muttered to Nick, "what with the timing and everything."

"Of course."

Carl gave Kennedy's shoulder an encouraging squeeze. "Cheer up. Let me drive you back to campus."

They slipped out of the office. "I got my car parked around the corner." Carl beeped the button on his automatic keys.

"What about Sandy?" Kennedy asked. "I didn't see her all morning."

"She left right after the service ended. Went to drop off a few things at the center, do a little planning for the dinner."

Kennedy slipped into the passenger seat of Carl's maroon Honda. He groaned as he plopped down next to her. "I'm getting too old for this," he mumbled. "Now where are those keys? I just had them."

She smiled to herself while she watched him turn his pockets inside out one by one, but all she really wanted to do was get back to her dorm and grab some lunch. She had to meet Reuben in an hour to finish going over their lab report. If they started right away, she might finish in time to get a decent chunk of her Russian lit reading done before crashing for the night. In addition to her calculus test, she had papers due in both her literature classes next week. When Carl's air conditioning blew in her face, she blinked her eyes and made a mental note to call her dad tonight about those contacts.

Carl finally found his keys under his leg as a phone beeped. Kennedy automatically opened her backpack before she remembered her cell wasn't there. "That's not me," she told Carl. "Did someone just text you?"

He fumbled for another minute before pulling out his thick cell phone. He squinted over his glasses. "Uh-oh." He was already dialing before Kennedy could ask what was wrong.

"Hi, babe. Are you ok?" He swung the car backwards out into a wide arch as he pulled out of his parking spot. Kennedy looked back over her shoulder to make sure they weren't about to ram into anything. Her shoulder slammed the passenger door when he straightened out and pumped the gas. "Sorry," he whispered to her.

Kennedy checked to make sure her seat belt was tight.

"No, no, no. I'm coming over right now." Carl was almost yelling. "Well if it's too dangerous for me, then I'm not about to just leave you there ... You're sure you're not hurt? ... Ok, we're already on our way ... Yeah, I've got Kennedy here with me. Stay put. And stay away from the windows, all right? Go in the back office and lock the door until I get there ... Fine, stay until the police get there then ... Be safe, baby. I love you."

His complexion had paled several degrees by the time he hung up. "Sandy's run into some problems at the pregnancy center. We need to stop and make sure everything's all right."

Kennedy saw the way the vein in his neck twitched and didn't ask for any more information. His knuckles were almost white against the steering wheel. She sensed it wasn't the appropriate time to joke about him missing his afternoon football game.

Carl sped the entire time and broke several other traffic laws as he weaved his way through the lazy weekend traffic. When he finally turned onto Elm Street, the whole sidewalk was littered with people. Some waved picket signs. Others shouted. Kennedy couldn't distinguish the words but felt the vibrations of their angry yells like a low, violent rumble. Down the road a ways were two parked police cars, their red and blue siren lights spinning in the midday sun.

Carl snaked his way into a parallel parking spot next to some yellow police tape. "Stay here." He slammed the door shut behind him and jostled his way down the sidewalk with fists clenched. Kennedy jumped out and followed him.

"What's going on?" he demanded as a policewoman walked up.

"Sir, this is a zoned area. Please stay behind the tape."

"My wife is in that building." Carl had to yell to be heard. Kennedy didn't notice until then the broken glass glistening on the pavement. Two other police officers were holding back crowds while picketers waved around signs with sayings like, *Keep Your Regulations Off My Uterus*, and *Pro-Choice or No Choice.* Kennedy stayed close by Carl's shoulder.

"Your wife's in there, you say?" the police officer repeated.

"She just called me a few minutes ago."

A young man hollered, "Hey, aren't you the pastor at that megachurch?"

Carl glared but said nothing.

The guy waved his hand in the air and pointed. "This is the pastor. The one who opened up the clinic."

A few people started shouting, and even though nobody made their way closer to the yellow tape, the policewoman grabbed Carl by the elbow. "Come on. Let's get you inside."

Kennedy stepped as gingerly as she could around the broken glass while trying to keep up with them. "Sandy!" Carl shouted as soon as they got into the center, but all Kennedy noticed were the walls splashed with crass pictures, angry slogans, and an obscene statement or two. It felt as if someone hit her in the gut and then left his fist there to fester.

"Sandy!" Carl repeated.

"I'll be back to ask you some questions later." Kennedy doubted Carl heard the police officer before she went out the front door.

"Oh, thank God they let you through!" At the sound of Sandy's voice, Kennedy pried her eyes away from the grotesque graffiti. Sandy rushed to Carl, the extra fabric of her floral dress fluttering around her ankles, and they embraced. Kennedy thought she saw Carl's broad shoulders tremble, but when they pulled apart, his voice was clear and resolute.

"Baby, tell me exactly what happened."

"I came straight from church. The protestors were already here, at least some of them. At first, I didn't even notice the broken windows. I thought they were just doing their picketing thing. You know, they've got as much a right to these sidewalks as the rest of us. I was going to walk my way in here and not let them bother me. Well, by the time I was out of the car, that's when I saw the glass. And some guy starts following me real close, asking me what I'm doing around the center, making rude comments. Then another woman, one of the protestors, started shouting at him, telling him he shouldn't intimidate me no matter who I am. Then she asks me what I'm doing here, and I tell her my husband and I opened this clinic, and she apologizes for the broken glass. Says it was like that when she got here, and if she had seen who did it she would have reported it to the police. Then she asks if I want to go in, and she just marches up with me, and tells me that we're women and we have to ..." Sandy's voice caught, and Kennedy stared at her shoes while Sandy continued. "Says we have to stick together, no matter if we have our political differences. And once she sees me safe in here, she tells me again she's sorry for the mess. And then she takes her *Hands Off My Uterus* sign and goes back out with the rest of them."

Carl and Kennedy were both quiet. Carl was running his hand through his wife's light brown hair, but Kennedy couldn't take her eyes off the walls.

"I just can't believe how insensitive people can be." Sandy shook her head. "They've got their right to picket. They've got their right to be heard. But they don't care about our rights, and now look at this mess."

Kennedy had been trying to figure out a particular image spray-painted on the wall. "What's up with the hanger? What does that have to do with

..." It felt like someone grabbed the inside of her stomach and twisted a full three-hundred-sixty degrees. "Oh."

"There's more." Sandy glanced over at her husband. "You want to see the worst now or later?"

"May as well get it over with." Carl followed Sandy to the back office. She was a tall woman but looked half a foot shorter by the time they arrived there.

Kennedy's nervous chuckle sounded out of place as it echoed against the walls. "What's so intimidating about a cookie?"

"I'm sorry, babe," Sandy whispered.

Kennedy glanced at Carl.

"Oreo," he explained in a lifeless monotone. "Black on the outside. White on the inside."

Sandy shut the door and pointed at the wall. "If it makes you feel any better, I got my own message, too." The room suddenly felt twice as small. Sandy had moved the wall calendar to cover some of the letters, but Kennedy could still see the huge red *N* and the bottom half of the word *lover* underneath.

Carl and Sandy held each other for several minutes in silence. Kennedy didn't know where to look or what to say. Indignation welled up in her chest like pressure building up in a sealed flask. These were her friends. From her earliest memories, the Lindgrens had been helping people, loving people, taking people into their homes. They didn't deserve any of this. She wondered what her dad would say. Would he have the words to make sense of this type of hatred and emotional violence? Kennedy wrapped her arms around herself again, but that did nothing to stop her trembling.

"Father God ..." Carl's words were loud and sounded completely out of place in the face of such darkness and shame. "I thank you for protecting my Sandy when she was here alone. And I thank you for the kind lady who helped her reach the center safely. And even though it tears me up inside God, I thank you for the jerk who insulted my wife on the sidewalk. I thank you for the stupid, blind, ignoramuses who desecrated our new center. Because somehow, I know you have a plan for them. And somehow, I know you love them. And if I have to be totally honest with you, Father, I have to admit that I would be just as lost and just as angry and just as hateful if you hadn't poured out your grace on me. So forgive me, Lord. Forgive me for the anger I feel. Forgive me for hating them for hurting my wife, making her feel unsafe."

Carl's voice caught, and Kennedy glanced up to see the tears splashing down his cheeks onto his wife's arms as they leaned their foreheads against each other.

"Forgive me, Lord, because I can't love these idiots like you do." Carl was crying softly now. Kennedy bit her lip, but that did nothing to contain her emotion.

"Lord, you're the King. You reign bigger than all this. You reign bigger than this center. You reign bigger than politics. You reign bigger than abortion or racism or intolerance or injustice. You reign bigger than the ignorance that has kept this country in darkness for so long. And now we're asking you to come into our little, humble, violated center today and show yourself bigger. Bigger than fear. Bigger than revenge. Bigger than any of their slurs or any of their hate speech or any of their rage. And be bigger than us, too. Bigger than our unforgiveness. Bigger than our hurt. Because, Father, you know we're hurting something awful right now."

There was no *amen*. Only a small, almost indistinguishable rushing in Kennedy's spirit. She opened her eyes. Carl and Sandy had already pulled apart and were laughing quietly at each other's tear-stained faces. Kennedy wasn't exactly sure what had just happened, but she recalled how insecure she had felt at St. Margaret's earlier. She thought about how small she had felt living with Secret Seminary students who risked North Korean death camps for the sake of the gospel. She thought about how envious she had felt when everyone around her was getting touched by God and she was left sitting in the bleachers to watch.

So maybe she hadn't lifted her hands in complete and utter abandon. Maybe she hadn't sung out her heart in ecstasy or faced a North Korean prison cell for her bold faith. But she had witnessed something more real than anything she had experienced since she returned to the States. She couldn't put a name to it and probably never could, but Kennedy knew she was somehow better for it, and she knew it was something she would carry in a sacred part of her heart for the rest of her life.

CHAPTER 7

Sandy made a list of paints for Carl to pick up from the store. Kennedy found a broom to sweep up the glass, but Carl didn't want her by the broken windows. "If you want to help, we still need to get these postcards ready to mail out. They're the invitations for the dinner on Thursday." He showed her how the post office needed them grouped by zip code, and Kennedy set to work, grateful for something constructive to put her hands to. She would be late meeting Reuben at the library, but she wasn't about to leave Carl and Sandy right now.

"Is everyone all right back here?" The voice was too good-humored, and Kennedy looked up to see the politician who had prayed at the service that morning.

"Wayne!" Sandy rushed to him with a hug. Carl stretched out his hand.

"I came as soon as I heard the report on the Christian radio." Wayne shook his head. "It's just horrible what they've done."

"Nothing a little paint and some new glass won't fix." Carl's voice was still tight.

"How in the world did you get through the picket lines?" Sandy asked.

"Well, I think I made a record. I was only asked for three autographs." Wayne flashed another dizzying grin.

"Autographs?" Carl asked. He leaned out of the office and let out a low whistle. "Well, what do you make of that? You had it easy, brother. Those weren't the picketers we had to walk through. It was all pro-choicers when we came."

"They're on the other side of the sidewalk now," Wayne told them. He locked eyes with Sandy. "You really should go take a look."

Kennedy followed Carl and Sandy into the waiting room. The police tape was gone. Half a dozen police lined either side of the road. All the protestors from earlier were on the opposite sidewalk, but those closest to the broken window had pickets with statistics about fetal development, Bible verses about God knitting children together in the womb, and slogans about protecting babies.

"That's quite a different view than when we arrived earlier," Carl admitted.

"I'll say." Wayne flashed a grin.

"You and your campaign didn't have anything to do with this new turn of events, did they?" Sandy asked with a smile in her voice.

Wayne flashed his white-toothed grin. "I don't speak for my managers. All I know is these picketers were here when I pulled up."

"Uh-huh." Sandy's voice was playful, and she smiled for the first time that afternoon.

Wayne smoothed out his hair and straightened his necktie. "Anyway, we're making a statement from here for the press in about half an hour."

"From here?" Sandy repeated. "They can't bring the cameras into this mess." Her eyes fluttered nervously to the walls.

Wayne frowned at the graffiti. "I guess we can do it up front by the window. I told my manager we should work in a little announcement about the fundraising dinner Thursday. Couldn't hurt to get you guys some more publicity."

"Unless the picketers scare off all the donors," Sandy mumbled under her breath, but Kennedy doubted the others heard.

"Well, then." Wayne clasped his hands together. "That's settled. What do we do while we wait for the cameramen?"

Carl caught Kennedy's eye and gave her a wink. "How would the soon-to-be governor of Massachusetts feel about stamping postcards?"

The mood in the center lifted minute by minute as they set to work. Once Kennedy finished the pile she was sorting, she figured it was time to head back to campus. If she got lucky and caught the T as it was pulling up, she might find Reuben still in the library. Before she could slip out, Wayne's phone rang.

He slipped his hand smoothly into his pocket. "I bet that's about the statement." The conversation was short. "They're ready for me out front." Wayne was beaming, and Kennedy wondered if Carl and Sandy noticed how fake he looked. Maybe it was a politician thing. Or maybe all the support and publicity he brought to their center helped them overlook his apparent insincerity. Whatever it was, Kennedy was glad for an excuse to leave before she had to watch him preen in front of a dozen cameras.

"I need to go, too." she announced. Sandy cast a worried glance to her husband.

"Maybe you better wait," Carl said. "After Wayne's speech, I'll drive you back myself. Your father would kill me if I let you walk out of here with hundreds of angry protestors looking on."

"I'm sure it will be fine," Kennedy insisted, but she looked at the Lindgrens' expressions and didn't want to burden them further. "I'm supposed to meet my friend," she explained, "but I guess a few more minutes won't kill anyone."

"Do you want to use the phone to let her know you're late?" Sandy asked.

"I don't have his number with me. It's in my phone, and that's somewhere in my dorm room."

"*His?*" Carl asked but stopped smirking when his wife nudged him in the ribs.

"Carl will drive you back as soon as Wayne's done posing for the cameras." Sandy gave Kennedy a gentle back rub. "And don't worry — he won't take more than a few minutes I'm sure. The last thing he wants to do is bore his audience."

Carl chuckled under his breath. Sandy was right. The speech was over in less than five minutes. Kennedy had expected the Lindgrens to both stop their work to listen, but they seemed content to keep on sorting postcards side by side.

"Did you wow them?" Sandy asked when Wayne pranced back into the center to a loud roar of both applause and angry shouts. He looked even taller than he had before he left.

"All I have to say is I hope something I said got through to the fools who vandalized your center." He shook his head, replacing his smile for an instant pout that became him just as well.

Sandy patted his shoulder. "Well, you keep focused on winning your election and don't worry about us. We've seen worse, you know."

Kennedy wasn't sure if she had seen worse or not and was sad to think that Carl and Sandy had.

"You heading out now?" Carl asked when Wayne started to button up his coat.

"Sure am. I wish I could stay to help more, but ..." He stumbled over his words for the first time, but neither of the Lindgrens seemed to notice.

Sandy put down her pile of invites and gave him a hug. "It's always good to see you. Thanks for taking time out of your campaign to check on us commoners." Everyone chuckled, and Kennedy was left guessing if Sandy meant to be sarcastic or not.

"Well, if you're heading out ..." Carl inserted, and Kennedy wished she could stop him with telepathy. "Would you mind taking Kennedy here back to her dorm at Harvard?"

"Harvard, huh?" Wayne's face brightened, and he spared Kennedy his first glance since showing up. "Sure thing. My car's out back."

Kennedy glanced at the Lindgrens, who were only a quarter of the way through the postcards they had to sort. Maybe it was just as well they both stayed here. Besides, she hadn't thought about it before, but now that Carl was marked as the director of the center, it might still be dangerous for him to walk out right now. Wayne was way too-high profile for someone to seriously bother. She said good-bye to Carl and Sandy and followed him out the center. The sound of the protestors increased, but Wayne put his arm around her, and whispered before she could shrug him off, "Don't listen to anything they say. Their words can't hurt you. All right?"

Kennedy nodded and tried to recreate the calm she had felt when Carl prayed in the center. Many of the pro-lifers extended their hands to Wayne, and others offered encouraging words about the election next week. He kept his arm around her like a shield as a photographer flashed a light at them and a reporter shoved a microphone in his face.

"Mr. Abernathy, is this one of the young women you would deny contraceptives and access to safe abortions?"

Wayne didn't slow down his pace but waved the microphone away.

They got to his car, which he circled once and studied with a frown. Looking for dents? Then he turned on his shiny smile and opened the passenger door. "After you," he stated regally.

The upholstery had that sort of new lacquer smell, and when Kennedy sat down, she found it hard to get comfortable because her pants kept sticking to the seat. Even the seatbelt buckle glistened. Kennedy wondered how many semesters at Harvard Wayne's car would pay for.

"You ready?" he asked when he got into the driver's seat.

Kennedy smiled in response, and he rolled out of the lot. They hadn't passed the outlying protestors when his phone rang. "Hey. I'm on the road. What's up?"

Kennedy let out her breath when they finally turned off Elm Street. She wondered how all the other shop and business owners felt about having their sidewalks turned into an ideological war zone.

"Good news?" Wayne was apparently one of those people who shouted into their cell phones as if that was the only way to be heard. "Those were my friends whose office was attacked ... Well, it's your job to worry about publicity, not mine. I'm just glad nobody got hurt."

He shook his head as he hung up. "My campaign manager," he explained with a sigh. "Acts as though this protest is Christmas Day for the campaign. Sympathy votes and all." He gave Kennedy a smile, a real one this time, the corners of his eyes wrinkling up attractively. "So, what are you studying at Harvard? I just hope it's not politics."

"Biology."

His eyebrows shot up. "Oh yeah? Pre-med?"

"Sort of. I'm part of their early-admissions medical school program."

"Good for you." Kennedy was relieved to note Wayne could actually sound sincere if he wanted to. "You must have worked hard to get accepted right out of high school."

Kennedy didn't feel like talking about herself, so she asked, "What about you? When did you get involved with pro-life stuff?"

Wayne chuckled. "That would be a better question if I were driving you all the way to DC. The short version is I did picketing, things like that from Roe v. Wade on. I was part of the first wave of the anti-abortion movement, but I got frustrated. We got a little bit of publicity, made a lot of people angry, and preached to thousands of choirs. That was it. Don't quote me on this, but it was actually a staunch pro-abortion advocate who helped me see the light. You ever heard of Sandra Green?"

Kennedy shook her head.

Wayne shrugged. "Yeah, she hasn't been around in a while, at least not making news like years past. She used to be a real big voice for the abortion camp. But she was talking about a new bill we were hoping to push through the State House. I was just wetting my feet in politics at the time, you know. But she said something I'll never forget. Knocked me right off my high horse. Said that the reason nobody wants to jump on the pro-life bandwagon is because it's a bunch of stuffy old white men who have never lifted a finger to help single moms. And it was true. At least for me at the time. And a lot of my acquaintances. What was the point of stopping abortions if I wasn't going to help support new mothers? That's how I got my initiation into the pregnancy center ministry. Made it my mission to give women a foundation, maybe alleviate some of the perceived need for abortions in the first place."

Kennedy didn't know how to respond. She had never looked at abortion in those terms before. In her family, it was simply wrong, morally and ethically, and that was all.

"You from a Christian family?" Wayne asked after a minute. He had a disarming way of taking his eyes off the road to look at her when he talked.

"Yeah."

"Well, you just stick to your values. Especially on a campus like Harvard. It's not easy. Even more so now than when I was your age. But you keep following what your mom and dad taught you, and you're going to be fine." That plastic smile flashed again, and they spent the last few minutes traveling in silence. Kennedy got the impression Wayne wouldn't remember her face in a week, but she was thankful for the ride. He pulled his car into the main campus entrance. "Is this close enough?"

"Yeah," she answered. "This is just fine."

"Well, God bless you." He raised his hand in a wave, and for a minute she expected him to hand her a pen or a campaign button or something. As his car eased back into traffic, Kennedy wondered if Reuben would still be in the library. Her dorm was on the way, so she figured she'd grab her books and her cell phone. She needed something quick to eat, too. Her stomach had been churning and grumbling ever since St. Margaret's.

She felt light as she bounded up the stairs to her dorm, grateful her lab would give her an excuse to shove all thoughts of the pregnancy center and Rose out of her mind. The door to her room was halfway open, and Willow crossed her arms as soon as Kennedy entered.

"Your boyfriend's been looking for you."

CHAPTER 8

Kennedy knew if she took the time to sit down, she wouldn't get up again, but her bed tugged her toward it with an almost irresistible gravity. She threw her lab books into her backpack.

"So Reuben was here? Was he upset?"

Willow shrugged. "Does that guy ever get upset about anything? He must take, I don't know, ten Prozacs a day or something. Is he a weed head?"

Kennedy shook her head, only half listening. "I left my phone here this morning so I couldn't call him." She glanced around her desk and rummaged through her top drawer. "Hey, could you call me? I still can't find it."

Willow let out a long, dramatic sigh that could have won awards if she had actually been on the stage, but she punched the buttons on her phone. "It's ringing."

Kennedy spun herself around in a slow circle. "I don't hear it."

Willow turned her cell off. "Maybe you let your batteries go dead."

"Yeah, maybe." It certainly wouldn't have been the first time. The problem was she didn't have Reuben's number written down anywhere. She looked at her clock. Over an hour late. "He must think I'm such a flake. When did he stop by?"

Willow ran a hand through her long hair, which this week was tinted a somewhat convincing ginger tone. "Half hour ago, maybe? I don't know. I've been busy."

Kennedy glanced at the army shooter game on her roommate's computer. "Looks like it," she mumbled. "Hey, did he say where he was going to be? Did he mention the library?"

Willow was already back at her sniping. A fake death cry rang out as a puddle of red pixelated blood splashed on her screen. She didn't respond.

Well, Kennedy would try to send him an email and then head to the library to see if he was still there.

Kennedy waited for her desktop to load and opened a granola bar. What had she had for breakfast? It seemed like so long ago. And she and Reuben had at least three or four hours of work ahead of them to finish up that report. All she really wanted to do was sleep off the stress of the day. She glanced once more at her bed. Maybe a few minutes ...

Wonk. Wonk. Wonk.

Willow wrinkled her nose and covered her ears. "What's that noise?"

The resident advisor from the boys' side of the hall poked his head through their open door. "Fire drill," he called out.

Kennedy groaned. She didn't have time for this. She grabbed her backpack and decided to head right to the library. She could email Reuben from the computers there if she didn't find him. Willow was moaning about having to start her level over again as she and Kennedy plodded down the stairs along with the other sluggish students. Several dozen were already outside by the time they joined the throng.

"So there you are."

Kennedy turned toward the sound of Reuben's voice and tried to muster the energy to smile. "I'm sorry about our meeting. It's been a crazy day."

She didn't want to go into any details and was thankful when Reuben just remarked, "Hey, things come up. No big deal."

"Well, I would have called. But I didn't have my phone with me. I just got back to my dorm a few minutes ago, and I still couldn't find it."

"No problem." Reuben's eyes twinkled, and Kennedy had to laugh at his endearing way of staying so composed. There wasn't much she suspected could make him mad, with the exception maybe of someone insulting one of his sisters.

"I was on my way to the library to look for you," she said. "Do you want to head there?"

"Sure." Reuben adjusted the straps of his backpack. "Did you print up the table from last week?"

Kennedy groaned. "I completely forgot. You know, things have been insane ever since that weird phone call Friday."

"Hey," Reuben insisted, "don't worry about it."

"We can go up now and grab it from my computer. Well, at least we can when this fire drill is over."

"So that's why you're all standing out here?" Reuben chuckled. "I thought somebody put something rotten in the vent and smoked you all out."

After a few minutes, the resident advisor shouted the all-clear, and Kennedy and Reuben headed up the stairs.

"Did your roommate tell you I stopped by?" he asked.

"Yeah. I'm sorry you had to come all the way over here for ..."

"You don't need to apologize any more. Your roommate's very nice, by the way. Strange maybe, but nice."

Yeah, that's Willow. Kennedy kept the thought to herself. When they got to her room, she sat down and pulled up the files they'd need on her laptop.

"You can grab Willow's chair until she comes back," Kennedy offered. "It should only take me a minute."

"Isn't this yours?" Kennedy heard the smile in Reuben's expression before she glanced over at him. "I thought you said you lost it."

She reached out for the phone he dangled between his fingers. "Hey, where was that?"

"Right here on your roommate's desk. I knew it couldn't be hers. She isn't the type to have John 3:16 on her phone case."

"No, I wouldn't," Willow remarked from the doorway.

Kennedy put the cell in her bag. "Reuben just found my phone on your desk."

"Huh." Willow shrugged. "All kinds of mysteries today."

"What other mysteries?" Kennedy asked automatically even though she was focused more on getting her file downloaded.

In her periphery, she saw Willow fling her hair over her shoulder. "I left around noon to find some breakfast. I know I locked up."

Kennedy pressed print and wondered if Willow's story had a point or if maybe she simply appreciated having a male audience member paying attention to her.

"Well, when I came back ..."

"Let me guess," Reuben interrupted. "Your door was wide open."

Willow pouted. "No. But it was unlocked. And I know for sure I locked it up."

Kennedy shrugged. "I've done that before. Maybe we should mention it to the RA. Might be the lock itself."

"Oooh," Willow exclaimed, "let me be the one to tell him. I've been dying for an excuse to stop by his room."

"You'd be better off going to Fatima. You know, the RA for the girls' hall?"

Willow shrugged. "The other one's cuter."

Kennedy rolled her eyes, and Reuben stifled a chuckle. "What?" Willow asked. "Just because he's a junior you think I can't get his attention?"

Kennedy snatched the pages from her printer. "Come on," she told Reuben. "Let's get this lab finished up, now that we've wasted half the afternoon."

"What?" Willow demanded. "You still don't think ..."

Kennedy's ringtone interrupted Willow's tirade. "Is that mine?" she asked, digging it out of her backpack. "I thought the batteries were dead."

"Guess it's your lucky day." Reuben headed for the stairs and Kennedy followed him out.

She didn't recognize the caller ID. "Hello?"

"Kennedy, honey, it's me, Sandy. I forgot to give you the cookies I made for you earlier. We were going to stop by and surprise you, but Carl lost the address you wrote for him."

"I didn't lose it," Kennedy could hear Carl object in the background. "I had it right here on the desk. On a purple Post-it."

"Well, anyway," Sandy breezed over him, "are you at your dorm now? Because I want you to have them while they're fresh. If I had been in my right mind, I would have sent them back with you this afternoon, but, you know ..."

Sandy's voice trailed off. As Kennedy walked toward the library with Reuben, she searched for something to say to keep Sandy from feeling guilty over homemade goodies. "That's really sweet of you. I'm actually getting ready to work on a lab report, but if you give me a call when you're pulling up to campus I can come out to the parking lot and meet you."

"I'm sorry we couldn't surprise you, sweetie. But you know Carl, always misplacing everything ..."

Carl's flustered reply was barely audible.

"Well, I'll see you pretty soon." Sandy's voice rang out strong and melodic. "We just have to finish up these postcards."

Kennedy was glad to note how much more chipper Sandy sounded compared to earlier.

"You know," Sandy continued, "I feel awful about this afternoon. Here you are, I haven't seen you since you were in my Sunday school class way back when, and we didn't even get to have a proper how-you-doing chat."

"Well, I know today's been a crazy day," Kennedy began and then stopped, reluctant to bring up the incident at the center.

"Don't you worry about us," Sandy prattled. "You know, Carl and I, we've been through hell and back more times than you've been around the sun. We're just thankful you weren't hurt, honey. And you weren't too shook up, were you?"

"I'm all right," Kennedy assured her, although thinking about that afternoon made her shiver in the autumn breeze. By the time Sandy was done talking, Kennedy and Reuben were already stepping up to the library.

Reuben held the door open. "That woman has a loud voice."

"That's the pastor's wife at the church I checked out this morning. I knew her a long time ago, before we moved."

Reuben didn't say anything else as they made their way to their regular study spot near the art history books.

"So, you want to talk?" Reuben asked when they both sat down.

"Talk about what?"

"Whatever happened today. Why you were so late. Why you started shaking on the phone just now."

"I wasn't shaking." Kennedy laughed nervously.

"Yes, you were. You want to talk?" he asked again.

She glanced at their books on the table. "Not really."

Reuben leaned back in his chair, crossed his arms, and studied her. "All right. Then let's take a look at that lab."

They finished up their report a few hours later over dinner. Reuben even managed to keep from spilling anything on their paper or getting dirty finger smears on any of the pages.

"You doing anything else tonight?" he asked as they walked together back toward Kennedy's dorm.

"I have to read a little more Dostoevsky. But that's pretty relaxing."

Reuben chuckled.

"What's so funny?"

"Not many people use *Dostoevsky* and *relaxing* in the same sentence, I imagine."

They said good-night, and Kennedy's legs felt as heavy as titanium as she trudged up the stairs. She was glad Willow was out. She could use some quiet time to herself. She gathered up her robe and shower supplies when her phone rang. *Not again.* She glanced at the time. It could be her mother. She groaned and put down her towel when she saw the number. She had been so busy with Reuben she'd completely forgotten about those silly cookies.

"Hi, Sandy," she sighed, trying to muster up some convincing resemblance to enthusiasm.

"Kennedy, it's me." When she heard the tension in Carl's voice, Kennedy overlooked her own exhaustion.

"Did you find out who the girl is?" She clutched the phone to her ear.

"No," Carl answered. "No, Sandy wanted me to tell you she's terribly sorry about the cookies."

Disappointment sank to the floor of Kennedy's gut like a concrete ball.

On the other line, she could hear Carl sigh, too. "We're just now leaving the center, believe it or not. We had the police to talk to, they went over the whole joint, then the reporters ..."

"It's all right. Tell Sandy I just had dinner, and I'm stuffed now, anyway."

"Well, she's still planning to get these cookies to you."

Kennedy wondered if maybe she should feign a diet or something so the Lindgrens would stop worrying. The gesture was nice, but Kennedy couldn't imagine how fretting over a plate of sweets could be beneficial to their health.

"Anyway..." Carl let out a nervous-sounding chuckle. "The reporters are wondering who's really behind the vandalism. One suggested Wayne may have planned it to garnish extra publicity."

Kennedy's whole face scrunched up at the thought of the politician. "Do they have any proof?"

"You know how reporters are," Carl answered. "Act like they're holding all the cards and you never know if they're bluffing until you see it all in print."

Kennedy didn't know much of anything about reporters, but she was sorry the Lindgrens had gone through so much today.

"Well, I don't want to bother you," Carl said. "I should let you go. Sandy just wants me to say she'll call you tomorrow about the cookies. We can't have her baking go to waste, you know."

Kennedy told Carl good-night and ended the call as her low battery light came on. That was weird. It was over halfway charged when Reuben found it that afternoon. She plugged it in and reminded herself to talk to her dad. Maybe it was time for a new battery or something.

She picked up her towel and stared around the room. What was it about being alone that made the back of her neck prickle? Had she gotten so used to having others around that solitude freaked her out and left her skin all covered in goose bumps? She glanced at the window to make sure the blinds were down, half expecting to see someone staring right at her.

What a crazy day. As she headed to the showers, she hoped tomorrow would be a little calmer.

CHAPTER 9

Exhaustion clung to Kennedy's limbs when her alarm rang Monday morning. She wasn't much of a coffee drinker but decided she might stop for something on the way to lab. Her roommate didn't have any classes before noon, at least none she regularly attended, so Kennedy got dressed as quietly as she could with the light from her desk lamp. Her phone beeped, and she hoped it wasn't a text from Reuben saying there was a mistake in their lab. They had to submit it in fifteen minutes. She looked at the message.

This is Nick from church. I have a question about that call you got.

How in the world was she supposed to concentrate on science after getting a text like that? Well, he'd have to save it for later. She started typing to tell him she was off to class but stopped. Lab wasn't over until noon. Could she really wait that long? Would she be able to focus on anything besides Rose? She was halfway down the stairs before she decided to call him back.

"Hey, Kennedy," he answered. "I got your number from Carl. Hope I didn't wake you up or anything."

"No, I'm on my way to class, though, so I only have a minute."

He made a sound like smacking his lips together. "Well, I started browsing through our youth group roster when I came in this morning. We don't have anyone named Rose, but if we assume she used a fake name, it looks like there are two girls who may or may not be our mystery caller."

Hope swelled in Kennedy's chest like an over-inflated balloon.

"Unfortunately, neither one is a perfect match."

Pop.

"One is a homeschool girl who's actually fourteen now. And the other is thirteen and *was* homeschooled until this fall when her parents enrolled her in private school."

Kennedy slowed down her pace as the science complex loomed into view.

"Like I said," Nick went on, "neither one is a perfect fit."

Kennedy sighed. Out of all the girls at St. Margaret's ... "Well, thanks for looking." She tried not to let the disappointment creep into her voice.

"Wait a minute," Nick went on. "See, both the girls were in a drama last spring. We've got the whole thing on video. I was thinking, if you wanted to meet me here, at the church I could show you the recording. Do you think if you heard her voice, you'd be able to tell if it was the girl you talked to?"

Kennedy knew for a fact she could replicate Rose's voice even in her sleep, since that's all she had done last night in her dreams. "Yeah, I could probably do that."

"I'm here until three and then I'm off to one of the elementary schools for Good News Club," Nick said. "Do you have time to come on by?"

"I can take the T and be there by about one." Kennedy's backpack hung heavy on her shoulders when she thought about the full schedule ahead. "Would that give us enough time?"

"Sounds perfect." She could hear Nick's smile from the other end of the line.

"Ok, talk to you then." She went to push the end button and saw her phone was already back down to half a battery after charging all night. Yeah, she definitely had to talk to her dad about a replacement. If she could find the time to get hold of him, that is. Kennedy wondered if her classmates from the East Coast realized how fortunate they were that they didn't have to worry about time-zone issues.

Kennedy saw Reuben waiting for her at the door to the science building and sped up. She probably wasn't any closer to figuring out who Rose was, but at least others were asking questions, trying to help.

The three hours of lab passed faster than they might have thanks to Reuben's good nature and humor. For bits at a time, Kennedy forgot about the pregnancy center and her upcoming meeting with Nick. She found herself laughing with Reuben on her way out of class, and part of her wished Carl had never asked her to get involved at the center in the first place. She was here at Harvard for her education, and if it hadn't been for some fortunate miracle and her lab partner's charming personality, she couldn't have made it through the past few hours without completely losing her focus. She was beginning to think that even if she had time for pregnancy center ministry, she didn't have the emotional capacity to juggle it along with her schoolwork.

"Want to grab some lunch?" Reuben asked. "I need to study more for calculus."

"I can't, I'm off to St. Margaret's, that church I visited. I have a meeting there."

"You're not in trouble, are you?" Reuben asked, his tone almost defensive.

Kennedy laughed. "No, nothing like that. We're still trying to see if there's any way we can figure out who called us the other night."

"That's still got you worried, doesn't it?"

She nodded. "Last night I kept jerking myself awake. I kept thinking I heard the hotline phone ringing again," she admitted with a chuckle.

"It's because you've got a big heart, my friend."

Kennedy glanced at Reuben, expecting to see his familiar sarcastic grin, but his expression was warm, considerate.

He stuck his hands in his pockets. "You know you can always come knock on my door if you need anything."

"Thanks." She forced a smile so he wouldn't think she was depressed on top of crazy. "I really appreciate that."

"What are friends for?" He elbowed her playfully on the side of her arm, and that old crooked grin spread across his face once more.

"I better go," she told him.

The underground T station was nearly as dark as a solar eclipse compared to the bright midday sun. Kennedy paid for her token and stood on the platform to wait. She hadn't expected to get so nervous. What if she heard one of the girls on the video and recognized Rose's voice? They could go to the police. They'd have enough evidence to warrant an investigation, right? Especially if Carl got behind them. Maybe he could talk Wayne Abernathy into using his political sway to get the case open. But what if the girl's uncle had already taken her to an abortion clinic? What if they were too late? Kennedy's stomach tried flipping itself inside out every time she thought about it. Who would be sick and depraved enough to violate ...

"Excuse me. Did you drop your book?" Someone tapped her back, and a man in sunglasses held out a paperback novel. There was a small scar running from his thumb joint to his wrist. She scanned the cover. Historical, by the looks of it, with a pretty long-haired brunette wearing a velvet gown on the cover, something Kennedy's mom might like. "No, that's not mine. Thank you, though."

He shrugged and went on. Kennedy wondered when she'd have time to start the next mystery her mom ordered her from Amazon. She glanced at the clock in the subway station. If she had planned ahead, she would have brought *Crime and Punishment* to read while she waited.

The redline train finally arrived, and after the short ride, Kennedy walked the last few blocks to the church. Her insides trembled a little when she stepped into St. Margaret's again. Some kind of psychosomatic response, she told herself and ignored the uncomfortable quivering. She was wearing a long-sleeved blouse covered by a loose sweater. At least Nick wouldn't see how much she was shaking.

She sped up as she neared his office. Now she was there, she wanted to look at the videos and leave. Nick's door was slightly ajar, but she knocked anyway and waited for him to call her in. He was wearing a T-shirt with a picture of Jesus smiling and drinking a Coke. "Boy, you look tired," he exclaimed.

She gave him a surprised look, and they both laughed.

"I'm sorry. Let me try that again." Nick cleared his throat. "Kennedy, hi. How are you? Do you want some coffee?"

Kennedy accepted his offer. She knew she must look as awful as she felt. To complete the picture, she had accidentally fallen asleep last night with her contacts in, and her eyes were now bright red as well as itchy. She couldn't remember the brand of eye-drops her dad got her the last time that happened, and she added it to her list of questions to ask him.

"So, I got the video up." Nick fidgeted with his pen. "Unfortunately, I watched it again, and Harmony has a few lines, but Alicia doesn't actually talk." He slid the cursor until somewhere about halfway through the video. "All right, here's where we hear Harmony."

He pointed his pen to a confident-looking teenager on the side of the screen who exclaimed in a melodramatic voice, "*I don't see why we have to do anything for her at all.*" The audio was pretty poor quality, but Kennedy shook her head right away.

"That's not her." The girl in the recording was bold. Outspoken. She could handle the spotlight in a way Rose almost certainly couldn't.

"All right. That was easy." Nick scrolled to another part of the video and leaned forward. "Well, here's what Alicia looks like. You can see her there behind that boy with the mike."

Kennedy squinted at the screen.

"If I remember right," Nick continued, "she'll come up front a little bit later in the show so you can get a better look."

He skipped ahead. "There. This gives a pretty good picture. I just wish we could hear her voice."

Kennedy frowned at the image. "Is this the highest resolution you've got?"

"Yeah, sorry about that."

She leaned forward. The girl wasn't as petite as Kennedy pictured Rose, but there was a shy look in her eyes. "Would you say she's pretty quiet?" Kennedy asked.

Nick nodded. "Yeah. Unless she's with her brothers or sisters. Those kids are like little Shriners when they get together, just without the hats."

"Shriners?"

"You know, those funny guys in parades ..."

The last parade Kennedy had seen was when she was about six, but she didn't say anything. It was just another one of those cultural references any other American her age would catch onto right away. Just another reminder she wasn't quite at home at Harvard as she hoped.

"Anyway," Nick went on, "Alicia's pretty quiet when she's by herself, but she can get rowdy when she's with her brothers and sisters. Her mom just had a new baby if I remember right. Makes nine or ten altogether now."

Kennedy had grown up as an only child and couldn't imagine that many kids running around one house. "And she's the one who's fourteen?"

"Yeah."

Kennedy peered at the photo one last time. Could you tell if a person was abused or not just by looking at a picture?

"Good family, you'd say?" she prodded.

"Yeah, I think so. Carl knows them pretty well."

"She said she was thirteen on the phone."

Nick shrugged. "I just thought it was worth mentioning, since their whole family is homeschooled."

Kennedy didn't say anything but sat staring at the monitor. There were at least a dozen girls on stage. Why couldn't one of them be Rose?

"That's not her, is it?" Nick finally asked.

She let out her breath. "I don't know. Part of me wants it to be, but ..."

He clicked off the monitor. "Yeah, I didn't think so, either."

They looked at each other for a moment. Kennedy knew she should go, but she was so tired.

"I know you're busy with school," Nick added tentatively, "but we have youth group on Tuesday nights. If you wanted to come by tomorrow, I could introduce you as a new helper for the junior high girls ..."

"What? Go in undercover?" Kennedy chuckled even though she didn't find the situation at all humorous. She wondered what her parents would say about the whole situation. Would they be proud of her trying to protect someone so helpless and vulnerable as Rose? Or would they tell her to mind her own business and focus on her studies? She had the feeling they would approve of her volunteer work until her grades started to suffer for it. She had already spent Friday afternoon at the center and Sunday at St. Margaret's. Now she was here again, and Nick was talking about her coming back tomorrow for youth group.

"I'm not sure," she confessed. "I really wasn't planning to get this involved in the first place."

"Yeah." Nick drummed the pen against his desk. "I know. Carl's really stressed out about it all, too, what with the election and everything coming up."

"What's the election have to do with it?" Kennedy asked. Two months in the States and she was already sick of American politics.

"Well, Abernathy is a high-profile candidate. Lots of people love him. And just as many hate him. We've had journalists poking around, attending services, asking Carl questions."

"I didn't even realize he attended here. I thought he just showed up yesterday to pray."

"No." Nick stretched his arms behind his head and leaned back in his chair. "His family's been coming here for years. He and Carl knew each other back in college, or something like that."

"Where is Carl?" Kennedy asked, looking around as if talking about him should make him materialize in the doorway.

"It's his day off. Well, technically, at least," Nick answered. "I think he and Sandy are cleaning up the center. I guess there was a lot of graffiti ..."

"I was there." Kennedy didn't want to remember those slogans on the wall. If she didn't have her Russian literature class later in the afternoon, she could stop by Elm Street and offer to help. Why couldn't there be an extra five or ten hours packed into every day? She stood with a sigh. "Well, thanks for showing me the video."

"Yeah, no problem." Nick stood up awkwardly, as if his body didn't know if he wanted to take the extra steps to walk around the desk or if he would see her out from where he was. He held up his hand. "Thanks for coming in. Sorry we didn't ..." He frowned. "Sorry it didn't work out. But God knows where she is, right?"

Kennedy forced a smile even though his words were a little too optimistic for her current mood.

God, if you know where she is, how hard would it be for you to give us a little clue?

She hugged her sweater tighter across her chest as she headed back out into the brisk autumn afternoon.

CHAPTER 10

Once Kennedy got back to her dorm, she spent half an hour before class studying for the next day's calculus test. She munched on dry Cheerios and thought about her meeting with Nick while she worked on her practice problems.

St. Margaret's was a big church. Why should it be so hard to find one girl? There should be at least a few dozen families who homeschooled, right? And none of them had a thirteen-year-old daughter? It didn't make sense.

When it was time for her to close her books and head to her Russian lit class, she still wasn't any closer to an answer. Maybe she should call Carl, see what he said. She had gone over her phone conversations with Rose hundreds of times already. Had she forgotten something — one little detail that could solve the whole mystery? During class, she listed each particular she could remember about the phone call and only heard half of what the professor said.

Reuben texted her that evening to see if she wanted to study math over dinner, but she feigned a headache and went back to her room. She really would have a migraine by the end of the night if she kept this up. She plopped down in her desk chair and heaved open her huge calculus book.

She gaped at the first problem for over ten minutes before she finally gave up. Maybe she should email her mom. Kennedy opened up her inbox. After gazing at the screen for another few minutes without typing anything, she finally shook her head and went to the St. Margaret's website. There had to be some kind of clue.

There was a little search box on top of the home page. Kennedy knew she wouldn't get any hits, but she typed in *Rose* anyway and waited for the computer to tell her the search term hadn't been found. She was wasting time. She still had to spend another hour or so on her practice problems if she wanted to be ready for her calculus test tomorrow, and she was now officially behind in *Crime and Punishment*, which she needed to finish in a week along with a ten-page research paper.

She followed the links to the photos page. There were plenty of pictures from the youth group, even though none of students' names was listed. What was she doing? Did she really expect staring at photos of strangers would help? Besides, if Rose was part of Nick's youth group, wouldn't he have been able to identify her?

But what if Rose only came to St. Margaret's with her family on Sundays? It would be impossible for anybody at a church that size to know everyone else. So how in the world could they find her? She thought for a moment about calling Carl, but he had been through so much the past two days. Now he and Sandy were probably going crazy trying to get everything ready for Thursday's dinner to celebrate the center's opening. It was going to be fancy, and having Senator Abernathy speak would draw a lot of people in as well, she suspected.

Some music. That's what she needed to focus. She typed in the address for her favorite online radio station. She still had to get those calculus problems finished.

The website loaded slowly, so she went back to the St. Margaret's page while she waited. She had taken almost all Advanced Placement classes during her senior year in Yanji and still graduated with a 4.0. So far at Harvard, she hadn't gotten lower than a 92 on any test or assignment. She could handle culture shock, weekly lab write-ups, and still find time to read a mystery or two a month. Why couldn't she track down a single girl? It wasn't like the city was overrun with homeschooled thirteen-year-olds named Rose. Maybe she would take Nick's suggestion and visit the youth group tomorrow night. Her study group was meeting until about 5:30. What time did Nick say she should come?

She clicked on the St. Margaret's calendar of events. *Youth group. Tuesday night, seven to nine.* Well, she might make it. If she wasn't already behind in every single class by then.

Something on the bottom of the calendar caught her eye. *Homeschool group field trip. Tour of the State House.* Straightening up in her chair,

Kennedy searched to see if there was more information about the homeschool group. She finally found a quick blurb under the women's ministry tab:

Our mission is to provide support to the homeschooling families in our congregation. We offer fellowship through field trips, cooperative learning experiences, and a quarterly homeschool moms' support group. Contact Vivian Abernathy for details.

Abernathy? What if ...? No, it couldn't be ... She did a quick google search for Wayne Abernathy. Her computer was running slower than normal, but by the time the image of his family finished loading, she had already read the caption.

Wayne and Vivian Abernathy with their two children, Noah (age 16) and Jodie (age 12).

Kennedy's pulse was the only thing in the room racing faster than her mind. The picture was dated. She quickly counted back. Nine months ago. She stared at the family. Vivian was tall, a woman who was obviously aging but still trying to cling to the last remnants of her youth. She had her arm around her son, who stood with a half-smile that made Kennedy guess he would rather be anywhere than posing for one of his father's campaign photos. The fingers on Vivian Abernathy's other hand intertwined tenderly with her daughter's wind-blown bits of hair. Kennedy looked at the name again. *Jodie.* She was quite a bit shorter and even more petite than her mom, as if a strong wind might erase her from memory. Her clothes were pressed and elegant, and her pearl earrings looked out of place on someone so young. Kennedy studied the smile and tried to guess if she was a happy child or not.

Jodie. Was it possible ...?

There were footsteps outside her door. Voices. The sun was almost down, and Kennedy hadn't turned on the lights. Her eyeballs were jabbing pain to the back of her brain after staring so much. How long had she been sleuthing behind her computer screen?

The door burst open, and Kennedy gave a little start. "Oh, it's you." She let out her breath when Willow came in. "I thought you were at rehearsal."

"I will be." Willow's voice was always dramatic but now had a strange sort of drawl to it. She walked lazily to her dresser and pulled out some nightclothes. "Don't wait up for me tonight, ok? I'll just take what I need and see you tomorrow."

Kennedy rolled her eyes when Willow burped.

"Don't you want to know who it is?" Willow hunched over and slumped an arm on the back of Kennedy's chair. "The RA from the other hall. I told you I was going to talk to him about that lock, right?"

Her roommate's breath reeked, but Kennedy didn't make any comments. It wouldn't be the first time Willow spent the night away.

"Good-night," she muttered as Willow hummed her way out of the room, leaving the door a crack open.

As soon Willow was gone, Kennedy started browsing Wayne Abernathy's personal webpage. A lot of the information had to do with the upcoming election, but it did include a brief bio. Married to Vivian, a lawyer before she left the workplace to raise their children. The page didn't say much about the kids but did give updated ages. *Jodie R. Abernathy, 13 years old.*

Something told Kennedy to exit out of her browser. This wasn't going to lead her anywhere, all this speculation. What good would it do? She needed to get to work on her calculus. She tried to guess what Carl would say if he knew what she was doing, knew what she was thinking. She should stick to reading Russian crime novels, not inventing her own conspiracies. Was she really that desperate to find Rose?

Her fingers were as stubborn as her mind, however, and they refused to slow down. *Jodie Abernathy,* she typed into the search bar, leaning forward in her seat as she scrolled through the results. Halfway down the second page, she froze.

Jodie Rose Abernathy, daughter of State House ...

Rose.

She didn't click the link. She didn't touch the mouse. She held her breath and felt like she might swallow her own heart. Suddenly, she wished Willow hadn't left for the night. She wished her parents didn't live on the other side of the world. She wished she wasn't alone in her room. She reached down for her backpack.

She had to call Carl.

But she never got the chance.

CHAPTER 11

"Is this Willow's room?"

Kennedy managed to swallow down a full-fledged scream and only made a little yelp when her door banged open. She had never seen the student before. He wore a long-sleeved flannel shirt and stared around the room wildly.

"Who are you?"

"Dustin. Are you Willow's roommate?"

Why didn't Willow ever pull the door completely shut? Kennedy sighed. "Yeah." She exited out of the webpages, and when a flush warmed up her face, she reminded herself she hadn't done anything illegal or shameful.

The stranger's eyes were everywhere at once and he scanned one side of the room to another. "There's been an accident. Do you know where her wallet is?"

Kennedy stood up only to remember she hadn't eaten anything since lunch except for some dry Cheerios. She put her hand on the back of her chair to steady herself. "What kind of accident?"

"She was hit by a car just a few minutes ago. The ambulance is on its way. They need her ID."

"I'll look." Kennedy had no idea where it was, but she felt better about going through her roommate's personal effects than letting someone else do it. Willow's top drawer had a journal Kennedy had never seen her write in, some homeopathic cough drops, a few sticks of unburned incense, and a picture of her hiking with some friends up a snow-capped mountain back home in Alaska. No ID anywhere.

Dustin rummaged through the things on top of Willow's desk. "Here. This must be her wallet." He slipped it in his pocket. "Do you ... I mean, she's your roommate. Do you want me to show you ...?"

Kennedy was already slipping on her shoes.

"She was at the crosswalk. The car came out of nowhere." He bounded down the stairs two at a time.

"You saw it?" Kennedy had to run to keep up.

"Yeah. Wicked crazy." Dustin looked back at Kennedy over his shoulder as they hurried past the dorms. "I hope she's ok. Are you guys close?"

Kennedy wondered how to answer that question. Willow and she didn't share any of the same moral values, but they respected each other's space and so far had co-existed just fine. A few times they even streamed an action movie on Willow's desktop to watch together. "Yeah, I guess so."

"Well, I'm really sorry." He froze. "I don't see the ambulance. Maybe they already got her to the hospital."

"What was wrong with her?" Kennedy wasn't sure she really wanted to know.

"I didn't see everything, but it looked pretty bad." Dustin pointed ahead. "I think I see one of the cars that stopped to help her. Let me go ask him what the paramedics said."

Kennedy jogged after him. When she caught up, he was bending over, talking to the driver through the open window. "This is her roommate." He turned to Kennedy. "There's a guy in the backseat who wants to ask you something." He opened the door, and Kennedy peered in.

"There's no one back there."

Before she could react, Dustin elbowed her in the ribs. She doubled over. He grabbed her shoulder. Air. She needed a little air. Then she would yell for help. She tried to gasp.

Strong, sharp fingers pressed into the back of her neck. She flailed out her arms, trying to remember those dumb self-defense videos her dad made her watch. How could she go for the eyes if she couldn't even keep her balance?

Her lungs filled noisily with air. "Help!"

Dustin kicked her hard in the belly. She fell into the backseat and immediately stopped struggling when he brought a small knife just centimeters from her chest.

"Shut up."

She took shallow breaths. Dustin put one leg into the car, and she scrambled backward away from him.

"Hold still," he ordered.

She bit her lips together to keep from squealing. *Breathe evenly.* She could almost hear her dad's voice. Back when she lived in Yanji, she thought his emphasis on crisis preparation was one of his strange, morbid quirks. How many other girls at her high school actually had to role-play kidnapping scenarios? At the time, Kennedy thought it had something to do with her dad's paranoia about being an American overseas. He seized the stories of one or two US businessmen getting captured for ransom and created a whole atmosphere of fear. Now, she was grateful for his words in her head.

Create as much noise as you can during the abduction itself. Well, that had failed. All she got out was one pitiful yelp. If making a scene didn't help, the best thing to do was stay calm. *They're going to be tense. You don't want to make them even more nervous.*

And so she sat as the car sped onto the road. When Dustin covered her eyes with a blindfold, she didn't resist. She tried not to wince when he raised her hands over her head and cuffed her wrists to the neck-rest behind her. When the car made its first turn, she counted her breaths. Over and over and over. Someone would come. Someone would free her. This wasn't China, with its corrupt police force and neo-communist justice system. This was America. God wouldn't allow them to actually hurt her. He couldn't. Her parents were missionaries. She had grown up singing praises in Sunday school. People prayed for her. People admired her. She wasn't the kind of person who could just disappear.

She shut her eyes, which made her feel a little less powerless in the blindfold. If it was going to be dark, it was going to be dark because she wanted it to be. She clung to her dad's words as if they were a personal guarantee of her own safety. *If they want a ransom, they have no reason to harm you.*

The car sped ahead as if nothing had happened. The man in the front said something to Dustin. Kennedy strained her ears. She had to pay attention. She could tell the police what their voices sounded like ...

But what would that do? She remembered her 911 conversation last weekend. The people there couldn't even trace a simple phone call. Besides, how did she expect them to rescue her when nobody knew she was gone?

The realization hit her in the gut like a cannonball, sending splinters of fear and dread and disbelief coursing through her being. *Nobody knew she was gone.* She took a deep breath.

This was going to be the longest night of her life.

Assuming she survived until morning.

CHAPTER 12

"My parents live in China. My dad has a printing business there." Kennedy knew she was rambling but couldn't stop the torrent of words from flowing out her mouth. She wanted them to know she was a real person, not a nameless victim. And if they were after money, she wanted them to accurately estimate what her family might or might not be able to afford. She tried to keep from thinking about her mom and how freaked out she would be to get a ransom call from overseas.

"I have a roommate." Kennedy was still blindfolded, but she turned to Dustin next to her. "She'll wonder where I am if I'm not back tonight." Did her voice sound convincing enough, or could he tell she was lying? Willow was out with her newest interest and wouldn't be back until sometime tomorrow. Kennedy could be gone for twenty-four hours or more before Willow started to get suspicious.

"I have a boyfriend." That was a lie too, but it sounded better than calling Reuben her lab partner. "We're supposed to meet in half an hour to study for a test." It didn't matter if that wasn't true, either. These men had to understand their plans would backfire. They had to understand she wasn't the kind of person someone could pluck off the streets and get away with it.

"You're going to text your roommate *and* your boyfriend." The driver in front had one of those heavy Boston accents Kennedy had previously thought were only from movies. "You're going to tell them your aunt in Maryland broke her hip and your parents begged you to go check on her."

Kennedy's blood froze and her hands chilled at the mention of her aunt Lilian. How could they know? She thought about when Dustin came bursting into her room and called Willow by name. They had obviously planned ahead. But why?

"I don't have my phone with me." Remembering all her dad's advice, she tried to keep her expression neutral. She didn't want to make them angry.

"We do." Dustin's voice was younger, not as gruff as the driver's. He poked her in the side with something small.

"You have my phone?" How had they managed that? Dustin had stayed on Willow's side of the room the entire time. Were these magicians and illusionists she was dealing with?

"It's a copy, stupid."

Flashes of the previous day flickered in her memory. Her lost phone. The fire drill.

"How can I text when I'm cuffed to the seat?" Kennedy tried to guess how fast the car was moving. If they freed her hands to write a message, could she dive out? And if she did, would she roll right into oncoming traffic?

"Don't give her the phone, idiot," the driver spat. "Do it for her."

She listened while Dustin typed on her phone, or the copy of it — another curiosity she had previously thought only came from movies.

A minute later, the phone beeped. "Reuben wants to know if you uploaded your titration results to the class database yet. Whatever that means."

"Yeah, I did it this afternoon." Kennedy tried to picture her dad's comforting face. Maybe if she pretended this was some role-playing test he had designed for her ...

From the front seat, the driver grumbled something or other about traffic. It was rush hour. Were they going out of the city, then, stuck in a sea of commuters?

The phone beeped again a few minutes later. "Willow says do you mind if someone sleeps in your bed while you're gone."

Her bed. The one she wasn't in right now. Would she ever see it again?

"Forget about that," the driver called back. "Who else do you need to contact?" he asked Kennedy. She felt the car turn. Was this the second or third right so far?

"I have a calculus test tomorrow. Then I have general chemistry."

"I don't need your whole stinking schedule," he interrupted. "Just tell me who's gonna miss you if you don't check in."

The more Kennedy thought about it, the more she realized Reuben and Willow were the only people who would care if she vanished. Had she really spent two whole months at Harvard and not made any other friends?

"My parents." Would her kidnappers let her call her parents? She tried to think of some sort of code, some way she could tell them she was in trouble. Her dad had come up with contingency plans in case the Chinese police raided their home in the middle of the night. Couldn't he have dreamed up a secret phrase to signal distress? If these men let her phone Yanji ...

"We already sent your mom an email," Dustin said. "You're incredibly busy studying, plus you have laryngitis so you can't call. Easy."

So they had access to her email, too. "Who are you?"

"Just shut up," the driver mumbled.

She had lost track of the turns by now and wondered if they were driving around in circles. She strained her ears to try to detect any background noise that might clue her in to her surroundings, but all she could hear were the generic sounds of traffic. That, plus the roar of her own pulse in her ears. At one point, she was certain she heard the faintest hint of a police siren, but it disappeared faster than a lightning flash.

And so she was left alone with her thoughts. Her thoughts, her fears, her racing heart. Were they going to hurt her? Were they going to kill her? They knew her roommate. They had access to her phone and emails. Why? If her parents were billionaires or something, it would make sense for someone to go to such lengths to track her. Hunt her down. But all this for the daughter of an overseas printer? Could it have something to do with her parents' secret missionary work in China, then? If it were a movie, she'd joke with her dad about how far-fetched and contrived it all was.

Her eyes were still shut, and she figured her dad would try to tell her to let her body rest. What was that about sexual predators and their first goal was to tire you out? But would these men really go through so much trouble just for ...

"My pastor will miss me," she blurted out. "We've been working on a ..." She didn't want to mention anything about the hotline phone. "We've been working on a big fundraising dinner for Thursday. He'll be expecting to hear from me."

"Not no more. You've already sent Carl a text telling him you have laryngitis and a research paper to work on all week."

So they knew about her pastor, too? Who were they? Kennedy's one ray of hope was that Sandy would see the text about the laryngitis and bring over some chicken soup or those ridiculous cookies she kept talking about. Otherwise it could be days, maybe a week or more, before someone reported her disappearance. What horrors would she endure in the meantime?

Would they even keep her alive that long?

She guessed about an hour passed before they parked, but she didn't know if the terror or the blindfold were playing tricks with her mind. It was breezy when they forced her out of the car. She strained her ears for clues about where she was. Why couldn't there be a train? Something to tell her where she was? Were they still in Massachusetts? The ground was hard. Pavement. That was a good sign, right? At least they weren't out in the middle of the woods where search parties could hunt for weeks and still find nothing. But if she got a chance to run, would there be any place to hide?

There were no sounds, no cars, no traffic. She imagined that some people in her position might call for help in case anyone was nearby, but she could hardly muster the strength to support her own weight. "Where are we?" Her voice was quiet, squeaky. She wondered if this was how Rose felt when she made that call on the hotline phone.

Rose. Was all that a dream? Had she made it all up? Could Rose really be Jodie Abernathy? Sitting behind her computer desk, Kennedy had been so certain. The age, the middle name, the homeschool connection. But now it all seemed so distant, so jumbled. Even if Rose was Wayne Abernathy's daughter, that still didn't explain why Kennedy was abducted, miles from her dorm, uncertain if she'd survive the night.

Unless ...

They started to walk, and Kennedy shoved thoughts of Rose aside. She had one goal — to stay alive. Once she returned safe and sound to her Harvard dorm, she would talk to Carl about her suspicions.

If she returned.

She heard the sound of something lifting, a garage door or something as heavy. "Go on." When it closed behind them again, the ground reverberated, and its thud echoed around the room. No, she couldn't escape out that way.

Her hands were still cuffed, and she raised them in front of her to keep from bumping into anything. She tried counting how many steps they were taking her, but her pulse was roaring far too loudly in her ears and she lost track. A trained detective might be able to listen to her accosters' footsteps and discern the exact size and style of shoe they wore, but Kennedy was clueless. Besides, how in the world would it help her escape to know if her abductor wore a size ten or size thirteen?

They descended a staircase, and the air grew even chillier. She guessed if they let her look she would see her own breath, choppy as it was. She tried to rub her hands together, but her wrists chafed on the cuffs. She couldn't feel any railings to either side of her and was afraid of tripping.

"Watch your step." She recognized Dustin's voice and actually welcomed his hand on her bicep. His grip was forceful, but it almost felt as if he were holding her, supporting her quivering legs, preparing to catch her if she lost her balance.

When they reached the bottom of the stairs, the gnawing feeling in her stomach had grown until her entire abdominal cavity was a vacuum, void of life, void of emotion, void of matter. They slowed to a stop.

"Sit here."

Kennedy's shin bumped a couch. She felt the scratchy fabric with her hands and turned her face away from the musty smell. How long had it been rotting down here? How many other victims had used it before? Was she alone? She pictured herself in a room as cold and bleak and empty as the holodecks in those sci-fi shows she sometimes watched with her dad. Blackness. On and on forever even though your body was in a room, enclosed by four walls. She lowered herself carefully onto the couch, half expecting a rodent to come scampering out from underneath, ready to complain at whoever disturbed his rest.

Someone grabbed her wrists. His hands were warm. Didn't he know it was below freezing down here? She might die of exposure if nothing else.

She let out her breath when he unlocked the left side of the cuff. She forced herself to thank him, but her voice was still so small, so scared. Had her dad known? When he dragged her through all those seemingly pointless training scenarios, when he grilled her about how she'd respond if she was ever abducted, did he know how small she would sound?

Unfortunately, the man with the warm hands didn't take off her other cuff but attached it to something metallic sticking out of the wall behind. She wanted to argue. They could trust her. She would cooperate. She wouldn't run. But they'd know she was lying. She reached up to finger her blindfold.

"Don't." It was Dustin's voice.

She let her free hand drop to her lap.

"That's better."

Should she bother to scream? Other than the knife he pulled to get her in the car, she hadn't noticed any other weapons. No guns to her temple like in a thriller novel. No long blades pressed up against her jugular. The men hadn't talked to anyone else since they came in. Were they the only two guarding her?

She licked her dry lips. What did it matter? Two men or fifty, she wasn't getting out of here. Not yet. But still, if they weren't armed, wouldn't that make a rescue attempt a whole lot more likely to succeed?

She heard the men shuffle away, listened to the rumble of their voices as they conversed in a low murmur somewhere far off. Were they deciding what to do with her?

She wished her father hadn't told her so many statistics about abducted women and what might happen to them. Which horrible fate would she face? A lifetime of slavery in an underground sex ring? Or would she end up in a freezer, cut into pieces and stuffed into bloody Ziploc bags? Would they find her next week at the bottom of the Charles River? What was the least painful way to be murdered?

She shook her head. She couldn't go on thinking that way. Instead, she listed the reasons she still had to be thankful. They could have hurt her even more getting her into the car. Her stomach felt sore, but she didn't think she was seriously injured. Bruised up a little, but what would that matter if she got out of here alive?

Who were they? Hired men, perhaps? Had the Chinese government heard about her parents' clandestine missionary work? Was she some pawn now in an international conflict? She chided herself for watching too many spy shows with her dad. If only this were more like those. Then someone like James Bond would come and free her and kill her captors without breaking into a sweat or getting his tuxedo stained with blood.

"You hungry?" the man with the gruff voice asked. He sounded a lot older than Dustin, but Kennedy hadn't gotten a good look at him before she was blindfolded.

The question startled Kennedy. What was this — a bed and breakfast for hostages? She was famished, and her mouth watered at the prospect of food, but she shook her head. *Tell them what you need*, she remembered her dad saying. But she didn't want to. She didn't want to be dependent on them. She didn't want to admit she would be here longer than a few minutes. She didn't want to acknowledge she was miles away from her dorm, maybe even in a different state, and nobody realized she was missing. How long before Reuben or Willow would get worried and start asking questions? A week? If these men had a copy of her phone and access to her email, couldn't they keep up the ruse of her disappearance indefinitely?

Maybe. But she wasn't going to accept that as a possibility. Right now, she was going to swallow down her heart, which kept threatening to leap out of her chest. She was going to ignore the rumbling in her stomach that felt as empty as the earth's upper atmosphere. She was going to think about pleasant things, like about the fact that God hadn't allowed them to force themselves on her, and she was going to plan a way to get out.

"Then we'll check on you in the morning," Dustin said. Footsteps receded in the direction of the stairs. And then Kennedy — who had spent the last ten years in Yanji with its half a million residents, who now lived in a dorm with four hundred other students and shared her meals with nearly two thousand other college first-years — was left behind in stifling, deafening, soul-haunting solitude.

CHAPTER 13

She never knew what complete silence was until now. Her ears rang with it. Her mind waited for something — a shout, a yell, the horrifying pop of gunfire.

Nothing.

She reached up and touched her blindfold again, half expecting somebody to grab her wrist and stop her.

No one.

"Hello?" The sound of her own whisper sent goose bumps shivering up her spine. She thought of her high school psychology class, about how people could actually go crazy from sensory deprivation. Was that what this was?

She took off the blindfold with her free hand, but it was as dark as it had been. She couldn't see her own fingers and wished she had it back on again. Somehow knowing for certain she was in utter darkness was ten times more frightening than being blindfolded and only suspecting it.

Think. She had to think. Calm her mind and look at her situation rationally. Like her dad would. She thought about the advice he gave the Secret Seminary students for handling solitary confinement. Develop a schedule. Keep a routine. Find some way to track the time. And pray.

Pray.

She thought about the refugees her parents had taken in back home. How many of them experienced darkness like this? What did they do? She thought of Hannah, the only girl who completed the whole Secret Seminary program. When Kennedy flew out to Massachusetts for college, Hannah was only a week or two away from returning to North Korea. Where was she now? Kennedy pictured Hannah's serene face. If Hannah were here, she would find a way to kneel in spite of the handcuff and spend the whole night in prayer — prayers for others probably, not even herself.

But Kennedy wasn't like that. She could never be as spiritually mature as Hannah or the other Secret Seminary students. She had never been asked to sneak into a closed nation where the penalty for evangelism was torture and death. She had never risked her life to share a Bible verse with someone else. At the All American Girls' High School, with all those preppy daughters of wealthy businessmen, Kennedy hadn't really shared her faith at all. That wasn't who she was. She liked watching action movies. She liked reading mysteries and shopping for clothes. She liked spending time with her friends. What was the crime in that? She still loved God, still believed in the Bible. She even had a vague notion of considering full- or part-time missions once she graduated from medical school in eight years. So why did it always feel like she wasn't doing enough?

She shivered from the cold and hugged her free arm around herself for extra warmth. Couldn't they have given her a blanket or something? Why had she been so stubborn and refused to tell them what she needed? She made a mental list of things to ask for when the men returned. Something hot to drink. A blanket. A pillow. She wondered how she was supposed to use the bathroom and thought again of how many others might have been chained all night to this very couch. Better ask for a sheet, too.

Her own materialism stared her accusingly in the face when she thought again about the members of her parents' Secret Seminary. What would they have requested? A Bible, no doubt. Well, she'd be surprised to find one of those here. This didn't seem like the kind of establishment the Gideons would keep stocked. This was definitely no hotel. If it was, she would order up room service, eat a big, fattening dinner, and lie down on a clean, puffy pillow ...

Why was she always so focused on her own needs, anyway? *Why can't you be more like Hannah?* She could almost hear her mother's accusing voice. Kennedy's mom spent hours each day with the Secret Seminary students, training, teaching, praying. Kennedy would come home from school and her mother would look shocked, surprised so much time had passed, surprised her own daughter was home and already interrupting their meeting.

Kennedy still spent time with her mom in Yanji, but it wasn't the same. It was always at night after her homework was done. Her mom would invite her to eat chocolate and watch old black and white movies in the bedroom. Kennedy wasn't part of the Secret Seminary, so nobody expected her to spend an hour on her knees praying. Nobody expected her to copy Scripture every day or memorize huge chunks of the Bible. Even when the North Korean students fasted, her mom still got up and fixed Kennedy breakfast each morning and gave her enough money to buy her lunch at school.

Why can't you be more like Hannah?

Kennedy gritted her teeth. She wasn't Hannah, and frankly, she didn't want to be. Why couldn't she be herself? She loved God. She prayed during the day and almost never ate a meal without thanking him for it first. So what was she missing? Why did it feel like she was never going to meet anybody's expectations?

When the first hot tear splashed onto Kennedy's arm, she tried to sniff all those negative emotions away. Sometimes she hated the Secret Seminary students, their courage, their commitment. She resented all the time her mom spent fussing over them, resented all the pride her mom lavished on them. Her mom was more impressed with the students for copying a book of the Bible than she was with Kennedy for being named valedictorian of her high school class. Her mom threw a lavish feast whenever a new refugee was baptized, and the whole household spent the day as if it were Christmas. What about when Kennedy got accepted into Harvard's early-admission medical school program fresh out of high school? She didn't get a feast or a new Bible or an impromptu worship service to thank God for her achievements. Instead, she got a few extra hugs, a whole backpack full of mystery novels for her summer reading, and a two-hundred-dollar gift certificate to her favorite online clothes store.

Even her dad babied her when he made her sit through the crisis training part of the Secret Seminary. The North Koreans would likely face interrogation at some point after returning home. He spoke about it as if it were a fact, and he gave them the practice and encouragement they'd need to endure. But even though he made Kennedy suffer through the exact same lectures and participate in the same role playing as the others, he didn't really think she could make it. That's why he made her watch those extra hours of self-defense videos before she left for college. With the Secret Seminary students, it was all about *turn the other cheek* and *love your enemies*. With Kennedy, it was *kick him in the groin* and *make a scene 'til someone comes to rescue you*.

Why? Because she wasn't cut from the same mold as the rest of them. She wasn't ever going to risk her life for Jesus. She wasn't ever going to be anything more than a Sunday-morning pew warmer. Her parents smothered her with gifts, let her go to dances and parties that no pastor's kid in the States would be allowed to attend, and only expected her to go to "church" in the den one morning a week. Maybe she was ready for more. Maybe her soul had been crying out for more, but her parents were too busy with their precious, anointed missionaries-in-training to notice.

And where was God? Where was he when she listened to her housemates in Yanji praying and asked him to make her as bold as they were? Where was he when she sat bored in church and begged God to fill her with the passion she saw in the refugees? When she was packing her things to move to Harvard, she prayed for Christian friends to meet her there. And God answered with Willow, the least likely student on campus to ever accept Christ, and Reuben, who claimed to be a Christian but refused to set foot in church.

Somewhere in the pit of her stomach, a howl threatened to rise. She kept it trapped in there for as long as she could. She clenched her jaw and tried to swallow it back down, but still it welled up from deep within her core, gathering strength and volume as it rose. It echoed against the walls, stinging her ears, chilling her marrow. She had never heard anything like it, not even in the movies. Almost animalistic, utterly hopeless, the sound of a spirit condemned to death.

By the time her tears ran dry, her ears still rang with its hollow echoes.

CHAPTER 14

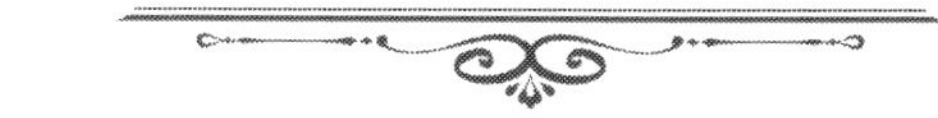

"Wake up. Come on."

She didn't know what time it was, day or night. She didn't remember falling asleep on the musky couch. All she knew was she definitely wasn't rested.

She squinted in the beam from the flashlight, too disoriented to try to create a mental image of the room. She recognized Dustin as he stood by the couch and waved the flashlight in her eyes. "We need your help."

Kennedy had to find a toilet, and she wanted to wash some of the grime off her face. She was thirsty. He shone the beam at her, and she tried to raise both hands to her eyes before she remembered the cuff.

"You've got some medical training, right?" His voice was smaller now, rushed and anxious like a nervous fox.

"I'm pre-med. It's just my first year." Her voice was scratchy. How long had she been asleep? She tried to remember if Dustin was wearing the same flannel shirt as when he captured her, but she had been too busy getting beat up and thrown into a car to pay attention to the color and pattern.

"We need your help." His tone was still authoritative. Demanding. But Kennedy sensed an underlying desperation.

"I have to use the bathroom." She was pleased that her voice didn't give out on her. She sounded put together. Confident. If only she could feel that way, too.

"We don't have time for this," he mumbled to himself as he pulled a key out of his pocket. "All right, I'm going to show you where the bathroom is. You try something funny, I shoot you. Got it?" He swept up part of his shirt to show Kennedy the bottom of some kind of holster. Her spine stiffened at the sight.

"Yeah, I understand." She hoped he didn't feel her quiver when he unclasped the handcuff. She shook out her arm, relieved to be free of her restraint. Her legs were unstable when he led her to the bathroom, a big rusty setup which was more like a huge walk-in closet that happened to contain plumbing.

"Go on."

He stood outside, and she squatted over the rusty bowl so she didn't have to actually touch it. She tried not to think about the sound of her pee echoing in that great big room for everyone to hear. Well, if Dustin was an experienced kidnapper, he would be used to it.

Once she was done she walked to the sink, still unsteady. The water smelled like sulfur and was so cold it stung her hands. She decided not to wash her face, but she forced herself to gag down a little sip from her palms. The icy chill sent pangs of torment shooting to the roots of her teeth. She might not get anything else all day.

Or was it still night?

"You done?" He pounded on the door, and Kennedy looked around for one more second. Sometimes in the movies, there was a small ventilation window or a pipe to climb.

Nothing.

She stepped out of the bathroom.

"We've got someone you need to look at."

Dustin put his hand behind Kennedy's back. She could smell his BO and decided he must be wearing old clothes. Her odor probably wasn't much better. How long until she was able to take a shower? And if it was in that rotten-egg water, she'd probably pass anyway.

"She's having some sort of asthma attack or something," he told her. "Choking and crying up a storm."

Kennedy wondered who he was talking about. Was this some sort of sex-slavery operation, then? Kennedy knew human trafficking was a huge problem in Asia, and her parents had even taken in a few girls who escaped from the hotel district in Yanji. But when her dad cited facts about forced prostitution in the US, she hadn't really paid attention. Something like that could never happen to her.

Could it?

"All right," Dustin called up the stairs. "Bring her down."

Kennedy heard the girl's wheezing, choking sobs even before she saw her in the poor light. She held her breath. What had they done to her?

"She won't hold still." Kennedy recognized the thick Boston accent of the driver. He came down the steps, struggling to carry the body that was kicking and flailing in his arms.

Kennedy's legs felt like they were supporting twice her body weight. There was no way the child was of age. Kennedy stepped forward, afraid the girl might thrash her way right down the staircase and break her neck.

"I need to talk to my dad!" She sucked in her breath in noisy, choppy spurts.

"She's been like this since we brought her in." The driver stepped into the light. He was older than Kennedy expected, built like a boxer and mostly bald. He glowered at Kennedy before he set the girl down on the couch. Kennedy cringed but didn't have time to think of all the germs and dust mites and rodents that probably made their home in its cushions.

The child covered her face with her hands and drew her knees to her chest. "I need my dad." Fitful sobs wracked her petite body.

Kennedy sensed the men's hopeful stares but forced them out of her mind. "It's all right," she whispered. "Everything is going to be ok."

The girl kept her face buried, and her shoulders heaved. "I don't want any more medicine."

Kennedy shot the two men a look, but they avoided her glare. "What's she talking about?"

"We have some pills. Doctor says it'll make her feel calmer. Anxiety medicine."

Kennedy didn't bother asking what sort of doctor would prescribe pills for a kidnapped child. "How long has she been here?" She forced an air of authority into her voice and stood up straight, stretching her spine tall.

"Half an hour. Maybe more."

"Have you had anything to eat?" she asked the child, who cringed when Kennedy touched her shoulder.

"She threw up on the way here," the bald man grumbled. "Gonna stink up the car for weeks."

Kennedy reached out one more time. If she could only get her to look up ... What had these men already done to her? "Here, let me feel your forehead, ok?"

The girl glanced up, and Kennedy's breath caught somewhere in the middle of her throat. She would have recognized that face anywhere, even without the pearl earrings. Heart fluttering, she did what she could to keep her expression neutral. She gave what she hoped was a reassuring smile. The girl's brow was damp with sweat but didn't feel feverish. Her collarbone strained with each irregular breath.

"I need more light," Kennedy told them.

"Plug in the lamp," the driver told his partner and jerked his flashlight toward the wall. Pain pulsed to the back of Kennedy's head as soon as Dustin switched the light on. She blinked. The girl's lips were outlined in grayish blue, and her mouth hung open in an inaudible little gasp. Her chest moved as if trying to inhale, but no air went in.

How long had they said this had been going on? "Is there a shower here?" Kennedy heard the worried strain in her own voice. "Something that could make some steam?"

"What good's that gonna do?" the driver demanded.

"It can open up all the airways. Help her breathe more evenly." Kennedy bit her lip while the men looked at each other.

"We don't got a water heater."

The girl's shoulders shuddered as her body attempted another jerky inhale. They had to do something.

"Is there a way to boil some water?"

The bald man shook his head, and the girl let out a long wheezy sob.

Kennedy reached for her clammy hand. "You can go buy a face steamer. They have them at just about any drugstore." Her heart was thudding loudly in her chest. Would they do that much? Would these kidnappers have the decency to help a little girl from suffocating on their mildewy couch?

"Get over here." The balding one gestured with his head, and both men moved to the base of the stairs and conferred in low whispers.

Keeping one eye on the pair, Kennedy stroked the girl's hair and whispered out of the corner of her mouth, "Is your name Jodie?"

The child bent over. The wheezing sound from her lungs made Kennedy vicariously faint-headed.

"Jodie Abernathy?" Kennedy asked again.

A single tear splashed into the girl's lap as her lungs forced a noisy gulp of air. Her breath was as choppy as a windy lake in the fall, but she didn't respond.

Kennedy wanted to hug her, to make her body into a shield that would ward off panic and terror. "It's all right to be scared," she whispered before Dustin stepped back into the light.

"Face steamer, it's called?"

Kennedy nodded. She didn't trust her voice. He returned to his partner.

"I think we've talked before." Kennedy kept her tone soft. She was afraid that saying too much might trigger another wave of panic. "Did you make a phone call from St. Margaret's on Sunday?"

Jodie sniffed and gave an almost imperceptible nod. A small jolt sent Kennedy's heart galloping one more time.

She had found Rose.

CHAPTER 15

"Do you know these men?" Kennedy had a hundred questions and probably less than a minute to ask them all.

"No." Jodie sniffed again.

Kennedy didn't realize she had been holding her breath until she let out the next torrent of queries. "Are you hurt? Did they make you do anything you didn't want to do? Did they ... did they force ..." She couldn't finish the sentence.

Jodie shook her head, and relief radiated out of Kennedy's core all the way to her fingertips, warming her whole body.

The older man stomped up the stairs. "Don't let them out of your sight," he called down.

Dustin didn't look over at Kennedy and Jodie. "I know."

Kennedy watched the older one pass out of view. Was he going to get the steamer, then? Jodie's breathing was a little quieter, and Kennedy hoped he wouldn't change his mind. She held Jodie for several minutes, keeping her eye on Dustin, who stood at the bottom of the stairs scowling.

She ran her hands through the girl's hair. "How are you feeling?"

"Thirsty." Jodie was quieter now and hiccupping.

Kennedy caught Dustin's eye. "I think she might be dehydrated."

He stared at Jodie for a few silent seconds. "I have some water bottles upstairs," he finally mumbled. "I'll get one when Vinny gets back."

Kennedy sucked in her breath. "What about the bathroom?" She tried not to wince when she remembered the taste of the sulfur water from the tap. "Could she get a drink there?"

"Whatever," Dustin huffed.

"Do you think you can stand by yourself?" Kennedy asked. She needed a chance to talk to Jodie privately. She stood up and then paused. Would

Dustin come over and stop her? After a moment of waiting to see if he would protest, she helped Jodie to her feet, and they shuffled together to the bathroom.

"Do you have any idea who these guys are?" Kennedy whispered once she shut the door. "Even a guess?"

"Uh-uh." Jodie's wide eyes blinked in the flickering light from the bulb.

"Are you having a little easier time breathing, at least?"

Jodie scrunched up her face. "I just ..." Her shoulders heaved with another choppy breath. "I just want my dad."

Kennedy didn't want to think about Wayne Abernathy and what his role might be in this whole scenario. "I'm sure you do." She should try to get more information. She should keep on asking Jodie questions until eventually the pieces fell into place. But she couldn't. Not when the little indent of Jodie's neck quivered each time she tried to inhale.

Kennedy rubbed Jodie's back. "Can you try to drink a little water?"

"I want my dad." Jodie took a noisy gasp in, and Kennedy paused to see if she would start hyperventilating again.

What could she say to keep her from panicking? There had to be some sort of encouragement, some sort of comfort she could offer. "You go to St. Margaret's, right?"

Jodie nodded.

"Well, you know how Pastor Carl and your Sunday school teachers are always talking about giving your worries to God?"

"Yeah." The response was appropriate, but Jodie didn't sound at all convinced.

"It's a good idea. He's here with us, you know." Kennedy wondered how long they had before Dustin ran out of patience. "The Lord's watching us right now. And I think he's going to help us get out of this." There was no real faith behind that last statement, but Jodie's body relaxed a little. "Do you know any Bible verses?" Kennedy asked.

"Psalm 23." Jodie wrinkled her nose when Kennedy turned on the water.

"Psalm 23's a good one." Kennedy did her best to infuse her tone with encouragement while Jodie cupped her hands and took a small drink. "Do you want to say it together?"

Jodie took a slow breath in and kept her face scrunched up after she swallowed the water from the sink. "*The Lord is my ...*"

"That's enough."

Jodie and Kennedy both jumped when Dustin banged on the door. Kennedy wasn't about to see how far his generosity ran. She stepped out of the bathroom, grateful to see he wasn't wielding his gun. "We were just finishing up."

He grunted in response.

Kennedy led Jodie back and didn't flinch when Dustin cuffed her left hand back to the metal hook that stuck out of the wall. He frowned at Jodie, and Kennedy wondered if he would cuff her, too. Would that start off another panic attack?

Instead, he went back to the wall by the stairs and spent the rest of the time before Vinny returned fiddling at the tool table and glancing at the stairs every so often. Kennedy's mind spun in multiple directions at once. What she really needed was more time to talk to Jodie about Wayne Abernathy, about his campaign, about any enemies he had made. She had read enough political thrillers and watched enough action movies with her dad to know a desperate candidate could do about anything, even stoop to kidnapping. But why had they grabbed Kennedy, too?

Her brain raced ahead, whizzing and gyrating. Puzzle pieces arranged themselves up in perfect rows faster than she had time to connect them all. A hot shower, that's what she needed. A hot shower, some tea, and a notebook to jot down all her questions. Right now, she felt she could fill a whole composition book with them.

"There weren't no face steamers there." The voice pierced the silence and made Kennedy wince. Vinny glowered down from the top of the stairs, his face set into an imposing scowl.

Jodie's tiny body quivered as he stomped down the stairs. Every step seemed to take twice as long as it should.

"It will be all right," Kennedy whispered, wondering if Jodie could guess how terrified she was, too.

At the couch, Vinny crossed his arms and scrutinized Jodie. "She looks better." Kennedy couldn't tell if Vinny was making a simple observation or if he had decided Jodie's condition was no longer serious.

Kennedy stared past his ear and clenched her sweat-drenched palms. "Well, that's the funny thing with asthma. Sometimes it gets better all by itself, and sometimes it gets so bad you'll end up in the hospital." She wondered if her roommate Willow would be impressed with her improv performance. Whatever happened, she couldn't let them take Jodie back upstairs alone. They had to stay together. *Are you listening, God?*

Vinny's phone rang, and he stomped off to the far wall to answer it. Jodie breathed in deeply. "I don't really have asthma."

"I didn't think so." Kennedy spoke out of the corner of her mouth. "But if they think you need more help, like you're sick or something, they might let us stay together longer."

Jodie nodded and her hand crept toward Kennedy's.

"They're probably not going to hurt us." Kennedy hoped her voice sounded more confident than she felt.

When Vinny got off the phone, he jerked his head, and Dustin joined him for another conference out of earshot.

Kennedy waited a minute until the men were absorbed in their hushed whispers. "When did you get here?"

"Just this morning." Jodie wiped her nose with her palm. Kennedy thought she had made a mistake in asking. Would Jodie start hyperventilating again? But she needed answers. She had to strain her ears to hear what Jodie said next. "I went to my uncle Anthony's to babysit. He was going to be out late, so he wanted me to stay overnight."

Revulsion bubbled up Kennedy's throat. "Do you spend the night with your uncle very often?"

Jodie shrugged. "Only since my aunt died. Sometimes he's out late and needs help with Charlie."

Kennedy focused her gaze straight ahead and waited until the swell of suspicion and disgust settled back down in her gut. "So does your uncle know you're here?"

"No." Jodie's eyes grew wide. "They came about an hour after he left. And I don't know what they did to Charlie." Jodie buried her face in her hands. "They might have hurt him."

Kennedy couldn't imagine being a thirteen-year-old and shouldering such a weighty responsibility. "Whatever happened isn't your fault." She prayed the Lord would give her the right words to say so Jodie could truly believe it.

"But he's so little. He just turned one last month." Jodie's voice hardly lifted over a whisper but was laden with terror. "He must have been so scared, and I wasn't there ..."

"You don't know if anything happened to Charlie, right? I mean, maybe he's just fine and safe at home."

Jodie shook her head. "But then he's all by himself. He doesn't even walk yet." A little sob forced its way out her throat.

"Well, maybe your uncle stopped by to check on you. Or maybe he called and you weren't there, so he went home. We don't know." Kennedy's whole torso was quivering again, but she hoped Jodie wouldn't notice. Her mind was spinning. If Jodie's uncle reported her missing, that would mean people were looking for them. They might get rescued, after all. She didn't want to raise Jodie's hopes, so she kept the thought secret and suggested, "Why don't you say a prayer for Charlie?"

Jodie dried her cheeks. "Do you really think that would help?"

Kennedy swallowed down her doubts. "I'm sure of it."

"You want me to pray right here?"

Kennedy glanced at Dustin behind the workbench and Vinny on the phone. "Don't worry. They're not paying attention."

"All right." Jodie collected her breath. "God, please help Charlie not to be really scared. And we hope he's at home right now and that someone's there playing with him so he stays happy. Amen."

Kennedy wondered at the simplicity of this prayer compared to the hour-long discourses she was used to hearing back in Yanji. Somehow, she figured these few sentences meant as much to the Lord as a whole treatise would have. Kennedy was about to add a prayer of her own when Vinny slammed the phone back into his pocket and stomped toward the couch, fists clenched, eyes glaring. She felt Jodie's whole body go rigid next to her.

"All right. Your little coughing fit's over. Time to take your medicine."

CHAPTER 16

Jodie shut her eyes and shook her head weakly. "I don't like those pills."

"I didn't ask if you liked them," Vinny snapped back. "Open your mouth."

"How many are there?" Kennedy asked when she saw more than one in his hand.

"Four. She's gotta take them all at once."

Kennedy had never heard of a dose that large for anxiety meds, especially for a child as small as Jodie.

"I don't like them," Jodie moaned again.

Even though her hand was still cuffed to the metal ring, Kennedy tried to position herself a little in front of Jodie. It wasn't hard since Jodie scurried behind her, scrunching herself up in between Kennedy and the couch cushion.

"Do you take these regularly?" Kennedy asked. If these men expected her to care for Jodie when she was hyperventilating, she was going to keep up her air of medical superiority at all costs. All the clues from the past few days — the phone, the uncle, the clinic, the kidnapping — played out in flashes in Kennedy's mind. They were racing to set themselves in logical order, and the closer she got to the full picture, the more dread grew and made its home in the center of her gut.

"My uncle gave me one after church." Jodie was curled up in the couch, and Kennedy could hardly hear her. "It made me throw up."

"What medicine is it?" Kennedy tried not to cower in front of Vinny, whose scowl radiated both impatience and contempt.

"I already told you. It's for anxiety."

Kennedy saw the hateful gleam in his eye. He was probably armed like his partner. She felt as nervous as she had as a child when she went ice skating on a frozen pond, trying hard to balance, all the while expecting the ice to crack beneath her at the slightest shift in weight.

"Can she take them after she eats something?" Kennedy tried to speak confidently without being too abrasive, either. "That might help with the nausea."

Time. Kennedy needed more time. Time to think. Time to sort out all her thoughts. And a snack for both of them wouldn't hurt, either.

Vinny's expression may as well have been etched in granite. "She takes them now."

"I don't need them anymore. I don't feel anxious at all." Jodie's voice was a pitiful little yelp squeaking out from behind the couch cushion.

"Your uncle Anthony says you need them."

At the mention of Jodie's uncle, Kennedy felt the floor had been slipped out from under her, like those inertia magic tricks when the magician pulls off the tablecloth.

"My uncle?" the child squeaked. "He knows I'm here?"

"We've been in contact," Vinny answered gruffly. "And he wants you to take your pills."

Kennedy scratched her cheek. Jodie's uncle. So he was involved. Thoughts collided against each other in Kennedy's brain as the pieces of the puzzle zoomed into place. The uncle. The same man who had overheard Jodie's phone call to the hotline phone. The same man who wanted her to get rid of her baby. Kennedy eyed the white tablets again as warning alarms screeched and squealed between her temples, unleashing a torrent of adrenaline and pure rage. Those weren't anxiety meds. How far along had Jodie said she was in the pregnancy? Five months?

Kennedy kept herself positioned squarely between Jodie and Vinny. "She can't take those."

He reached out to push her out of the way, but Kennedy slapped the pills out of his hand. He grabbed a fistful of her hair and jerked her head to the side. Before he picked up the fallen tablets, she tried to sweep them away with her foot.

"Wait! They're not safe this late." Kennedy clawed at his forearms as Vinny pinched Jodie's cheeks together.

He forced her mouth open. "Take them."

Kennedy winced as the handcuff cut against her wrist, but she hardly registered the pain. Anger, fright, and horror all mingled together, poisoning her blood, tinting her vision. She tried to knock Vinny's hand out of the way. Dustin appeared behind the couch and forced Jodie's mouth open once more.

"She can't take them." Kennedy reached with her free hand to scratch at Dustin, but he only strengthened his grip on Jodie's jaw. Gurgling noise came from the back of Jodie's throat. Dustin was holding her head so tight the veins in his forearms popped up.

Vinny loomed over them both, towering over Jodie with the pills in his hand. Kennedy tried to kick him away. He clenched his fist, and then pain splintered across Kennedy's temple. Her head jerked back right before Vinny punched her again in the gut. For a moment, she was paralyzed. She couldn't see. She couldn't breathe. She sensed the commotion around her but couldn't process any of it.

"Hold her head steady," Vinny growled.

"I'm trying."

Kennedy could hear the strain in both men's voices. Jodie was still struggling, but what chance did a thirteen-year-old girl have against two armed men? A toxic, murderous fury boiled over from somewhere deep within Kennedy's core, and she kicked Vinny in the shin. He cursed and lunged at her. She let out a roar and kicked him once more, this time in the groin. He dropped the pills and fell on the couch.

Jodie cried out once when he landed with his elbow on her midsection.

The room fell silent except for Jodie's tiny sobs. With her toe Kennedy nudged one of the pills under the couch and snuck her other foot over two more. She couldn't find the fourth. The pained grimace on Vinny's face morphed into a mask of rage, and hatred dripped from his entire countenance.

"You little ..."

Kennedy tried not to shrink back. *God, you have to get us out of here.* Her heart was thudding violently, pounding as if its one purpose in life was to beat its way out of her chest.

"Where are the pills?" Vinny spoke each word slowly, allowing his malicious venom to lace every syllable.

Kennedy tried crushing the two pills underfoot with her shoe, but they were too durable.

"She kicked one under the couch," Dustin declared.

"Stand up." Vinny's voice was now eerily controlled.

Kennedy got off the couch but had to lean over Jodie since one of her wrists was still cuffed. Her face was a few inches away from Jodie, who cried softly into her hands. *I'm sorry*, she wished she could say. *I'm so sorry.*

"Pick up your foot."

Kennedy shut her eyes. *Forgive them Lord, for they know not what they do.* Only that didn't apply here. Vinny knew exactly what he was doing. Was he really that deranged? Did he hold such little regard for Jodie and her safety? For the life she carried? Didn't he know what those pills would do? How could he work for someone related to Wayne Abernathy, whose name was synonymous with the pro-life movement in Massachusetts? So was Jodie's father involved, too? A dozen potential scenarios, each more troublesome than the previous, whirled their way around Kennedy's mind in a convoluted, dizzying blur.

She let out her breath, defeated, and took her foot off the two pills she had tried to hide. *I'm sorry, Jodie. I'm so sorry.*

Vinny kept his eyes on Kennedy. She could feel the heat from his stare boring into her forehead before he jerked his head at Dustin. "Pick them up."

Dustin came around to the front of the couch.

"Check and see if you can find the others," Vinny ordered.

A lone, silent tear slipped down Kennedy's cheek. She couldn't bring herself to look at anyone. What was the point of reaching the top of her high school class if she had to stand by and do nothing while a poor, victimized child was forced to swallow abortion pills that would kill her child and ravage her body? What was the point of studying in college until her eyes burned if she couldn't help a little girl or the baby she was too young to carry? She forced herself to look at Jodie's heaving shoulders. What was the point of worshipping a God who wouldn't lift his finger to rescue these precious souls?

The thought was blasphemous, but for the moment she didn't care. How could Christians understand the evil that flourishes in this world and still walk around with their happy smiles and talk about God's blessings? How could Christians confront such brutal, beastly violence and then fold their hands and thank God for his providence? She bit her lip to keep it from trembling and guessed what her dad would say:

And we know that all things work together for the good of those who love God. Well, Kennedy loved God. She had given up her rights to a "normal" American childhood and watched her parents start their Secret Seminary overseas. She had sacrificed time she didn't have to volunteer at the pregnancy center, and now she might never go back to her dorm. She might never talk to her mom or dad again. Another tear leaked down her face.

She didn't fight when Dustin bent down inches from her and picked up the pills. She didn't stomp on his fingers or try to kick his nose when he swept his hand under the couch and found the two others. Up until now, she thought the phrase *pick your battles* referred to minor compromises to help you get along with your family members or roommates. She hadn't ever stopped to think that sometimes you have to give up the most worthy of battles, the battles that deserve to be fought, the battles that hold life and dignity and innocence captive.

Dustin stood up. Vinny reached his hand out. "You will take these. Now." He fixed his gaze on Kennedy. "And you won't get in the way."

Kennedy didn't have the strength to cringe.

Jodie took the pills in her hand. In her eyes, Kennedy saw the same resigned sadness that squeezed and wrung her own soul as if it were a soppy-wet rag. "Can I have some water?" Jodie's voice was quiet, but it didn't tremble.

Vinny glared for a second longer and then strode to the tool table and grabbed some sort of thermos. As he stomped to the bathroom, Kennedy stared down at the floor.

"Here," Vinny grumbled when he returned, splashing water when he thrust the cup in front of Jodie.

She raised her eyebrows once at Kennedy. That single, trusting, hopeful look stabbed Kennedy's heart like a thousand guilt-laced arrows. She blinked back her tears and gave the child a nod. *Forgive them, Father, for they know not what they do ...*

Jodie uncurled her legs out from beneath her. She put her feet on the floor and reached for the cup. Kennedy's throat threatened to collapse on itself. Part of her wanted to force her eyes away. The other part wanted to brand each small detail into the recesses of her memory. Maybe God could forgive Jodie's uncle and kidnappers for what they were forcing her to do, but Kennedy never could. She steeled up her heart, fortified its chambers with walls of cool, calculating wrath, and wondered if she had ever really understood the phrase *righteous indignation* until this exact moment.

The thermos trembled in Jodie's hand. Kennedy sucked in her breath, steeling herself.

The tin cup clattered on the floor. The water splashed out and sprayed Kennedy's leg. The pills made the smallest of thuds when they hit the ground. Jodie yelped and jumped to her feet. Everyone stared at the front of her pants.

She was covered in blood.

CHAPTER 17

Kennedy forced a deep breath into her lungs even though her diaphragm threatened to spasm. Her head felt light. Whatever energy she still had left seeped out of her body and dissipated into the air.

Ignoring the spinning in the center of her brain, Kennedy balled her hands into fists and glowered at Vinny. "What did you do?" She recognized a hint of hysteria sneaking into her tone but couldn't control it.

Vinny was still frozen, his angry scowl cemented in place. Kennedy couldn't stomach the sight of him, but she met his glare with open hostility. That was another difference between her and the Secret Seminary students. Hannah and the others might be able to love their enemies. But if she ever broke free, Kennedy wouldn't sleep until Vinny was either dead or rotting away in a general population prison, where she hoped the inmates' sense of vigilante justice would only prolong his suffering.

She narrowed her eyes and thought about the big pit bull terrier that lived next door when she was a little girl. *If he meets your stare, don't be the first to look away.* She didn't know how long her face-off with Vinny would have lasted because after a few seconds, Jodie sunk back on the couch with a moan. "My stomach hurts."

At the sound of the tiny whine, Kennedy and Vinny both turned to the couch. Jodie's hands were clasped around her midsection. The wet spot of blood on her lap was even larger than before.

Contempt heated up Kennedy's whole body. *Stay calm*, she told herself. *Remember, you're still their prisoner.* She took another breath and swallowed down her disgust. "Would it be all right if I took her into the bathroom?" She remembered the men credited her with some degree of medical knowledge. "She might have gotten injured when you fell on her."

Vinny looked aside. "You have five minutes," he growled without changing his facial expression. A jerk of the head sent Dustin fumbling with the handcuff key.

When Kennedy was free, she put her arm around Jodie. "Do you think you can walk?"

Jodie grimaced. "It hurts."

"I'm going to stand up first, and then I'll help you, ok?" Kennedy blinked over her dry contacts. She pulled Jodie to her feet, and the child let out another whimper.

Kennedy was so weak she could hardly stand up straight, but she managed to shuffle toward the bathroom, half dragging, half carrying Jodie. A few steps away from the door, she lost her footing and nearly stumbled. She clenched her jaw shut to ward off the frustrated scream that threatened to jump from her throat. Why were they here? Why was any of this happening? And if Jodie needed real medical intervention, what in the world could Kennedy do about it in this cold, musty basement?

Please God, we need a miracle. We need to be rescued. Kennedy grew up learning God had amazing plans for her. When she heard stories of believers who went through incredible suffering or persecution, she figured that they were the unlucky ones like Job, but in the end they too would have their reward. She assumed her own life would continue on as always, paved with blessings, filled with abundance, sheltered from tragedy, free from fear. Could it really be that last week the biggest stress was the calculus test she was now missing?

She thought about *Crime and Punishment.* What would Dostoevsky say about her situation? Probably not much. Her case was one more petty injustice in a world teeming with suffering and evil. Kennedy had never felt so insignificant, so invisible. She bit her lip, repositioned her weight, and helped Jodie take the last few steps to the bathroom.

"Five minutes," Vinny repeated behind them.

Kennedy shut the door. A whole day, a whole week of prayer wouldn't have prepared her for any of this. What was she supposed to do now? How was she supposed to help Jodie? Kennedy wanted to find the man who came up with the catchphrase, *God wouldn't give you more than you could handle,* and laugh in his face. Or maybe shake him by the shoulders.

Jodie dropped to the ground when the door closed. Kennedy cringed when she thought about how many bacterial colonies were thriving down there. "Do you want to sit on the toilet or something?" Not that it was any cleaner.

Jodie stared into her lap. "I'm bleeding."

"I know, sweetie. I think something ..." Kennedy stopped herself. She didn't know what was going on. Had Vinny hurt her when he fell on her? Or was it something else? "I think we just need to see about getting you cleaned up. Can you come up here?" She patted the back of the toilet bowl and immediately wished she hadn't.

Jodie glanced at the toilet the same way Kennedy might have stared at the Demilitarized Zone between North and South Korea after someone told her she should race across it. But she couldn't leave the girl on the floor, could she?

"I think I wet my pants," Jodie finally confessed.

"Don't worry about that. Let's get you up here, and we'll see if we can clean you up some." Kennedy doubted the men had a change of clothes here.

After she helped Jodie onto the toilet, she opened the bathroom door a small crack. Dustin was standing outside, but his gun was still concealed. "She's bleeding pretty heavy." Kennedy's face warmed with humiliation, and she kept her eyes low. She didn't want Jodie to think she was embarrassed, and she forced her voice to sound natural. "Can we have some pads?"

Dustin looked over his shoulder at Vinny, who was tinkering again at the work table. "What do they need?" he grumbled.

"Pads." A small hint of pink dusted the tips of Dustin's ears.

"Pads what?" Vinny yelled back. "Pads of paper?"

Dustin looked once to Kennedy before answering, "No, pads. You know. For girls." The last two words came out reluctantly.

Vinny slammed his wrench onto the table. "You go get them, then."

Dustin didn't object. Kennedy wouldn't have either, not when Vinny used that tone of voice. Dustin went up the stairs without saying anything else. Kennedy reminded herself to try to gauge how long he was gone. That might give her some clue how far away they were from real people and real stores. She wasn't sure exactly how that knowledge could help her, though. What they needed was a real SWAT team with real tactical gear. She thought about Dustin's gun and wondered what other weapons the men had stashed around here.

With Dustin gone and Vinny tied up with whatever project he was working on, Kennedy and Jodie could have a little privacy. She shut the door the rest of the way. Jodie was still clutching her stomach, and in the artificial light from the bulb hanging overhead, her skin looked a strange shade of grayish green.

"This hasn't been a very good day for you, has it?" Kennedy was half joking and didn't really expect a response. She didn't know what else to say. She had dozens of questions, but any one of them would remind Jodie of their awful situation. Another panic fit was the last thing either of them needed. "How's your stomach feel?"

"A little better, I guess." Jodie offered Kennedy a weak smile. "Thanks for being here."

Kennedy forced herself to chuckle. "I could say the same to you, too. I definitely wouldn't want to be alone right now." She didn't know how late it was but figured it was some time Tuesday afternoon. At school, she would either be cramming for calculus or taking that test. It seemed silly now, all the time and energy Kennedy had spent worrying and stressing over her GPA.

"So, you know what you were saying before?" Jodie began. "About God being with you?"

Kennedy had never had a serious conversation — or a conversation of any kind — in a bathroom with someone who was bleeding on the toilet, but what was it she had told Reuben a few days ago? *First time for everything*. She waited for Jodie to continue.

"Well, I was wondering. Do you think, I mean, do you think he's with you even when you do something bad ... like have an abortion or something?"

The question hit Kennedy like a kick to the gut. So did Jodie know the truth about the pills? "Sweetie, what your uncle tried to make you do ... that wasn't your fault, you know. You didn't have any control over that."

"Yeah, but ..." Jodie bit her lip. "I actually told him I would. Have an abortion, I mean."

Kennedy hoped if she ever got out of here that God would keep Jodie's uncle in another country, preferably on another continent. Kennedy didn't want the guilt of murder on her hands, but she sure felt capable of it every time she thought about Anthony Abernathy. She couldn't let Jodie know though, so she nodded and asked, "When did you tell him that?"

"Well, he said that if I let him take me to this clinic after church that he'd ... well, he's going to France this Christmas. And he said he'd want me to go and be Charlie's nanny while he's there, and I've never been to another country, so ..."

Jodie nodded and kept her gaze on the grimy floor.

"And so after church my parents thought I was just going to play with Charlie for a few hours, but we took him to his grandma's and went to the clinic instead."

"What happened there?" Kennedy felt like she was reading an overly-violent scene in a novel. Her initial reaction was to skim past it all, but her brain forced her to pay attention to each word so she didn't miss anything. Instead of speeding up past the gruesomeness of it all, her mind slowed down as if it wanted to absorb the horror in small bits at a time.

"Well, I started crying. It was hard to breathe."

"Kind of like this morning?" Kennedy asked.

Jodie nodded.

"That's a panic attack, sweetie. It feels really scary, but you've just gone through a whole lot. It's your body's way of showing you it's frightened." Kennedy realized then she didn't know half of what Jodie had endured. Almost all of it was still conjecture. "It's a natural reaction for someone who's gone through as much as you have."

"I told them I didn't want to do it." Jodie's voice trembled a little. "I was screaming. My uncle had to hold me down." She hung her head.

Kennedy's skin tingled with rage. "Did he force you?" She had been horrified by the video her dad made her watch once about abortions, and that was when she was a senior in high school. She couldn't imagine what it would be like for a thirteen-year-old girl to have to suffer first-hand through something so traumatic.

Jodie shook her head. "No, he would never do that."

Apparently Jodie had a higher opinion of her uncle than he deserved, but Kennedy kept the thought to herself.

"He went outside for a minute to talk to the nurse. And then he came back and gave me a pill. He said I had a case of nerves — that's what the crying was about — and that I should take it to feel calmer. But it didn't help. I started throwing up really bad. Not just like the morning sickness, either."

Kennedy still couldn't get used to the idea that she was standing in a bathroom talking to a junior-higher about things like morning sickness and abortion clinics.

"Is that why you didn't want to take the pills the guys out there gave you?"

Jodie sniffed and nodded. "I've just been feeling so bad lately. I went to this forum online, and it said morning sickness usually goes away after the first twelve weeks, but it didn't."

"Well, I can see why you maybe thought that having an abortion was the only option." Kennedy hated saying the words. What kind of life had Jodie led to think there wasn't anything else she could do? On the other hand, given her age, given her family situation and the media hype over the upcoming election, would carrying the child have been any less horrific and traumatizing? "I'm proud of you, though, for changing your mind. That must have taken a lot of courage."

Jodie sniffed. "I didn't do it for the baby or anything, you know."

"What do you mean?"

"The nurse said they'd have to do an ultrasound. See how old the baby was. And I ..." Jodie sniffed again and turned her face. "I didn't want my uncle to know. He only thinks I'm six weeks." Jodie's voice was so quiet Kennedy had to lean down toward her a little.

"Why did you tell him that?"

"I didn't want to get Samir in trouble. He was ... he ... we were good friends. But our parents didn't like us spending time together." She kept her eyes to the ground. "Last summer his family sent him to a boys' home in Vermont. I think they just wanted to make sure we couldn't be around each other. I haven't talked to him since then."

"I'm sorry." Was there anything else for Kennedy to say? None of this made any sense.

Jodie looked up shyly. "If my uncle knew I got pregnant that long ago, he would have thought the baby was ... Well, you know. And he'd be mad at Samir. Really mad."

Something about Jodie's tone didn't fit with the rest of the story. Of course, it was unnaturally bizarre talking to someone so young about boyfriends and abortions and pregnancies, but was that all, or was there more to it? Was Jodie telling her everything?

Jodie sucked in her breath. "That's why I said I didn't want the abortion after all. I didn't want the nurse to do the ultrasound and tell my uncle how old the baby really was."

Kennedy tried to swallow. Why did she live in a world where girls so young could get pregnant in the first place? "We all make mistakes," she stammered. She thought about her junior-high crushes. Sure, they felt like real love, but she couldn't imagine going to bed with someone at that age. "I know if you're really sorry for what you and Samir did ..."

Jodie scrunched up her face. "But we never did anything."

Kennedy felt like she had when she first moved to Yanji, trying to understand the new language, knowing she had missed something important but unable to figure out what. "So Samir's not the dad?" She felt like a bigger dolt than she had when everyone in her calculus study group figured out how to derive differential equations before she did.

Jodie shook her head. "No. We never even kissed. I didn't want Uncle Anthony to think Samir got me pregnant. But he and I ..." She lowered her eyes again. "We didn't do anything like that. He's not even a Christian. We liked each other a lot, but neither of our parents would allow it. Besides, we both knew it would be wrong."

So she lied to her uncle to protect a boy who couldn't possibly be the baby's father?

"Guess you're surprised." Jodie let out a mirthless laugh that could have come from somebody much older. "With my dad being so pro-life and all."

Kennedy thought her next words out very carefully and kept her gaze fixed to discern Jodie's reaction to each syllable. "Well, if Samir's not the one who got you pregnant ..." she began tentatively.

Jodie turned her head and sat up a little straighter. Did she know what was coming?

Kennedy's hands started to sweat, and she wiped them on the sides of her pants. "You don't have to tell me anything if you don't want to, but I think it would be helpful if I knew." Her mouth felt suddenly very dry. She swallowed before she began again. "Sometimes adults don't know the right way to treat their daughters or their nieces, and they ... What I'm trying to ask you is if your dad or maybe your uncle is the one who ..."

There was a banging on the door. "Times up."

Jodie let out a loud, choppy sigh. Kennedy was just as ready to end the conversation there, at least for now. She was sure that hadn't been a full five minutes, but she was in no position to argue. She eyed Jodie's stained clothes. "What you want to do about your pants?"

Vinny pounded on the door again. If he grew too impatient, nothing could stop him from coming in before Jodie was dressed.

"We're getting ready right now," she called out in the least hostile tone she could stomach. She frowned at Jodie. "I'm really sorry, but I think the only choice is to put your old clothes back on for now. At least when the other guy gets back with some pads ..." She let her voice trail off and wondered for the hundredth time that day how she had gone from a volunteer weekend receptionist to a hostage in this huge, impenetrable cell.

Jodie could move more easily now, and she only needed a little help to keep her balance as she dressed. Kennedy helped her roll up some toilet paper to serve as a makeshift pad and tried not to cringe when Jodie put on the bloodstained things. It was better than wearing nothing at all.

A second before Jodie finished pulling her pants up, Vinny barged into the bathroom. "I said time's up," he growled. Kennedy avoided his eyes and linked her elbow in Jodie's. They walked back to the couch, and Vinny's phone rang. Kennedy hoped she could continue her awkward conversation with Jodie, but he just looked at his screen, swore, and jammed the phone back into his pocket.

"It's cold." Jodie sat and hugged her arms around herself. She was shivering. For a minute, Kennedy thought about asking Vinny for a blanket, but she decided to wait. Maybe Dustin would be in a more agreeable mood when he came back with the pads. It seemed nearly impossible for their situation to improve in any way, but she could always hope.

CHAPTER 18

Jodie curled herself up in a little ball on the couch, resting her head on Kennedy's lap. Kennedy stroked her hair and remembered cuddling with her mom like that in front of the TV when she was a little girl. But she couldn't think about her mom right now. She couldn't think about her friends she left back on campus or the homework assignments she was missing. She only had the mental stamina to worry about Jodie.

Thankfully, Jodie didn't seem to be in as much pain. The cold was her only real complaint. While they rested and waited for Dustin to return, Kennedy inventoried all the information she had stored up over the past few days. Dustin and Vinny were working for Jodie's uncle, and he was the one who wanted Jodie to take those abortion pills. Did he know what they would do to her body? If he knew how far along Jodie really was, would he still make her take them? Was he willing to risk his niece's life simply to keep the family from scandal? Was this whole act a desperate struggle to save his brother's campaign? Or would things be different if he knew the real age of Jodie's baby?

Since Jodie's friend Samir wasn't the dad, who got her pregnant in the first place? It was possible Jodie was lying, but Kennedy couldn't picture someone as quiet and demure as Jodie sneaking around with boys behind her parents' backs. Jodie had made a comment on the phone about her dad. What was it that she had said? At the time, Kennedy would have guessed she was being abused by her own father. She had only talked with Senator Abernathy for a few minutes and came back with conflicting impressions. On the one hand, he seemed as plastic and insincere as she would expect from any other politician. Even if he wasn't directly responsible for abusing his daughter, wouldn't he be close enough to his brother to know what a dangerous influence he was? But then Kennedy thought about the way he talked about his work in the pro-life movement, the concern he showed not only for the unborn babies but for the moms who carried them. Could he really be so two-faced to abuse his own daughter or stand by while her uncle tried to bribe her into having an abortion? Was there any possibility he was completely innocent in the matter?

Whether or not Jodie's dad was involved, her uncle definitely was. She had a low enough opinion of Anthony Abernathy to immediately suspect him. Anyone capable of kidnapping and forced abortions was capable of child abuse, right? But why did he go through the trouble to have Kennedy kidnapped, too? Even if he knew about Jodie's call to the pregnancy center, he didn't have any way to link that conversation back to Kennedy. Unless ...

The sound of smashed glass crunching on the pavement echoed in Kennedy's mind. The sight of the graffiti, the heaviness in the air when Carl and Sandy surveyed the destruction and vandalism of their new ministry building. Was that Anthony's doing, too? Was it his way of getting back at the center for taking a call from his niece? Or was there more to it than that?

What if he had been at the center looking for the phone records? What if he was trying to find out who it was that took the call? But Kennedy hadn't filled out any paperwork while she was there. Even if Jodie's uncle or one of his stooges broke into the center, how could he have known Kennedy was the one with the hotline cell? Then she remembered — Carl writing her name down on the big wall calendar, Kennedy jotting down her dorm room number on the purple Post-it. From there, it would have been easy enough for Anthony to find her room, check up on her contacts, bug her phone. But would he really have gone through so much trouble to keep the press from learning about Jodie's pregnancy? Politicians' daughters got pregnant every day, didn't they? Of course, this would be more sensational since Jodie was so young and her father was the most conservative gubernatorial candidate the state may have ever seen, but it would pass, right? Nobody paid attention to the tabloids for that long. If the election wasn't in a week, would Kennedy still be sitting here today?

She thought about the internet search she had been doing when Dustin barged into her room. She was seconds away from calling Carl about her suspicions. How could Anthony have known? How could Dustin and Vinny have gotten there so fast? Unless they had been watching more than her phone. Kennedy's whole spine went rigid at the thought. So was all this to cover up the pregnancy, then? Or was there more to it? Incest? Statutory rape? Child abuse? She remembered Nick saying the press was lurking around St. Margaret's looking for a scandal. They would have gotten one, too, if Anthony's men hadn't caught Kennedy when they did.

Her thoughts about St. Margaret's led to others. If they bothered kidnapping Kennedy, why would they stop there? What if they went after Carl or Sandy, too? The Lindgrens had all the same information Kennedy did when she went to meet with Nick in his office.

Nick. She tried to think through their conversation. Had either of them mentioned the Abernathys? Wasn't it Nick who told her they went to St. Margaret's in the first place? If Anthony's men suspected Nick might reach the same conclusions as Kennedy, would they get rid of him, too?

Jodie shifted on the couch, and Kennedy rubbed her on the shoulder. "Are you holding up ok?" she asked. It was a stupid question. Nothing was ok about any of this.

"My feet are really cold."

Kennedy had just decided to risk Vinny's wrath by asking him for a blanket when his phone sounded again. This time he grunted and answered it reluctantly. "Hey, Anthony."

"That might be my uncle," Jodie whispered. Was that hope in her voice? "Do you think he's going to tell them to let us go?"

Was she still so naïve? Kennedy didn't want to lie. "I don't know." Kennedy couldn't believe Anthony tried to deceive Jodie into thinking those pills were anxiety meds. She tried to listen in to Vinny's conversation, but all she could catch were snippets of mumbled words that made no sense when strung together.

The door to the top of the stairs swung open. As Dustin came down, Kennedy tried to guess how long he had been gone. Forty minutes? Maybe a little more. What did that tell her about their location? What did that mean about their chances of rescue or escape?

The starchy smell of French fries reached the bottom of the stairs before he did. He carried two McDonald's bags. Kennedy swallowed a whole mouthful of saliva as the fatty aroma swirled around in her empty stomach.

When was the last time she had eaten? And how could she watch Dustin and Vinny dining in front of her when she was so hungry she hardly trusted her legs to support her weight anymore?

To her surprise, Dustin threw one of the McDonald's sacks at her when he passed by, along with a plastic shopping bag. Even if she wanted to, she couldn't ignore the greasy smell wafting up to her nostrils, so enticing she could almost taste it. She passed Jodie the package of pads when Vinny called out, "This time she goes by herself."

Kennedy didn't argue. "Think you can make it?" she asked.

Jodie nodded.

"Let me know if you need anything," she whispered when Vinny wasn't looking. "I'll save some of the food for you."

Jodie was walking more smoothly now. Kennedy's fingers trembled as she broke the burger in half. It took all the self-control that she possessed to refrain from eating the entire meal. She finished her portion in a few ravenous bites and tucked the rest of the food away to save it for Jodie. Her hands still shook when she was done, but she reminded herself that Jodie would need the iron and the calories more than she did.

Vinny and Dustin were still eating their meals over by the table. What were they working on over there, anyway? Kennedy took advantage of the silence and tried to pray. She thanked God for providing the much-needed food and for helping Jodie feel a little better. After that, her mind was racing too fast to formulate any sort of cohesive request. She hoped God understood anyway. Didn't her dad say God knows what we need before we ask him?

There was a buzzing sound from upstairs, and Vinny turned to Dustin. "That's Anthony. Keep an eye on them." Vinny stomped up the stairs. So was Anthony actually here? Would he dare to show himself to his niece, or would he keep hiding behind his stooges like the coward he was?

Kennedy watched Dustin as he finished up the last of his fries. He must have sensed her staring, because he turned to her and announced with a full mouth, "She's still going to have to take those pills."

Kennedy wondered if Jodie could hear from the bathroom. How long was she going to take in there? Was she all right? "She can't do that. It's not safe." She tried to talk loud enough so Dustin could hear without having her words carry to every square inch of the room. Why couldn't he come closer?

Dustin shrugged. "Vinny's going now to talk to her uncle. She's taking them."

For a minute Kennedy wondered what would happen if she grabbed the pills and swallowed them herself. It couldn't be more dangerous for her than for Jodie, could it? But they would stop her before she could carry through. If she could only reason with them ...

Kennedy stood up, studying Dustin's expression as she took a few steps toward him. He kept eating, so she went a little farther until she was a foot or two away from the workbench. At least now she didn't have to yell across the room. She lowered her voice and kept her ear strained to hear when Jodie or Vinny returned. "Those pills only work when a girl is a few weeks pregnant. If you take them later than that ..." What would happen? Kennedy didn't know, so she'd have to bluff. "If you take them later than that, it's really dangerous for both the mom and the baby." That made sense, didn't it?

Dustin shrugged. Of course, he wouldn't care about the baby's life. But didn't he worry about what Anthony Abernathy would do if Jodie died or ended up in the hospital?

"If you don't believe me, I can look it up for you. Do you have internet down here?"

Dustin's eyes narrowed suspiciously.

"I'm telling you, those pills could kill her."

Dustin put down his fries. "You give me the information, and I'll look it up." There was a laptop computer on the far side of the work table, and Dustin drummed his fingers on the wooden platform while he waited for it to start.

"She said she's already five months along." Kennedy tried to keep her voice sounding reasonable, but now that she could see what was going on at the work bench, she grew even more nervous. Weapons were strewn across the wooden platform. Parts of guns, boxes of ammo. She tried not to stare as one incessant question raced through her mind — if Dustin planned to let her live, would he have allowed her to see his stockpile?

Kennedy glanced at the screen as it lit up and saw what looked like blueprints for a building. Was that where they were keeping her? If she got a chance to study it, could it teach her how to escape? Dustin quickly closed the browser and opened up a Yahoo search page. "Well?"

Kennedy couldn't remember the name of the drug. "Look up *abortion pills and second trimester*," she told him and shot a glance at the staircase. She was sure if Vinny came down now he would be furious to see her by the workbench. Dustin was staring at the keyboard while he typed, and if Kennedy had any idea what to do with a gun, she might have been able to grab one before he had time to react. What was the point of her and her dad watching all those action movies if she never learned the first thing about handling real weapons?

"All right." Dustin strained his neck forward as he stared at the screen.

Kennedy noticed he had misspelled most of the words in his search, but Yahoo still brought up the name of the pill she was looking for. "That one." She pointed. He squinted, and Kennedy saw a small knife on the table, gleaming in the bluish glow from the screen. Did she dare?

Dustin clicked on the link and then looked at Kennedy. "Now what?"

She got a little closer. Her fingers were near enough to brush the knife's leather sheath. "Click there, under *frequently asked questions*."

He stared blankly until she tapped the screen to show him the FAQ tab.

She let her eyes skim the bullet points briefly. "There it is. See? The pills are only designed for use in the first seven weeks. She's way beyond that."

"How do you know?" he scowled.

"Well ... she told me."

Dustin let out a short laugh, but he shut up in an instant as soon as Vinny shouted down the staircase. Kennedy froze and wondered if he would be angrier at her for leaving the couch or at Dustin for letting her up in the first place. Would they cuff her again?

Dustin's eyes grew wide, and he scurried to the bottom of the steps. "What do you need?" He seemed as eager as she was to keep Vinny from coming downstairs.

Kennedy ignored the danger warnings screeching from her brain and grabbed the knife. She slipped it into her pocket seconds before Dustin came back to the bench.

"You need to get back to the couch," he told her in a low growl. She hurried as fast as she dared, wondering if the knife's outline would stick out and give her away. Should she hide it in between the cushions maybe? Why did they have to make jeans so tight these days? She tried to pull her sweater down to cover it.

She sank back on the couch as Jodie opened the bathroom door and shuffled back to her seat. Kennedy hoped Jodie would be a little more comfortable now that she was cleaner. "Everything go all right?" she asked.

Jodie nodded and rubbed her arms. "Yeah. I'm just cold. And tired."

"Get some rest." Kennedy wondered how long they had before Vinny made her take those pills. After that, who knew what would happen? "You can lie down here again if you want."

Jodie put her head on Kennedy's lap. Kennedy bit her lip. *God, if you're listening at all, we're still here. And we're still waiting for that miracle.*

CHAPTER 19

Jodie was asleep by the time Vinny came back downstairs. He stomped louder than normal on the steps, and he cursed more vehemently than usual when he stepped on some sort of wrench that had fallen on the ground by the workbench. She couldn't hear what he and Dustin were fighting about in their hushed whispers, but she saw by their body language they were both angry. Not a good time to make either one of them more upset.

"Fine." Vinny spat and trudged to the couch, his large hands balled into fists that looked as hard as granite. Did he know about the knife? Had Dustin told him she had seen their weapon stash?

"Why'd you tell Dustin the pills won't work?"

They still thought she had some sort of medical expertise, so she did her best to pack confidence into her tone. "She's already in her second trimester. Those pills won't be effective at this stage." That would probably be a better deterrent than anything else. Kennedy watched him frown and quickly added, "It would be very dangerous for her, as well, since they're not designed for this late in the pregnancy."

"Her uncle told her to take them."

"I talked to her just a little bit ago." Kennedy kept her voice even. "She said she lied to her uncle about how far into the pregnancy she really was."

Vinny glared at the girl sleeping with her head on Kennedy's lap. What was he going to do to her? A protective instinct, stronger than hunger or fear or cold, surged from Kennedy's whole body. She pictured it wrapping itself all around Jodie while she slumbered, shielding her, comforting her. For a moment, Kennedy wondered if that's how her own mother felt toward her. Could you really live your whole life with such a strong desire to defend someone whose future and fate rested entirely out of your control?

Wouldn't you go mad? *Please, God. Aren't you listening? Can't you do something?*

Vinny scowled. Kennedy's heart pounded in her chest, so loud she wondered if he could hear it. But a calming presence floated past her, a whisper of comfort breathed over her. Was this what Christians sometimes talked about when they said they felt the Holy Spirit?

There was no majestic opening of the heavens. There was no loud rumble of thunder. Her body still shivered until her back and abs were sore. But she felt invisible arms of protection covering her, spreading all the way over to Jodie, whose eyelids were almost translucent while she rested. Was God really here? Kennedy wondered if this was how the Secret Seminary students felt when they faced arrests or interrogation. Was this why they never showed fear? If the feeling could have converted itself into something tangible, she would have reached out to pocket it, saving it for whenever she needed it in the future.

She held her breath, certain something must happen soon. Maybe God would send an earthquake to crack open the walls and let Jodie and her escape. Hadn't he done something like that once in the Bible? Kennedy couldn't remember the details. Or maybe Vinny would have a heart attack and they could rush right by him and flag down someone to help. Or their rescuers could storm the place. Someone as well known as Jodie Abernathy couldn't go missing for long before every member of the police force was out looking, right?

Kennedy waited. Nothing. Vinny reached into his pocket. She knew what he was going to do before he pulled out the four white pills. The gentle awakening in her spirit passed, leaving her colder than before. She strained her senses. Could she catch the feeling once more before it deserted her forever?

Vinny cleared his throat. "Wake her up."

A harsh, biting winter replaced the peace from seconds ago. Kennedy doubted that any amount of prayer could ever warm her again. The air itself felt less dense, the room darker. The chill in her body seeped farther down into her bones.

"Wake her up," Vinny repeated.

Kennedy thought about the knife. Its image zipped through her mind before she could stop herself. Did she have the courage? Could she fight him off?

No. The thought didn't come from her. For a second, there was something almost familiar about it. The calming presence returned long enough to assure Kennedy she hadn't imagined the whole thing. It deserted her as fast and unexpectedly as it came, but there wasn't room for doubt. *No.*

Something was tugging at her heart — an invitation to trust. A chance to let go of her own ideas, her own self-reliance. A picture flashed in her mind of a giant canyon. There was no bridge offering easy passage across, but there was a path going through it. Through the thorns that threatened to scratch and cut into her skin. Through the darkness that clung to her like a winter chill. Through the heaviness of mourning, the weightiness of grief. There was no bridge, but there was a path, dangerous, rocky, terrifying.

Kennedy shook Jodie. "You need to wake up now."

CHAPTER 20

Jodie's eyes blinked open. "What?" She sounded groggy, like Kennedy's roommate Willow did nearly every weekend when she finally woke up.

"They want you to take the pills now." Kennedy tried to seize some of the peace, some of the comfort from before and wrap her words up in it. She didn't know how or why, but she knew — as certainly as she knew that the earth was round or that her parents loved her — things would work out all right. Was there a way to make Jodie believe it, too?

Lord, please give her that same comfort. Give her the same trust. Unfortunately, it was yet another prayer whispered in vain.

Jodie clutched Kennedy's arm. "I don't want those."

Kennedy stroked her hair. "I know." What else was there to say? "I know."

"I can't."

Vinny let out a huff of air. "Enough whining. Now do it."

"I can't," Jodie repeated, shaking her head weakly from side to side.

"I told you ..." Vinny roared, but he didn't get to finish. A high-pitched squeal sounded, louder than any smoke detector Kennedy had ever heard. Both she and Jodie clasped their hands to their ears. A red light on the wall strobed, making shadows dance and flicker. Vinny muttered angrily under his breath and raced to the workbench. Dustin had already grabbed one of the guns and was sprinting up the steps. Vinny snatched two others and rushed right behind him.

Kennedy freed her arm from Jodie's clutches. If she didn't act now, she would never have the courage. She sucked in her breath, leapt up from the couch, and dashed to the laptop. *Please start up. Please start up.*

The screen lit within seconds. Kennedy let out the air she had been holding. She forgot all about the pills. She forgot all about the serenity God had poured out over her spirit a few minutes earlier. She had only one mission.

A browser was open to some sort of list. If there was more time, she might have tried to figure out what it was. She opened a new tab and typed in the web address for St. Margaret's, mentally chiding Carl for not giving his church a shorter name. What would Vinny do to her if he came downstairs now? It didn't matter. She had to find a way to get Jodie free. The siren blared. The screeching noise fired agony into her ears. She had to move fast. As soon as the webpage came up, she clicked on tab to leave a comment. She didn't know if the messages went right to Carl or to some receptionist, but that didn't matter as long as it got to someone fast. She had to tell them where she was. As far as Carl knew, she was really busy with school, and her voice was too hoarse to allow her to talk on the phone. Her fingers trembled as they flew over the keyboard. It took all of her self-control to leave the misspellings there instead of wasting the time to correct them.

It's Kennedy. I'm here with Jodie A. Two men are keeping us in a basement.

There was so much more to say. She wanted to tell him how long of a drive it took to get there. She wanted to tell him that when Dustin went to the store, it was a little over half an hour before he returned. She wanted to tell him the names and descriptions of the men involved, including Anthony Abernathy. But there was no time. If either of the men came down and saw her at the laptop ...

She clicked the send button only to have the computer protest because she hadn't entered a valid email. She grumbled at the website designer, then blasted in her address — typos and all — and exited out of the browser. For a second, she worried that she had also closed down the page Dustin and Vinny had up, but there it was again. Some sort of itinerary, maybe? She wondered if she should switch the laptop to sleep mode or if it was better to let the screensaver start on its own. Why hadn't she thought of that before? If they saw the screen on now, they would know she had done something. For a moment, she considered cuffing herself back by the couch so if they accused her, she could deny it. But of course they would remember if she were handcuffed when they left. Wouldn't they?

Her heart was throbbing when she got back to the couch, and her stomach was twisted in a knot. For the first time, she was glad she hadn't eaten that other half of the burger. Her legs were weak and unsteady, like stalks of limp celery.

Jodie stared at her wide-eyed, her hands still over her ears. "What's going on?"

Kennedy wished she knew. The alarm continued to shriek. Had someone broken into the complex? Was that why the men both grabbed their guns before they raced upstairs? Or could this be some sort of a drill? If it was an attack, did the men plan to leave the two girls down here to fend for themselves? Kennedy wished the siren would stop, but she didn't want Dustin or Vinny to come downstairs until the laptop's screensaver kicked in again. And what would she say if they noticed something was different about the computer? What if they questioned her? Was there any sort of excuse she could come up with to stay out of trouble? Her lungs constricted, and she had to force air in and out of her chest while her mind raced through its different options. What if she told them she was worried about Jodie and went online to research medical conditions that might cause her bleeding? She glanced over. Jodie's skin tone had improved. Her eyes looked tired and nervous, but she didn't appear to be experiencing any pain or discomfort.

Could she tell them she had an assignment due today and was checking up on the status of one of her classes? No one would believe that a hostage, however much of a perfectionist, would sneak onto a laptop to check on homework. The only thing to do was hope that either the screensaver would kick in on time or they would be so worked up over the alarm they wouldn't notice.

"Why did they run upstairs?" Jodie asked.

"I don't know." For a minute, she considered telling Jodie this was all some sort of a drill. But what if it really was a rescue attempt? What if someone had noticed one of them missing and tracked them to the complex? Someone could have followed Anthony Abernathy if he came here earlier to talk to Vinny. Someone may have witnessed Kennedy's abduction on the side of the road. And of course, if anyone realized that Senator Abernathy's daughter was kidnapped, the city would throw all its resources into finding her as soon as possible.

Now that sirens were shrieking in her ears and the red strobe light was pulsing pain to the back of her head, Kennedy almost wished things were back how they had been. She didn't know what was going to happen. She didn't know if whatever battle might be raging upstairs would work its way to the basement or not. She thought about the weapons stockpiled on the workbench. How long could Vinny and Dustin hold off a rescue team?

She stood up. "I wonder if we should go wait in the bathroom." She tried to think of something to say to keep Jodie from feeling frightened. No matter how fast her heart was racing, no matter how her lungs burst at the thought of fresh air, this might be some sort of a drill or internal conflict. Still, she wanted to get Jodie someplace a little safer, a little more protected. "Maybe we could find a way to clean up your clothes."

Jodie didn't answer. Her eyes were wide, and her hand was cold when Kennedy helped her to her feet. "Do you hurt at all?" They shuffled toward the bathroom, and she wished Jodie would hurry. Kennedy's whole body was tense, and her ears strained over the alarm for the gunshots she expected to explode behind her at any minute.

When they got to the bathroom, Kennedy shut the door behind them. There wasn't anything she could use as a barricade. Now what? Jodie looked up at her with trusting eyes, and Kennedy's heart felt like it had been wrung dry. *Lord, how am I supposed to help her? How am I supposed to help either of us?* She remembered the peace that covered her before the alarm sounded. Why couldn't she carry that calm around with her all the time? She wondered if other Christians, more mature believers, lived their entire lives in a constant state of awe, perpetually aware of the presence of the Holy Spirit. She thought about people like the Lindgrens or the Secret Seminary students. What would they do if they were here now? Sing hymns? Drop to their knees in prayer? The only thing Kennedy felt capable of doing was throwing up.

"Oh." The color drained from Jodie's face.

"Are you all right?"

"I think I need to pee."

Kennedy faced the door to give Jodie some privacy. She almost offered to step out and wait, but her hands grew clammy at the thought of going back into the room where that red light sent shadows dancing wildly across the walls. The grease from the fast food she had eaten threatened to turn against her. "Take as long as you need," she told Jodie. "I don't mind."

What was going on upstairs? When would Dustin and Vinny come down? What would they say when they found both girls in the bathroom? Kennedy hoped the screensaver had kicked in by now. At any rate, she would rather have them mad at her for taking Jodie to the toilet than for tampering with their computer.

Jodie made a little moaning noise.

"Is everything all right?" Kennedy asked without turning around.

The tiny little *yes* that answered back was anything but convincing.

Dear God, Kennedy prayed. She was sick of asking for rescue. She was sick of experiencing tiny glimpses of peace that didn't last. She was sick of trying to maintain a trusting, positive attitude when the whole world around her was spiraling down to hell and madness.

Dear God, she began again, *just get us out of here.*

CHAPTER 21

"Maybe it was a fluke."

Kennedy's spine stiffened when she heard Dustin's voice. There was a series of six short beeps, but Kennedy's ears still rang even after the alarm fell silent.

"You don't get flukes with a ten-grand security system," Vinny grumbled.

"It might have been nothing." Kennedy detected a sort of questioning hopefulness in Dustin's tone. "Hey, where'd they go?"

Kennedy's spine tingled as footsteps neared the bathroom, and she jumped a little when someone pounded on the door.

"We're almost done," Kennedy called out quickly, afraid they might barge in.

"Get outta there." Vinny pounded on the door again. "Now."

Somehow, he was less intimidating when she didn't have to look at his face. "She's not feeling well." Kennedy opened the door a crack and slipped out so he wouldn't feel compelled to come in.

"What's wrong with her now?"

"She's been on the toilet since the alarm went off." Kennedy could judge by Vinny's expression that she shouldn't have mentioned the sirens. "I think she's passing a lot of blood," she hastened to add.

Vinny shrugged. "That's why Dustin went to the store. Give her a pad and get back to the couch."

Kennedy gripped the doorknob, clenching her teeth to keep her mouth shut.

"And be quick about it." Vinny's warning made her blood seethe, but she turned around, swallowing her contempt.

Jodie hadn't moved but sat on the toilet with her eyes closed.

"They need you to get dressed again." She hated to rush Jodie, but she didn't want to get Vinny more upset. He was tense enough already, like a shaken can of soda about to burst under all that extra pressure. She looked around the room. "Do you need another pad?"

Jodie grimaced, as if the sound of Kennedy's voice hurt her ears. She held her finger up for silence. Kennedy waited. Was she getting worse?

Kennedy walked over to the toilet and put her hand on Jodie's shoulder. Jodie sucked in her breath at the touch.

"What's wrong?" Kennedy had a hard time keeping the panic out of her voice. She looked down. The water in the toilet bowl was dark red. For the second time in the past ten minutes, Kennedy regretted eating such a greasy meal.

Jodie whimpered when Kennedy tried to help her to her feet.

Kennedy let go. "Vinny says you need to come out." How could she get Jodie up?

"I can't," Jodie squeaked.

Kennedy felt dizzy. *This is just like school,* she told herself. *It's like studying for a math test when you have over a hundred pages of reading, a paper, and a lab all due the next day.* Panic was a luxury she simply couldn't afford. She had to assess the problem, figure out what needed to be done, and take care of everything so her world kept on spinning. That's all this was. Just like school. The setting was different, the teachers more cruel, and the stakes were measured in human lives instead of grade point averages, but the route to success was exactly the same.

"Can you tell me what's wrong? Where do you hurt?"

Jodie put her hand on her stomach. Kennedy did the same and felt it tighten up like a concrete ball drying in fast-motion. Jodie grimaced and shut her eyes again.

"It's going to be all right." Kennedy forced herself to smile even though Jodie wasn't looking at her and wouldn't have noticed. "I'm going to get you a new pad, and then I'm going to help you get back to the couch."

"Get out," Vinny declared, and Kennedy only had enough time to position herself between the toilet and the door before he barged in.

"She's not ready!" Kennedy spread out her arms, as if that would give Jodie an extra measure of privacy.

"I said time's up," Vinny snarled.

Kennedy didn't want to move. She wanted to stay there as at least a partial shield blocking Vinny's view, but she couldn't help Jodie from where she was. *Please, God. Can't you just make him go away?*

Kennedy had lost count of how many prayers God had failed to answer so far today. Blinking back tears of angry frustration, she walked toward the wall and pulled out a new pad from the package in the corner. Jodie's eyes were still closed, and Kennedy wondered if she realized Vinny was in there with them at all.

"Come on," Kennedy urged. "We need to get you up."

Jodie was taking short, shallow breaths. Tiny pearls of sweat beaded on her brow.

"What's her problem?" Vinny demanded, and Kennedy imagined how rewarding it would be to watch him get shot point-blank like in the movies. She was surprised by the heat of her hatred. Had she grown so vengeful she could actually wish him dead?

Yes, she could.

"I think she might be ..." Kennedy lowered her voice to keep Jodie from overhearing, even though she doubted Jodie was paying attention to anything. "I think she might be miscarrying."

Vinny shrugged. "Good."

Didn't he understand? Didn't he realize? There was no way Kennedy could deal with a medical crisis of this magnitude. Anger boiled up in her gut like the contents of a pressure cooker. "No, that's not good. This little girl is five months pregnant, and she's hemorrhaging in this filthy bathroom."

"She's not hemorrhaging," Vinny remarked, and Kennedy wondered if he knew the meaning of the word.

As if on cue, Jodie let out a little groan, and Kennedy heard something plop into the toilet.

Vinny snapped his head back to Kennedy, his nose wrinkled up, his eyes darting from her to the bowl. "What was that?"

"I think it might have been a blood clot." She braced her queasy stomach and peeked down to confirm her suspicions.

Jodie was ashen. She gripped her midsection. Kennedy reached out to tell her to try to relax when Jodie shifted her position slightly.

"You need to get her to a hospital. Now." Kennedy stood as tall as she could, even though her leg muscles quivered and threatened to buckle right out from under her.

"But the baby's dead, you say?"

Couldn't he see Jodie was in trouble? Did he have no conscience, no sense of remorse or compassion? Kennedy had heard stories from the North Korean refugees in Yanji about horrifically evil people, but somehow in her mind she had compartmentalized those villains. They lived in dictatorships. They thrived in nations with godless, immoral laws and horrific records of human-rights abuses. Not in America. Not in big cities like Cambridge or Boston. And they didn't prey on girls like Kennedy and Rose, girls from Harvard, girls from important families, girls from churched backgrounds.

She reached out and felt Jodie's forehead. It was cool and clammy. Even her skin had a strange, sick-smelling odor that immediately reminded Kennedy of those horrible visits so long ago with her grandmother in the hospital. She brought her hand back and balled it into a fist, hoping Vinny couldn't see how much she trembled.

"She's losing way too much blood. She has to get medical treatment."

"But the baby's taken care of?" Vinny pressed. Was that all these monsters cared about? A dead fetus so Wayne Abernathy could continue his political career? Was murdering a child a reasonable price to pay to avoid a scandal? And even if Vinny had no regard for the baby's life, didn't he care that Jodie could bleed to death in his disgusting, germ-infested bathroom?

"I don't know." Kennedy felt like throwing up her hands but kept them planted firmly at her sides. "I'm not a doctor." Couldn't he see how serious this was? The pointed sheath in her pocket jabbed into her leg. She envisioned herself wielding the knife, demanding that Vinny take Jodie to a hospital, but her mind answered back with a snapshot of their arsenal of weapons in various stages of assembly on the workbench. A move like that would be suicide. And if something happened to Kennedy, Jodie would lose the only advocate she had left.

"I don't feel good." Jodie reached her arm out and used Kennedy's shoulder to hoist herself up a little. Kennedy tried to adjust her position to block the child from Vinny's view. If he wasn't going to help, couldn't he grant them some privacy? Kennedy tried to think back to her physiology unit in AP Biology from high school. What were you supposed to do if someone was losing that much blood? She couldn't think of any answer except get them to the emergency room as fast as possible.

Jodie raised herself up but stayed positioned over the toilet. There was too much blood. Too many clots. Even if she had been wearing pads, Kennedy guessed she would have soaked through several just in the past few minutes. For the first time, she was glad Vinny was still here. Couldn't he see?

He wrinkled his nose. "You two will have to clean up the mess when this is over." He turned to leave.

"I can't ..." Jodie's face was the shade of chalk dust. Her eyelids fluttered. Her pupils rolled up until for a second only the whites showed. Her body swayed. The scene played before Kennedy like freeze-frame animation, displaying itself in millisecond shots one after another. Jodie reached toward Kennedy before she swung off balance. Kennedy's muscles weren't ready to support her extra weight. They both dropped to the floor, and Kennedy's knee took the brunt of both their falls.

"Are you all right? Sweetie, what's wrong?"

Jodie's head lay in her lap again, but it wasn't anything like a little bit ago when they rested together on the couch. This time, Jodie's eyes weren't closed in the heavy slumber of the weary. She had passed out, the gravity of her condition written in the pallor of her sickly gray face. Kennedy stared at Jodie's chest and counted five awful, spirit-draining seconds before it rose. She held the girl's clammy wrist. Her weak, fluttering pulse reminded Kennedy of a dying butterfly's last desperate attempt at flight.

In the silence that followed, Kennedy could hear Vinny swallow. "I'll go call her uncle."

CHAPTER 22

The next few minutes could have lasted an hour or more. When Vinny left the room, the unmistakable feeling of total isolation weighed down Kennedy's whole body. What if Jodie died? How much blood could a person lose and still survive? She sucked in her breath at the sight of the puddle pooling around Jodie's body and knew they were in need of a miracle.

She lay Jodie's head flat on the ground, hoping to keep some of the blood going to her brain. Wasn't there something about elevating the legs as well? Or would that cause more blood to flow out? She wasn't sure. Her fingers never left Jodie's wrist, and she fully expected that frantic flutter to cease any minute. How long could your heart keep up such an impossible pace? She knew the basics of CPR but had never taken a class. And was it different on an adult than it would be for a child?

A child. A child who should have never been pregnant in the first place. A child who should have never found herself a pawn in this dangerous political game, where her family members held no regard for her safety. What had her uncle been thinking? Even if it wasn't the pills he prescribed that did this to Jodie, Kennedy would hold him guilty for it. All of it. No thirteen-year-old should be forced to endure a fraction of the trauma Jodie had suffered.

Kennedy thought about the articles from her dad's pro-life magazines. She thought about all those testimonies, victims of rape who carried their babies to term and found room in their hearts to love and nurture them. Or the story Willow told her about the lady who died because she delayed cancer treatment that would have killed her child. Kennedy felt like the biggest hypocrite who had ever volunteered to work for a pregnancy center. She couldn't find room in her heart to worry about the baby. She only had the energy and psychological fortitude to care about one thing right now, and one thing only — Jodie's safety. If she ever saw Carl or Sandy again, the first thing she would do was resign her position at the center, insignificant as it was.

The seconds passed. The puddle of blood widened, seeping into Jodie's shirt, creeping its way toward Kennedy's shoes while she crouched on the floor. In eight years, Kennedy would have the medical skills necessary to handle situations far worse than this. She would know exactly what to do. She could save Jodie's life. Maybe even the baby's. But time wouldn't hold still until she got her medical degree. This emergency was happening right now. Kennedy was just a first-year in college. An undergrad. She had never set foot in a med-school class. She had never completed a single rotation. She had no idea how to start an IV, how to stop a patient from hemorrhaging. She didn't know how many chest compressions you were supposed to do during CPR. And she still didn't really understand what she was doing here. Had God allowed her to be kidnapped just so she could care for Jodie? Why couldn't he have kept them both safe in the first place?

Her body trembled violently, as if all those prayers the Lord left unanswered that day sat festering in her blood like a toxin. Her teeth chattered noisily, her breathing grew shallower. What would Vinny say if he came back to find Jodie and her both passed out on the floor? And what in the world was she supposed to do now? Even if she knew a way to help Jodie, even if she possessed the magic knowledge it would take to stop her bleeding or save the baby inside her, how could she execute any of those lofty plans when it felt like she was going to suffocate?

Kennedy gasped noisily in time with her shivers. The blood beneath Jodie widened with each passing minute. Kennedy had to fight the irrational fear that she would faint dead away if the puddle made it all the way to where she squatted. How many blood-borne pathogens were there, and what were the chances of someone as young as Jodie carrying one of them? Careful not to let her sleeves drip down, she swept her hand against Jodie's forehead and had to watch her chest for the next ten breaths to assure herself the girl was still alive. She was so cold to the touch, it was almost as if Kennedy had reached out and encountered death's forerunner seated on Jodie's brow.

"She's in here."

Kennedy never expected Vinny's voice to bring such a surge of relief. She tried to stand up but was too dizzy. How had she gotten so weak? Was it actually her blood pooling all around them, her life source draining out of her in a steady, unstoppable stream?

"What'd you do to her?"

Kennedy had never seen Jodie's uncle before, but he had the same build, the same hairline, the same square jaw as his brother. He was taller than Vinny and skinnier, someone who might have passed for a male model if he were ten or fifteen years younger, or the kind of actor who would make middle-aged housewives swoon.

"What happened?"

Kennedy didn't know if Anthony was talking to her or not. Either way, she didn't have the strength to respond.

"We think she's having a miscarriage." Vinny's voice lost a little bit of its brusque edge as he glanced up at Anthony Abernathy.

"So you got her to take the pills after all?" It was worded like a question but came out definitively like a statement.

"No, this happened before the pills."

Kennedy wondered if Vinny was going to tell him about the fight, about how he fell on top of Jodie. She doubted it.

Anthony shrugged. "Well, it got taken care of one way or another." He spoke casually, as if someone had made plans to take the subway but ended up hopping on a bus instead. "Now why's she on the floor like that?"

"She's hemorrhaging." Kennedy's voice came out steadier than she expected. "She needs to see a doctor."

Jodie's uncle frowned. "Unfortunately, I don't think that's possible. What can you do for her from here?"

I've already done everything I can think of, Kennedy wanted to scream. Which was basically nothing except for lowering Jodie's head so the blood didn't have to travel against gravity to get to her brain.

"She passed out from all the blood loss. She's ..."

"Yes, I hear that's natural with miscarriages." Was he even listening? Did he care? Or would he stand here and watch his niece bleed to death?

"I'll send Dustin out for some ibuprofen. That might help if she wakes up with cramps."

"She's not sleeping!" This time Kennedy did allow her voice to rise. "She passed out. She may already be in shock." A blanket. Why hadn't Kennedy thought to cover her up with a blanket? It's what the first responders always did in the suspense novels she read, at least.

Anthony frowned. If he gave her another shrug, it might invigorate her enough that she could summon all her strength and attack him with her bare hands.

"Look at the toilet." Kennedy pointed. "Look how much blood she's lost in there. That's on top of all this." She gestured to the floor. "And that's just from the past ten minutes or so."

Jodie's uncle fingered his chin. "That's a lot." He said it thoughtfully, as if they were discussing a late commuter rail. "But a fetus that small should pass easily enough." He scratched his chin again.

He still had no idea.

"Her baby is five months old. She's over halfway through the pregnancy." Kennedy's voice was steady, but she felt like she was screaming at a small child who refused to accept common-sense reason.

At this point, Kennedy expected one of two things to occur. Anthony would either maintain his stoic demeanor and refuse his niece medical care, or he would spring into action and make rapid plans to get her the attention she needed.

He did neither.

His indifferent stare morphed almost instantaneously. The dull, apathetic eyes narrowed, boring hatred into his niece's body. The muscles in his face and neck all seemed to flex at once, making some of the veins pop up underneath the smooth skin. The formerly calm, placid voice was now laced with disgust. "The lying little brat."

His alteration occurred so dramatically, his words spewed out so vehemently that Kennedy nearly lost her balance. Still managing to maintain her squat, she stuck out both arms so she wouldn't topple onto the dirty floor. She had no idea what brought about the sudden change, but she understood now why Jodie lied to him about the pregnancy.

Anthony stomped out of the bathroom, nearly plowing Vinny over on his way. He stormed back a few paces later. "Five months you said?"

Kennedy bit her lip. She wanted to believe Jodie was telling the truth about her relationship with Samir. Now she wasn't so sure. Maybe the two kids really had been together. Had she just betrayed Jodie's trust? Well, the uncle had to know at this point. He had to realize how serious this was.

Anthony kept pacing and lifted his eyes to the ceiling. A few seconds later, he punched the wall, exclaiming more loudly, "Five months!"

A tiny gurgle of a cough made them all fall silent and lean toward Jodie.

"Is she waking up?" Vinny asked.

They stared expectantly for several seconds, but there was no more movement. Kennedy kept her eyes on the girl's chest, as if she could keep Jodie's lungs functioning by sheer willpower.

"She needs a hospital," Kennedy whispered.

"She doesn't deserve it." Anthony resumed pacing the length of the bathroom in two strides at a time, swinging his arms as he went. Vinny had to avoid him more than once. "To think of all that planning, the lengths I went to cover up for a deceitful little ..."

So was he going to let her die, then? Is that how this was all going to end?

"Five months." Anthony shook his head and muttered under his breath. "So she was with him that whole time. The sneaky, conniving, spoiled brat. Five months."

Kennedy did her best to keep from getting in the way of his boots as he paced. For a minute, she imagined what would happen if he slipped in the puddle of blood. The whole scene played out like a bad *Three Stooges* sketch. Only there was no comedy in this drama.

"She lied to everyone." Anthony slowed down and crossed his arms. "If she had told me the truth ..." He glanced at Kennedy. For a moment, his eyes reflected a pained, tortured sadness. He shook his head, and the tenderness was replaced with calculating malice. "If she wasn't family, I'd let her bleed to death right here."

For the first time in her life, Kennedy realized how grateful she was for her own mom and dad, how glad she was that her definition of *family* bore no resemblance to Anthony Abernathy's.

He bumped into Vinny's shoulder when he started to pace again. "She's been with that toad this whole time. I told her parents that little Muslim was no good. They should have sent him to Vermont as soon as I told them to, then this wouldn't ..." He shook his head and waved his hand in the air dismissively. "Take her to the hospital. And tell her that if she even drops a hint as to who she really is, I will find her Arab boyfriend, and I will murder him. Got that?"

Vinny bent down, and Kennedy wanted to protest before he jostled Jodie up in his arms. Shouldn't they call the paramedics instead? Shouldn't they have a stretcher and someone trained to transport patients in such critical condition? But there was nothing she could say. At least Jodie would get the help she needed. Kennedy hoped it wouldn't be too late.

"Well, that's out of the way," Anthony growled, fixing his gaze on Kennedy. "Now get up. You're coming with me."

CHAPTER 23

Kennedy's mind processed the danger before her body had a chance to fully respond. She slapped Anthony's hand away when he reached out. He lunged and grabbed a handful of her hair. She barely managed to break his hold.

Scampering backward, she made it to the wall before he seized her collar and yanked her to her feet.

All those videos her dad made her watch on self-defense were a complete waste of time. How could she be prepared for something like this? How could she fight back when she only felt like throwing up or curling into a ball and trying to disappear into the air?

He tightened his hold, and her collar cut into her throat. She tried to swing herself around. He was too strong. She aimed a clumsy kick at his shin that did nothing to loosen his grip.

"You think fighting's going to get you anywhere?"

She choked back her scream and pictured Jodie's unconscious body being carried out of their prison. She would get the medical attention she needed. At least she wasn't here to witness her uncle's brutality.

White spots floated in Kennedy's field of vision. She tried to reach back and claw at his face, but his hold was too tight. Would she pass out now, too?

She thought about the knife in her pocket. Did she dare use it? Could she ever find the intestinal fortitude? She glanced down at the blood clots on the floor. Bile rose in her throat.

"Let go of me." She scratched at his forearm and felt like a schnauzer fighting off a grizzly.

"You should have never gotten involved in any of this."

She tried to turn her face away from his nauseating breath.

"It was never your business to poke around in," he snarled.

Kennedy's head felt like it was about to float up like a helium balloon. She clutched at the front of her shirt, trying to give herself some breathing room. She could hardly think straight. The battle was lost. It had been lost the minute Anthony entered the room.

He turned his neck and bellowed out the door. "Dustin. Get over here. Now."

The younger man appeared seconds later. "Yeah?"

"Once we clean up here, you're going to Vermont. Take care of that Arab boy."

Dustin nodded. Kennedy was terrified to see him leave. She would have rather faced a hundred Dustins instead of one angry Anthony.

"Jodie said they were never really together." The words squeaked out of Kennedy's mouth.

She felt Anthony shrug behind her. "She lied."

Was Dustin going to go kill him, then? No, there was no way these men planned to let her live. She knew too much. She had seen too much. She thought of her parents, how devastated they would be. How long until they learned the truth? She wondered if Reuben or Willow would really grieve, or if it would only weird them out to have known the victim of a brutal murder. Her only consolation was that Jodie had made it out safely.

"Why?" Kennedy croaked. She had to get him talking more. She had to keep his mind on anything but her. She had to breathe. "Why are you doing any of this?"

Anthony's laugh fell flat in the room. "Jodie is my niece. I love her like she was my own flesh and blood."

There was something in his tone — something almost possessive — that made Kennedy shiver. Should she expect any less from a beast like this? It didn't matter. As long as he kept babbling, she could inhale. As long as he kept babbling, his attention and his wrath weren't focused solely on her.

"You know if this gets out, it's going to hurt her dad's campaign even more than the pregnancy would have."

He sniggered. "You think I'm doing this to help my brother?" His words dripped with cruelty. Did men like this really exist outside of horror novels? Did men like this have souls, or were they empty shells possessed by fiends and demons, intent on wreaking havoc on anyone and anything unfortunate enough to get in their way?

"Come on. Get moving." He nudged her forward without releasing his hold.

Kennedy glanced down and took a careful step around the bloody sea on the floor. What was going to happen now? It was like waking up from one nightmare only to fall back to sleep and dream something horrifically worse.

Anthony's voice held a hint of malicious humor. "You know, you shouldn't ask so many questions. One day you might learn something that ..."

His boot skidded in the puddle of blood. His arms flailed out. One foot slipped out from under him. He crashed to the messy ground, knocking Kennedy over with him. Her reflexes were quicker than his, and she jumped out of his way before he could get up.

"Don't move." The force in her own voice startled her. The knife was out of her pocket, out of its sheath before she could change her mind. She held it out with a shaking hand and backed another step closer to the door.

He made a move to stand, but she tightened her grip on the weapon.

"I said don't move."

Anthony's eyes widened, and then he let out a laugh that rang out and echoed eerily against the walls. "Or what?"

Kennedy felt the blood drain from her face. Why had she brought a weapon into this deadly scenario? How many seconds would it take him to seize it and use it against her? Would she bleed more or less than Jodie when he was done?

Anthony narrowed his eyes angrily. "What are you going to do, girlie? Stab me to death?" Another laugh, like two pieces of silverware scraping against each other, setting her teeth on edge.

What should she do now? What could she do? She was about to risk an impossible dash out the bathroom when she heard the door by the stairs crash open.

"FBI!"A whole army of voices burst out at once. They shouted, made loud demands as a horde of boots stampeded down the stairs. How many were there? A dozen? A hundred?

"Drop your weapon!"

Two single pops sounded, and Kennedy let the knife clatter to the floor. Instinct told her to fall to the ground, but she wanted to stay as far away from Anthony as she could. She sucked in her breath and pressed against the wall.

Everything after that happened all at once. There was no slowing down the perception of time like she read about in books. First, Anthony swiped the knife and sprang to his feet. He spun around behind Kennedy and held the blade to her throat.

A second later, at least half a dozen men in dark gas masks materialized in the doorway, aiming assault rifles at them both.

CHAPTER 24

"Sir, drop the knife."

The rest of the team fell silent, and only the man in front spoke. His tone was calmer now, even though Kennedy's ears still rang with the sounds of the men's angry bellows and ultimatums from a moment earlier.

Anthony wrapped one arm around her chest. She could feel him breathing hard behind her and wasn't sure if she was the one quivering so much or both of them. She held her breath, trying to creep away from the blade pressed against her skin.

"Sir, you need to drop the knife. Now."

Kennedy wondered why the agent was so reserved. Couldn't he see what was happening? Couldn't he tell she was less than half an inch away from death? How far down was her carotid artery? And once Anthony made the fatal slice, how long would it take to die? Would it feel like drowning? Would it be peaceful, like falling to sleep as the world around you slowly went black? Or chaotic — gasping for nothing as you felt your life spurt out of you pulse by pulse?

The men in the doorway looked to Kennedy more like one cohesive unit of death than individual men. Their eyes were all fixed on Anthony. She wished one of them would look at her. They were trained for rescues like this, right? So why weren't they acting? Should she duck so they could get their shot? They must have good aim and quick reflexes. They'd make sure to hold their fire until she was out of the way.

Wouldn't they?

"Hold still." The leader was talking to her even though his eyes hadn't moved off of Anthony. Had he anticipated her thoughts? Why couldn't someone tell her what was going on? A little nod, a slight hand gesture — something to convince her they were going to take care of her?

Kennedy was trembling so hard she feared she might slice herself open on the blade. She could feel the cold pressure against her skin, but it hadn't cut into her yet. At least she didn't think it had. These men wouldn't let Anthony go that far, right?

Why were they so still?

"Don't take another step closer, or I'll kill her." Anthony was still breathing heavily, but his voice didn't quiver.

"You'd be dead before you finished."

The words didn't comfort Kennedy at all. What did these men care more about — getting Anthony, or keeping her safe? When she stared into their hard, calculating faces, she had serious doubts. This wasn't anything like in the movies. There was no fast-paced soundtrack, no pops of gunfire syncopating in the background. In fact, it was almost completely silent except for the sound of her heartbeat pounding in her ears.

Anthony gripped her more tightly from behind. The movement from the men in black was barely perceptible. She didn't know if she actually saw it or only sensed the increase in tension. She sucked in her breath. Were they going to shoot? Was he going to cut? She knew too much. Even if Anthony was about to die, what would stop him from taking her down with him?

Apparently, the team leader's thoughts weren't that far from hers. "We have a medical team assembled right outside this building," he told Anthony. Kennedy knew she should feel relieved, but then again she didn't relish the thought of getting cut open at all. Was he trying to boost her confidence? "The girl would get immediate attention. And you would rot in hell. Your choice."

Anthony let out a loud sigh. Hope tried to emerge from its steel cocoon where Kennedy had buried it deep within.

"All right." Some of the tension seeped out of Anthony's strained muscles. "We'll do this your way."

Kennedy waited. Wasn't there supposed to be a rush of relief like they talked about in books? Shouldn't the men's faces relax? If she had to guess, their expressions were even more strained now. Or was it her imagination? Was the worst really over?

He removed his arm from across her chest.

"Easy," the team leader warned, but Kennedy didn't know which one of them he was talking to. What was she supposed to do now? Was she really free? "Easy ..."

She didn't trust her legs and waited for some sort of sign from her rescuers. If Anthony was letting her go, why did he still hold the blade to her neck?

"Lower that knife." The rescuer sounded like someone telling the high tide to calm itself and take a time out.

Hope for freedom merged with some sort of primitive, fear-laced instinct. Kennedy held her breath as Anthony slowly moved the knife away from her throat. So he really was giving in. It was over.

A second later, the saturated silence was broken by a chaotic din as everything erupted into noise at once. Someone shouting, "No!" A dozen gunshots or more. The sound of Kennedy's own scream.

Next the shock of fiery, glowing, diabolical pain as Anthony plunged the knife into her back.

CHAPTER 25

There were voices, murmurs that sounded like they were coming from underwater. Tension. Worry. Would the nightmare never cease?

A high-pitched electronic wailing. Ceaseless. Relentless. Enough to drive you crazy if you let it.

Pain everywhere. Hot pain, as if a fiery lance still sizzled inside her. Over and over and over again.

People shouting commands. Hands poking here, prodding there. She wasn't ready to wake up yet.

"Kennedy? Sweetie? Can you hear me?"

The voice pulled her out of some dark, murky mire. She returned slowly, reluctantly. The light overhead burned. Why was someone shining the sun in her eyes?

"She's waking up." The gush of enthusiasm sounded out of place as the nightmare begrudgingly loosened its hold.

She blinked. Her eyes were even scratchier than normal.

"It's me, sweetie. Sandy. And Carl's here, too." The voice was pleasant, kind. If Kennedy had any tears left in her ducts, she might have let them flow.

A hand held hers. A voice, strong as the wind. Bold as the ocean. "We're glad to have you back."

She tried to focus. Carl. She didn't recognize where she was. Was this the next chapter of the nightmare, a short reprieve before it dragged her back down in its clutches to the abyss?

"You're all right, sweetie." Sandy swept some hair off Kennedy's brow. "You're going to recover just fine."

"You're a very lucky young lady." Carl beamed at her with a sort of paternal pride.

"What time is it?" The words made sense in her mind, but she couldn't tell if they came out right.

"Excuse me." At the sound of the authoritative voice, Carl and Sandy stepped aside. A man in a police uniform strode over to Kennedy's bed. "I'm Detective Drisklay. I see you're waking up." He took a noisy sip from the Styrofoam cup he was holding.

Details of her kidnapping and rescue crept back into her memory. When she recalled the knife stab, she was thankful she didn't feel anything but tired. Tired and groggy. How much time had gone by? How long had she been passed out? She wiggled her fingers. Everything was working fine. Now she had to check her ...

"I can't move my feet." She hadn't meant to sound so panicked.

The detective cleared his throat. "Blame the anesthesia. The blade really couldn't have made a safer cut ..."

Kennedy looked around for something she could vomit into.

The detective stirred the coffee in his cup. "Now that you're awake, I have some questions to ask you."

"Beg your pardon, officer." Carl's tone was respectful, but his words were resolute. "She's just survived an abduction, a major injury ..."

Kennedy wasn't sure how Carl's retelling of all her recent trauma could help anything.

"What my husband is trying to say," Sandy jumped in, "is that maybe you could give her a little more time to recover. She just woke up not a minute ago. I imagine she wants to talk to her mom and dad ..."

Kennedy's throat constricted painfully at the mention of her parents.

The detective frowned. "Unfortunately, we have reason to believe that ..."

"I'll do it."

Three pairs of eyes stared down at her.

"I'll answer your questions." Kennedy still didn't feel like her tongue was working quite right, but they seemed to understand her.

"You don't have to," Sandy crooned. "Don't feel pressured ..."

"I already heard him make plans to kill somebody. A friend of Jodie's." She sucked in her breath. *Jodie*. She tried to sit up, but it was as if all her core muscles had gone on strike. "He sent Jodie to the hospital. She was passed out. He had tried to get her to take ..."

Detective Drikslay held up his hand. "We got the girl as soon as they came out of the complex. We were already there waiting."

"That was some fast thinking you did, contacting us on the church website." Carl was glowing as he stared down at her with his arm around his wife.

"We had plans to storm the complex for other reasons," the detective explained. "We would have jumped in with gas until we learned they were also holding hostages."

"What you did on that computer may have saved both of your lives," Sandy gushed.

Kennedy didn't care about any of this. "Where is Jodie now? Is she all right?"

"Your little friend will be just fine." The detective stared at his coffee, and Kennedy immediately noticed his use of the future tense. She looked to Carl and Sandy.

"She lost a lot of blood." Carl had such a different appearance when he wasn't smiling. "She's in another part of Providence right now getting a transfusion."

Kennedy detected the heaviness that seemed to crouch down on everyone's shoulders. She already knew the answer to her next question. "And the baby?"

Carl shook his head. "By the time she got here, it was too late."

"It was her uncle." Kennedy fixed her eyes on the detective, wondering if he was going to write that down on the little notepad in his breast pocket. "Anthony. He wanted to force her to have ..."

"We know all about Anthony Abernathy." The detective scowled. "But I'm curious about what you said about killing someone."

Kennedy told him how Jodie didn't want her uncle to realize how far along in the pregnancy she really was. "Jodie said the boy wasn't really the father, but her uncle would think it was. She didn't want to get him in trouble. They mentioned a boys' home. Vermont, maybe?"

Detective Driskslay nodded. "We'll look into it."

Kennedy wanted to see Jodie. She wanted to hug her, apologize for not finding a way to help her sooner. How much did one little girl have to endure? And then after she assured herself Jodie really was safe, Kennedy wanted to sleep for a very, very long time.

But she couldn't. Not now. There was still work to do. "Jodie's uncle told one of his men to go and ..." Could she bring herself to speak the words? "He told Dustin to go and kill that boy." Had she really just said that? Had it all really happened? If she weren't here lying in a hospital bed, if she didn't have such vivid memories of the cold, the hunger, the knife stab, she might have thought it was a dream that felt a little too real.

"Well, you don't have to worry about that," the detective assured her. "Anthony Abernathy and Dustin are dead. Killed on the scene."

Kennedy shut her eyes for a minute. Would she ever forget? Could she ever forget? "What about the other one? Vinny."

"He got away, but we suspect he's injured. The important thing is you're safe, and so is the girl."

"Her family knows by now?" Kennedy wondered how Wayne and Vivian Abernathy would respond to a crisis like this. What would it do to their picture-perfect family? She hoped Wayne would have the decency to stand up for his daughter instead of worrying how the events would impact his campaign, but she had her doubts.

"I just got back from praying with them." Carl sounded tired. "I think they're blaming themselves for what Anthony did. They never suspected."

"She was babysitting over there all the time," Sandy added. "They thought he just needed the extra help since Moriah died. They had no idea ..."

The detective cleared his throat, and Sandy took a step back. Kennedy tried to follow the gist of the conversation as he asked her more questions, but she never felt like she could grasp what was really going on. Her head felt as heavy as her calculus textbook when he finally left, mumbling something about sleeping off his coffee.

"I suppose we should be going, too." Carl helped Sandy into her sweater.

"What, so soon? I thought the party was just starting." The voice sounded familiar, but Kennedy couldn't place it until she saw the hair.

"Nick!" Sandy spread out her arms and gave him a hug. "That's nice of you to stop by."

He ran his hand through his dreads. "Well, I got Carl's text, and I figured I'd stop by right after youth group and see how everything's going." He gave Kennedy a little wave. "How d'you feel?"

She was too tired to smile but tried to give him a reassuring nod. "I'll be just fine."

"You bet she will." Carl clapped Nick on the back.

Nick looked around the room awkwardly. He wore a bright orange Hawaiian shirt over a T-shirt with Jesus and his disciples all piled into a white Honda. The caption at the top read *In One Accord.* Kennedy probably would have been glad to see him if she weren't so exhausted. She wasn't certain she'd remember any of this in the morning. How long had it been since she had slept the whole night through?

"So the media is kinda going crazy over all this." Nick didn't seem to know where to focus his eyes, which darted from Carl to Sandy to the various objects lying around the room.

Sandy winced, but Nick went on with his explanation.

"I guess they're saying now Anthony Abernathy was on some sort of rampage. Trying to sabotage his brother's campaign."

Carl shrugged. "Everyone's desperate for a scoop."

"No, that's what he said before he ..." Kennedy swallowed. Had she really remembered right? She could still hear the shouts of her rescuers and the sound of gunfire when she shut her eyes. Her whole body sank farther into her hospital mattress at the thought of Jodie and all she had gone through.

"I still don't know how someone so close to Wayne could do a thing like that," Sandy breathed.

"That appears to be the question of the day." Nick put one foot up on a little hospital chair near the wall and drummed on his bent knee. "Some are guessing it has more to do with protecting his own hide than anything else."

Carl made a motion to the door. "Maybe we should talk about this more on our way out."

"That's a good idea," Sandy replied.

Nick offered a sheepish good-bye. Kennedy wanted to tell them she didn't mind. She was dying to understand it all herself. But her vision grew blurry as she watched them gather up their things, and she was asleep before their voices died out in the hall.

CHAPTER 26

A nurse came in sometime in the middle of the night and recorded Kennedy's vitals. Whatever medicines they had given her were starting to wear off, and she itched and tried to get comfortable for another hour before dozing off again. In the morning, a nurse checked her bandages one last time and told her she would get her discharge papers ready. "Your pastor said he'd come pick you up in about an hour."

Kennedy wondered what it would be like to go back to the real world after an ordeal like this. Would she ever feel safe on the streets of Cambridge again? Would she ever feel safe in her own dorm? She thought about the pregnancy center, about the big Thursday dinner that would go on as if none of this had happened. Could people really go on living in such blissful ignorance? She couldn't. Like an over-stretched rubber band that can never resume its original shape, she couldn't close her eyes again and forget it all.

Her dad would tell her he had been right all along, of course. He would probably chide her for following Dustin the night he came to her room. Kennedy had been worried about Willow, that was all. And her compassion could have killed her. She wouldn't mind, though. Her dad could rage for an hour as long as Kennedy could hear his voice. As long as she could sit with the phone to her ear and listen to that strong, familiar, lecturing tone. All the homesickness of the past two months collected itself into one massive swell that came crashing down with tsunami-like force all around her. It wasn't like drowning. It was like being hit by a ten-foot brick wall.

"Excuse me. Do I have the right room?"

Kennedy squinted at the man in the doorway.

He smiled. "So here you are. Remember me?"

There was something familiar about that red hair. The guy from the subway. The journalist. What was he doing here? He gave her a casual smile and strode to her bedside.

"I saw your picture come up on my news feed. I never forget a face." He held up his camera case.

Oh no. Was he here for pictures, then?

Kennedy raised the back of her hospital bed so she was sitting up. At least she was in her street clothes already. What was he doing here? She wasn't sure if she should be talking to the media at all. Or was that only what they told victims in novels?

"I'm not here to interview you or anything." He patted his bag and kept it closed.

Kennedy stared. So he was a mind-reader, too? Or was he just used to people not trusting him because he was with the press? "It's just that I don't meet too many young people from Jilin Province. And, well, I guess when I saw you were involved in all this, I wanted to check in. Make sure you were all right."

His endearing smile only took away a fraction of Kennedy's misgivings.

He sighed. "Well, what do the doctors say?" He eyed her hospital room with a calculating, meticulous care. Was he some kind of Sherlock Holmes? What could his trained eye learn about her condition simply by observing her surroundings?

"I'll be just fine. Maybe a week or two of taking it easy. You know, after I catch up on all the homework I missed."

He crossed his arms. A little dimple dented his right cheek when he smiled. "I was a lot like that my first year, too."

She didn't ask him what he meant. She thought she was already learning.

He shook his head. "So you probably heard Anthony Abernathy was shot."

A shudder started in the base of her back and sped up her spine. She winced when it reached the spot of her injury.

"They're saying he did it because of his wife."

Kennedy felt her face scrunch up in about a dozen unasked questions.

He leaned forward. "Moriah Abernathy? Did you guys hear about her over there in Yanji?"

The name sounded vaguely familiar, but Kennedy couldn't place it.

"Anyway, she was pregnant when they diagnosed her with aggressive cancer. She refused chemo. No abortion, either. She died a few weeks after her son was born."

"Charlie."

"Pardon?"

Kennedy shook her head. "Never mind. So this is all some sort of vengeance because his wife died?"

He tightened the strap of his camera case. "I guess he figures if she hadn't gotten so much pressure from the pro-life camp, his wife wouldn't have been so adamant. Maybe she would've gotten the medical care she needed."

Kennedy wondered if it was the exhaustion or the pain meds that were most responsible for fogging up her brain.

He leaned forward. "Between you and me, there's chatter about other motives for hiding the girl's pregnancy, too. Selfish ones. Meant to hide incriminating evidence, if you catch my drift."

Kennedy squinted. Did he mean what she thought he meant? And if so, was she really surprised?

"But that's all spec at this point. You know how it is."

No, she didn't, but she wasn't going to tell him so.

He leaned against the end table by her bed. "You hear about the computer they recovered?"

She still hadn't figured out if this was an interview or some strange and unexpected courtesy call. If it was an interview, he was revealing lots and gleaning hardly anything, at least nothing she was giving him verbally. What was it her dad always said about Kennedy trusting strangers?

"I guess it had all kinds of incriminating evidence," he went on. "Wayne Abernathy's itinerary, blueprints of his election headquarters. Sounds like they were also planning to target some pro-life fundraiser later on this week."

Kennedy couldn't keep her poker face and felt her eyes grow wide. "But they stopped it?"

He shrugged. "As far as I know. I'm sure they'll have extra security just in case. You might want to tell your pastor to plan for more guests."

A nurse bustled in before Kennedy could figure out how he knew so much about her and about the whole situation. "I'll have to ask you to leave," she told the reporter. "We have some discharge directions from the doctor to discuss."

He cracked another wide smile, his dimple pierced his cheek, and he was gone before Kennedy learned his name. She had a hard time focusing while the nurse went over all the paperwork. She wished she could go home to her parents for a long weekend. Why couldn't they live closer?

The nurse left, and Kennedy reached over for the Bible on her nightstand. Had someone left if for her there? She couldn't remember seeing it last night, but she had been so drugged up and exhausted she could have missed anything. There was a note inside the front cover.

To Kennedy ~ Psalm 139.

Psalm 139. It sounded like a passage she should be familiar with. The pages crinkled as she turned them.

You have searched me, Lord, and you know me. How many times in Yanji had she ached for God to show himself to her, for him to let her know he cared for her, not only the missionaries and evangelists of the world?

You know when I sit and when I rise. She looked back on the past thirty-six hours. The whole time, God had known where she was. He had a plan to rescue her all along.

You perceive my going out and my lying down. You are familiar with all my ways. Her life, as isolated and lonely as it had felt for the past few months in the States, was an open book her heavenly Father had memorized. There wasn't a lab write-up, a calculus problem, a late-night snack of dry Cheerios that he didn't know about. And he loved her.

Kennedy was only halfway through the Psalm when Carl nudged open the door carrying a colorful bouquet of flowers and brandishing a huge smile. "Grab your things. Sandy insists you spend the next few days with us while you recover."

Kennedy wanted to argue. She wanted to tell him that she needed to get back to her dorm, back to her classes. She couldn't even guess how far behind she already was. But the dull ache in her back had grown exponentially since she woke up until she was sure she could feel Anthony behind her, stabbing her in the same spot repeatedly whenever she shifted her position. The doctor had assured her it would get better and ordered her to rest. Well, there wasn't time for that. Not with labs and calculus and *Crime and Punishment* ...

"She's already baking you muffins." Carl rolled a hospital wheelchair to the side of the bed. "She said the food back in your dorm won't heal you up half as fast as her home cooking." He reached his hand out and helped her down. "You ready?"

There was no point arguing. "Yeah." Once in the wheelchair, Kennedy put the new Bible on her lap. She had to swallow twice before she could trust her voice again. "I'm ready."

CHAPTER 27

Kennedy spent that day resting on the Lindgrens' couch, napping in their guest room, and assuring her mother over a series of five different phone conversations that she really was safe and unharmed. She nibbled her breakfast, finished about half of her lunch, and by evening was so hungry she cleaned her dinner plate twice.

Kennedy got in touch with her professors and wasn't expected back in class until Monday. She had some work to do in the meantime to keep from falling too far behind, but Carl and Sandy insisted she stay at their home through the end of the weekend. Kennedy surprised herself and didn't protest.

On Thursday morning, Sandy drove Kennedy over to her dorm so she could pick up her books. The door to her room was slightly open. Kennedy's body shook at the memory of what had happened the last time she was there.

"So, our little celebrity finally makes her grand stage debut." Willow's face lit up when they entered, and she stood up from her desk. Her hair was already a darker shade than it had been at the beginning of the week. She took a step toward Kennedy. "I'm like not gonna injure you if I give you a hug or something, will I?"

Kennedy blinked. Her dad had ordered her a new set of contacts that would arrive in the mail in a week or less. "No, just be gentle." She smiled. It was the first time she and Willow touched each other, at least as far as she could remember.

"So, you selling your book rights yet or anything?"

Kennedy winced at the shouts and gunshots bursting from Willow's computer game.

"Oh, sorry about that." Willow reached out and shut the monitor off.

Kennedy looked around. Besides Willow's hair color, nothing had changed. There were her books on the shelf, her bag on the floor. She could tell by one of the lights that her laptop hadn't even been shut down properly. Her phone — the real one, not the clone — was right there on her desk where she had left it.

"Do you want me to pick out a few outfits for you to bring back with us?" Sandy asked.

Kennedy had forgotten Sandy was there. "That would be great." So far, she had been wearing Sandy's old house dresses, which were comfortable enough on her back but not exactly what she'd consider her own personal style. She had already seen the way Willow raised her eyebrows at the oversized floral thing she was wearing today. "By the way, Sandy, this is my roommate Willow. This is Sandy, my pastor's wife."

She half-expected Willow to go into some tirade about the horrors of organized religion, but Willow simply waved her hand and gave her stage-ready smile. Kennedy pointed out the books she'd need, and Sandy packed them in a little duffel. To Kennedy's surprise, Willow remained where she was instead of plopping back down behind her computer. "So you skipping town or something? Going into witness protection?"

Kennedy laughed. "No. I'm just going to be staying at Sandy's for another few days until I'm recovered."

"Well, I know you're going to be wicked busy because you're a huge over-achiever that way, but you need to make time for me to take you to the L'Aroma Bakery so you can tell me everything that happened. You know, before your memoir hits the bookshelves and everything."

Kennedy wasn't sure if Willow was being sarcastic or not, but she could sense the genuine concern behind the words. "Yeah, I'd like that." It might be a while before she was ready to talk about it all, but she was glad Willow would be there to listen when the time came.

"Oh, by the way, your boyfriend's been stopping by ... I don't know, like every other hour to see if you're back. He said he's called you a dozen times or something, but your phone battery must've died. Again."

Kennedy felt Sandy's curious stare at the mention of the word *boyfriend*. Well, even though they weren't dating, it was sweet that Reuben was so worried about her. She made herself a mental note to call him at the Lindgrens'.

Sandy refused to let Kennedy carry any of her things back to the car. As soon as they were on the road, Sandy stole a quick sideways glance. "*Boyfriend?*"

Kennedy tried to keep her voice casual. "He's just a good friend. My lab partner."

"Just a friend?" Sandy asked with that same playful tone. "Just a friend that stops by every hour on the hour to see if you're ok?"

Kennedy felt the smile creep up on her face before she could stop it. Part of her wanted to change the subject. Part of her looked forward to getting her phone charged and hearing Reuben's easy-going voice and cool accent again.

Sandy put on some worship music, and they drove for a while without saying anything. Kennedy didn't know how she could ever show her full appreciation to the Lindgrens for everything they'd done for her. She wished she didn't have to have this next conversation, but she may as well get over it. It wasn't going to get any easier later.

"You know, I've been meaning to tell you and Carl ..."

Sandy reached over and lowered the speaker volume.

"I think I'm going to put my volunteer work on hold."

Sandy turned a corner. "Well, that's fine by us. We figured you may need time off after all you went through."

"It's not just that." Could Sandy ever begin to guess what was going on in Kennedy's heart? Kennedy hated to acknowledge it even to herself, but there was no way she was worthy to rejoin the pro-life movement. Not now. Probably not ever. As they drove, Kennedy told Sandy about the doubts that had plagued her since she took the first call from Jodie. "I just don't really know where I stand on abortion at this point. I know it's wrong. I know it's taking an innocent life. But, I mean, what about someone like Jodie? She's so tiny. I don't think her body would have been able to carry a baby to term, and even if she could, I wouldn't have wished that on her."

Sandy was quiet. Kennedy expected her to come back with a Bible verse or a pro-life platitude to cover over all of Kennedy's doubts and uncertainties like a miniature Band-Aid. The silence was unnerving, so she kept talking.

"There was a point when I realized they wanted to give Jodie the abortion pills, and a little part of me was sad that she was too far along in the pregnancy to actually take them. I mean, wouldn't that be infinitely easier on her body?"

"Easier?" Sandy repeated, and Kennedy stared out the passenger window.

"I don't know. I just, I wanted Jodie to be safe." She was shaking. Could Sandy tell? The singer on the radio crooned quietly about God's glorious majesty, and all Kennedy could think about was the puddle of blood on the floor of that bathroom.

She waited for Sandy to respond, for her to say it was normal to doubt. It was normal to feel the way she did. But Sandy only turned another corner and said, "We have one more quick stop." It wasn't until Kennedy saw the blue signs on the side of the road that she realized where they were headed.

When they parked in front of Providence Hospital, Kennedy's legs refused to move. *I can't do this*, she wanted to say, but she couldn't find the breath to form the words.

Sandy put her hand on top of Kennedy's. "There's someone here who's been asking to see you."

Two silent tears streaked unchecked down Kennedy's cheeks.

Sandy insisted they borrow one of the hospital's wheelchairs since Jodie was staying in the children's section, two towers over and four stories up. Kennedy and Sandy made their way through hallways painted in bright primary colors, watched a clown performing for a few dozen kids in hospital gowns, and passed dozens of patient rooms, but they still reached their destination before Kennedy was ready.

"Are you all right?" Sandy asked.

Kennedy blinked her eyes, and Sandy rolled the wheelchair in.

A nurse was busy adjusting some funny gadgets on Jodie's feet. Jodie looked even smaller in her hospital gown. A shy smile inched its way across her face. "Hi."

Kennedy sniffed. "Hi."

Sandy wheeled the chair right up to the bedside. The nurse silently excused herself, and Sandy exclaimed loudly, "You know, I've been needing to find a restroom since we left the house. I'll be back."

Kennedy had no idea what to say. One of Jodie's arms was bruised near the indent of her elbow. The other had an IV hooked up to it. Her face was puffy, but she looked stronger and had better color. She was sitting up in her bed and looked as embarrassed and unsure of herself as Kennedy felt.

"How ..."

"Did you ..."

They both began at once, and both stopped at the same time with nervous chuckles.

"How are you?" Kennedy finally asked. Their voices were hushed, as if Dustin and Vinny were right outside the door, listening in on everything they said.

"I ended up needing surgery. They ..." Jodie swallowed and stared at her Curious George sheets. "They, um, they said I'll be able to go home in a few more days."

"That's great news." Kennedy tried to sound positive but knew she had failed.

"I'm glad they got you out safe," Jodie said. "My dad told me as soon as he heard."

"Me, too." Kennedy tried to swallow. "I ... Well, you were really sick. I was happy to hear you made it to the hospital."

They stared blankly, and a few seconds later they both let out another round of nervous laughs, still under their breaths, still hushed, still haunted by the memories they both shared.

"You probably need your rest," Kennedy finally stated. When would Sandy get back? Why had she ditched her here?

"Yeah, my mom's been sleeping with me at night. Oh!" Jodie's eyes widened. "Did you hear? It looks like we'll probably be able to adopt Charlie."

Kennedy forced a smile. "That's great news." As hard as she tried, she couldn't drag any degree of enthusiasm into her voice.

"Yeah." Jodie's expression fell flat again by degrees. "I was really glad to hear that. He was fine, by the way. The day I was babysitting, I mean. He was fine. The police found him at his grandma's." She cleared her throat.

Kennedy glanced at the clock. How long was Sandy going to take?

"You know about my uncle?"

The question caught Kennedy off guard. Was Jodie asking if she knew he was dead? Or something else? She nodded tentatively.

Jodie let out her breath. "The doctor said something about giving the baby a DNA test. I guess you can do that even after ... Well ..." She bit her lower lip and stared past Kennedy. "At least Samir won't get in trouble. Once they get the results back, I mean."

"So it really was ...?" Kennedy couldn't bring herself to complete the thought.

Jodie let out what sounded like a bad imitation of a laugh. "I didn't want to tell my parents, you know, because I thought it might hurt the election."

Kennedy didn't know what to say. From their first phone conversation, there had been a connection, a certain camaraderie between her and Jodie she couldn't explain. Now, she felt like they were slipping apart, pulled away from each other by a gravity far too strong for either to resist.

"It was a boy, you know." Jodie's voice was a small hush.

Kennedy felt her face scrunch up awkwardly. The corners of her eyes felt warm.

"A little, tiny baby boy," Jodie breathed, staring past Kennedy's shoulder.

"I bet he was beautiful." Kennedy tried to cough but ended up making a painful choking noise deep in the back of her throat.

"I told my mom ..." Jodie let out her breath nervously. "I told my mom I wanted a picture. He just, he was so perfect. Do you think that's weird?"

Kennedy shook her head but couldn't form any words.

"I decided to name him Wayne."

Kennedy tried to say she thought it was a perfect name, but she wasn't sure she got it out right.

"They even let me hold him for a minute or two. I talked to him. Just a little. I told him I was sorry for thinking about, well, you know. I told him

I hoped he wouldn't forget me." She looked over at Kennedy with shining eyes. "I want him to remember me when I get to heaven. Because when I'm there, I know I'm going to recognize him right away. Don't you think?"

Kennedy didn't know who started crying first. She didn't know who reached out for whom. But when Sandy came to the door, Kennedy was up on Jodie's bed. They were curled up into each other's arms and sobbing, mourning little Wayne, releasing all the fear and trauma of the past few days. Kennedy cried for Jodie's lost innocence, for the depravity that made such a sweet child suffer unimaginable torment, for the cruelty that spilled over into a world Kennedy had previously assumed was safe.

Sandy caught Kennedy's eye and pointed to the hallway, mouthing, *I'll be out here.* Half an hour later when their tears were dried up, Jodie said her mom would stop by with Charlie to visit soon. She and Kennedy both chuckled a little again as they said good-bye, and then Kennedy let Sandy wheel her back to the car. They didn't say anything on the way home, but the silence filled Kennedy's wounded, weary soul like words never could.

CHAPTER 28

As soon as they got back to the Lindgrens', Kennedy took her pain meds and went to the guest room to lie down. Carl and Sandy would be busy that afternoon getting ready for the pregnancy center's big dinner. It would be Wayne Abernathy's first public statement since his daughter's kidnapping. They had to make a last-minute room change because even St. Margaret's huge fellowship hall wasn't large enough to accommodate both the guests and the press who would be there. Nick recruited a bunch of kids from the youth group to stop by after school to set up tables in the sanctuary. There would be extra security too, although everyone assumed with Anthony dead and the computer confiscated the attacks wouldn't proceed as planned.

"You're welcome to come with us." Carl took a noisy slurp of soup that Sandy had whipped together for a late lunch.

"I'll see how much reading I get done this afternoon." Kennedy was glad when Carl didn't push the issue any further. The thought of being there with so many people left her paralyzed.

When the time came to set up the church, Carl asked Kennedy again if she wanted to come. "If you're not ready now, one of us could swing by and pick you up a little before six. No problem."

Sandy laid her hand on her husband's shoulder. "I think she needs to rest."

In this case, Kennedy was happy to let Sandy answer for her.

"Well, just text us if you change your mind," Carl called out as he went to the bedroom to hunt for his lost keys.

Once the Lindgrens left, it was the first time Kennedy was alone since the kidnapping. She hobbled around to make sure both the front and back doors were locked. She wasn't in the mood to read, and *Crime and Punish-*

ment wasn't the right kind of book for a day like this anyway. Her usual spy or thriller novels wouldn't be an adequate distraction, either. Would she be stuck reading historical romances like her mom for the rest of her life? She heated up a bread roll Sandy left for her, glanced at some of her reading for her general chemistry class, and tried to remember where she had put that Bible someone had left her in the hospital. She found it a minute later in the guest room and returned to Psalm 139.

For you created my inmost being; you knit me together in my mother's womb. Kennedy sat staring at the words. Shouldn't they speak to her? Shouldn't they mean something at a time like this?

I praise you because I am fearfully and wonderfully made. What did Jodie's baby look like? She almost wished Jodie had offered to show her the picture she had. Was he a tiny version of his mother? Kennedy tried to swallow away the lump in her throat with another bite of bread.

When I was woven together in the depths of the earth, your eyes saw my unformed body. God had loved that baby. She knew now that Jodie had, too. Was that what pastors and politicians meant when they spouted off terms like *sanctity of life*?

All the days ordained for me were written in your book before one of them came to be. All the days. Did that include baby Wayne's days in the womb? Had he been knitted together in time to know how much God loved him? To know how much his mom loved him, scared and young and ill-prepared as she was?

Kennedy's eyes hurt. She shut the Bible and thought about calling Reuben. She wasn't quite sure why she hadn't yet. Part of her was scared he would ask too many questions. Another part of her didn't want to admit anything had changed. She didn't want to talk. Especially about the past few days.

Kennedy checked her phone. Tomorrow, Carl would take it in to get the surveillance bugs removed. Did she really want to use it yet? She stared at her empty plate and her assignment notebook for another twenty minutes before she finally picked it back up and found Reuben's name in her contacts.

"It's about time I heard from you!" There was both relief and good humor in his voice.

Kennedy couldn't help laughing. "I'm sorry. It's been a busy few days."

"I'm sure it has. I'm hearing all about it right now, actually."

"What do you mean?"

"Check out Channel 2 News and then call me back."

Kennedy wasn't sure she wanted to hear some newscaster recount the horrid details of her and Jodie's capture. She was sure they wouldn't spare Jodie any courtesies on account of her age. She knew Carl had been right. Anything that might stink of scandal this close to the election was going to make huge headlines.

Reuben had already ended the call. She didn't want to spend the rest of the night in such suffocating silence, and she knew Reuben would probably want to know how many details from the news report were accurate. Part of her wondered the same thing. Fortunately, the Lindgrens' TV was one of the old-fashioned kinds that were really easy to use. She flipped to channel 2 and saw Wayne Abernathy's face instead of the floating head she expected. The news ticker at the bottom flashed details about Jodie's capture and child-abuse allegations against the late Anthony Abernathy, but Kennedy was paying too much attention to Wayne's speech to try to read them all.

"I've been the front-line man when it comes to the war against abortion for some time now. It's a cause I believe in deeply, a cause I've fought for zealously." He was wearing a red, white, and blue tie and one of those little American flag lapel pins. Fitting for a pre-election speech.

"Unfortunately, my commitment to the pro-life movement has had a price, a price my wife, our children, and our extended family have had to pay. Last year, many of you blessed us with your condolences, prayers, and well-wishes when my sister-in-law passed away. Moriah was a beautiful, angelic creature, who chose to delay chemotherapy treatment when she discovered she was pregnant. Her choice was a personal one, not forced upon her by any pastor or priest or politician. It was a choice her doctors may have disagreed with, but they respected it as a choice that she alone could make."

Kennedy leaned forward to listen.

"Moriah died shortly after giving the precious gift of life to my little nephew, Charlie. Our memories of her will be of a woman who was strong, courageous, who found strength in God and wasn't afraid of dying. Everyone who knew her suffered when she passed, but none more than her husband."

Wayne cleared his throat. He would probably make a good actor. Kennedy could picture him on stage next to Willow.

"I'm sure most of you by now have heard of the charges and allegations brought against my brother, Anthony. Charges of vandalizing the new Cambridge Community Pregnancy Center, whose opening we celebrate tonight. Charges of targeting my campaign in order to stop the pro-life cause in our state. And, unfortunately, charges that hit much closer to home."

Kennedy turned up the volume so she wouldn't miss a word.

"My daughter, as you have already heard, was pregnant when she was abducted Tuesday morning. It was as much as a shock to us as it was to you, believe me. Unfortunately, Anthony learned about the pregnancy before we did and tried to convince our daughter to kill her unborn baby. He eventually resorted to kidnapping her with the intention of forcing an abortion. We assume it was an attempt to smear my campaign. Any motivations beyond that are purely speculation at this point, and I ask that in deference to our family's privacy and to our daughter's young age that none of us allow the spread of ungrounded, malicious rumors."

Staring past the blinding, dazzling spotlights and camera flashes, Kennedy was surprised at how many wrinkles were on Wayne's face. Not something she noticed the other times she had seen him.

"I would like to publically thank God as well as the FBI team who responded at the rescue scene to ensure my daughter and the other hostage involved were delivered to safety. Unfortunately, injuries sustained during my daughter's abduction resulted in a spontaneous miscarriage. Please note that this was not the result of an elective abortion, and that if her mother and I had known about her condition ..." Here his voice caught. He took a drink of bottled water. "We would have done everything in our power to give our daughter a safe and healthy pregnancy. We would have opened our arms and our home to give our grandson a loving, caring childhood. I would also like to take this chance to publically announce that even if our daughter had gone through with the abortion procedure like her uncle wanted, we would have loved her unconditionally, just as God loves his own children."

Kennedy's throat was parched, but she didn't want to get up for a drink. Not yet.

"Because of these recent events, I have decided to withdraw from the gubernatorial race next week. My priority right now is to be with my family, to ensure my daughter gets the rest and healing she needs, and to protect our privacy during this difficult time. My wife and I have also assumed guardianship of my nephew, Charlie, and we will be busy helping him adjust to life without either his father or his mother. For those of you inclined to prayer, I ask you to remember us."

The next few minutes were filled with questions from the press and comments from the newscaster, who was a little zealous in reporting that one of the kidnapping suspects was still at large. Kennedy finally turned the TV off, wincing as she stood up from the couch. Her back was stiff. She thought she could use a hot shower but wasn't sure she had the energy to move down the hall.

There was a knock on the door. Kennedy froze.

"Kennedy? You in there?" Her heart raced as fast as spinning electrons. She grabbed her phone, ready to call 911. "Kennedy?"

If she could slow down her heart to remember where she had heard the voice before ...

"It's me, Nick. From St. Margaret's."

Kennedy shuffled toward the door, still not sure how she felt about the intrusion into her evening of solitude. "Hi." She held the door open but couldn't mask the question in her voice. Nick looked halfway normal in khaki pants and a dark blue sweater. He could have passed for any one of Cambridge's thousands of young men in casual work attire if it hadn't been for the dreadlocks. What was he doing here?

"Carl sent me. He says they have way too much food, and he wants you to come get your fill." Nick lowered his voice. "But Sandy wants you to know it's totally fine if you stay home and rest. She'll make sure Carl doesn't give you a hard time for it."

Kennedy thought about all the schoolwork she had to catch up on. She thought about Reuben, who was probably expecting her to call him right back. Was she ready to return to St. Margaret's? To the pregnancy center? She thought about her former resolve to distance herself from the pro-life movement, thought about the time she spent with Jodie in the hospital, the tears they shed over baby Wayne, the verses she had read a few minutes earlier. Did she know how she felt about abortion now? It was still wrong, but when she tried to articulate why, all she could picture was baby Wayne as he must have looked in Jodie's arms. Was that enough? It would have to be, at least for now.

She offered Nick an uncertain smile. "Let's go."

She reached to grab her coat off its hanger, but Nick stopped her. "Let me help you with that." She was glad to not have to twist herself into it.

The phone rang. "Can I meet you at the car?" she asked Nick. "This will only take me a minute or two."

"Sure thing. I'll take your bag and meet you there."

Kennedy didn't even look at the caller ID before she answered. "Hey, Reuben."

"That was some crazy story."

Would she ever be able to look back over the past few days without shaking? "Yeah, sure was."

"You ok?" His words were laden with concern.

"I'm really tired. My stitches are itching, too."

"Ouch. When are you coming back to campus?"

"This weekend sometime. I should be moving around a lot easier by then."

"Can I get you something? Heating pads? Pain meds?"

Kennedy let out her breath. It was good to hear his voice. "How about the notes from today's chemistry lecture?"

"Consider it done."

They talked for another minute about nothing important and made plans for Reuben to stop by the Lindgrens' tomorrow evening with his lecture notes. Kennedy warned him to come with his appetite since Sandy would almost certainly force him to stay for dinner.

They hung up, and Kennedy zipped her coat. As she locked Carl and Sandy's house behind her, she thought about tomorrow, and peace wrapped itself around her like a warm blanket. She was glad Reuben hadn't asked for any more details about the kidnapping. It was therapeutic somehow to talk about something as mundane as school.

Kennedy limped down the driveway and balked when she saw Nick standing in front of a VW bus that looked about as old as her dad. "You actually drive this?"

He grinned and held the passenger door open. "It's the youth group van, actually. I prefer my bike, but I didn't think you'd be up for a ten-mile ride."

She chuckled, even though the movement shot pain through her back muscles and made her cringe. "Yeah, maybe not."

He tapped the hood, which had a painted picture of a tie-dye Jesus fish about to swallow up a cartoon-style shark. "What do you think?"

Kennedy was too overwhelmed by so many colors to form a personal opinion. "Is that Michelangelo?" She pointed to a picture of a Ninja Turtle surfing with a Bible in one hand.

"Nah. Donatello. I was going to make it Jesus, but Carl pulled the senior pastor card on me and said it would be irreverent." He tapped the windshield. "I did get the Peter, James, and John bobble-head set, though. You can see it better once we're inside."

"So you did all this yourself?" Kennedy eyed the sunset scene painted on the passenger side. Looking closer, she saw the individual Bible verses stenciled in to form the branches of a palm tree.

"Like it?" he beamed.

"It suits you well," was all she could manage.

Once she was inside the bus, Nick handed her the seatbelt and shut her in. She thought about Reuben, about her calculus test, about the mounds of homework she would tackle starting tomorrow. After everything she had already been through, would she ever get stressed out over a test again?

Yes, she probably would. Life would turn back to normal, she'd get caught up in her studies, and in a month, a semester, maybe a year, she'd wonder if anything could be more nerve-racking than having two tests, a paper, and a lab all due in the same week. She would never forget Jodie or the time they spent together in that basement, but she didn't have to relive that moment every day of her life. As Nick drove to St. Margaret's, the future opened out before her like a brand-new novel with limitless possibilities for adventure, blessings, and growth between its covers.

She couldn't wait to see what the next chapter would contain.

Paralyzed

"Whoever dwells in the shelter of the Most High
will rest in the shadow of the Almighty."
Psalm 91:1

Paralyzed

First Printing November, 2015
Cover design by Damonza.

www.alanaterry.com

CHAPTER 1

Loud.

Why was it so loud? Kennedy's knee-high boots clicked against the hard floor of the science hall. She glanced over one shoulder and then the other. Who was staring at her? She sensed his presence, felt his eyes — ominous black beams boring into her soul. She looked around, but all she could see was the crowds of students, milling, giggling, oblivious to fear and danger.

She should warn someone. There had to be almost a hundred students filing into the lecture hall to take their chemistry final. Didn't they know someone was watching them, waiting for them? No, waiting for her. Everyone else was safe. Kennedy was his only target. She glanced behind her.

Her imagination, or something far more insidious?

She longed for the days when stress meant finishing a paper by its deadline. There had been a time when her biggest frustration was working out a calculus equation so her TA wouldn't get mad at her for not showing her work. Was it really only six weeks ago that her little safety bubble had imploded around her?

When she left China to head for college last August, she had expected drama. Occasional tiffs with her roommate. Maybe a little dating awkwardness. The loneliness that would come from being on the other side of the world from her missionary parents. She was ready for that, just as she had been ready for the academics. She hadn't graduated first in her high school class by sitting around texting her friends or streaming videos all day. When she got off that plane last fall and took the airport shuttle to Harvard, when she tipped the driver and rolled her two suitcases up the stairs to her dorm, she had felt mature. Adventurous.

She was prepared.

Kennedy clutched her book to her chest. It was part of an old Ivan Turgenev collection she had picked up at the antique book shop near Boston Common. She had always been a big reader, but she couldn't breeze through action novels anymore. She hadn't even tried a mystery since Vinny kidnapped her. She stuck mostly to works by dead authors from centuries past. During her first semester of college, she had lived through more suspense than she had ever experienced from a thriller. She wondered if she'd ever be able to pick one up again. How had she once considered that kind of reading enjoyable?

"Hey there."

She recognized her lab partner's slightly accented voice, but her body still jumped.

"I'm sorry." Reuben frowned. "Are you all right?"

Kennedy let out her breath and didn't bother to blush. Not in front of Reuben. He had seen her at her worst this semester — he had seen her *through* her worst, really. She gave her best attempt at a smile. "I'm fine. Just a little anxious about the final."

Reuben glanced at her book. "I thought you were done with Russian lit for the semester."

Kennedy followed him into the lecture hall. "I am. I just brought this with me to read when everything's done."

Reuben snatched the volume out of her hands. "Actually, you're not going to have time for that."

Kennedy focused on grabbing it back so she didn't have to acknowledge the crowded, noisy lecture hall, with its endless rows of chairs, the perfect place for a kidnapper to blend in with the crowd. Professor Adell wouldn't be able to tell who was and who wasn't actually enrolled. If Vinny wanted, he could sit hunched over behind a test for the whole period, wait for Kennedy to finish, follow her out of the science building ...

After she was kidnapped that fall, her dad signed her up for a self-defense course, but Kennedy had done what she could to get out of it. She had been preparing for midterms by then, still struggling to make up the work she missed while recovering from her injuries. She didn't want the constant reminder of her own hopelessness, the powerlessness she felt while cuffed downstairs in that cold basement. She promised her dad she would enroll in the class during spring semester, but his message was as clear as an Erlenmeyer flask: Take self-defense, pass the course, or else fly back to China. He also ordered her some pepper spray, which he expected her to carry around wherever she went, even to the dorm bathroom and back.

At first, she tried to write her dad off as paranoid. But when Detective Drisklay started talking about security measures and even mentioned the possibility of witness protection, she realized how dangerous it was to have survived an attempted murder while one of the culprits was still at large. What could she do, though? Her self-defense course did more to creep her out than to instill confidence. The class focused on warding off one unarmed attacker. If or when Vinny came after her, it wouldn't be that simple.

"... celebrate the end of the semester," Reuben was saying.

Kennedy's head felt as though it was spinning, an electron buzzing around the nucleus in its nebulous cloud orbital, constantly in motion. Constantly searching for the perfect energy level, still rushing around madly after finding it.

"That sounds great." Kennedy wondered what she had agreed to.

"Where are you going?" Reuben asked. Kennedy loved his clipped Kenyan accent, but now she could barely hear it over the drone of so many dozens of students waiting to take their final exam, waiting to see which of them would pass on to next semester and which would become one of the leagues of Harvard pre-med dropouts. So much noise. So much bustle. Enough to drown out a muffled scream or the shot of Vinny's gun.

Kennedy slipped into an aisle desk near the back of the room. Reuben stared down at her. "Why all the way back here?"

Kennedy and Reuben had spent their semester in this lecture hall in the two center seats of row three, but now when she looked at their usual place, all she could think about was how many students would fill up behind her, students she couldn't see. Students she didn't know.

She shrugged. "I thought it might be nice to be in the back today, you know, just so we can be that much closer to the exit when we're done."

"We'll still have to walk to the front to hand in our papers."

Kennedy didn't respond but swung her knees to the side so Reuben could slip in beside her. He passed her a stick of gum. "Hey, if I get stuck on a problem, can I take a peek at yours?"

Kennedy chuckled. She and Reuben were both getting good grades, but he managed to do so without giving himself an ulcer. While Kennedy recovered from her injuries after her kidnapping last fall, Reuben had been there, talking her through the lectures she missed, encouraging her through the quizzes she had to make up.

He leaned toward her. "Just remember, nothing can be harder than that calculus final yesterday."

Kennedy didn't even want to think about it. She had one focus now. Finishing chemistry. The very last exam before semester break. It didn't matter that Vinny had tried to kill her less than two months earlier. It didn't matter that he had evaded Detective Drisklay and the scores of police officers searching for him. It didn't matter that her parents were working in China and couldn't afford to fly Kennedy home for Christmas. It didn't matter that she would be lucky if she passed yesterday's calculus test with a B. All that mattered was that in an hour and a half her last final would be over. She still had laundry to wash. She still had clothes to pack. And there was that meeting with Detective Drisklay in the morning before she left for her aunt's. But she didn't need to worry about any of that right now. She had excelled in chemistry this semester, even more than in her AP class in high school back in Yanji. This was her day to outshine even her own high expectations.

Professor Adell stood in front of the room. She was an eccentric old woman. Some whispered she was one of the few remaining Holocaust survivors; others said her parents immigrated and she was born after the war ended. Nobody quite knew how she had gotten so involved in chemistry, but it was impossible to deny she had found her passion. After filling up the chalkboard with notes during her lectures, instead of pausing to erase the whole thing, she would throw the eraser into her right hand and switch to writing with her left. Her students couldn't tell if she was originally right- or left-handed; the writing was atrocious either way.

She was a great scientist and decent lecturer, but not much of a motivational speaker. "Take your tests. Turn them in when you're done. No noise." Those were Professor Adell's only instructions, and she passed the exams out to the students in the front. Kennedy stared at the back of everyone's heads. Was someone here who shouldn't be? Someone who had sneaked in just to watch Kennedy, make sure she didn't leave the science building alive?

The stack of chemistry finals eventually made it to Kennedy and Reuben in the back of the hall.

"Good luck," Reuben whispered, clicking the back of his mechanical pencil.

She pried her eyes away from the other students. She had to focus. She took a deep breath and skimmed the problems on the first page. She could do this. It would be fine.

A tickle in the back of her throat. Was she catching a cold? No, she couldn't get sick. She was flying to Baltimore tomorrow to spend Christmas with her aunt. It wasn't the same as going home to her parents in Yanji, but at least she'd be out of the Boston area. Vinny couldn't reach her there, could he? Of course, he could hack into the Logan Airport system, look up her flight plans ...

No, she couldn't think like that. She had a test. A test she was supposed to ace. That's all that mattered. There were a hundred people here. She was safe.

She cleared her throat, and another student a few rows ahead coughed back at her. She licked her lips, felt Reuben's glance, and attacked the first problem.

She was halfway through the second page when it came again. That tickle. Why hadn't she thought to bring a water bottle? Or a cough drop? She tore off a corner of her test and spit out her gum. She let out three coughs, loud enough for Professor Adell to frown at her from the front of the lecture hall.

A nice deep breath. That's all she needed. But when she tried, her lungs refused to expand and convulsed instead. More stares. She coughed again.

Reuben turned his head. "Are you ok?"

"I just need a drink," Kennedy whispered, and a student in the middle of the room let out a loud, "*Shhhhhh.*" Kennedy raised her hand, but Professor Adell was already glaring at her. Kennedy pointed to the back doors. The drinking fountains were just around the corner. Couldn't she run and come right back? Adell took a few seconds to respond. Did she think that Kennedy was going to cheat? That she had stashed some formula or answer sheet outside the lecture hall? If she had wanted to do something like that, she could have just brought it with her to the test. Who would notice one dishonest student out of so many?

Finally, Adell gave a curt nod, and Kennedy slipped out of her chair, thankful she was near the back. She knew Reuben was watching, probably worrying about her, but before she could give him a reassuring smile, another coughing fit seized her, and she ran up the stairs trying to stifle it.

In the hallway, she coughed so hard she thought she'd throw up. Doubled over, hacking on the floor, she pictured the young girl who had been kidnapped with her. Hopelessness wrapped its unyielding, icy tentacles around Kennedy's body. She couldn't stop the coughing, just like she hadn't been able to stop the bleeding in that ice-cold basement. Helpless. Victimized. Paralyzed.

She still had to finish her test. She couldn't let her mind sink to these depths. She would pray. She would find a way to take these thoughts captive. She was shaking now. Her whole body was trembling, reminding her of the pit bull who lived next door to her growing up who would thrash his head and growl until Kennedy ran home in tears and hysterics to her mother's arms.

She stumbled to the drinking fountain and waited for her breathing to calm down. The first attempt at a drink failed and sent snot-flavored juices burning her sinuses. By the third try she could manage a few sips. She didn't dare a deep inhale, but she could take a few short breaths before she had to cough again.

This was ridiculous. She had a final to finish. Her last test of the semester. If she didn't get back to the lecture hall soon, Adell really would accuse her of cheating.

She just needed to pray more. Isn't that what Christians always said? You're in trouble? Pray about it. Your parents are so busy training underground missionaries they don't even care that you brought home another straight-A report card? Pray about it. You're ready to take your last final of the semester, but a horrible cough has got you trapped outside in the hall because you know the moment you walk in you're going to become one gasping, wheezing, hacking mess?

Pray about it.

Well, Kennedy did pray. In fact, she had been praying all semester, at least since she got back to campus after her kidnapping. Praying for relief from the nightmares. Praying for the scar on her back not to stand out so glaringly on her pale skin. Praying for her body to stop trembling at random times, interrupting her studies, flashing her back to that cold, dark basement.

By now, Kennedy was all out of prayer energy. Besides, didn't God know what she needed before she even asked? Didn't he see how needy she was right now?

Pray about it. So simple to say. So hard when you actually have to pick up one boot and plant it in front of you. So hard when you've got to pull yourself out of murky water so deep you can't even see the bottom, so muddy you're stuck before you realize you're sinking one deadly centimeter at a time. The suffocating, soul-starving fear that grips you in the middle of the night when you should be asleep but wake up gasping, drenched in sweat and certain your assailant is staring into your second-story window, waiting until you drift off to sleep again before he finishes you off for good. That's what Kennedy had been trying to pray against, but it was like trying to send a rainstorm back up to the troposphere with a broken umbrella.

She pulled back some of the hair that had fallen out of her ponytail and counted. Five seconds since her last cough. Maybe she was ready now. She had been accepted out of high school into Harvard's early-admissions medical program, but that offer was contingent on her GPA. If she failed general chemistry, even with high scores in all her other classes, she would probably end up on academic probation. Maybe even flunk out of the pre-med program altogether.

The itch tickled its way up her throat once more, and Kennedy decided she'd take another sip from the fountain and then go back. Until she threw up or got thrown out of the lecture hall for distracting other students, she would finish that final, and she would get the A she had worked for all semester, the A she deserved.

A door opened, and for a moment Kennedy worried some cocky TA would come out and shush her for making so much noise in the hall, but all Kennedy saw was a bald head and two mean, brooding eyes that widened as soon as they met hers. The door shut. The face disappeared. Kennedy's stomach dropped to the floor of her abdominal cavity.

She would have recognized that face anywhere.

Vinny.

CHAPTER 2

This was no time for her body to give out. Her heart pounded in her chest like the horrible thumping in that Edgar Allen Poe story, and her legs propelled her past the drinking fountain and out of the science center before she realized her coughing had stopped. Her boots pounded on the pavement, their echoes crashing in her ears. Could she hear Vinny behind her? Would he chase her, or would he just gun her down? Zigzag. Shouldn't she run in a zigzag? Somewhere in her dad's crazy crisis training, didn't he say something about it being easiest to shoot someone if they were running in a straight line?

But what if Vinny was coming after her on foot? She didn't have time to waste on cute little twists and curves and slithering snake patterns. She had to get somewhere safe. She couldn't slow down. She had to get to shelter. If Vinny had a gun, would she hear it and then feel the hot fiery pain in her back? Or would it happen all at once? Was there really such a thing as dying instantly like the police reports claimed? Could you ever die so quickly you didn't even realize what had happened?

Ahead of her, someone unlocked the dorm. Just a little more exertion, and she could reach it before the door closed. "Hold it!" she tried to yell, but she was going so fast her voice got lost somewhere behind her.

The door shut just as Kennedy slammed into it. She didn't take the time to look back. Vinny would be on her any second.

Someone opened the dorm from the inside, and she darted in, not even pausing to glance at her savior or mumbling, "Excuse me."

Up the stairs, two by two, hoisting herself up with the handrail when her thigh muscles got too tired. *Please let Willow be in. Please let Willow be in*, her mind begged, and she strained to see down the hall. Was the door open just a little? That would save at least twenty seconds if she didn't have to stop and fiddle with her keys.

Please be open. Please be open.

Yes!

Kennedy pushed through the door, slammed it shut behind her, and threw back the deadbolt. She jumped to her roommate's side of the room just in case Vinny shot straight through the door.

The police. She had to call the police. She reached around for her backpack. It wasn't on her shoulders. She had left it in the science hall. She needed a phone. Where was Willow's?

At that point, Kennedy first noticed her roommate staring at her from her bed. Under the covers beside her was someone Kennedy had never met. At the beginning of the semester, she might have been surprised, but right now she didn't care what Willow was doing or who she was doing it with. She just had to let the police know Vinny was after her.

"I need your phone."

Willow raised an eyebrow.

"I'm sorry," Kennedy panted. "It's an emergency. And ..." She turned her back. "Well, sorry for barging in."

Willow swept her blanket off. "Don't worry. We're still decent."

Over the course of the semester, Kennedy had grown to enjoy Willow and her carefree style, but right now she needed someone whose brain functioned faster than a viscous gelatin. "I just saw Vinny," she panted. "I need your phone."

Any minute, Kennedy expected to hear Vinny pounding on the door outside. She wondered how much damage she'd do to Willow's computer if she slid it and the whole desk against the door as a barricade. Why was Willow just reclining there with that dazed, questioning expression? Didn't she realize Kennedy was the one person Vinny wanted dead more than anyone else?

"Where is your phone?" she panted.

"You say you saw Vinny?" Willow's voice was softer than normal. Subdued. Almost gentle.

"I ran all the way here." For just a minute, confusion mingled with the acidic fear that raged and foamed in Kennedy's stomach. "He was right behind me."

Willow stood up. Slowly. As if she was afraid of hurting Kennedy if she moved too fast. She reached out her bejeweled hand. Softly squeezed Kennedy's shoulder with those long, painted nails. "That cute journalist you'd been talking to stopped by this morning. You know, the ginger?" Willow stared at the wall behind Kennedy and took a deep breath. "He wanted to ask if you'd heard the news. Vinny's been in custody since last night."

CHAPTER 3

Adrenaline oozed out of Kennedy's pores. She sank down in Willow's chair.

"You sure?"

Willow twirled a strand of her wavy hair around her finger. "Yeah. I thought about texting you, but I didn't know if you'd get too distracted from your finals."

Kennedy sat up a little taller. "Well, he must have escaped or something. He must have gotten out and come here and ..."

Willow leaned over to her computer and went to Channel 2's website. She pointed at the man whose face was plastered on the home screen under the headline *Kidnapping Suspect Caught in North End.* "This him?"

Kennedy glanced at the picture. "Yeah." Her legs wobbled, and she turned away.

Willow scrolled down. "He's most definitely still in jail."

Kennedy slouched down and swallowed. Why did she feel like crying? This should be good news. It should be great news, except for the fact that she just ran a quarter of a mile from a phantom. A bald nothing.

"Hey, maybe you should go."

For a minute, Kennedy thought Willow was talking to her. She had forgotten about the boy in the bed.

"No prob." He got up and tucked his shirt into his pants. "Call you tonight?"

Willow kept her eyes on the computer screen. "Nah, I'm going to Cape Cod with some buddies for a few days."

"Maybe after that?"

His voice was hopeful, but Willow still didn't look up. "Yeah, happy Hanukkah. Or Christmas. Or whatever."

Willow's friend gave Kennedy a slightly apologetic glance, unlocked the door, and headed out.

Kennedy stared at her lap. "Sorry for ruining your date."

Willow clicked off her monitor. "Don't worry about it. Seriously. He had wicked bad breath."

Kennedy laughed but knew it sounded forced and artificial. "I really don't know what happened. I seriously thought ..."

Willow flicked her wrist as if swatting the rest of Kennedy's apology away. "You don't need to say anything. You had a horrible semester. You got kidnapped, watched some little girl nearly bleed to death, had a crazy dude with a knife ..."

"I get it."

"Anyway ..." Willow stared at herself in the little mirror on her desk and adjusted her hand-crafted earrings. "At least your imaginary friend waited to show up until you were done with your final, right?"

Kennedy blinked.

"You were finished with the test before you did your little sprint in those cute boots, right?"

Kennedy shook her head.

"Hey, it's ok." Willow sounded like she was talking to a puppy with a hurt paw. "You can always explain to your professor what happened. With everything you've been through ..."

How could Kennedy have been so stupid? Didn't she know Vinny wouldn't dare risk showing himself in broad daylight in a building full of witnesses? Why had she run? And how many people saw her acting like the fool she was?

"It's all right," Willow repeated.

What should she do? She couldn't go back to the lecture hall and expect to pick up right where she left off. The test started over half an hour ago. Even if the professor let her back in to finish her exam, it didn't seem fair to the other students, and there was no way to explain the circumstances to Adell without distracting the entire room. Besides, Kennedy was tired of all the publicity. Her image had been splashed all over the news last fall, and even now she could almost hear the thoughts of people who stared at her a second too long: *That's the one who got kidnapped. That's the one they got with that little pregnant girl.* She didn't need to rehash the entire scenario. She needed to move on.

Forgetting what is behind, straining toward what was ahead. Wasn't that how the Bible verse went? She had been trying to memorize Scripture lately, Scripture she could turn to whenever she recalled Vinny's face, the feel of the unforgiving handcuff biting her wrist. She had spent so much mental energy over the past six weeks convincing her parents she was fine. If only she could reach the place where she believed it. Where was the victory Pastor Carl talked about in his sermons? Where was the freedom, the dramatic deliverance from fear and the nightmares that plagued her?

"... cute lab partner of yours?" Willow's voice interrupted Kennedy's thoughts, and she tried to recreate the entire sentence.

"What about him?"

Willow let out a dramatic huff. "I said, would you be more comfortable explaining it to the professor if he came with you?"

Kennedy went to her own desk and turned on her computer. It was nice of Willow to try to help, but her suggestions were about as effective as salt dumped into a solution when it's already past its saturation point.

"I'll just email Adell," she replied. "See what she says."

"Don't forget to play the whole I-was-kidnapped card. If I were you, I'd be milking that for all it's worth, and I'd have signed for that book deal, too."

Ignoring Willow's remarks, Kennedy let her computer start up. Adell would understand, right? She'd let Kennedy take the test tonight. Or first thing tomorrow before she met with Detective Drisklay. Maybe Willow had a point. After everything Kennedy had gone through, a little slack wasn't too much to ask for, was it?

Willow came up behind and rubbed Kennedy's back. "You sure you don't want to come with us to the Cape? Might help you relax a little. Get some of that tension out of your neck."

She started massaging the deep muscle, and Kennedy cringed.

"You are so tight up here." Willow dug in even deeper. "It's like your neck has turned into the dumping grounds for every single negative emotion in your body."

Kennedy turned around to face her. "You don't need to worry about me. I'm all right."

Willow raised her eyebrows. "Really? Well, I still think you should come with me. You should see the cabin we got. It's wicked posh. We have room in the car for one more."

Willow made for a good roommate and even a decent friend, but her crowd of noisy, boisterous theater majors made Kennedy feel like a drop of oil floating in isolation in a lava lamp. She mumbled something about meeting with the detective in the morning and went back to typing her apology to Professor Adell.

Kennedy stared at her half-composed email and glanced at the time. The test would probably go for another half an hour, maybe more. She could go back and finish it right now if she had the chance. Why had she let her imagination play such a horrid trick on her?

She reread her email but still wasn't happy with the finished product. She deleted everything she wrote about running away from Vinny and just said she had been coughing too much and didn't want to disturb the class. How would Adell react? Would she think Kennedy was just trying to get out of her work?

Well, there was nothing else she could do. Not right now. Except maybe start that laundry and pack for Aunt Lilian's. It would be a short hop to Baltimore, nothing like the flight between China and the States. She could take one or two volumes of her antique Turgenev set to read on the plane. She just hoped it'd be enough to keep her mind off everything else. *Forget what's behind. Strain toward what's ahead.* If she could block out her memories from last fall, that basement, everything would be fine. She could live that victorious Christian life she heard everyone talk about. She could even be a witness, a living example of how God helps people overcome adversity. If she weren't petrified by public speaking, she could even become a motivational speaker. *If God can bring me through a kidnapping and attempted murder, he can carry you through whatever problems you're dealing with today.*

If only she could bring herself to believe it.

"Well, I've gotta get going." Willow leaned down and pecked the air by Kennedy's cheek. "Promise me you'll relax a little, ok? Especially with them catching Vinny and all. I mean, that's really good news. Oh, and get in touch with that reporter. He's cute." Willow picked up her bag and glided out, leaving the door a crack open behind her.

Kennedy's heart dropped slowly, like crystallized honey sinking in a cup of tea. After a brainless eternity staring at her computer, she got up and gathered her laundry into a heap. There was so much to do before she flew out. Why had she let it pile up this high?

A couple of minutes later, the computer dinged at her, and she glanced at her screen. Professor Adell had already replied.

Medical excuses may be permitted at the discretion of the professor provided a note from the campus medical center verifies the necessity of said provision.

That was all, no names or greetings or *hope you're feeling better*. Not even an automatic closing or signature at the bottom. Kennedy reread it, each time wishing for more information. She hadn't ever been to the campus medical center. She didn't know if she needed to bring her parents' insurance card or write a check or what. And how much would it cost? She had spent most of her discretionary funds at the used bookstore downtown. Well, it was either visit the clinic or fail the final. Maybe she could conjure up another coughing fit for the doctor or nurse and get a quick excuse. Why couldn't she be like Willow? Her roommate could probably convince someone she was dying of meningitis to get out of a test.

Kennedy buttoned up her new leather coat, an early Christmas gift from her dad, checked Harvard's webpage to remember where she was supposed to go, and headed to the medical center.

CHAPTER 4

Kennedy opened her mouth for the middle-aged doctor in his white lab coat. She stared at his little flashlight and performed all the other tests he doled out. She didn't have to overact to make her movements slow and lazy. As soon as she got out from the wind and sat down in the clinic, exhaustion clung to each individual ligament like hoarfrost.

"You said your throat's been hurting?" He frowned, and Kennedy felt about as nervous as she had been during her phone interview with Harvard Medical School's early admissions application committee.

"It's a little better now, I guess. It was just during the test. I kept coughing, so I went into the hall to get a drink, and it got worse."

He nodded his head slowly and studied Kennedy over his glasses.

"Then I went back to my room." Why had she told him that? He didn't react, and she didn't have any choice now but to go on. "And, well, it got a little better then."

"And then you came here?" he asked. "For what? A prescription?"

"I started to worry I might have strep," Kennedy recited the little white lie she had formed on the way over. "I'm supposed to fly to my aunt's tomorrow, down to Baltimore, and, well, I thought maybe I should get checked out before I went on a plane." She squirmed, wondering how many germs were on the table bed where she sat.

He kept his pen poised over his clipboard but didn't write anything. "And how did your test go? Did your coughing interfere with your final?"

Kennedy tried to meet his eyes, but her gaze settled somewhere near his salt and pepper mustache. "Well, I started coughing right in the middle. It was hard to breathe, and I didn't want to disrupt anyone, and, well, I just left my paper there."

"So you're looking for a medical excuse?" His voice was steady and somewhat bored, but Kennedy felt her palms clam up.

"I told the professor I'd be willing to retake it."

He frowned. "I see ..." He glanced down at his clipboard. "Kennedy." He paused, and she knew from his furrowed brow what was coming next. "Kennedy Stern. Where have I heard that name before?"

She stared at her lap, wondering if he'd come to the realization on his own or if she'd have to jog his memory.

"Kennedy Stern," he repeated. "Aren't you the girl who was ..."

He paused, leaving Kennedy to finish on his behalf. "Kidnapped."

He nodded. "Well, I'm glad you're back safe and unharmed."

There was that tickle again. Was she going to have another coughing attack here?

"You say you had a hard time breathing. Has that happened to you before?"

"No, not that I can ..." Kennedy stopped.

Guilt must have been etched on her face, because the doctor leaned toward her. "Yes?"

She sighed. "Well, there was one time. A few weeks after I was ... after I got back to campus." She glanced up to make sure he understood. He nodded, so she continued. "I thought I saw someone in the student union. Turns out it was nothing, at least I think it was. But I started running, and I was coughing then, too. Had a hard time catching my breath again."

She didn't mention the tears. The sobbing that convinced her she was on the verge of hyperventilating. She didn't mention barging into her dorm room in the middle of Willow's make-out session with a student from the theater department. Kennedy's mortification snapped her out of her panic, but thankfully her roommate wasn't upset. "He was really sweaty and gross, anyway," she insisted. A little while later, once Kennedy stopped trembling, Willow suggested, "Maybe you should see a shrink or something."

Kennedy had shoved the suggestion aside. After all, she was a Christian. She needed to pray more, that's what she needed to do, not talk out her trauma with a therapist who would stretch her out on a couch and make her relive those twenty-four hours all over again. She forced herself to focus once more on her schoolwork, carried her pepper spray wherever she went for the next week, and did a decent job of forgetting about the whole cafeteria episode. Still, she didn't eat any hot meals for a while and subsisted on dry Cheerios, Craisins, and microwave popcorn until she could enter the student union without shaking.

None of that had anything to do with getting a medical excuse to Professor Adell, though, so she shrugged. "That's all."

The doctor didn't look convinced, but he mercifully didn't press the issue. "So you had a hard time breathing this afternoon. And coughing?"

She nodded. Hadn't she just told him that?

"Wheezing?" he asked.

"No." She didn't mention the gasping. That was easily enough explained because of how fast she had been running.

"Any other changes?" he asked, finally looking up at her. "Heart rate? Chills? Drop or increase in body temperature?"

"I don't know." More frustration crept into Kennedy's voice than she had intended. It's not like she had stopped sprinting to check her vitals.

He pursed his lips and squinted while he scribbled on his pad. "I'll email your professor a medical excuse. When did you say you fly out?"

"Tomorrow." Kennedy wondered why it felt like she was back in high school and he was writing her a detention slip.

"Well, then, within your first week on campus next semester, I want you to make an appointment with one of our therapists. I'm writing you a prescription for counseling right now."

"Counseling?" Couldn't he have handed her a bag of cough drops, given her a note for Adell, and wished her happy holidays?

He ripped the page noisily off its pad and handed her the slip. His handwriting was large and scrawling, nearly as sloppy as Professor Adell's, but the largest words right in the middle of the page were as clear as a beaker.

Post-traumatic stress disorder.

"That's not an official diagnosis," he explained. "But after what you've been through, it's worth ruling out."

Kennedy's throat constricted.

"You've had a rough semester." He glanced at her meaningfully. "That's nothing to be ashamed of."

"I'm not ..." Kennedy began but stopped. If she tried defending herself, she'd look even guiltier. She forced a smile. "Thank you."

He answered with a half-smile of his own, and she walked out the room, conscious of his eyes on her. How did normal people walk, those without PTSD? Could he tell if she was infected just by her gait? She wasn't sick. She wasn't stressed. Well, no more stressed than usual. And besides, it was finals week. Who wasn't anxious, at least just a little?

The sun wasn't setting yet, but the sky was that shade of grayish pink only seen in winter as Kennedy trudged back to her dorm. She would rather have made up the final first thing in the morning. Counseling? Was he serious? *Give a quack a white coat, and he thinks he can read souls all of a sudden.* Kennedy was a Christian. She didn't get traumatized. Worried, maybe. Stressed, for sure. But full-scale trauma? That was for POWs and war veterans and all those firemen who saw thousands die the day the Twin Towers fell. Not girls like her. No, Kennedy had the Bible, and she had prayer. Maybe she just hadn't been trying hard enough. She gripped the prescription slip, braced herself against the biting wind, and hurried to her dorm.

She stomped up the stairs, certain all she needed was a night of solitude. A night without Willow and the ridiculously dramatized shouts and cursing from those silly shooter video games her roommate always played. A night without worrying about homework or lab papers or due dates. A night just to herself, just her books, her fuzzy pink bathrobe, some hot chocolate, and ...

"So there you are!"

She recognized Reuben's voice and took a moment to collect herself before turning around on the staircase.

"I've been looking all over for you." He held up her backpack. "You forgot this."

She was glad he didn't ask specifically about the test. She didn't want to think about it. "I, um, I went to see the doctor about my cough." She crumpled the paper even more tightly in her fist.

"What did he say?"

They were at Kennedy's door by now, and Reuben stopped while Kennedy fidgeted with the lock. He followed her in without invitation and plopped down in Willow's beanbag chair.

"Well?"

Kennedy had already lost the progression of the conversation. "Well, what?"

"What did the doctor say? About the cough?"

She tossed the wad onto her desk. "Wants me to go to counseling. He thinks I have PTSD or something." She half expected to feel a warm surge of relief when the words were out, but all she could feel was the quivering in her abdomen and the hot sting of embarrassment.

Reuben didn't smile and didn't frown. He looked right into Kennedy's eyes far too long for comfort. "That's an interesting suggestion," he finally stated without emotion.

"Interesting?"

He cocked his head to the side. "Well, do you have any objections?"

The question caught her off guard. She had been prepared to defend herself if he said it was a good idea. Instead, she had to rethink her arguments and failed to come up with anything coherent.

"It sounds to me like you're in need of some serious holiday cheer." He grabbed her scarf and held it out.

"What are you doing?"

"You and I are going off campus. We need to celebrate the end of the semester, the start of the Christmas season. With this." He reached into his back pocket and pulled out two tickets.

"*The Nutcracker*?"

"It's an American holiday tradition. And since this is my first Christmas in America, I decided we should go."

She wanted to smile. Wanted to laugh. Wanted to give him a hug to thank him for being that thoughtful. But she was so tired.

"Don't you like ballet?"

She couldn't bear to disappoint him. She wrapped the scarf around her neck and grabbed her book bag.

"The show doesn't start until seven." He grinned. "Which gives us just enough time to stop by Common Treasures and get you a few more books. What do you say?"

She was tired. Far more tired than she wanted to admit. But she wasn't traumatized. *Forgetting what is behind, straining toward what is ahead.*

Forcing a smile, she followed Reuben out the door and checked the lock behind them. There was a lightness in her step she hadn't known in months. Maybe a night out was just what she needed.

CHAPTER 5

"What do you think of this one?"

Kennedy looked at the book Reuben held up. She loved the antique smell here, even though she figured the workers at Common Treasures Books were probably at risk for developing lung cancer or some other tragic malady from spending their time in the dust and mildew.

"*Catcher in the Rye*?" She frowned. "I read that once in tenth grade. Could barely understand it. Baseball and trains, right?"

Reuben chuckled. "Close. Except it was fencing."

"Oh, really?" Kennedy asked. "I could have sworn it was baseball."

"Well, there's the part where ..." Something else caught Reuben's eye, and he snatched another book off the shelf. "I loved this one!"

Kennedy gawked. "*Lord of the Flies*? Are you serious? That made me want to barf."

Reuben was already flipping through the pages, thumbing back and forth, letting his eyes skim over the passages. "This was the very first book I read in English literature."

Kennedy had nothing to say and strolled around the bend to another section. Reuben followed reluctantly. She pointed to the spine of an old hardback copy of *Pride and Prejudice*. "You know, I never did get what all the hype was over Mr. Darcy. He was just a rich, eccentric introvert, but about half the girls in my high school had major literary crushes on him."

Reuben raised an eyebrow. "Really? I found the whole thing dry and hard to follow."

"It's not hard to follow." Kennedy was already scanning other titles on the shelf. "Oh, they have *Little Women*." She pulled out the book. "You know, I think my grandma gave me an edition with these same illustrations. I wonder what I did with it."

Reuben opened the front cover and pointed at the price penciled in the top corner. "You should find it. That's enough to pay for next semester's textbooks."

Kennedy gently placed the volume back on the shelf. "You know, this is one of the only two novels I've read that's actually made me mad."

Reuben checked the time and slipped his phone back into his pocket. "Really? Why's that?"

"I just always thought Jo should have married Laurie. I was furious when she turned him down." She watched him button up his coat and asked, "Is it time to go?"

"Pretty soon. Show starts in twenty minutes."

Kennedy placed the book back on its shelf and bundled up. "Well, next time we come here, we need to find something that we've both read and we both like."

Reuben held the shop door open and nodded at the owner. "We might be here for days if we tried that."

The wind had picked up, and Kennedy tucked her scarf into her leather jacket to keep it from flapping in her face. She increased her pace. They hadn't spent very long at the bookshop, but it was the first time in weeks she hadn't thought about classwork or finals or kidnappers or anything horrible like that. The campus doctor didn't know what he was talking about. She didn't need therapy. She just needed a chance to relax.

The Opera House was only two blocks away from Common Treasures, so they walked instead of taking the T. Kennedy asked Reuben how he spent Christmas in Kenya, but the wind was howling so loud she had to stand practically shoulder to shoulder and hip to hip with him to hear his response.

"We'd always go up country to my grandfather's farm." He shrugged. "It wasn't all that different from family gatherings here, I assume. We walked to church on Christmas Eve. Didn't get home until after midnight. On Christmas Day, my grandfather's first wife would butcher one of the cows, and then we'd all ..."

"You butchered a whole cow?" Kennedy recalled how much of a fuss her mom made over a fifteen-pound turkey.

"Well, I didn't. Grandmother did."

"How did your family go through that much meat?" Kennedy didn't know if Kenyans "up country" would have freezers or even the electricity to run them. Reuben had talked a lot about growing up in the city, but this was the first time he had mentioned anything outside Nairobi.

Reuben laughed. "You'd be surprised at how fast a hundred people can eat a cow."

Kennedy leaned forward. "Did you say a hundred?"

"Around there. It changes each year depending on who's gotten married, who's had a new baby, and who's passed away."

Kennedy thought back to the largest family gathering she could remember. It was probably her grandma's funeral. The wake was for relatives only, and she guessed there were twenty people there, certainly no more. Before she moved to Yanji, getting together with "family" usually meant her grandma, Aunt Lilian, Uncle Jack, and sometimes Uncle Jack's two teenagers who spent every other holiday with him. Kennedy had figured it out once when she was younger. They were her step-cousins-in-law, and once Aunt Lilian and Uncle Jack split up, she had to tack an *ex* to the front of that and make the title longer and more confusing. She hadn't seen them in over a decade and couldn't remember the older boy's name anymore. Still, they were the closest thing Kennedy had to extended family around her own age.

"So where do a hundred people sleep?" she asked, thinking about how uncomfortable Aunt Lilian's roll-away trundle bed was.

"Wherever we can."

Kennedy's mind was reeling, like water molecules zipping around in a steaming pot. "I still can't imagine having that many cousins. How many aunts and uncles do you have?"

Reuben furrowed his brow. "I'm not sure. I counted once, but I probably forgot a few."

"Well," Kennedy tried again, "how many kids did your grandparents have?"

"Twenty-three."

Kennedy's eyes grew as wide as the pipette bulbs in her chemistry lab. "Your poor grandma!"

Reuben laughed. "Well, that number was spread out over three wives."

"Three? That's a lot of times to be widowed."

"No, three at the same time. They're all still alive. It wasn't all that unheard of back in his day, you know."

"Really? They still do that there?"

"Not so much anymore, but yeah, in the past it was common." Reuben's voice had grown even softer, so Kennedy could hardly hear him over the wind.

"Will it be hard for you not going back this year?" she asked.

He looked away. Quickened his pace. "It wouldn't be the same even if I went back now."

A heaviness clouded the air between them like fog in a beaker. She had known Reuben long enough to recognize these brooding moods of his. She forced false enthusiasm into her voice. "Well, it's like I already told you, if you don't want to spend Christmas by yourself, I'm sure my pastor and his wife would love to ..."

"Thanks, but it's fine. Really. Here we are." Reuben was apparently ready to end their conversation as soon as they arrived at the Opera House, and Kennedy didn't press matters. They passed through the line and joined the other *Nutcracker* enthusiasts filing in to find their places.

"I thought it would be more crowded in here," Reuben stated as an usher led them to their seats in the highest balcony.

Kennedy was glad to hear him sounding more like himself. He could never stay very serious for more than a few minutes. She stared down at the hundreds of empty chairs below. "Maybe everyone's running late. That wind is awful."

Reuben leaned forward, his eyes wide.

"Do they have shows like this in Kenya?" she asked.

He didn't seem to hear her question over the sound of the tuning orchestra. "Look down there!" He pointed. "I think I just saw one of the dancers when the usher opened that door."

Kennedy hadn't seen anything. "That's probably the entrance to backstage or something."

"I wonder if we could go in there."

Before long, the lights dimmed, and Reuben finally sat in his seat. His right leg bounced like pressurized carbonation in a jar of soda. Kennedy was glad they were this high up or else he might have run right onstage in his enthusiasm. She had never cared all that much for *The Nutcracker*. She had seen it a few times in Manhattan before her family moved to China, but it had never really enthralled her. Still, she was glad to be here with Reuben, glad to get her mind off everything that had plagued her recently.

When the orchestra began its first strain, Reuben sucked in his breath. She had to smile. As much time as the two of them had spent together over the past semester, she had never considered him the type to love ballet so much.

The first colorful dancers graced the stage, and he was completely lost. Sometimes she caught him keeping beat with one hand as if he were an assistant conductor. During the nutcracker's fight with the Rat King, Reuben leaned forward in his chair so far she was afraid he might topple right off the balcony. As soon as the curtain closed for intermission, even before the lights came on, he sprang to his feet. "Let's go!"

"What are you doing?"

He grabbed her hand and plucked up both their coats. "There's empty seats down there. I want to see everything closer."

On a normal night, Kennedy would have protested. She would have brought up issues like ticket prices and cranky ushers and would have forced Reuben to see reason. But his enthusiasm was catching. Besides, this was her night to throw worry to the wind and let it blow away into the Charles River, never to bother her again. They raced down the plush staircases to the lower level. A white-haired usher gave them both a quizzical look but didn't say anything when they scurried down the aisle.

"How close were you planning to go?" Kennedy whispered as Reuben rushed toward the front.

"As close as we can." He stared for a minute, paused, and squinted at the rows. "Over here," he finally said. "This area was pretty empty."

"Are you sure nobody was here?" Kennedy asked as he set his coat down on one of the chairs in the fourth row.

"If someone was, we'll just say we forgot where we were and move somewhere else. No problem."

Kennedy wanted to protest, but Reuben wasn't even looking at her anymore. He was staring straight up at the huge dome ceiling, with all the graceful cherubs and dancers frolicking in the painted clouds.

"I've seen some beautiful things back home," he breathed, "but not like this."

Kennedy had to admit it was gorgeous. If it hadn't been for Reuben, would she even have thought to look up?

"So, are you having a good time?" he asked.

Kennedy set her leather coat across the back of her chair. "Yeah." She took in a deep breath, thankful she hadn't had a single coughing fit since her exam.

The lights dimmed, the hum of conversation died down, and the sounds of the orchestra softly tuning their instruments billowed out to Reuben and Kennedy's new seats. Thankfully, nobody pestered them for their chairs, and none of the ushers seemed to notice or care that they had slipped so close to the front even though they only carried cheap student tickets. Reuben's leg bounced even more quickly when the curtain opened and revealed the ground fog and majestic backdrop of the Land of Sweets. For the entire second act, during the parts where she might have been tempted to lose herself in daydreams, Kennedy just glanced over at Reuben, saw his enraptured expression in the dim lights from the stage, and decided this was a perfect evening out.

Now that she thought about it, this was the first time she and Reuben had been off campus together without their textbooks and lab assignments in tow. She couldn't even remember a meal in the student union with him that didn't consist of at least some degree of studying. Had she really been so serious all semester? Layer after layer of exhaustion and anxiety lifted off her shoulders as she sat, mesmerized and enchanted just like Clara beside the prince.

When the curtain closed, Reuben clapped so loud it shot vicarious pain to Kennedy's palms. He didn't say anything as they got their coats and worked their way back to the aisle. Kennedy was about to follow the crowds out the main doors, but Reuben took her by the elbow.

"Wait a minute. I want to see something."

She hesitated before he dragged her to the side door he had spotted from the balcony. A short, stocky usher with spectacles scowled a few feet in front of it. He had a clipboard in his hand and was talking to two well-dressed adults. After a minute, he put his hand to his earpiece and then waved the patrons through.

"Back here," Reuben whispered. "Just act like you know what you're doing." Bypassing a few others who had formed a short line, he slipped in behind the two going through, and Kennedy followed, expecting any minute to hear the angry protests of the old man.

The door shut behind them.

"We made it." He tightened his hold on her arm.

Kennedy didn't know whether to laugh or chide him. "I can't believe you actually did that."

He ran, tugging her down a set of stairs to a hallway and down a small side corridor, giggling like a guilty child.

"Come on." Reuben pulled her arm again. "I want to see if we can meet some of the dancers."

"I really don't think we're supposed to ..." Kennedy stopped as a whole flock of little girls scurried past.

"Aren't those the ones who came out of that woman's dress?" Reuben waved at the ballerinas, who hardly noticed him. He ran down the next hall, and Kennedy followed behind, feeling lighter and more playful than she had in years. In all her time living in Yanji, had she ever done anything this spontaneous?

Reuben hurried straight ahead, but she thought she heard someone behind them. The near-sighted usher, maybe, ready to put an end to their mischief? She stopped and spun around, her heart gripped with foreboding. Nobody was there. She let out a sigh and turned back toward Reuben.

He was gone.

The hallway was infinitely narrower than she remembered it. Why did they keep the lights so bright down here? She had turned so many times she couldn't figure out where she was anymore in relation to the rest of the Opera House. Was this beneath the stage? There were no marked exits, no friendly old ladies with flashlights ready to show you the way. Where did Reuben go?

The tickle returned to the back of her throat. She hadn't thought to bring any cough drops. Not even a water bottle. Where had he run off to? Why hadn't he waited?

A chill covered her whole body although she was wearing her new coat. What if someone had followed them? What if they saw her go down beneath the Opera House? A sort of *Phantom-of-the-Opera*-type menace who would entrap her beneath the theater and hold her hostage in his cold, cement cell? Her wrists chaffed with the memory of handcuffs, and her lungs constricted without forcing out any air.

Where was Reuben? Had someone attacked him?

Her diaphragm spasmed. She couldn't inhale.

A door slammed shut. Was someone locking her in? Would she be stuck down here forever? Would anybody even know she was gone?

Help.

She slipped up to the wall for support. She couldn't hold herself up anymore. Had someone sucked all the air out from the basement?

Her cellphone. She could call Reuben. Call the police. Somebody would get her out of here. Somebody ...

She fumbled through the zipper pockets of her backpack. Where was it?

Her fingers finally clenched the phone, which she had flipped off during the performance. She punched it on. Why did they take so long to start up again? A light flickered on the screen. A familiar, ominous tone.

No!

The batteries were low.

There was still enough power to make one call, wasn't there? *Please let there be enough.* She found Reuben's number in her contacts.

Please pick up.

Tiny bars danced across the screen. What was taking so long? She fought the urge to fling the phone to the ground. There wasn't enough reception down here.

Three short beeps, and then her screen flashed with the message: *Call failed.*

Fear jolted through her entire body. What if this was a setup?

"Kennedy?"

She jumped, flinging her bag around. It hit Reuben in the gut.

"Oof."

She forced herself to laugh, swallowing away the lump in her throat. "Don't scare me like that!" Did she sound like someone who had just been startled? Or did she sound like someone about to have a nervous breakdown?

"I'm sorry."

She sighed as her breath came back to her in a rush. "I didn't know where you went." She blinked her eyes. She had been taken aback, that was all. A little jolt. Nothing to worry about. Nothing to be ashamed of.

"I should have told you, but I thought you were behind me. Look. I just got a picture with the old guy. The uncle or grandfather or whoever he was." He showed her the picture. "Come on, I want to get one with both of us."

Kennedy shook her head. "You know, I'm actually getting really hungry. Do we have time to stop for something to eat?" Anything to get out of this basement.

"Angelo's Pizza?"

Kennedy forced excitement into her voice. "Perfect."

Reuben pointed. "I saw an exit back here. I think it goes right to the street level."

Kennedy followed a pace behind, squeezing back her hot and silent tears of shame.

CHAPTER 6

The wind whipped and howled around them when they emerged on a side street in back of the Opera House. Reuben stood a little in front and shielded Kennedy from the biting wind.

"That was so fun."

If Kennedy knew Reuben, he wouldn't stop gushing about the show until next semester.

He let out a contented sigh. "Ready for pizza?"

They made their way to the T station. Kennedy just wanted to get out of the cold. Loathing and humiliation clashed together in her gut. When would she stop acting like such a baby? Maybe she really was coming down with something.

Reuben hummed a little tune from *The Nutcracker* as they waited for the T, and Kennedy wondered what her friends from high school would say if they saw her today. At the All American Girls School in Yanji, she earned a reputation for being responsible and studious. Now, the same young woman who took four AP classes her senior year and still graduated as valedictorian couldn't sit through a simple general chemistry final without breaking down into a sobbing, coughing, hallucinating mess.

What was she doing wrong? She was praying. God knew how much she was praying these days. She had never been one for Bible study, at least not like the Secret Seminary students her parents trained in China, but for the past few weeks she had read her Bible nearly every morning and had memorized a dozen passages or more.

Forgetting what is behind, straining toward what is ahead. It sounded so simple. And if that's really what God wanted her to do, why hadn't he given her the ability to follow through? She was so busy on the weekends she didn't always make it to St. Margaret's Church, but she was there at least a few Sundays each month, and she went over to Pastor Carl and Sandy's for dinner a couple times, too. As far as she knew, she was doing everything right. By the book. Exactly what any Sunday school teacher or VBS leader would tell her. Prayer and Bible study were the keys to the victorious Christian life. So why was she floundering, flailing her arms and still sinking into the miry muck of anxiety? She couldn't remember the last time she had slept the whole night through. She didn't always remember her dreams, but she often woke up in the middle of the night drenched in sweat.

Dear God, what am I missing? I'm trying so hard.

"What are you thinking about?"

Kennedy had almost forgotten Reuben was still there and fumbled for a response. "Oh, I was just wondering if Professor Adell will want me to retake the test in the morning."

"I don't think you need to worry about your final. Even if you have to take it again, you'll do fine, like always."

The Green Line train pulled up to the platform. Kennedy didn't say anything else. Reuben followed her up the steps of the car, and they found seats toward the back.

Neither spoke as the subway chugged along noisily. When it came to the next stop, a heavyset woman in a huge fur coat climbed up the steps, panting from exertion. "Phew, that wind is really howling up there," she announced to nobody in particular. She caught Kennedy's eye and stared a few extra seconds before sitting across from her.

Another man came on, thickly built, slightly bald. His eyes passed over Kennedy, but he didn't smile. Had she seen him somewhere before?

"What will you be reading over break?" Reuben's voice startled her, but she hid her surprise.

"I've still only made it through two of the Turgenev books." She glanced at the man, who was sitting near the emergency lever. He opened up a newspaper, and Kennedy looked away.

The fur coat lady still stared at her quizzically. Finally, she leaned forward. "Excuse me, but are you that girl from the news? The one that got kidnapped last fall?"

Kennedy's spine stiffened, and she wished those transporters from her dad's favorite sci-fi shows were real so she could beam herself straight to bed. Instead, she just gave a quick nod.

"I thought so." The woman folded her arms across her massive chest. "You know, I'm very good with faces. As soon as I saw you, I knew you had been on the news. Terrible thing, isn't it, what happened to that little girl?"

Reuben leaned over and whispered in her ear, "We can get on another train at the next stop if you want."

Kennedy shook her head. She was a gifted, mature, capable young woman. Isn't that what all of her high school teachers had written in their letters of recommendation to Harvard? What kind of straight-A pre-med student couldn't handle a little chitchat with a nosy stranger on the T?

"You're shaking," Reuben whispered.

She wished he hadn't said anything because now she could acutely feel every single muscle tensing. At one time, she had joked with Willow that all this trauma would be worth it if she got a six-pack out of it, but in reality she had put on a few extra pounds. Probably due to the late-night crunching on Craisins and dry Cheerios.

"You know," the fur lady continued loud enough for everyone in the car to hear, "my husband and I are big supporters of Pastor Carl's mission to unwed mothers." Her earrings jingled ostentatiously as she nodded her head up and down. "A great ministry."

Reuben stared at Kennedy in concern. Sometimes his sympathy was harder to bear than her own mess of emotions. He would get to looking at her like she was a dying butterfly about to take its last flutter. How was she supposed to forget about the past and move on when everyone kept reminding her about it?

"I was telling my husband," Fur Lady continued, "those women sure need our help. You know, back in my day, when a gal got pregnant, she would either marry the boy or she'd put the baby up for adoption to be raised by a real family. Nowadays, it seems like all these girls want is a baby or two, no matter if there's a dad in the picture or not. The state pays more with each kid, you know, and then of course these girls go and demand child support. You get enough babies lined up and make the state and those dads all shell out their cash, and you can make a good living without lifting a finger."

Kennedy bit her lip and glanced around. The man near the exit glared from over the top of his magazine. Just a few more stops. If she could handle complex computations during a lab titration without using a calculator, she could keep her mouth shut for a few more minutes on the T with a rude, loud-mouthed busybody.

"In fact," the woman prattled on, "I was at the store just the other day, and one of those welfare moms came up with her coupons ..."

The T jolted to an unexpected stop, and the woman let out an unbecoming expletive. The lights flickered once and then went off.

"What was that?" she screeched, her voice rising to an even more annoying pitch, somewhat akin to a silver fork scraping against a ceramic plate.

"Must be having some kind of problems with the T," a man answered. Several passengers pulled out their phones and let the light from the screens pierce through the darkness.

Kennedy tried to ignore the fluttering in her heart. Things like this probably happened all the time. Nothing to worry about. Nothing at all. She scooted a little closer to Reuben.

"Maybe it's the wind," someone suggested. "Coulda blown down the electrical lines."

"Welcome to Boston," muttered another.

Beside her, Reuben sat as calm as always. He was probably enjoying the extra time to think about his favorite scenes from *The Nutcracker*. She pressed her hands to her throbbing temples. There was too much work to do. She still wasn't packed for her trip to her aunt's tomorrow, and she had to be up early to meet with Detective Drisklay. She had to get in touch with Adell to see if she needed to retake the exam tomorrow morning or if it would count as an excused absence. She'd be a little disappointed if she didn't have to take it at all. What kind of school would let someone out of a final because of a cough? It wasn't fair to the other students. It wasn't even fair to Kennedy, given the hours she had spent studying.

"How long until we start going again?" asked the woman in the fur coat. "Shouldn't the conductor say something on that system of his?"

"Power's out," a passenger mumbled. "No way for him to tell us anything."

"So we just stay here?" Her voice rose higher. Kennedy wanted to cover her ears.

"They'll get it up and going soon enough."

"Are you cold?" Reuben took off his parka.

"You really don't need to. I'm all right." Why did she always do that? Why did she always pretend that she was hanging on better than she really was?

He draped his jacket around her shoulders. She stretched her arms into the soft nylon. His warmth still clung to the inside, wrapping her up like a foam insulator around a lab flask. Like a warm hug on a cold, blustery night.

"Any minute now," he said. "We'll be moving again soon."

His coat smelled like the student union. The student union and all of Reuben's favorite foods. Pizza, Doritos, plenty of bacon. The faint scent of smoke.

Smoke?

"What is that?" the fur lady screeched as grayish fog filled the car from the bottom up.

The passengers jumped to their feet in a noisy, confused jumble. Everyone spoke at once. Kennedy held her breath. What was going on?

"Where's it coming from?" someone asked. A few passengers coughed.

"There. I see something over there." Several phones flashed their lights to a corner of the car where smoke piled more densely around the fur lady's feet. She let out a little wail and rushed on her high heels to the far side of the T as the smoke billowed up to the level of their waists.

The smell was stronger, a mix of melting plastic and something else that stung Kennedy's sinuses. Most of the passengers covered their faces with their scarfs or sleeves. Reuben held her arm. How were they supposed to get out? *She glanced around, trying to guess what her dad would do in a situation like this. He had safety protocols for any type of crisis — getting kidnapped, getting mugged, getting carjacked. Before she left for Harvard, he even made her role-play what she would do if a professor threatened to lower her grade unless she slept with him. All those ridiculous hypotheticals, all that paranoid crisis training, but he never once thought to tell her what to do if she got stuck on a burning subway car during an electrical outage.*

The smoke swirled higher and stung her eyes. She hid her face in the collar of Reuben's parka. Her empty stomach swirled, and voices flew by her, hardly perceived. *The extinguisher ... Pull that pin ... What if it's electric ... Aim toward the bottom.* Shouting. Chaos. Kennedy tried to conserve her breaths. She had to get out.

The strange, almost sweet smell of the fire extinguisher spray. The sound of a dozen passengers sighing as one, but Kennedy's lungs remained paralyzed in her chest.

No, not again. Not here.

More voices. Relief and fear mingled in their tones. *Got it ... Still smells like smoke ...*

She coughed. That wasn't the extinguisher fluid stinging her lungs.

Still just as bad ... More smoke ... Out of spray.

"Open the doors!"

Banging on windows. A walking stick swinging overhead. The thud of glass refusing to give.

The man who had been reading the magazine jostled the lever of the emergency exit. Fresh air. Everybody surged toward the opening. *Ladies first ... Make room ... Not all at once ...*

Hands reaching out, grabbing her shoulders, propelling her forward. All she could think about was getting out of the car. Out of the tunnel.

Watch your step ... Gonna be all right.

She hopped off the train, and another passenger held out his hand and helped her to a small sidewalk running alongside the tunnel. Bending over, she coughed until her lungs were clear, thankful the choking didn't set off another crying fit. She was safe. She was off the T. Everything was going to be just fine.

CHAPTER 7

It took Kennedy a moment or two to adjust to her new surroundings. She was standing on some kind of platform, narrower than a city sidewalk. She touched the wall to steady herself and immediately snatched back her hand, her spine prickling at the thought of all the germs she had just contracted. She reached instinctively for the Germ X in her backpack, only then remembering she had left her bag on the T. She rubbed her grimy fingers together, her nose and cheeks crinkling in disgust.

She stepped farther down the platform. If she had her phone with her, she could have shined some extra light on the path, but of course she had left that behind in her backpack as well. It would be easier to keep her cell in her pocket like every other college student she knew, but the thought of all that radiation sitting right next to her made her skin feel hot and scorched.

Any minute, she expected Reuben to materialize beside her. What was taking him so long? And why didn't the MBTA keep some kind of emergency lights down here, anyway? It was so dark. She shut her eyes and inhaled. It was all right. She was in a subway tunnel. They had encountered some technical difficulties, but the T lines were so old, the cars so decrepit, this was probably a regular occurrence. Maybe the MBTA would give them all free passes for a year or something as recompense.

So much smoke. She hadn't known a car could fill that fast.

Kennedy took another few steps away from the train. What if the smoke had come from a bomb? What if it exploded? She thought about the action movies she and her dad liked to watch together, how the hero would leap forward as a fireball blasted behind, outlining him in glorious shades of red and orange. The explosion always gave an extra push but never really injured anybody. Maybe a few scrapes, a small bruise if the directors wanted to be gritty. But Kennedy knew the science behind an explosion in an enclosed space like this. It wouldn't matter if she was five feet away or fifty. She inched down the platform to put more distance between herself and the train. She didn't see any flames. That was a good sign. When would Reuben come out?

Submerged memories forced their way to the surface of her mind. Handcuffs, the sharp metal digging into her wrist. The ache in her back from spending a whole night chained on the couch. The crawl of her skin in her squalid surroundings. Images of lice and bedbugs and rodents growing to IMAX proportions on her brain's mental projector. She hurried farther away from the train, picking up speed as her boots clanked against the cement.

She was panting now. She heard the sound of her own breathing but couldn't control the rate. Cold. Why couldn't they at least give her a blanket to wrap up in? The feel of a small child shivering next to her, a child far too young to be trapped with her, a child Kennedy could do nothing to help.

She drew in a sharp breath. She was in a subway station, not handcuffed in a cement basement. It was dark because she was in a tunnel, not because her captors had blindfolded her. She was still free. Nobody was keeping her here against her will. She could walk away whenever she wanted. Nobody would point a gun at her or pull a knife to make her stay.

Forgetting what is behind.

The heat of anger mingled with the chill of fear, and her gut sizzled with steam at the spot where they met. Why couldn't she get over these silly anxieties? She could tackle twenty-two credits this semester, find time to take her self-defense class, and even read a few books a month just for fun. Why couldn't she get a grip over her own thoughts instead of letting them trap her into the past whenever they felt like tormenting her?

The old has gone, the new has come. Kennedy quoted one of the verses she had memorized during a recent quiet time. *Take every thought captive* was another good one. That's what she had to do. Seize her thoughts. Seize those horrible, relentless memories. Lock them up where she could control them. Give them nothing but water to sip, deprive them of warmth, feed them only on fear. Fear that she would never be rescued. Fear that her captors would murder her and nobody would find out for weeks. Fear that she would have to stand by and watch an innocent child die at the hands of godless, soulless monsters.

She pressed her fingernails into her palms. No, this wasn't the way to walk in victory. This wasn't the way to find her freedom and deliverance. If God could take the sins of the world and throw them into the sea of forgetfulness, surely Kennedy could do the same thing to a few old memories that still haunted her. If she only knew how. More prayer, maybe. More Bible reading. She had gotten so busy with finals she had let her spiritual disciplines slide. That's why she was suffering now. That's why she felt like the wild rabbit, crouching in plain sight with no hope of shelter or safety, knowing the fox would pounce with its razor teeth but unable to guess when.

Steps on the sidewalk. She felt the vibrations just a yard or two away. "Reuben?" she asked, her voice quiet. So uncertain. "Is that you?"

No answer. Kennedy held her breath. What had her self-defense instructor said? She couldn't let her brain shut down when she was scared. She had to channel that fear and turn it into positive survival energy.

"Is someone there?" She sounded more like a mouse, her words a pitiful squeal.

No, that wasn't who Kennedy was anymore. She didn't have to be afraid. She knew how to protect herself. She even had her pepper spray. Wait, that was still on the T along with everything else. Why hadn't she remembered to take her backpack with her?

"Don't get any closer. Stay where you are." She tried not to sound too forceful. What would people think of her? It was probably just another passenger getting off the train. How had she gotten so far from the main group in the first place?

She hurried down the walkway. The footsteps echoed behind. She glanced over her shoulder. "You need to stop following me." Kennedy spoke assertively like she had practiced in her class. She had been so self-conscious those first few times she had to stare her instructor right in the eye and say ridiculous things like, "Get back five feet," or "No, you're making me uncomfortable, and I want you to leave." But nothing had been as awkward as the simulations when they brought in male volunteers to attack the students. She hoped to never suffer through something that humiliating again, whether in a controlled role-play setting or in real life.

Hot breath tickled her neck. Or was that just her imagination? If she reached out her arm, she would know for sure if someone was there. But what if he grabbed her? What if Vinny had escaped custody? What if he followed her and was just waiting for the chance to get her alone?

She wouldn't be victimized again. She had to get away. She wouldn't let him catch up to her. A footstep on the concrete. Not a fabrication. Not this time. It was real. Real as the scientific method. Real as her parents' love for her. Real as death. In the pitch darkness, she rushed ahead, running her fingers along the grimy wall so she would know which way to go as she sprinted down the walkway. What did contracting a few germs compare to getting murdered?

How close was he now? And why couldn't she have remembered her pepper spray? She strained her ears but only heard the slap of her boots on the walkway, the sound of her own panting, the pounding of her heart valves in her pericardial sac. She didn't want to stop, couldn't slow down, but she had to save her strength. She needed energy to fight back when he caught up. She couldn't hear him, but that didn't mean he wasn't coming.

Any second now.

CHAPTER 8

Kennedy rehearsed every lesson from her self-defense class in fast motion, promised herself never to roll her eyes at her dad for all his unsolicited safety advice. Legs in a crouch, back hip at a slight angle. Hands up, ready to block, ready for a blow. Should she go for a throat strike with the fingers or palm strike to the chin? Her ears pounded as her heart plunged blood and oxygen and adrenaline to every muscle cell in her body.

Kennedy stood as still as the fetal pig corpse she had dissected in high school. She prayed for protection, not in actual words but in that unspoken language of desperation, hopes shot heavenward with the full expectation God could understand and decipher her soul's chaotic pleading. She strained to pick up the slightest noise around her. Nothing. Not even the voices of the people evacuated from the T.

Why had she separated herself from the group? She should have raced back toward Reuben and the others the second she suspected someone was following her. Even if that sped up the inevitable confrontation, she would have been close enough for people to help. For people to hear her scream. Now she was cut off. Stranded. Completely unprotected. No witnesses. How far had she been running? What would happen if they found her body on the tracks tomorrow morning? Fears of radiation and cancer aside, she vowed to never ride the subway again without carrying her phone in her pocket. Her phone and her pepper spray.

Stupid. Stupid what you do when you're so afraid your neural circuits shut down one after another like a domino effect of idiocy. Isn't that what her self-defense instructors had warned her about? Isn't that why they ran her through all those painfully awkward simulations, so she could think straight when her veins flooded with epinephrine and her mind clouded with the rush of fear?

Kennedy took a deep breath. There was nothing to hear, nothing around her but perfect stillness. If she didn't know better, she might have thought herself the only human in a twenty-mile radius. She should go back. The farther she went down the rail, the more she distanced herself from people who might help her. If there really was someone after her in the first place. What if this was just another attack, a trick of her brain that now seemed to think trauma was a normal, everyday part of life, something to fabricate if reality didn't provide enough danger?

Part of her wanted to reach out, touch the phantom that had scared her so badly, figure out exactly what had made her run. Probably not even a person at all. She thought about *Little House in the Big Woods*. As a little girl, she had giggled wildly at the part when Pa was walking home late and saw a bear blocking his path. After a terrifying standoff in which the bear didn't move a muscle, Pa finally charged it with a stick only to find that he had been having a stare-down with an old tree stump. It had been hilarious back then, picturing Pa with his big broad shoulders and his long scruffy beard getting scared by a silly shadow. Kennedy had never thought until now about the way his heart must have thudded underneath his flannel shirt, how his thoughts must have turned homeward to Ma and the girls, wondering if he would ever see their faces or hold them in his arms again.

Kennedy shook her head. How had she let her own silly fears drive her this far down the tracks? It was probably the stress of finals week. Her meeting tomorrow with Detective Drisklay. How long until she could forget about the entire ordeal and get on with a normal life?

It was silly to stay here and shiver in the dark. She had to get back to Reuben. He was probably worried about her by now. What would he say when he found out she had run so far on account of a few unfamiliar sounds? Kennedy smoothed his coat she was still wearing. It was time to go back. He might tease her, and then it would be over. At least she'd be safe. She'd probably been safe all along. Now she just wanted to get back to Reuben, get back to campus. Tomorrow would be another long, busy day. The semester was over, and now she wanted to relax. Get back to her dorm, maybe read a little from her Turgenev book, grab a snack, and then go to sleep. She could take her laundry to Aunt Lilian's and wash it there.

She still couldn't believe what she had done. What would her self-defense instructors say if they saw what a coward she had been? How would they chide her for running away from the group of potential witnesses instead of toward them? That silly class probably made her even more paranoid than she needed to be, all those scenarios she had to act out, all that talk about what horrible situations she might find herself in one day. Just like Pa and the bear in the woods. Only it had been a tree stump.

She stepped slowly at first, thinking up the least embarrassing way to tell Reuben why she had freaked out and run a quarter mile or more in an unlit underground tunnel.

She let out her breath, the sound of her sigh even louder than normal in the enclosed space. She thought about the chapter in *Les Miserables*, the fifty pages or more Victor Hugo devoted to verbose descriptions of the underground sewer system in Paris. How would Hugo paint the tunnels beneath the streets of Boston if he were alive today?

Yes, she would think about *Les Miserables*. Even before she read the book, her mom took her to see the Broadway show when they still lived in New York. She had loved the music as a child and let the lyrics run through her mind. Another few minutes and she'd be back with Reuben. Then they could go back to ...

Slam. The thud of a shoe pounding the pavement. So there was someone after all. He was behind her now. How had he circled around on the other side? It didn't matter. She was running, pushing forward, lunging ahead.

Noise. She needed to make noise. There wasn't time to recall those forceful sayings she had practiced in self-defense. So she screamed. At least she tried to. It came out more like a squeal. It didn't sound particularly bold or courageous, and it wasn't even loud. Not as loud as his boots smashing into the cement. Any minute now, she would get tackled from behind, but she didn't have time to plan and visualize how she would fight him off. Getting away and making as much ruckus as she could — that was the only plan.

She surged forward, her heart close to bursting from exertion. Her only other feeling was the pain in her shins, the sting in her lungs. He was right behind her. She pictured him reaching out his hand, knew he was about to jerk her to a dead stop, braced herself so the whiplash wouldn't be so bad. She arched her back, as if gaining another centimeter or two of distance could delay the inevitable.

Please, Lord, get me out of this.

"Watch out!"

By the time she realized the voice was in front of her, she didn't have a chance to slow herself down. She slammed into him, and her breath rushed out of her chest. They both stumbled. He grabbed her by the shoulders to keep them both from falling, and all those simple moves she had practiced in self-defense deserted her. There was no reflex reaction, no autonomic response. Instead, she froze, and he gripped her by both shoulders. Almost as an afterthought, she tried to thrash her body to throw him off, and for a minute, she was afraid they'd both topple over the edge onto the rails below.

"Calm down." He wrapped his arms tight around her, and her brain stopped trying to recall how to get out of a bear hug and instead focused on his voice. "It's me."

"Reuben?" Saying his name unleashed a torrent of tears, and he held her, whispering comforting words that made her feel even more wretched.

Kennedy shook her head. "Someone was coming."

Reuben took out his cellphone and let its glow fall on the tracks and walkway around them. "I don't see anybody."

"I was being chased. He was right ..." Kennedy stopped. *Pa and the bear.* If she could have turned into a corrosive acid, burned a hole into the cement, and disappeared from sight, she would have.

"I'm sorry." She sniffed, afraid to get some of the snot from her runny nose on Reuben's coat.

"Another episode?" Reuben offered quietly.

She turned her face away. God was merciful to have turned off the lights. Now she wouldn't have to look Reuben in the eye. Not yet, anyway. She would have been willing to stay there in the darkness forever, but once she started breathing a little calmer he said, "We're only a few hundred yards from the Boylston station. You think you're ready to walk?"

"I'm sorry," Kennedy repeated. This was supposed to be a fun night. Why couldn't life be more like the chem lab? If you didn't get it right the first time, you could just dump everything down the drain and start over fresh. "I'm such an idiot."

"No, you're not." The good-natured teasing never came. The playful jabs, nothing. "You've been really stressed out. This kind of thing doesn't mix well with stress. You know?"

No, Kennedy didn't know. Reuben could talk about *this kind of thing*, but what was it really? She recalled the large, scrawling letters the doctor wrote on the notepad. *Post-traumatic stress disorder.* But he was wrong. He had to be.

"You ready?" Reuben asked and shined the light from his cell on the walkway in front of them.

Kennedy swallowed through the tightness in her throat. "Yeah. I'm ready."

When they passed the train car, the smoke was gone. The conductor and a firefighter pointed their flashlights at the tracks. Most of the passengers had gone. Kennedy was thankful she didn't have to meet anyone's eye.

"I got your backpack," Reuben told her, patting the straps on his shoulders. This was the second time he had retrieved her bag for her when she had one of her ... *episodes*, or whatever they were. Any other night, she might have made a joke about being careful so this sort of thing didn't become a habit, but her humor as well as her energy were stuck back there in the subway tunnel, pounded into the ground where her feet had smashed the pavement. Her heart rate was steadier now, but her stomach churned with the bitter aftertaste of humiliation.

"What's that light ahead?" she asked.

"I think that's the Boylston station."

Kennedy squinted. "I thought the power was out." She would have preferred the darkness, at least for a little while longer.

Reuben slowed down. "I heard the conductor and the firemen talking. It sounds like the problem was localized. Something on the subway grid." He adjusted the straps of Kennedy's backpack. "Do you still want that pizza?"

"No, thanks." There was only one thing Kennedy wanted to do — get home and forget this night ever happened. Maybe Reuben was right. Maybe she should talk to somebody about her episodes. She hated the idea of rehashing her abduction all over again, but could it be worse than being a slave to these fears? How many more tests would she miss? What would happen if she fell victim to an attack while working with dangerous chemicals in the lab?

When they stepped into the lights of Boylston station, Kennedy wished she could wrap her scarf around her entire face, not just her neck. She avoided Reuben's eyes and everyone else's. Could these strangers tell just by looking at her that she was crazy? Maybe even delusional?

What was wrong with her? Was it just stress from finals, maybe? Lack of sleep? Or was she truly losing her mind? No, crazy people never worried about going crazy, did they? It was only sane people who questioned their sanity, right?

Home. Well, at least the closest thing she had to a home in the States. Willow would be at Cape Cod for the next few days before she flew back to Alaska. Kennedy wouldn't have to answer any questions, engage with anybody. Home. She glanced at the map of the T. Five stops and one transfer would get her back to her dorm in half an hour or so. Maybe less if there were no more delays. Could she do it? Could she force herself to step onto another subway?

Just a malfunction, she told herself, but her lungs still stung with the memory of smoke, and her pulse quickened at the sound of an oncoming train. What if she had lost her balance running away from phantoms in the dark? What if she had landed on the tracks and knocked herself out and nobody found her before ...?

Reuben slipped his hand into his pocket, flipped casually through his wallet. "How would you feel about taking a taxi?"

Kennedy didn't know how shallow her breaths had grown until her lungs let out one prolonged, choppy sigh. "That sounds like a really good idea."

CHAPTER 9

"You don't need to keep telling me you're sorry." Reuben leaned against the doorway of Kennedy's dorm room. "Did you know you apologized five times in the taxi?"

Kennedy still wished Reuben had let her pay the fare. She was thrilled to be as far away from the subway system as possible, but it wasn't as if Reuben had a whole lot of discretionary income. She didn't, either, but she would have felt less guilty about plunking fifteen bucks on a taxi ride back to campus if it had been her money, not his.

"So, you're really all right?" Reuben stalled at the door. On any other night, Kennedy might have thought it was sweet. Right now, she only wanted to get to bed. All the energy she had exhausted getting ready for finals had finally caught up to her. She was drained, sucked dry like a pile of old Craisins left out on her desk. She needed sleep.

"Maybe we can hang out again when I get back from Maryland," she suggested. "Rain check?"

"Rain what?" Reuben was even worse at American idioms than she was.

"Rain check. Since tonight didn't work for pizza, we can do it when I get back from Maryland. Deal?"

Reuben flashed her a thumbs up. "It's a deal."

"I promise I won't chicken out on you next time."

"Chicken?"

"Never mind."

Sleep. She wanted to sleep. Her bed beckoned to her with its own irresistible gravity.

He stepped into her room and gave her an awkward half-hug. "Merry Christmas."

"You, too." Heaviness sank in her gut, disappointment over their failed night out mingling with her own embarrassment. She plopped onto the bed. Why did she always do this to herself? She had let her own anxiety and nerves ruin her evening out with Reuben, and now she didn't even have the strength to pack her bags for tomorrow. The morning would come all too soon.

She set her alarm for seven. That would give her time to start her laundry and see if Adell wanted her to come in for her final. And then she had to be at the detective's by ten. Why hadn't she asked him if they could get together after Christmas vacation? With Vinny in custody, what was the rush?

Her head hit the pillow, and she wondered how many cavities she'd end up with if she went a night without brushing her teeth. She'd have to get up soon, but she'd take a minute or two to rest her eyes first. She deserved at least that small indulgence, didn't she?

The whole dorm was as still and lifeless as a dish full of fruit flies etherized into temporary comas. Everyone had already rushed home to their moms and dads, to their decorated houses and colorful Christmas trees. The silence was like pin pricks in Kennedy's ears, and she missed the ticking of the grandfather clock in her parents' house back in Yanji.

Just a few minutes' rest. Then she'd get up and do something productive. She couldn't sleep the whole night away ...

All she could focus on was the exhaustion in her limbs and the gnawing emptiness in her gut. They hadn't fed her in almost a day. Water. Just a little sip of water.

Tinkering. Stockpiles of weapons. Men fiddling by the workbench. Arguing in hushed tones.

Blood. A whole river of it. How could someone so little lose that much?

Lights. Flashing. Strobing. Ringing sirens. Never stopping.

Breathe. She couldn't breathe.

Kennedy opened her mouth and inhaled noisily. Oxygen flooded her brain, jolting her into consciousness. She sat up in bed, gasping. Her body was cold and clammy with sweat. She hadn't even taken her black boots off.

The ringing continued. Her phone. She glanced at the clock. Past eleven. Who would be calling now?

She flipped on her desk lamp, which cast dim shadows on Willow's side of the room. She checked the caller ID.

"Dad?" Her voice was croaky from sleepiness. She hoped he couldn't tell how confused she felt.

"Honey, where are you?" His voice was even more tense than normal.

"I'm in my dorm."

"Did you lock yourself in?"

Kennedy rubbed her eyes. Did her dad really think a safety drill at this time of the night would help anything?

"Did you lock yourself in?" he demanded again.

Kennedy let her eyes drift slowly to her door. She couldn't even remember what time it was when she lay down. "Mmm-hmmm," she lied, staring at the unbolted lock.

Her dad let out his breath in a sigh that did nothing to relieve the strain from his voice. "I was just on Channel 2's webpage. Have you heard about Vinny?"

Kennedy contemplated whether it was worth getting off her soft mattress to lock herself in. She probably should, she decided without moving. "Yeah. They caught him just yesterday." Or was it two days ago? She couldn't figure it out. Was it tomorrow yet, or still today?

"Not that. They say he's been working with a partner. A man who's wanted for questioning. Sounds like he was part of the plot last fall."

This was news to Kennedy, but she still didn't understand why it couldn't have waited for morning. "I'll ask Detective Drisklay about it tomorrow." Was that the only reason her dad had called?

"Is your computer up?" he asked.

"No, I've been asleep for the past couple hours." Had it really been that long? She had only meant to take a little catnap.

"Well, I'm emailing you the news page. It's got a picture of the man. I want you to take a good look at it. If he was involved with everything that happened, he's not going to want you talking to the police, or anyone else for that matter."

"Yeah, I'll take a look." She stood up. Her back was as tight as a spring scale.

"I'm sending it now. Check your email as soon as we hang up."

"I will." She shoved some dirty clothes into her laundry bag. Her back and leg muscles ached. Had she really been running that far in the subway tunnel?

"All right, sweetheart. How were your exams?" he added, almost like an afterthought.

"They went fine." Kennedy was ready to forget about them.

Her dad paused for just a moment and then added, "Well, have a safe trip to your aunt's tomorrow. Remember, call ..."

"I'll call you as soon as the plane lands," Kennedy interrupted. "Talk to you later."

"I love you, sweetie."

"Love you, too."

Kennedy put the phone on her desk. Stupid laundry. Stupid dreams. Stupid evening. For a minute, she wondered if Reuben was awake. Well, she wouldn't bother him now. She needed time to let her bruised pride heal over. She'd get back to campus in a few weeks in time to start a new semester. She and Reuben would take general chemistry, chem lab, and calculus together again, and things would go just like this term. Joking in the cafeteria. Late nights in the library. Frantic texts the day before a lab was due. It almost would have made things easier if he had laughed at her in the taxi. Now, she was mortified not only by her own behavior but by his undeserved compassion.

Kennedy fumbled through her desk looking for spare change for the laundromat. Her phone buzzed with an incoming text.

Emailed you the link. Did you get it?

She had already forgotten about the news from Channel 2. When would her life stop being ruled by current events her dad read from halfway around the world?

Reading it right now, she typed back, but her phone powered off before she could send it.

Stupid battery.

She thought about going back to bed. Her dad had only said there was another potential suspect. If the police thought she was in danger, they would have called to let her know. Just like her dad to ruin a perfect nap with his paranoia.

Still, if she didn't give him some sort of response, she'd never hear the end of it tomorrow. She clicked on her computer and waited for her inbox to open. There was a note from Adell telling her she could take the test when she got back to campus in January, and there was another note from her Russian lit professor. She had gotten an A on her paper on Raskonikov and the Christological symbols in the epilogue of *Crime and Punishment*. "If you were a grad student, I'd encourage you to get your ideas published." It was a somewhat indirect compliment, but Kennedy would take it anyway.

After shooting back quick replies to both professors, she clicked on the email from her dad. No notes attached, no *Merry Christmas, sweetheart*, just the web address for a Channel 2 webpage. She opened it up, hoping it wouldn't take too long to load. She needed to get her clothes washed.

Additional Partner Identified in Boston Kidnapping Case. At least when she got to Maryland, nobody there would remember the incident. Even if they did, they would consider it old news.

She skimmed the text, her eyes darting down the screen so she could tell her dad she read the whole thing. Four paragraphs down, she froze. The computer was still loading the bottom half of his face, but she recognized his eyes immediately.

Cold. Icy green like frosted grass before it's covered by snow and trampled by sleds.

The picture kept loading. High cheeks. Angular nose.

Tight jaw. Lips drawn in a narrow line.

The man from the subway.

A noise in the hall. Kennedy whipped her head up from her computer screen in time to see her doorknob turn.

CHAPTER 10

She imagined screaming but was too petrified to make an actual sound. She pictured herself running behind the door so that when it swung open she would be partially concealed behind it. But her feet fastened to the ground like a slide on a microscope stage, held in place by unyielding metal clips. Her scream stuck between her throat and her mouth, closing off her trachea so she couldn't breathe.

She watched the door swing toward her, clutched her phone as if it could ward off an attack. Blood drained from her head to her limbs, which still refused to move.

"What are you standing in the middle of the room for?"

At the sight of her roommate, Kennedy's breath whooshed out of her lungs like wind through the subway tunnel. The paralyzing power of fear melted, and embarrassment heated her face. She steadied herself against her desk and clicked off her monitor. "Oh, you startled me, that's all. I was just talking with my dad."

Willow raised an eyebrow and glided in, leaving the door partially open behind her. *Lock us in here*, Kennedy wanted to scream. She forced a smile. How many times would she humiliate herself before the night was over? "What are you doing? I thought you were going right from Cape Cod to the airport."

Willow tossed her long raven waves over her shoulder. Of all the hair colors Willow had gone through this semester, Kennedy liked black the best. It reminded her of those smooth onyx gems her grandmother used to buy for her at the little knick-knack shop in upstate New York. Kennedy had loved the soft feel of the stones, which could stay several degrees cooler than the ambient temperature.

Willow tossed her duffel bag onto her bed. "The partying was lame."

Kennedy tried to hide her surprise. Willow hadn't talked about anything besides her trip to the Cape during all of finals week. She and about a dozen of her theater friends had rented a little cottage, and Willow had rattled off their inventory of entertainment plans — both legal and illegal — nearly every night like a bedtime prayer.

"Besides," Willow continued, "I got a text from this guy I met at the bakery. He thought it might be fun to get together, so I left early." She plopped onto her mattress and studied her fingernails which were painted with the swirling colors of the aurora borealis. "Anyway, what'd you do tonight? Eat Cheerios and stick your nose in a book?"

Kennedy had to chuckle at how well Willow knew her. "Actually, I was out with Reuben. We saw *The Nutcracker.*"

"It's about time you two finally started to date."

Kennedy fidgeted with some old papers on her desk. Maybe she should clean up a little before she left for Maryland. "It wasn't a date." Kennedy's back tingled at the spot where she knew Willow was staring.

Willow let out a dramatic sigh. "You two are so cute together. Just going slow like you both have all the time in the world. It's adorable."

Kennedy's brain was too groggy to defend herself or Reuben.

"Anyway," Willow prattled on, smacking gum while she talked, "you know I totally respect your morals and everything. Because if I didn't, I would have figured he was gay or something and that's why you hadn't hooked up yet."

Kennedy's whole stomach scrunched as if someone was trying to twist excess water out of it. She hoped her expression was more neutral.

"Boy, you look tired," Willow exclaimed and kicked off her shoes. "Are you ok? Wait." She stood back up. "He didn't hurt your or anything, did he?"

Kennedy was itchy beneath her sweater. Itchy and sweaty. "No, nothing like that."

"Good. Because, honestly, from the looks of it, you're either doped up or something freaked you out. So what is it?"

Kennedy inhaled choppily. Maybe she needed acting lessons from Willow. "Nothing. I'm fine."

Willow raised her eyebrows, which were about as thin as two blades of grass.

"It's just my dad," Kennedy explained. "I guess he read in the news that there's now another suspect at large."

Willow frowned. "He give you one of his famous freak-out safety speeches? Well that explains the shell-shock." She chuckled. "For a minute, I was worried it was serious."

Something buzzed, and Kennedy flinched at the noise.

"Geez, woman. You're as jumpy as a poodle in heat." Willow reached into her pocket and smirked at the screen. "It's just a text from the guy I met. He's an actor. Hey, let me get on your computer. I want to see if he's got an IMBD page." She turned on the monitor and froze when the Channel 2 page leapt onto the screen. Her eyes widened, and she brought her blanched face closer to Kennedy's computer screen. "Where'd you get this picture?"

Unease splashed at the bottom of Kennedy's gut and sent waves of fear rippling outward. "That's the guy I told you about. The one they think helped mastermind things last fall." Even now Kennedy couldn't bring herself to use words like *kidnapping*. "I forget his name. Something kinda ethnic. Guido? Giulio?"

"Gino." Willow's voice, usually dripping with melodrama, was terse. Expressionless.

Kennedy's legs felt like they were supporting one of Boston's looming concrete overpasses. "What are you talking about?"

Willow pointed at the computer screen, but Kennedy didn't even want to look. What venom dripped from that photograph? What new threats would she discover in that pixelated image?

Willow slammed her fist on Kennedy's desk. "No, no, no, no, no." She pinched her forehead between her thumb and forefinger. "The jerk!" If Kennedy had been critiquing one of her roommate's plays, she would say Willow was overdoing it. Willow held out her hand in the universal sign for *Don't freak out on me*. "That guy in the photo, that's the one I met at the bakery. The one I was supposed to ..." Willow scrunched up a large handful of her jet-black hair. "We've been texting all night, making plans for tomorrow. I gave him our dorm number and everything."

CHAPTER 11

Kennedy's diastolic blood pressure must have dropped at least twenty points. She didn't yell. Raising her voice might attract whatever fiend her roommate had invited. *Seriously? Seriously!* Willow was always hooking up with strangers, but a random man at least in his thirties she met at a bakery?

"When's he coming over?" Kennedy's voice quivered, but she didn't care. Disgust and fear warred against each other in her stomach. It was a miracle she didn't have a dozen ulcers after a semester like this.

"We weren't going to meet until tomorrow," Willow answered. "You know I don't do that kind of stuff until you're out."

Kennedy shut her eyes. *Think*. She had to think. Come up with a plan. Which was harder than it sounded after functioning on a few hours of sleep each night. Why did her parents have to live so far away?

Willow picked up her duffel. "Come on. Are you already packed for tomorrow?" She grabbed Kennedy's backpack and shoved it at her.

"What are you doing?"

"We're not staying here," Willow answered. "We'll spend the night with Toby."

"The RA?"

Willow put her shoes back on, but Kennedy still hadn't moved.

"Let's go." Willow stopped tugging on her laces. "Look, Toby and I will behave ourselves. I promise. Nothing funny. Now hurry up before Gino decides to pay a surprise visit."

Kennedy stared around the room, uncertain what to take. She still had that mass of laundry, and her clean clothes were strewn sloppily in her drawers. Her mind was swarming, like a chemical reaction that clogs up if you introduce too many reagents at once. She stared at her dead cellphone, her lifeline to her parents. To emergency responders.

Willow was right. They should both go somewhere else. But would they be any safer down the hall? The men who abducted her last October were chillingly high-tech. They had bugged her phone, hacked her computer. What difference would it make if she were in her own dorm or five rooms down when Gino came after her?

But what other choices did she have? She couldn't ask Reuben to put her up for the night. It would be ridiculously awkward, for one thing. For another, she didn't have his phone number memorized and couldn't call him until her phone charged. Where was the plug?

"You're stalling." Willow's hand was on the doorknob, her penciled eyebrows slanted down.

"I just can't figure out what would be best." With all the crisis training her dad put her through, you'd think she'd be more prepared to make these sorts of snap decisions. Maybe he was right. Maybe she just wasn't ready to be out on her own yet. "Do you think we should call the police?"

"Of course. But not from here." Willow's features softened, her eyebrows resumed their regular position, and she sighed. "I know this is all my fault. And I'm really sorry. I thought that he ... well, he wasn't what I expected. Now I just want to make things right and make sure you're safe, ok? If you're not comfortable at Toby's, then let's find somewhere else to go. Do you have any other ideas?"

Kennedy's stomach rumbled once. Why couldn't this have been a normal night? She should be asleep right now.

Willow's hand rested on the doorknob. Waiting. Waiting for Kennedy to make up her mind. Only she didn't know how. Kennedy half-expected Willow to come up with a sarcastic jab, but her roommate just stood there. Watching. Waiting.

Kennedy's mind churned like a centrifuge in slow motion. Reuben's wasn't an option. She didn't really have any other friends on campus. There were students she smiled at, a few in her calculus study group she might eat lunch with if they happened to be in the student union at the same time, but nobody else she could call a friend. In fact, she was closer to Pastor Carl and his wife than to anyone else on campus.

That was it.

"What about my pastor's house?"

It wasn't the ideal scenario. Carl's phone number was stuck in her phone as well, and it would be almost midnight by the time they got there. Well, how many times had he and Sandy told her to let them know if there was ever anything she needed? This was definitely something she needed.

"Do you think you could drive me over there?" Kennedy didn't have the route memorized, but she could point Willow in the right direction and let her phone charge up on the way.

Willow frowned, and Kennedy wondered if she'd throw another one of her fits about the evils of organized religion. "I'm thrilled you have somewhere off campus to go," she started, "but I parked all the way in J lot. So that would mean you and me walking at least ten minutes in the dark in a windstorm that's so loud nobody could hear you scream more than ten feet away, and most of the student body and half the security staff have already gone on break."

The temptation was strong to plop down in bed and worry about everything in the morning. She could talk to the detective, head out of state for a few weeks. No, that wasn't going to cut it. Call the police, maybe? See if they could get her some protection? She hated running to them like a damsel in distress, unable to take care of herself, but if she explained that she had actually seen that man on the subway — a subway that ran out of power and filled with smoke ...

Kennedy's head spun, threatening to knock her off balance. The smoke in the T, the invisible phantom in the tunnel, the chase ... So it had been Gino that whole time. The power outage, everything. That hand she was sure was about to reach out and grab her. Only he didn't. Why? What had stopped him? What had saved her?

No, she couldn't think about those things. *God, why have you left me here to deal with all this myself? You tell me to be brave, and then you throw convicts at me ...*

Willow's voice was as soft as her gently waving midnight hair. "I know it's not easy, but I think we need to go. Let's at least head to Toby's. We'll call the police from there, ok?" she coaxed, as if Kennedy were a toddler afraid of getting wet in the kiddie pool.

Kennedy took a deep breath. The plan made sense. She picked up her phone charger and her coat.

Footsteps pounded up the hall. Footsteps coming closer, headed straight to their room. Kennedy froze, staring at the door Willow had left a crack open.

"Kennedy!"

The door burst open.

CHAPTER 12

Kennedy would never believe any of those suspense novels that had the heroines screaming in every chapter. Her breath caught in her throat, every muscle in her body seized up at once, and she stood paralyzed, staring at the form in the doorway.

When she saw Pastor Carl, she wasn't sure if she wanted to throw herself into his arms for a bear hug or collapse on the ground like a lump of gelatinous mold.

"You know him?" Willow asked. She had snatched the hardcover Bible off Kennedy's shelf and held it high above her head.

"It's ok. This is Pastor Carl." She laughed nervously, picturing Willow swinging the huge book in an attempt to ward off an attack. Silly as it looked, it was more than Kennedy had thought to do. "What are you doing here?"

Carl was winded. He put his hands on his knees and bent forward at the waist. "Your dad called me. Explained about that Gino guy, said he was implicated somehow with everything. He asked me to check up on you. I called at least a dozen times and couldn't get through, so I drove over here." He glanced at Willow, who was now holding the Bible at waist level. "You can put that down, Miss. I know a thing or two about defending myself from Bible thumpers."

For the first time in Kennedy's memory, Willow looked sheepish, and she replaced the Bible on its shelf.

"And as for you, young lady." Pastor Carl clasped Kennedy on the shoulder. "You're coming home with us. We'll drive you to Logan tomorrow in time for you to fly to your aunt's."

Kennedy wasn't about to argue. She glanced at Willow, who seemed eager for the chance to excuse herself. "Don't you think you should come, too?" she asked.

Willow shook her head. "Nah. I still might head over to Toby's. You know, just in case."

"You should still call the police." Kennedy studied Willow's eyes. Was she going to take care of herself? "Or do you want me to do it?"

Willow pouted. "No, I will. I'm the one who made a mess of it."

"What are you getting the police involved for?" Carl looked from one girl to the other. "What's been going on?"

"It was me." Willow's voice was completely deflated. "I met this guy, and I thought he was ..."

"Willow might have accidentally given our dorm room information out, that's all," Kennedy jumped in.

Carl frowned. "You need to come with us too, then. I'm not about to leave you alone by yourself ..."

Willow picked up her duffel. "I'm all right. I was just leaving anyway." She swung the bag over her shoulder.

Just the thought that Willow had talked with anybody involved in the events of last fall curdled the blood beneath Kennedy's skin. "Be safe," she whispered and did her best to offer a reassuring smile.

"Hey, I'll be just fine." Willow pulled her hair behind her ears. "It's not me they want, remember?"

"That's right." Carl prodded both girls into the hall and shut the door behind them. "That's why Kennedy's coming with me, and you're welcome to as well," he added to Willow.

She flashed one of her stage smiles to reveal dazzling white teeth. "Don't worry about me." She lowered her gaze and stared at Kennedy. "You be careful now, all right?"

"I will." Kennedy wondered why it felt like they were saying good-bye. Break was only a few short weeks. "You, too," she whispered and followed Carl down the stairs.

CHAPTER 13

Kennedy couldn't remember the last time she had seen wind like this. It howled around her face, wrapped around her legs, and threatened to suck her breath away.

"I parked just around here." Carl had to shout to be heard.

Kennedy clutched her leather coat across her, wishing for the warm softness of Reuben's parka again. She followed Carl around the corner and saw his maroon Honda.

He fidgeted with the keys until the doors unlocked. "Gonna have to take this baby in soon to have someone look at the wiring. Every time I signal left, the wipers go on."

Kennedy didn't care what they were driving as long as it got them out of the cold and off campus. How could Willow have been so naïve? Giving their dorm number to a total stranger ...

She had to stop thinking like that. It wasn't Willow's fault. Ok, so maybe it was, but she hadn't acted in malice. Willow was like an untrained puppy. You couldn't really get mad at her, and even if you did, it wouldn't last for long.

Carl strapped the buckle across his chest and pulled it. "Darn thing never gets tight enough." He tugged a few more times and then seemed content. "You ready?"

She nodded.

"Let's go."

There was hardly any traffic. Kennedy had never been on the roads at this time and wondered if they'd have to worry about drunk drivers. At least it was still a weeknight.

Carl turned down the volume to his talk radio station. "So, you've had an exciting evening, by the sound of it."

Kennedy stared at the picture of Carl's grandkids taped to the dashboard.

"You wanna talk about it?" He gave her a quick glance.

No, she didn't want to talk about it, but she knew she would anyway. That was just the way Carl was. He wouldn't make a single demand, probably wouldn't say more than a dozen words, and Kennedy would end up baring her entire soul before they reached his home in Medford.

Carl drummed a little beat on the top of the steering wheel. Kennedy knew he had lived through his share of both trials and excitement. He played pro football for a few years before settling down as a pastor. He started St. Margaret's only five or six years ago, and it was already one of the largest churches in the Cambridge area. New Englanders were by nature fairly tolerant, but she knew he and his wife had experienced a decent amount of flak in the past for their interracial marriage. Maybe that's why he was so easy to talk to. In all their conversations this semester, he had never once made her feel judged. She shut her eyes for a minute, wishing the night would end.

"I hate these silly rotaries." Carl leaned forward and squinted his eyes as he curved onto one of the Boston area's many circular intersections. "Why can't they just put in a traffic light like normal cities?"

Kennedy was surprised at how few Christmas decorations were out, nothing at all like when she was growing up in New York. The one or two businesses that sported lights were about as polished and appealing as a Charlie Brown Christmas tree.

"So you finished your classes finally? How'd they all go?"

Kennedy sighed. She knew Carl would find a way to get her talking, so she may as well stop resisting and get it over with. "I ended up getting an extension for my chemistry final." She told him about her episode during the test. "I felt pretty stupid when I heard they caught Vinny. I mean, I should have been ecstatic with news like that, but really I was just embarrassed."

Carl didn't respond as he whizzed right over a speed bump. The car jostled and made a loud scraping sound that made Kennedy wince.

"So I had to make an appointment at the clinic to get a medical excuse, and the guy I talked to thinks I should have some counseling when I go back for spring semester."

Carl looked over at Kennedy and rushed through a yellow light. "Really? What kind of counseling?" There was a strain in his voice that made Kennedy even more uneasy.

"Something to do with PTSD. You know, probably thinks I'm still not over the whole thing last fall."

"And are you?"

"Traumatized?" She had to fight off her indignation. "No. It could have been a lot worse."

"No, I mean are you over it?"

Kennedy was shaking now. She hoped Carl didn't notice and hugged her arms across her chest. "I mean ... I don't know. I'm trying to move on. That's all."

Her throat constricted.

"I've been praying." Her voice was defensive, but she didn't care. "And reading my Bible. A lot. And I know that if I keep that up, I'm going to be fine. I don't need to sit on a couch and talk with some shrink about what happened."

She sniffed. *Please don't cry*, she begged herself. That was all she'd need to convince Carl she was as big of a basket case as everyone else thought. Tears spilled out from the corners of her eyes, but she looked out her window and refused to acknowledge them.

Carl was silent. The radio talk show host was drawling on about something or other in the Middle East, and then the next minute he moved on to the American public school system. Didn't Carl realize there were at least a dozen stations playing Christmas music this time of year? Kennedy remembered teaching carols to the North Korean refugees who lived with her family in China. On Christmas Eve, they had all sung a Korean version of *Silent Night* a capella in the den, and the sound had given Kennedy chills.

A small black car revved its engine as it sped past them, swerving in its lane, and Carl muttered something about crazy Boston drivers. The radio host was complaining about a new tax proposal when Carl finally spoke up, his voice soft and subdued. "The Bible never says you have to forget something to heal from it."

Kennedy wiped her nose on her sleeve.

"God promises healing, but sometimes that can take years." Carl handed Kennedy a Kleenex. "Sometimes, it doesn't come until the afterlife," he added, almost to himself.

"I just wish that ..."

Kennedy stopped herself. Wish what? That she had never gotten abducted? That her dad didn't constantly freak her out with his safety paranoia? That her roommate hadn't given Kennedy's room number to the one person connected to her kidnapping who remained at large?

"I just wish I could go home." A tear splashed onto her seatbelt buckle.

Carl slowed down and passed her another tissue. "You've had a rough semester. It would have been hard for you even without getting kidnapped."

Kennedy wished people would stop using that word. She didn't need to be reminded of what happened to her last fall. Her nightmares did a good enough job of that.

Carl slowly curved the Honda up an overpass ramp. "You shouldn't be hard on yourself. Just because you're a Christian doesn't mean you ..."

The black car in front of them slammed to a stop. There was a terrifying crunch accompanied by a jolt. Kennedy sucked in her breath as Carl's forehead bashed into the steering wheel.

CHAPTER 14

"Are you all right? Is anything broken?"

Kennedy had never heard Carl sound frightened before. They were at a dead stop in the middle of the overpass, but he shot his hand out across her chest, as if he wanted to shield her from the impact several seconds too late. The wipers turned on automatically and screeched loudly against the dry windshield.

"I'm all right." She was a little sore on her shoulder where the seatbelt had seized up, but she didn't think she was injured.

There was a small cut on Carl's forehead, but he opened the door and stepped outside. "I'm gonna see if the other driver's all right. What in the world ..." He slammed the door in the middle of his sentence and walked up to the car ahead, smoothing down the front of his coat.

Kennedy opened her door and hopped out, too. If the driver was hurt, Carl might need an extra set of hands. She patted herself down and checked Carl's fender, which was obviously dented, but at least it hadn't buckled all the way in. Good thing Carl hadn't been driving any faster.

The wind rushed across the top of the overpass, and Kennedy took a few steps away from the edge so she wouldn't lose her balance. She was about to join Carl when the door to the black car ahead opened, and a muscular, slightly balding man jumped out.

Gino.

Her body whipped around and started running before her mind had fully processed the danger. She wasn't about to wait and see if Carl's Honda started up after slamming into Gino's car. She sprinted right past it and hurried down the ramp. There were no sidewalks here, but it didn't matter. She had to get as far away from him as possible.

And then she'd need to find someplace to hide.

Cold, wind, and panic were foreign to her now. Her lungs ached, but she didn't dare slow down or look back. She thought she heard Carl calling behind her, but she couldn't be sure. He was probably worried, probably would attribute her actions to another attack. It didn't matter anymore what he thought. If only this were another episode. She would face shame and humiliation every day of her college career to learn this was another phantom her mind had conjured up.

Maybe the other times were just ghosts from her trauma, but this was different. Her mind was surprisingly clear. There was no coughing, no choking, no sobbing like in the science hall. No, this wasn't some psychological hiccup.

This was real.

She had never driven in Cambridge before. She didn't even have a license. She hadn't been paying attention when Carl was driving and had no idea what street she'd be on once she got down off the overpass ramp. It didn't matter. As long as she got to safety, she didn't care where she was.

The street was mostly bare, no houses, only a few storefront businesses that were all closed for the night. Traffic was slow, but there were headlights ahead. Should she flag someone down? What if it was one of Gino's men? What if they had been following for backup, and now they were coming straight toward her?

Tires screeched and squealed on the overpass above. The wind moaned and whipped past her cheeks. She had to stay alert. She could run underneath the overpass, but that would be an obvious hiding place. The sidewalk was lined with streetlights. Why couldn't the city conserve energy at night like they did near her grandma's house in upstate New York?

Her options were limited, but the worst plan of all was to stay put. She had to keep moving. She thought she heard a crash behind her but couldn't slow down to look. *Just move. Just move.*

Her hair had fallen out of its clip and was smacking her face. She would never buy another pair of winter boots again — no matter how cute or stylish — without checking first to see how well she could run in them. There was a side street just ahead. If she could get to it ...

She strained every muscle. Forced her lungs to push through the pain. *Please, God. Just give me a little more strength.*

Her feet pounded the pavement, shooting fire up her shins as she rounded the corner onto a little residential road. This was perfect. Backyards. Fences. Even a doghouse a few homes down. Any shelter would do if it hid her from Gino.

She slowed her pace. The rest of her body was hot and sweaty from running so hard, but her face was raw with cold. Her leg muscles and lower back ached. How many times had she run in the past twenty-four hours?

Warm shame melted the icy cold on her cheeks. What if ...?

No, this wasn't like the other times. That really had been Gino getting out of that car. She had seen him once on the subway. She had seen his picture again online. She couldn't have made a mistake like that.

Could she?

And what about Willow? Willow said she recognized him, so it wasn't all in Kennedy's mind. He really was after her, right? Or what if her own paranoia had rubbed off on Willow, as well? Had her dad been giving Kennedy so many safety speeches that her roommate got infected, too?

What would she say to Carl?

Carl.

Where was he? She had just left him. She had just run right past ...

The sound of gunfire. She had never heard it before in real life, only in Willow's silly video games and the movies she watched with her dad, but there was no mistaking it. Were they shooting at Carl? Her feet took off beneath her, thrusting her forward. If she could just make it to that dog house ...

The sound of tires squealing. A car taking the corner way too fast. She wasn't going to make it in time. The light from the headlamps caught her, and she skidded to a stop, too petrified to keep running, too frightened to turn and face him. In her periphery, she caught sight of the little black car pulling up along the curb.

She listened to it stop, forced herself to turn, and quivered as Gino strolled out as if he had all the time in the world, swinging his gun back and forth in his hand. What would he do? Make her kneel with her hands behind her head? Shoot her execution-style? What if he abducted her again? What if they took her somewhere ...

The loud blaring of a horn broke Kennedy's fear-induced paralysis, and the crumpled front end of Carl's Honda whizzed toward her. She dashed across the street, but even as she ran, she knew she wouldn't make it in time. Gino would shoot. He would kill her.

Crack.

She prayed the noise of the gun firing would wake up someone in the neighborhood. They would call the police, check the license plate, maybe get the entire scene on video.

"Get in!" Carl shouted at her, and she scurried around to the passenger side and flung open the door as another gunshot split the air around her. As soon as she was in the car, Carl slammed on the gas, and they jolted ahead.

"Buckle up." His voice was rigid. His whole body radiated tension as he leaned forward and gripped the steering wheel. "I haven't driven this fast since college."

CHAPTER 15

The Honda lurched forward, squealing ahead of Gino.

"He had a gun." Kennedy was breathing hard, her brain branded with the image of the firearm swinging low in Gino's hand.

"Take a deep breath and calm down," Carl told her. How could he talk about calm at a time like this?

"But he had a gun."

Carl swerved around a corner. "So let's be thankful we're both alive and focus on staying that way."

He yanked the steering wheel the other way, and Kennedy was thrown against her door. The wipers still smeared across the windshield.

"Sorry about that," Carl muttered.

"Do you know where this road leads?" Kennedy held onto the bottom of her seat.

Carl glanced in the rearview mirror. "Looks like we're gonna learn."

He turned down the next side street and clunked over three speed bumps. The sound of the car's bottom scraping against the pavement zinged pain through Kennedy's ears all the way to the roots of her teeth. It was probably a ridiculous gesture, but she pushed down the lock on her door.

"Good idea." Carl did the same.

"Do you know how to get out of this neighborhood?" Kennedy asked after he turned down yet another road and sped past a school.

"If I had to guess, I'd say it's this way."

She wasn't reassured. "He's still following us," Kennedy announced, stealing a peak in the mirror.

"Yup." Carl sounded tense but not necessarily afraid. Since he was a pastor, did that mean he was more prepared to die than the average church-goer?

They sped through a stop sign, and Kennedy clenched her jaw. She couldn't relax it even when she tried.

Carl looked both ways before swinging out of the subdivision onto the main road. "You should see if you can get a license plate number."

Kennedy turned around, expecting to be shot in the face the moment she faced Gino's car. The Honda whizzed past the streetlights so fast that they had almost a strobe effect. She could only see one or two characters at a time but figured she could rattle them off if she had to.

"Do you have your cellphone?" she asked.

"It's in my pants." Carl adjusted his weight to one hip. This was no time to be prudish. She reached into his back pocket and pulled out his little black flip-phone. Her fingers only shook a little as she dialed. Everything would be fine. She'd call the police. They'd send the squad cars to save them in a minute. Two at most.

"It's going through." She held her breath and waited for the operator's voice.

"*We're sorry. All lines are busy at this time. Please hold.*"

It had to be some kind of joke. This wasn't customer service for some mail-order clothes catalog or online bookstore. This was serious. Life or death. And she was on hold?

"They're busy." She could hardly believe the words herself.

Carl nodded. "Must be this wind. The power's out in Medford. Our house was hit for a little bit earlier. Whole neighborhood went dark for half an hour or more."

"So people are calling 911? In the middle of the night?"

Carl was winding down one street after another, and Gino was working hard to pull up in the lane next to them.

She glanced out her window. "He's getting closer." She could see the black car in the other lane. There was no way Carl's little Honda could outrun him.

"Don't worry about Gino." Carl kept his eyes on the road.

"But he's got a gun," Kennedy reminded him. She had no idea how long Carl's old car could keep up this kind of pace and hoped the engine wouldn't give out. Were cars like horses? Could you work one until it fell over dead?

"I know." Carl's voice was calm and steady. "But he's got to focus on his driving. It's not like in the movies. You can't drive and shoot at the same time."

Kennedy hoped he was right. What would a full-time pastor know about those kinds of things, anyway? She glanced out the window right as they sped under a street lamp. The driver was scowling behind the wheel, quickly gaining on them and about to pass on the right.

"That's not Gino." Confusion slowed her mind. Her body tingled with an electric fear. "It's someone else."

The back window rolled down.

"He's in the backseat," she squealed.

"Duck!"

Kennedy could hardly hear Carl's shout over the sound of her own scream. Glass shattered on top of her as the window exploded. Shards rained down in her hair, in her eyebrows.

Kennedy screamed again as a second shot rang out.

"I'm gonna get us on Main Street. The police station's that way."

"Oh my God, oh my God." For the first time, she realized that phrase wasn't only using the Lord's name in vain. It could also be a prayer.

"Tight curve," Carl warned. He leaned into the steering wheel with his whole body, and Kennedy cried out in pain as her arm bashed against the door.

"Hallelujah!" Carl exclaimed. "We lost them!"

Kennedy glanced in the passenger mirror. The black car had missed the turn, but she only felt a slight breeze of relief because her arm was firing pain all the way down to the bone.

"You all right?" Carl asked.

Something was sticky. Something was ...

"I'm bleeding." She held up her fingers as disbelief swirled around in her gut. "I'm bleeding." She hadn't realized how terrified she was until she heard the tremor in her voice.

"From the glass?" Carl asked. His words were coated in hope that only thinly veiled his own fear.

"I'm bleeding." Her breaths became shallow. She reached up and turned on the overhead light. "I think I've been shot."

CHAPTER 16

"All right," Carl whispered. "All right."

Panic laced his voice, mirroring the panic that swelled up inside her.

"Let me just think. If I take Riverside to Governor's Ave, I can get you to the hospital. You need to apply pressure. You need to ..."

The pain hadn't been that bad until she realized what it was. The shoulder of her leather coat was torn. She couldn't even see skin beneath, just blood. What kind of diseases would infect a wound like that? She looked at her arm again, and her vision blurred.

"I don't feel too good." She had time to turn her face away from her injury before throwing up. It wasn't until her stomach was empty that she realized what she had done.

She didn't dare raise her eyes to Carl but stared at his dirty pants leg. Where was that Kleenex he had given her?

"I am so sorry," she stammered. "Here, let me help you ..."

"Don't worry about it." Carl didn't take his eyes off the road.

"I'm really, really sorry," she repeated, her fear and pain giving way to the mortification that warmed the pit of her stomach, shouting blaring accusations in her ear.

"It's ok."

She had never seen Carl so serious. Was he mad at her? Of course he was. If it hadn't been for her, he wouldn't be sitting in a smelly mess. His car wouldn't be all smashed in, and they wouldn't be fleeing for their lives. She'd be lucky if he ever spoke to her again. She'd probably have to find another church and ...

"Sandy did that, too, you know."

"What?"

"When she was in labor with Jordan and I was driving her to the hospital." His voice was lighter now. A little more like normal. "Puked all over herself, the car, my arm." He let out a little chuckle. "Man, the orderly who met us at the ER, he took one look at her, went back inside, and came back with some gloves and a face mask just to help her in the doors. Can't blame the kid."

Kennedy laughed, but the jerky motion made her shoulder hurt even more.

"We're just a few minutes away from the hospital, kiddo." Carl squeezed her knee. "You just hang tight." And then, in his comforting deep voice, Carl started to pray. He thanked God for keeping them safe and asked him to keep Gino far away from them. He prayed for the police and all those impacted by the power outages. He prayed for the doctors and nurses they would soon meet, and asked that if it was God's will they could have a chance to spread the love of Jesus to them.

He had just said "Amen" when Kennedy heard a car speeding up behind them. She turned in her seat, wincing with pain, expecting to see Gino's black vehicle.

"Oh, thank you, Lord," Carl breathed.

Kennedy never expected to be so relieved at the sight of blue and red flashing police lights. Carl pulled over and jumped out of the car, raising his arms in the air.

"Hurry!" he called, keeping both hands high. "She's been shot."

CHAPTER 17

Kennedy wanted to get out of the van, too, but there was so much glass around her she couldn't move. The police were here now. That was what really mattered. They would find Gino, put him behind bars where he belonged. Kennedy could go to her aunt's tomorrow — or was it technically today by now? When she returned to campus next month, she wouldn't have to worry about panic attacks or post-traumatic stress disorder or anything like that. Gino would face justice. So would Vinny. And she could focus on school.

Everything would return to normal, and she would be just fine.

"All right, miss, let's take a look at your arm."

A mustached policeman leaned down near Kennedy's splintered window. He shined the flashlight at her.

"Nope. That ain't glass." He straightened up, cocked his head, and muttered something into the walkie-talkie on his shoulder.

Kennedy bit her lower lip. Sure, she was in pain, but it wasn't anything the doctors couldn't handle. Nobody was freaking out about blood loss or anything like that. If her injuries were life threatening, she would know it, right? It wasn't anything like getting stabbed in the back with a four-inch blade. Her arm hurt, but what was a little pain as long as the people who wanted her dead were in custody?

Wait, they were in custody, right?

"Did you find Gino?" she asked. "The one in the black car?"

The officer lowered himself back down by the window. "Easy now. We'll have plenty of questions. But let's start by looking at that arm of yours." He frowned and mumbled something else in code on his radio. What did that mean? Did it mean she was dying? No, he'd be applying pressure if she was at risk of bleeding out, not standing there with his chin in his walkie-talkie, right?

"Did you get Gino? He's the guy they just said was another partner in the kidnapping."

"Kidnapping?" The officer shined the flashlight in Kennedy's face. "You the other girl?" he asked after a pause. "The one they picked up with Abernathy's kid?"

Kennedy nodded, and the officer let out a slow whistle under his breath.

"All right. So this Gino just started chasing you guys in his car? What were you doing out so late?"

She wasn't sure where to start. At her chemistry final? In the subway? In her dorm room? Had that all really just happened today? Or yesterday. Why did everything get so jumbled and confusing in the middle of the night?

Kennedy gave the officer a brief rundown of her evening, starting with seeing Gino on the T.

"You were on that subway? We got word someone sabotaged it. Cut the power and set off a smoke bomb to get people freaked out."

"That must have been Gino." Even saying his name made Kennedy nauseated. Her arm throbbed. "Once we got off the T, I thought someone was following me." She didn't want to admit to the police how far she had run in the tunnel. If it really had been Gino, though, how was she still here? Wouldn't he have attacked? Maybe she started running at just the right time. Any farther down the walkway, and ...

The officer frowned. "Why didn't you call the police when you recognized him?"

"I didn't know who he was. Not yet. But then I got back to my dorm, and my dad sent me the link from Channel 2 with his picture, and I recognized him then, and then my roommate did, too."

He interrupted with questions every few sentences, but eventually the entire report came out, culminating with the car chase.

"And did you get a license plate number?" He frowned again, and Kennedy wondered if he thought her whole story was a farce. Could her mind have made something like this up? She glanced at the window shards on her lap, winced as the pain deep in her arm radiated throughout her entire right side. No, this was no PTSD episode.

"I saw the license plate." She tried to recreate the image in her mind like a photograph. "I had it in my head, and then I tried calling, but you guys were busy …"

She heard the accusatory tone in her own voice. Where had the police been when she needed them?

The officer pursed his lips together in what Kennedy guessed was some sort of approximation of a smile. "Well, if you're ever in the same situation again, try shouting the number out loud."

"What, so I don't forget?" Kennedy couldn't recall a single thought that had rushed through her brain after Gino shot through the window. How could she have remembered something as obscure as a license plate number?

"No, so we can pick it up. We were listening to you guys the entire time, you know."

"You were?"

He nodded. "Our dispatch operator got on shortly after you called. At first we thought we had a hostage situation, thought you were being forced somewhere against your will and had managed to put out a call. Then we put enough pieces together to realize you were being chased, and they sent us out after you."

"But how did you find where we were?"

"Ain't too hard if the driver names you the cross streets and tells you exactly where he's headed."

Good old Carl. So had he known? Was that why he had been naming the streets?

A female officer came up to the window. Carl followed her, and Kennedy caught the gleam in his eye as a car approaching in the opposite lane lit up his face in its headlights.

"They found the vehicle and have the suspect in custody," the officer told her partner.

Kennedy let out her breath. Everyone had something to say, even Carl, but Kennedy just sat, letting relief wash over her like water from a hot bath.

The excited cacophony was interrupted by the siren of an ambulance speeding toward them.

“Good.” The policeman leaned down. “EMTs are here. They’ll get you fixed up just fine.”

CHAPTER 18

Two men rushed to Kennedy's window and started shouting questions at her.

"Can you breathe?"

"Are you able to move your fingers?"

"Do you hurt anywhere near your neck or back?"

She wished they'd just get her cleaned up and let her get some rest, but they kept up the barrage for five minutes or longer.

"All right," one of them said. "We'll get you on the stretcher and take you to the hospital. Won't take long. We're just a few miles away."

"I can walk without a stretcher."

He looked at her dubiously.

"Really," she insisted. "I'm fine." She unbuckled her seatbelt to prove her point.

"No, don't do that, miss." He held out his hand.

She ignored the gesture. "I'm all right. I don't need a stretcher."

He gave a little shrug. "Ok." He turned and called to the other EMT, "Leave it there. She's gonna walk."

"You sure?" he called back.

Why did everyone treat her like a fragile china doll about to shatter?

She swept some glass chunks off her lap and held onto the car door to raise herself to her feet. The world spun for a second or two and then settled down again. She smiled at the EMT. "See?"

He shrugged. "All right. This way." He gestured toward the ambulance.

"Doesn't that seem a little overkill?" she asked. "Carl could drive me in his car."

He turned and eyed the maroon mess. "That thing? Does it still run?"

"It got us this far."

"Well, we really need you in the ambulance. We have some paperwork to go over on the ride."

Kennedy didn't argue anymore. The sooner she complied, the sooner this whole ordeal would be over. She walked herself to the back of the ambulance and eyed the gurney, thankful she wasn't so injured she needed something like that.

Her shoulder smarted a little as she hoisted herself into the back and sat in one of the seats along the side.

The paramedic cleared his throat. "Actually, we're gonna need you on the stretcher."

"You're kidding, right?"

He shook his head. "Standard policy. It's got the best straps. Safer than the seats." He walked over and propped up the back. "If it makes you feel better, you don't have to lie down."

He was just doing his job, Kennedy had to keep reminding herself. She felt about as useless as a discarded Petri dish as he strapped her down. It was all right. Before long she'd be asleep in a nice bed.

"How you doing, sweetheart?" Carl stepped onto the ambulance platform and gave her a paternal smile.

"I'll be fine."

"You need anything?" he asked. "Want to call your mom? What time is it over there, anyway? Think she'd be awake?"

The last thing Kennedy needed was for Carl to call her parents back in Yanji and freak them out. She'd fill them in once things quieted down. "No thanks." She tried to smile, remembering she was the one guilty of ruining Carl's whole evening.

The paramedic took a step toward Carl. "You're welcome to follow us to the hospital, but we're ready to roll out, so I'll need you to hop down."

Carl folded his arms across his chest and stared at the man. "She is not going out of my sight."

He frowned. "I'm sorry. We only transport immediate family. And I, uh ... well, you, um ... You're not actually related, are you?" He glanced nervously from Kennedy with her pale-white skin to Carl's dark complexion. If she hadn't just been shot in the arm, Kennedy might have enjoyed watching his discomfort.

Carl took a step forward, puffing out his chest to hint at the kind of beast he must have been in his football days. "You don't think I could be her father?"

The paramedic eyed Kennedy once more. "He's your dad?"

Kennedy just wanted to get to the hospital. She didn't care if Carl came with her or followed in his car. None of that mattered. She just wanted to get her injury taken care of, and then she wanted to sleep for a very long time.

"Sir?" The policewoman came up and addressed Carl. "We still have a few more questions, and then you'll be on your way."

"She's not going out of my sight," Carl repeated.

The officer took a breath, glanced at Carl's hard-set face, and sighed. "We'll caravan, then. You follow the ambulance. We'll be right behind you."

Carl nodded. "Good. Because there are men out there who are ready to break every law in the book to keep her from testifying against them. She's not going into that hospital without an armed escort. Whoever wanted her dead might guess she was shot. Hospital would be the first place they'd look for her."

"Wait a minute," Kennedy inserted. Had she heard them right? Was the exhaustion making her brain fuzzy? Or perhaps it was the blood loss. She hadn't thought she had been wounded that seriously. "You said you had Gino in custody."

The policewoman frowned at Carl and then turned to Kennedy with a sigh. "We caught the driver. Unfortunately, he didn't fit the description of the suspect we're looking for."

Carl put his hand on Kennedy's stretcher. "They've got patrols out looking for Gino right now. He's probably on foot. Trust me. He's not gonna get far."

Blood drained from Kennedy's face and mingled with the bile in her gut. She wasn't going to dwell on Gino right now. What was it about positive thinking having healing powers? Hadn't she read an article like that in her psychology class? Or was it something her roommate had said? It sounded like something Willow would dream up.

Carl held Kennedy's gaze. "I'll be right behind you guys. You all right with that?" he asked.

Kennedy nodded even though she was too tired to try to smile. "That sounds fine."

After he hopped down, the paramedic swung the two doors shut. He glanced at Kennedy once and then back at his own hands after he buckled himself in. "So, wait, he's not really your dad, then, is he?"

Kennedy shook her head. "No. He's my pastor."

The young man's cheeks flushed red, and the ambulance sped off to the whining of its own sirens.

CHAPTER 19

Kennedy wished the doctors and nurses believed her when she told them she was all right. She wasn't even bleeding anymore. Why couldn't they just clean her up, tape on a massive Band-Aid, knock her up with painkillers, and let her go to sleep?

A team of a dozen or more nurses met her as soon as the paramedics wheeled her into the back doors of the ER. One shoved a stethoscope to her chest. Another clipped a plastic clamp to her pointer finger. People were shouting, running. She felt like she was on an old episode of one of those medical dramas her mom watched.

She tried to look back to see if Carl was there, but a nurse reached down and pinned her on the stretcher.

They sped her to a little room separated from the main hall by a hanging curtain. A doctor in full gear snapped on his second blue glove when they wheeled her in.

"All right." He gestured at one of the nurses. "Let's cut that coat off her."

"What?" Kennedy tried to sit up, but the same nurse held her down once more.

Another nurse reached into her pocket and pulled out a pair of scissors with a little metal ball at the end.

"Not sure how these will work." She held up Kennedy's sleeve.

"You can't cut my coat," Kennedy insisted. "It was from my dad."

"You know it's ruined already, right?"

Kennedy bit her lip while the nurse sliced away at her early Christmas present. It didn't matter, she told herself. She just wanted to get this whole ER visit over with.

"Oh, look at that."

She didn't understand the nurse's tone. Why did she say it that way?

"That's all?" another asked.

"Probably could have saved the coat."

Hadn't Kennedy tried to tell them?

The doctor gave a few orders, and everyone left except for the nurse with the scissors.

Just doing her job, Kennedy repeated to herself over and over.

"Well, looks fine to me." The doctor also stood up. "Dolores here will clean you up, and then when the police are done with whatever questions they've got, I have no reason to keep you here."

He left without any sort of good-bye. Kennedy didn't even get the chance to thank him.

Dolores set to work, spraying her wound with a big can of saline and spreading a large blob of antibiotic ointment. The area burned hot, but the pain was bearable. Nothing like when she was in the hospital last fall.

"So, you a student around here?" Dolores asked.

"Yeah." Kennedy didn't necessarily like telling people she went to Harvard. That kind of confession automatically made certain people assume she was a preppy rich kid.

Dolores kept her eyes on the wound and opened a package of sterile gauze. "Whatcha studying?"

"I'm pre-med." It sounded silly to mention here. Right now, Kennedy didn't even have the know-how to clean a wound like hers.

Dolores frowned and muttered, "That'll pay the bills."

Kennedy didn't say anything. This wasn't the first time someone had mentioned money when they found out she planned to become a doctor. She wasn't sure how much she believed the common perception that every MD was filthy rich. With all the student loans she was accumulating, she wondered if she'd have enough disposable income to buy her own white coat once she finally graduated med school.

Dolores was wrapping some brown stretchy cloth around the gauze when someone pulled back the curtain.

"Here she is."

She immediately recognized Carl's voice. She had been wondering if they would let him back here. Behind him was Detective Drisklay with his salt and pepper beard and coarse mustache.

"So, I guess our ten o'clock meeting got moved up a few hours." He took a drink from a steaming Styrofoam cup, and Kennedy recognized the scent of coffee that followed him wherever he went. She wasn't sure if he was in a good mood or not. She had never seen him either happy or sad and wondered if he even had an emotional life to speak of. "Well, since we're both here, I've got a few questions for you." He sat down on the doctor's swivel chair and whipped out a notepad.

Dolores finished her work and excused herself with a promise to come back with painkillers and Kennedy's discharge papers. Carl crossed his arms impassively by the curtain, reminding Kennedy of her childhood pet schnauzer when he tried to act territorial. Tonight might turn into an amusing memory when she looked back on it, but right now all she hoped was to stay awake to answer whatever questions Drisklay had for her.

"So, they tell me the wound was pretty superficial."

Kennedy nodded. "Just a graze."

He frowned. "You're lucky, then."

She wondered what history lay behind his hardened gaze.

"How long have you known Gino?"

"I just met him tonight. I mean, I never met him. He was just there chasing us. Oh, and before that he was on the subway."

The detective frowned and didn't write anything.

Kennedy decided to order her thoughts more logically. "I didn't know who he was until tonight. I didn't even know there was another partner involved. I saw the news before I went to bed, and then I realized I had seen him on the T earlier. Green Line."

"Which branch?"

Kennedy had a hard time keeping all the different lines straight. "Whichever one goes to the Opera House."

Detective Drisklay frowned. "That would be E."

She nodded. "E, then."

"Inbound or outbound?"

"We were headed back to campus."

"Inbound." He scribbled a little more. "And you hadn't seen him before then?"

Kennedy stopped herself from shaking her head too soon. Hadn't the man looked familiar on the T? Or was that just her memory playing tricks on her? How did witnesses in crime novels keep such great track of faces and details?

"I think he looked a little familiar, but I can't be sure."

Detective Drisklay kept his pen poised over his notebook. "So you've had previous encounters with him? Did you see him working with Vinny?"

As hard as she tried to forget everything that happened to her last fall, she couldn't get Vinny's face out of her mind. She sometimes replayed whole segments of her captivity at a time, as if a big projector screen took over her brain and went over every minute detail. She was certain she hadn't seen Gino with them.

"No, he wasn't there." She frowned. Where had she seen his face? Maybe her memories were jumbled. Maybe she really hadn't recognized him on the T. None of it made sense.

"He had a scar." Detective Drisklay rolled back his sleeve and drew an imaginary line from his thumb down past his wrist. "Here on the right hand. Ring any bells?"

Kennedy frowned. Maybe if she had more sleep ...

"Well, if you remember, we'll come back to it." Drisklay flipped a page in his notebook.

If Drisklay was anything, he was thorough. Eventually Dolores poked her head in, handed Kennedy a huge pill and a miniature Dixie cup of water, and sneaked back out. Carl even left his station at the curtain to sit down in one of the hard plastic chairs lining the wall. He didn't exactly doze, but every once in a while, Kennedy caught his eyes glossing over right before he shook his head and jerked himself back to attention.

Drisklay picked Kennedy's brain completely clean of every detail from the past twenty-four hours. Finally, he took the last long swig of coffee, which must have been room temperature by now, and stood up. "I appreciate you taking the time to see me."

It wasn't as though Kennedy had much of a choice, but she returned what she hoped was a polite smile. Where was Dolores? She was ready for those discharge papers so she could leave.

Drisklay pulled on a pair of black winter gloves. "By the way, we've got men out looking for Gino now, but we're making provisions for your security after your discharge."

Carl leaned forward in his seat. "What exactly does that mean?"

"I understand Miss Stern will be sleeping at your house."

Carl nodded. "That's right."

"We're going to send out a car, maybe two, to keep watch at your place tonight."

Carl let out a sigh. "Well, then, I'll give you my address."

The detective patted his pocket. "Already got it. The men are on their way there now making everything secure."

Carl's whole upper body tensed. "I got my wife at home."

Drisklay gave a respectful nod. "They don't need to go in or wake her up or bother your wife at all. They'll just walk around the premises, make sure any entrances are secure."

Carl glanced nervously at his watch. "Maybe I should call her." He stood up and excused himself.

Drisklay turned his attention back to Kennedy. "As for you, I imagine you'll want to sleep in tomorrow instead of coming downtown like we planned."

Kennedy was too tired to do anything but nod.

"That's fine. I'll call you around noon."

"I'm supposed to fly to my aunt's at four. Is that going to be a problem?"

Drisklay frowned and buttoned up his coat. "We'll talk about that tomorrow."

Kennedy tried to ignore his ominous tone.

A young nurse in Betty Boop scrubs popped in almost as soon as the detective left. "I've got your discharge instructions." Her voice was far too chipper for this time of day. Night. Whatever it was. She gave Kennedy a big grin. "My guess is someone's ready to go home, huh?"

CHAPTER 20

"How are you holding up, kiddo?" Carl certainly looked different behind the wheel of his Honda when they weren't getting gunned down by a crazed criminal.

"I'm exhausted." Kennedy shut her eyes. All the nurse had given her after the horse pill was some directions about changing the bandages.

"Well, the good news is we'll be home soon. And just so you know, Sandy's probably still awake," he warned. "She'll want to see for herself that you're well taken care of."

Kennedy was glad for the warning. If Carl's wife was awake, it would take ten or twenty minutes at minimum to tell the entire story over tea, but Kennedy could handle that. The Lindgrens were about as close a thing to family as Kennedy had in Cambridge, and Christmas season was a lousy time to be alone. At least Drisklay didn't need her downtown tomorrow morning so she could sleep in.

Kennedy kept checking the rear-view mirror, and she caught Carl doing the same on more than one occasion.

"You'd think we're a bunch of loons," Carl joked when they both glanced up at the same time. "Throwing glances over our shoulders every chance we get."

It felt good to laugh even about something as dangerous as a murderous stalker. Kennedy kept reminding herself about the officers Drisklay had promised to send to the Lindgrens' house. Nothing was going to happen tonight.

When they got to Carl and Sandy's, the police car was already out front. Carl opened the garage door but stopped in the driveway and lowered his window when a tall officer headed over. The man kept one hand on his belt and walked over in that special slow gait Kennedy had previously assumed was just for cops in movies.

"Mr. Lindgren." He nodded at them both through the window. "Miss Stern."

"Thanks for being here." Carl held his hand out.

The officer didn't make eye contact but kept scanning the whole perimeter while he shook Carl's hand. "We don't want to bother you any. We already took a look around. We'll be the first to know if anyone tries something funny."

Carl nodded. "I appreciate that. I'll just pull in the car then."

"Yup," the policeman replied. "You just go about your night like normal and try to forget we're here."

Carl rolled his window halfway up and paused. "Oh, if we run into problems, do we call you or 911?"

The officer lowered his gaze as well as his voice. "If you run into problems, we'll know it before you even have a chance to yell."

The answer wasn't as reassuring as Kennedy might have hoped. Still, she was thankful to be home, or at least some semblance of it. Anywhere safe with a bed was good enough for her.

Carl pulled the Honda slowly into the garage and then came around to help Kennedy out of the car. She could walk just fine on her own, but she didn't mind having Carl to lean on. Something about his closeness was reassuring. He escorted her up the garage steps and into the kitchen, where the hot smell of cinnamon and vanilla mingled together and set her mouth watering.

"It's about time you showed up!" Sandy exclaimed, wiping her floury hands on her apron. "Those men outside were making me nervous."

"Just remember they're here to keep us safe." Carl gave her a peck on the cheek.

"I know." Sandy waved a spatula in the air. "But it still gives me willies."

He reached out and rubbed the back of her neck.

"Kennedy," she asked, hardly noticing his affections, "do you feel up for some cookies and milk? I have tea, too, if you'd prefer. Oh, and these cinnamon rolls are fresh. I made them this morning."

A few minutes later, they were all seated at the dining room table with fresh desserts and mugs of hot, steaming tea. Kennedy put an extra spoonful of sugar in hers, figuring she deserved it after a night like this. In the background, the Lindgrens' radio crooned about a white Christmas, and the wind howled outside.

"Any more problems with the electricity while we were gone?" Carl asked.

Sandy took a sip of tea. "No, thank the Lord. Only that little episode before you left. I unplugged the TV, though, just in case."

Carl leaned back in his chair, and Kennedy wondered how he could be so calm. Didn't he remember everything they had gone through? Gino had tried to kill them. They would be dead right now if it hadn't been for a major dose of luck.

No, not luck, Kennedy had to remind herself. Had she even bothered to thank the Lord for bringing her through a night like this?

Sandy asked Kennedy about her semester and her finals, and Kennedy was grateful she didn't have to talk about Gino or tonight's excitement. After a little more small talk and two more cookies, music from *The Nutcracker* faded in on the Lindgrens' radio, and Kennedy strained to remember if it had really been tonight she had gone to the ballet with Reuben. She sure would have a lot to tell him when she returned to campus in January.

"Oh, you got Justice's old spot, didn't you?" Sandy pointed to the numerous nicks in the wood. "That boy would fidget with his knife the whole meal through. It's a wonder he ever grew. Boy hardly ate a thing."

"How many kids do you guys have?" Kennedy asked. When Carl led her parents' church back in New York, she remembered the Lindgrens having a large family, but she could never keep track of how many there were.

Carl and Sandy exchanged frowns and both gave different answers at the same time.

"Thirteen."

"Six."

They chuckled, and Sandy reached over to pat Kennedy's arm. "We did foster care, and then we adopted some at different ages."

"The correct answer," Carl answered with his mouth stuffed with cinnamon roll, "is three biological, three adopted, and a whole lot of other sons and daughters of the heart, even if the state doesn't recognize them."

"Well, and some of them wouldn't claim us anymore, either," Sandy added, taking a sip of tea.

Kennedy looked from one to the other but could only guess at the chaos, the heartache, the drama, the fullness, the joy that had been the Lindgrens' family life. She wondered if either one would say any more, but they were both staring at their plates quietly. Had Kennedy said something wrong? Had she opened old wounds?

"And how many grandkids?" she finally asked. Wasn't that a subject grandparents loved to talk about? She remembered Pastor Carl's office, all the hand-drawn pictures and professional portraits he had up of his grandchildren.

"Five," he mumbled into his mug.

Sandy raised her eyes to meet Kennedy's. "Six," she corrected softly. "Five here with us, and one little one with the angels in heaven."

Carl took a loud gulp of coffee and clunked his mug on the table. "That was delicious, dear." He scooted his chair back noisily and kissed Sandy on top of her head. "It's been a long night."

Kennedy frowned. Why was he leaving so abruptly?

Sandy took his hand in hers, and a tender look passed between them. "You sure?"

His face softened. "You know me, baby. I get grumpy without my beauty rest." He gave a little wink and kissed his wife once more. "Love you."

Sandy pecked his hand before letting it go. "I won't be long."

"Yes, you will," he laughed. "Just don't keep Kennedy up. Remember, she's had the hardest day of all of us."

"I'll behave myself," Sandy promised and blew him a kiss.

The floorboards creaked under Carl's weight as he shuffled down the hall.

Kennedy stared into her plate, uncertain what she had done to make Carl leave. "I'm really sorry." She kept her voice low so he wouldn't overhear. "I didn't realize ..."

"Of course you didn't, sweetie." Sandy stood up and brought the platter of cookies over to the table. She set two more in front of Kennedy without asking. "Of course you didn't." Sandy swept her hair over her shoulder and sat down with a loud sigh. "Have I ever told you about our daughter, Blessing?"

CHAPTER 21

"Carl was doing campus ministry when we met," Sandy began. "Anyway, we got married and knew right away we would have a big family. We just figured between us and the Lord we had plenty of love to share, and that's what we wanted to do.

"So our first two kids were born while Carl was serving as a campus minister, and our youngest came when his daddy was just starting seminary. Well, like I said, we thought we'd keep on having more and more, but I had some complications delivering Justice. Pretty major ones, actually. So we knew God had closed the door for us, at least biologically speaking.

"Well, it was right around that time when I read a report about Romania and the orphans there, and I showed it to Carl, and we both decided that was the next step for our family. We wanted to do everything just right. I talked with some folks who had adopted from overseas, read up on the subject. Prayed our heads off. I still remember the day I walked the kids to the post office to mail out our application packet. I was more nervous than I had been on my wedding day. And I was talking to the kids — they were still little, but we talked about it all the time. Talked to them about how we could open our home to a new brother or a new sister, and they had so many questions, and our little girl Bridget wanted to know what orphanage *she* had come from, which of course led to all kinds of interesting discussions."

Sandy smiled at the memory. "And then we waited."

Kennedy remembered how hard it was waiting to hear back from all the colleges she applied to. That had been torturous enough.

"Three weeks later, we got our notice in the mail." Sandy glanced down at the table and ran her napkin over an imaginary smudge. "The adoption agency declined our application. Romania wasn't open for interracial couples to adopt."

Kennedy leaned forward in her seat. "What? That's ridiculous."

Sandy shook her head slowly. "The sad thing was, after all we had been through already, neither of us were that surprised. Disappointed ... absolutely. Felt like one of our children was stolen. But surprised? Well, let's just say Carl and I had seen a lot worse by then."

"Like what?" Kennedy had studied the American Civil Rights movement in high school, but it always felt like any other period of history — long-ago events that only historians and a few great-grandparents remembered or cared about. She counted back the decades. Had Carl and Sandy lived through that tumultuous mess?

Sandy sighed loudly. "Oh, it's no secret what we've been through. But it's not necessarily the happiest of subjects."

Kennedy took the hint and tried to remember how the conversation had turned down this depressing rabbit-trail in the first place. "Well, what about your daughter?" she asked. "Blessing, you said her name was?"

A smile shined through the darkness that had obscured Sandy's face. "That's right. Blessing. See, after the whole Romania incident, we stopped thinking about formal adoptions. We figured until the world was ready to give us the same parental rights they gave any other adoptive family, well, we weren't going to put ourselves out there to get hurt dozens of times all over again." She chuckled. "So we became foster parents."

Kennedy didn't know what was so funny about the remark but offered a little smile.

"Well, that first year I forget just how many kids we had. See, some were through the system, but then others heard we had an open-door policy, and boy, did we see some beautiful children those first years. Our own kids loved it. They were all little social bugs. All loved having temporary brothers and sisters to live and play with. Always cried when they left. All of us did."

She glanced down the hallway at the long rows of photographs before continuing. "Anyway, like I said, at that point we weren't looking into formal adoption. We just figured the Lord would send us the kids that needed a home, and we'd take care of them for however long God needed us to. Well, it wasn't as easy as all that. Politics, CPS, ugly custody battles ..."

Her voice trailed off. Kennedy didn't know much about the foster system but sensed it must be trying to bring in kids like that, never knowing how long they'd stay, never knowing what kind of baggage they carried with them.

"Anyway, we got Blessing when she was twelve years old. We had just started the Redemption Temple church plant in New York at that point. Times weren't easy, and money was especially tight that year, but we got the call and knew we had to take her in. Her mom had been out of the picture for years. Dad had never been in the picture from as far as we knew. Wasn't even listed on the birth certificate. She had been living with her grandma somewhere upstate, and from what we could gather, her grandma was a decent, God-fearing sort. Well, when she died, Blessing got passed from one relative to the next. Happens so often. And let's just say that being someone's aunt or uncle or step-dad's ex-sister-in-law doesn't make you qualified to be a guardian. By the time we got Blessing, she was so broken. So broken, so hurt ..."

Sandy stuck out her finger to touch a cinnamon roll. She made a comment about them getting cold and would have gotten up to reheat them if Kennedy hadn't declined multiple offers for seconds.

"Anyway," Sandy went on after Kennedy finally convinced her she was full, "she came to us, and we knew she was ours. Not that we didn't love the other foster kids who came to us. We did, and even if I say so myself, I think we did right by most of them. But Blessing was different. We knew — just as sure as we knew Bridget and Jordan and Justice were ours — that Blessing belonged in our family.

"It didn't happen right away, and later we realized how lucky we were that it happened at all, but we adopted Blessing when she was fourteen. She was a lively little thing. Lively and headstrong and stubborn, and we loved her to death. She had some problems with the church youth group. Said she thought the people there treated her like a charity project instead of a person, and looking back, I think she was probably right. I think there were things we could have done differently for her if we had really known. But none of us understand these things going into it, right?"

Kennedy nodded even though she had never been in an even remotely similar situation. The closest experience she had with guardianship was when her friend in high school asked her to watch over her fruit fly specimens in the lab while her family went on vacation to Germany for a week.

Sandy poured more tea into both their mugs before continuing. "Well, when she was sixteen, she ran away. We hadn't been fighting. There weren't any boyfriends, not that we knew of. She just had the heart of a runaway. We looked and looked. Redemption Temple even gave Carl a three-month sabbatical. We went everywhere. When we finished searching the city, we went up and down the East Coast, following leads, not finding anything. It was Carl who did most of the travelling, actually. I had to stay home with the other kids. We had adopted another little boy by then from the foster system as well, and we just couldn't uproot everyone to go looking in crack holes, if you'll pardon my language."

Kennedy had to take a sip of tea to hide her bemused smile.

"We finally found her right under our noses in Manhattan. With the exact same uncle who was the reason she finally ended up in foster care in the first place. They were both homeless, living in some kind of tent neighborhood somewhere near Alphabet City. Carl never told me all the details. They were too gruesome. He knew as her mom I just couldn't handle them all.

"She was strung out. Addicted to all kinds of street drugs. God knows how she and that uncle of hers were supporting their habits. I have my guesses, of course, but there are some things better not asked. So Carl found her, but he didn't drag her home. He didn't beat up the uncle, but God knows he deserved it. He just asked her, 'Sweetie, d'you wanna come home?' Simple as that. He'd been a pastor for quite some time now, and he knew a thing or two about those kind of addictions and how they work. You don't just save someone who's not ready to be saved."

Sandy stirred her tea while she spoke. "And Blessing told him no. No, she didn't want to go home. Didn't want to go back to the rules and the snobby youth group kids and the stuffy church where she was expected to act like a perfect pastor's kid. Redemption Temple was like that back then. I don't know if you remember very well. Really, I would have felt the same way probably if I had been in her shoes. So Carl told her, 'We love you, we're glad to know you're safe, and would you mind giving us a call maybe once a month or so just so we don't get too worried?'

"So he came home, and I have to tell you I wasn't as level-headed about the whole thing as my husband. I resented him, truth be told. Back then I didn't understand why he didn't just drag her home. She was our daughter. She belonged with us. It wasn't a pretty time in our marriage."

Kennedy had a hard time picturing the Lindgrens really struggling in that area. For as long as she had known them, they were affectionate and doting, much more romantic than her own parents ever were.

"Well," Sandy continued, "I finally decided all I could do was pray. We needed Carl back home, and the church needed its pastor again. So that's what I did. I prayed. I know it never came close to what Christ suffered, but I think I've got a little more appreciation for what Jesus went through in Gethsemane after that season. A few months later, there she was, there on our doorstep, looking sad and timid and scared. Just like the prodigal, only I hadn't seen her coming at a distance or I would have hitched up my skirt and ran to her just like in the story.

"She didn't say much. We didn't ask much, not at first, at least. We were just glad to be a family again. She had to detox. I've never seen a soul suffer like that, not in my entire life. There's no explaining it, especially when it's your own daughter there, fighting her demons. And when I say demons, I mean demons. 'Course I could pray for her, help the battle that way, but the struggle really was hers. I couldn't go there with her. I would have, though. Carl and I both, we both would have traded spots with her in a heartbeat had God allowed it. But he has his reasons.

"She stayed clean the first time about four months, if I remember right. And then it was just repeat, the whole thing all over again. The disappearing. The looking, except this time Carl couldn't take time off work. The waiting. Each time the phone rings, we think it's the police calling to ask us to identify our baby girl's body in a morgue."

Sandy's voice caught, and she inhaled the steam from her tea.

"And then she'd come home, always more broken than the last time. The detoxes were just as awful, just as soul-wrenching to watch, but it was easier now for her to go back. Easier to relapse. But it was easier to find her, too. She always ended up with the same crowd. Same bad-news uncle. Same sad story all over again."

Kennedy didn't know what to say. It made everything she suffered during her first semester of college sound like a carousel ride.

"Well, I'm probably making it out a lot more awful than it was, but really there were good times, too. When she was clean, she was great to be with. Good company for me. We were taking in a lot of medically-fragile babies back then, and I honestly don't know how I could have survived without her smiles. She'd get up early to make my morning tea, and we'd have a few minutes together quiet before the babies woke up. But all it took was one trigger, one bad day, one phone call from an old friend, and she'd be out of our lives for months.

"We did everything we could think of. We tackled the problem from every angle. Took her to counseling. Took her to a deliverance ministry team from a church in Waltham. Sent her for eight months to a Christian girls' home in Vermont. That's probably the longest she stayed clean.

"It was when she was in Vermont that she wrote to tell us the real reason she ran away that first time. She was pregnant, just some boy at school Carl had warned her to stay away from, but she hadn't listened. And she was scared of what those church ladies would say, and looking back at how the women of Redemption Temple used to be, well, I don't blame her. And so instead of taking the problem to Carl and me, she ran off and took care of it herself. Thought she found the easy fix, but she was scarred. So scarred.

"That's how Carl and I got involved in pro-life ministry, actually. We wanted to understand what Blessing was going through. We really did. Back then, people didn't talk about things like post-abortive syndrome. I had never heard the phrase. But we realized if Blessing was suffering something that awful, how many other girls were, too? And then, we got to thinking, we were really grieving that baby we lost. It wasn't just Blessing who lost a child. We lost a grandbaby, too. Our first grandbaby. A grandbaby we would have loved and cared for and even helped raise if Blessing had just asked us. And we were grieving, which got us thinking that other moms and dads and grandmas and grandpas were probably going through the same thing.

"That girls' home in Vermont was really good for her. Taught her to take responsibility for her own actions, but they also helped her find healing from some of the things in her past. Things that had happened to her early on that no child made in God's image should ever have to endure. Really good folks. We still support the ministry there. That's how highly we think of them. Anyway, she almost made a whole year in Vermont before she crashed, but when she finally did, it was worse than all the other times combined. Reminds me of that story of the demon who leaves a house and then returns with seven other friends, all stronger than the first. We went a few years not even knowing if she was alive. She was twenty before we heard from her again."

Kennedy shook her head. No wonder her own dad freaked out so much at the thought of sending her off to college alone. "What's she doing now?"

Sandy smiled. "She's living in Boston. Got a job at a bank. Been working steady there for four or five years now. Just got promoted last fall. She's the assistant branch manager, or something like that. She's dating a nice young man. They're living together, but I told Carl after all she's gone through, we're not going to make a big deal about that. She's got a little boy. He's five. I watch him three days a week." Sandy leaned over and pointed down the hall. "That's his picture right there. First one in the middle row."

Kennedy smiled at the portrait of a precocious-looking youngster in a three-piece suit. He had his hand on his hip and a smirk on his face that yelled mischief. Kennedy guessed he kept Sandy's hands plenty full when he was over.

"He's a sassy one," Sandy mused. "Spoiled, too, but bright as a lightbulb."

Kennedy looked down the long hallway of photos, wondering how many other stories lay behind each one. She was about to ask how many foster kids they had taken in all together when Carl's voice boomed from the back room. "Princess, you need to let that poor, exhausted child get her sleep."

Sandy pouted. "I suppose he's right. You're probably tired, aren't you? Ready for bed?"

"I think that sounds like a good idea."

Sandy scooted her chair back. "You know where the guest room is. I left a nightgown in there if you want and a dress you can wear in the morning. It's loose. It shouldn't bother your bandage one bit."

"I really appreciate everything you've done."

Sandy waved her hand in the air and made a little *pshaw* sound. "Don't mention it. Oh, I should have asked you earlier. Do you want me to find you a toothbrush?"

All Kennedy wanted to do now was sleep. "It'll be all right for just the night."

"You sure?" Sandy put her hand on her hip and eyed the empty plate. "That was a lot of sugar."

"Yeah, I just don't want you to worry about ..."

Before Kennedy could complete her thought, Sandy was two steps down the hall. "No trouble at all, sweetie. Just stay there. It won't take me more than a minute."

Kennedy slumped down in her chair, figuring she could probably fall asleep right there if Sandy took too long. She always knew there was something special about the Lindgrens' home. Every time they had her over for dinner, or when she had spent a long weekend here recovering from her injuries last fall, she had noticed its peaceful, welcoming feel. At the time, Kennedy thought it was just because she was so homesick, and the Lindgrens were the only people she knew before arriving at college. Now she wondered if there was something more to it, if Carl and Sandy's generous and hospitable spirits just made the place seem inviting to everyone who came in. A house with spare toiletries just in case someone needed a place to stay.

Sandy padded down the hall, holding out a toothbrush and travel-size tube of toothpaste. "Here you go, sweetie. I told you it wouldn't take long."

CHAPTER 22

Sandy gave a good-night hug. Kennedy wouldn't have been totally surprised if she had offered to tuck her in bed. Kennedy went to the bathroom to brush her teeth and heard Sandy padding down the hall in her fuzzy slippers. She felt like she was already sleepwalking by the time she made it to the Lindgrens' back room. They kept the bed ready at all times, day or night, to welcome the tired and needy. Kennedy wondered how many others besides herself had found shelter here in this past year alone.

It was late. Kennedy shut her eyes. She didn't even have the energy to change into Sandy's nightgown. All she wanted was to sleep. To sleep and forget that tonight had ever happened. She would do things so differently if she had a chance to start her college career over again. So differently. She had flown to the States with so many plans. So many expectations of what her college experience would be like and what she'd get out of it. Her high-school self had fantasized about meeting a boy, falling in love. She had quickly discovered there simply wasn't time for romance, not for a pre-med student like her. Reuben was the closest thing she had to a ...

No, she didn't want to think like that. He was such a good friend. So encouraging. So fun. His humor and easy ways made him the perfect juxtaposition to her uptight personality, which is why they got along so well in the lab. He was a great study partner. A great friend, really. And she didn't want to ruin that by dwelling on ...

She snuggled under the blankets but couldn't lie on her right side. Her arm wasn't throbbing anymore, but it still smarted when she adjusted her position, as if the skin was being stretched too far apart near the wounded area. If she could just get to sleep, her body would forget about the pain. She could spend hours in blissful delirium.

It was so quiet here compared to the Harvard dorm. No students stomping by. No voices in the hall. No music or shouting from the other rooms. Kennedy thought back over her first semester. Academically speaking, everything had gone pretty well. Everything except her chemistry final, at least. The only class she wasn't totally sure about was calculus, but most of that was her TA's fault, since he expected her to show her work a different way than she had learned in high school.

Harvard hadn't been exactly what she expected. She figured a school like that would have a large Christian group, but she only went to one worship gathering early in September. The songs were all unfamiliar, and none of the students introduced themselves to her. She hadn't gotten very well plugged in to Carl's church, either, but part of that was her own fault. Sundays were just so busy with study groups and lab write-ups and catching up for her literature classes. That didn't mean she wasn't making time for God, though, did it?

Was that why she was still having a hard time getting over everything? Was it because she hadn't been as faithful going to church as she should? St. Margaret's was just so different from what she was used to back at her parents' home. Each time she got back to campus after going to Carl's church, she had to sit and read for an hour or two just to unwind. It was like sensory overload, with the loud music and the dancing video screen. And so many people. How could anyone even get to know anybody at a church that size?

Still, a command is a command. Maybe that's why she was still struggling so much. She had gotten really consistent with her prayer and Bible study, which made her wonder why God still hadn't taken her problems away. Was God waiting to heal her — to help her truly forget the trauma of last fall — until she made church attendance a higher priority?

Well, if that's what it took, she'd be there every week without fail. She just wanted to move on.

Her arm ached. She didn't know if the horse pill from the ER was wearing off, or if her conversation with Sandy had been enough of a distraction to keep her from the discomfort. She should be thankful. It was a minor wound as far as bullet injuries go. That didn't take away the burning though, the smarting that throbbed and radiated throughout her whole upper body. Pain seeped through her veins all the way to her spine. No matter which way she turned in bed, she couldn't ease the sting.

Tylenol, maybe? The nurse told her she could take some over the next few days for the pain, but Kennedy hadn't thought to ask how soon she could take one after swallowing that monstrous tablet in the ER. She had assumed she would get to the Lindgrens' and sleep straight through the night. Well, the nurse hadn't advised her against taking something.

She sat and rubbed her eyes to clear her fuzzy vision. She was dizzy. Why couldn't her body just relax? She hated to think of bothering the Lindgrens, but she needed something to help her sleep. Maybe they kept something in the medicine cabinet. Her legs were heavy as she walked to the bathroom. It felt as if the night would never end. She was thankful for the food and warm tea in her belly, but she would have preferred it if her dad hadn't called her back at her dorm in the first place, if Gino had never found out where she was, if none of this had happened at all.

She imagined telling Reuben about it over pizza and Coke in the student union. It would be old news by the time she saw him again. Maybe she'd even relate the whole story without shaking.

She rummaged quietly in the bathroom cupboards, wishing for a robe or extra blanket to ward off the winter chill that hung all around her like condensation on a lab flask. No medicine there. The kitchen, maybe? She sneaked down the hall, unwilling to bother Carl and Sandy, and looked at the microwave clock. Not quite three in the morning. What was she doing awake? Even her busiest nights studying for a test or finishing off a research paper on campus almost always saw her in bed by this time. Exhaustion clouded around her head like a thick New England fog, but she was also jumpy, as if she had gone to bed after drinking a full cup of coffee. Was it something in the medicine from the ER? The stress of the night? The danger that lurked in the dark corners of the Lindgrens' house?

She pulled back the blinds of the kitchen window. The police car was still parked out front. She couldn't see the men inside, but took comfort knowing they were there. Nothing could hurt her now. Nothing could get her here.

"Stop right where you are, or I'll shoot."

The words chilled Kennedy's blood. The back of her neck tingled as she turned slowly around.

"Kennedy?"

The surprised look on her pastor's face might have made Kennedy laugh if he hadn't been pointing a gun at her. He quickly lowered the weapon.

"I'm sorry," he was stammering.

"It's all right."

"No." He held up his hand. "No, I just got so nervous with those cops out front, and then, well ..."

Kennedy just wanted to get his mind off his own embarrassment. After all, she was the one who had brought all this trouble to his doorstep and into his house. "It's ok. What do you have a gun for, anyway?"

He shifted his weight. "That? Oh, well, it's a long story, actually. It looks more like ..."

The door leading to the garage burst open, and two policemen barged in, weapons raised. Kennedy instinctively raised her hands above her head. Carl let his gun clatter to the floor and did the same.

"Everything's ok, officers." Carl's face was nearly the shade of his Honda in the light from one of the men's flashlights.

"It was just a mistake," Kennedy hastened to explain. "I came out to look for some Tylenol, and, um, I think I startled everyone. I'm sorry."

The men looked tense but lowered their weapons.

"You got a permit for that?" the older one asked Carl.

He let out a little chuckle. "Actually, I was just going to tell Kennedy ..."

"Carl? Is that you?" Sandy came bustling in, tying her bathrobe sash around her waist. Her brown hair was in a long French braid that wound around and fell over one shoulder. "Is everything all right out here?" She stopped when she saw the officers standing near the door.

"Looks like everything's just fine, ma'am."

"Well, thank you for being diligent." Sandy gave a nod that was far more dignified than Kennedy could have offered if she had been the one in fluffy pink slippers.

The older policeman nudged his partner. "Well, if that's all ..." He let his voice trail off and tipped the brim of his hat.

"Oh, nonsense." Sandy bustled into the kitchen, threw on the lights, and opened the fridge. "Since you're already inside, you better grab a few cinnamon rolls. It'll only take a minute or two to heat them up."

The men looked at each other.

"You've had a long night," Sandy reminded them.

"You go wait back outside. I'll be out in a few," the older one said.

"I'll send extra rolls out with him when they're ready." The young man had already shut the door to the garage behind him when Sandy shouted, "Do you want some coffee, too? I have cream and sugar."

The middle-aged officer hooked his fingers in his belt loop and leaned forward on his toes. "Well, since I'm here, mind if I have a look around?"

"Go right ahead," Sandy answered with her face in the fridge. "The bathroom's down the hall and to the right."

Carl positioned himself in the policeman's way. "Now, wait a minute. Using the pot's one thing, and you're welcome to it. But searching the house, you guys need a warrant for something like that, don't you?"

Sandy stood up. "He's just trying to help us out."

"I know that." Carl gave a nod of respect. "And I'm mighty thankful for that, but it's the principle of the thing, see? Today, we let you come in and walk around for our own safety. Tomorrow ..."

"Tomorrow what?" Sandy interrupted, wiping her hands on the sides of her robe. "Tomorrow they come back to see more pictures of the grandkids?" She nodded at the officer. "Feel free to snoop around as much as you'd like. Makes me feel safer knowing you guys are looking out for us at times like these."

The officer shot a quick glance over to Carl, who nodded his acquiescence. Somehow, just being in the same room as the policemen sent Kennedy's insides quivering like the little bowls of Jell-O that Reuben loved so much.

He sauntered down the hall.

Sandy pecked her husband's cheek. "Sorry, hon, but you know sometimes you just gotta accept the help when it's there."

That was the last either of them said of their disagreement. As the policeman sauntered down the hall, Sandy opened her arms to give Kennedy a big hug. "Sorry if all the fuss woke you up. You must still be exhausted."

"Actually, I think I caused it. I came out here to see if you had any Tylenol or something ..."

Sandy pouted. "Of course, sweetie. I should have thought of that myself. And are you still hungry? We've got cinnamon rolls and more cookies, too." She frowned. "Or can I fix you some real food. Not junk."

Kennedy didn't want to be rude. Right now, she wanted to swallow a few pills that would take the edge off her pain and then go to sleep for the next twenty-four hours.

Sandy opened the fridge again and leaned down. She reached back and pulled out a Tupperware. "Carl forgot his lunch the other day. It's chicken soup." She propped the lid open and took a sniff. "Oh, yeah. That's still good. Want me to heat you up a bowl?"

"I'm fine, really. I just wanted a Tylenol if you have any."

"Why, sure. Carl, you go get that pill bottle. It's in my bathroom cupboard, hon."

A few minutes later, the older policeman left with leftover soup, a whole plateful of cinnamon rolls, and cookies to share with his partner outside. Sandy took the pills from Carl, handed them to Kennedy, and was trying to convince her to sit down for a full meal when the lights flicked off.

"That wind." Sandy reached for Kennedy's hand. "You sit tight. We've got flashlights in the drawer over here. Hold on just a sec."

Kennedy listened to the sounds of Sandy's rummaging and the wind howling outside. She was thankful she wasn't out on the streets and wondered how many children like the Lindgrens' daughter Blessing were stuck outside on a night like this.

Sandy flicked on a flashlight. "Here we go." She brought another one and set it in front of Kennedy. "Well, I guess maybe this is God's way of telling us it's time for bed. What do you think?"

"That's what I've been saying all along," Carl inserted.

The Lindgrens hugged Kennedy good-night, and she dragged herself down the hall to use the bathroom one last time before bed. Why did this have to happen so close to Christmas? She wondered if Reuben was asleep now and thought about him spending Christmas break alone in his dorm. Maybe she should call him tomorrow. Had she brought her phone charger?

After washing her hands and face one last time, Kennedy made her way back to the guest room. As she passed the Lindgrens' bedroom, her neck tingled at the sound of her name. She slowed down and strained her ears.

"... through so much."

She couldn't hear all of Carl's response, but she made out the words *police* and *detective*.

"I don't think it'll go that far. They were so close to that Gino guy tonight. They'll find him."

Carl cleared his throat. "Well, if he's still at large, she's not flying to her aunt's tomorrow."

"I know," Sandy answered back. "She'll be disappointed spending Christmas away from family."

"She'll stay here."

"Of course she will, but it won't be the same. From her perspective, I mean."

Kennedy turned to head back to her room. She had to get some sleep.

" ... gotta think about witness protection," Carl added.

Kennedy stopped.

"Don't you think it's a little early for that?"

Her pulse sped up like a rocket blasting off into space.

"... up to the detectives, obviously, but if tonight's any indication, these guys aren't going to stop until they've silenced her. Permanently."

Kennedy's mind was screaming at her to run back to bed before someone caught her eavesdropping, but she was paralyzed, as if Gino were in the house with her, studying her every move. A cat stalking a helpless mouse before it makes its fatal pounce.

For a single, impulsive moment, she imagined throwing open the door to Carl and Sandy's room and flinging herself under the blankets like she had done in her parents' bed in New York after waking up from a nightmare.

Only Sandy and Carl weren't her parents.

And this was no nightmare.

She had to turn around, but she was afraid. Was it Carl's comment about witness protection that got her so spooked?

The police were right outside, she reminded herself. Nothing could happen.

Her stomach twisted in her gut. What if Gino got to the policemen first? What if they were already slouched over in their cars, their leftover soup spilled on their laps, their throats slit like in some gruesome horror flick?

No, this wasn't a movie. This wasn't anything like that. The police were here. Their job was to protect her, and she just had to get back to bed. The Tylenol would kick in soon. Everything would look different in the morning. Sleep and daylight were cures for so many fears and anxieties. She held her breath and turned around. Slowly. As if she'd be invisible to any intruder as long as she didn't make any sudden movements.

The hall was still and lifeless. The dozens of pictures lining the Lindgrens' wall stared at her. She could be back to her room in twenty steps or less. Why was she acting so silly? She was an adult now. She didn't have to live her life in this sort of fear. She was a Christian. She had victory over fear. Over trauma. Over terror.

She put one bare foot in front of the other, feeling guilty and sheepish now for eavesdropping at the Lindgrens' door. Was she a ten-year-old again?

One day, she'd tell Reuben all about it, and they'd laugh. He could tease her about it if he wanted, but instead he'd say something nice and comforting, something to soothe over Kennedy's embarrassment.

She opened the door to the guest room. Never had a bed looked more inviting. Her arm was already starting to feel better. A placebo, maybe? She didn't think Tylenol worked that quickly. It didn't matter. All she needed now was sleep.

She shut the door gently behind her but couldn't relax. Outside, the wind howled. A tree branch scratched the window. Had the police noticed that when they did their rounds? Did they realize how easily someone could climb the tree, enter through the window and ...

No, she couldn't think that way.

The Lord is my shepherd. I shall not be in want.

Wasn't Psalm 23 supposed to make everyone feel warm and fuzzy inside?

She wondered what her mom was doing right now. She sometimes thought about her at the most random times. She stretched out in the bed, wrapping the blankets around herself. The Lindgrens kept their thermostat lower here than at the dorms on campus. Or maybe it just felt colder from the sound of the wind howling outside.

Sandy's story of her daughter had gotten Kennedy thinking about anyone unfortunate enough to be sleeping out on the streets, especially during a windstorm like this. How many teens had she passed this semester in the T station who didn't have anywhere else to go for shelter? All this while Kennedy studied at Harvard, ate three square meals a day and all the snacks she wanted until she was well on her way to earning the notorious freshman fifteen pounds. It wasn't fair. It wasn't right.

If Kennedy had learned one thing about life this past semester, it was that the world was a dangerous, cruel place full of dangerous, cruel people. Kids kidnapped. Girls victimized and abused. Families homeless. Addicts selling themselves on street corners, addicts who had parents who loved them just as much as Carl and Sandy loved Blessing.

There was so much ugliness. People suffering so many different forms of indignity. Besides Carl and Sandy, what was anyone doing about it? What was Kennedy doing about it? Sure, one day she hoped she'd become a doctor, and she'd have plenty of opportunities to help people then. But what about right now? She wasn't lifting a finger to help anyone less fortunate than she was, and the last time she tried she ended up getting kidnapped.

She shut her eyes, trying to block out the noise of the howling wind and her accusing conscience. She couldn't do anything for anybody as exhausted as she was. She would feel better in the morning. She just had to get to sleep.

Why did knowing the power was off make the dark that much more threatening? This was supposed to be her first semester of real independence. How had she grown so afraid?

She had to force her mind and her body to relax. Sandy's story about Blessing and all the hardships the family endured must have gotten Kennedy thinking too hard. Worrying too much. There would always be Blessings. There would always be souls needing to be saved. Kennedy couldn't help them all. And if she didn't focus on herself, taking care of her own body and getting the rest she needed, she wouldn't be able to help anybody.

She took several deep breaths, deliberately relaxing one muscle after another. She was finally warming up underneath the blankets. Everything was all right now. She was cozy. She was cared for. She was safe.

A noise from beneath the bed. Kennedy jostled. This was ridiculous. She wasn't a child anymore. She was sick of being scared. She shut her eyes and focused once more on her breathing.

Slow.

Steady.

She curled underneath the blankets with her back to the window. The wind could howl. The storm could rage. She was relaxed. She would let peace wrap itself around her like an extra layer of warmth. Everything was fine now. Everything was ...

"Don't move."

A hand wrapped over her mouth. She squirmed, thrashing her legs, but he leaned over and pinned her down.

"Not a sound."

Kennedy had never heard that voice before. There were no lights in the room to see his face or form. Still, she knew exactly who it was.

Gino.

CHAPTER 23

"Get up."

She obeyed. Something hard pressed up against her back. She should scream. That's all she had to do. Just scream. Scream and alert the Lindgrens. The police would come, and Kennedy would be safe.

Right?

Safe. Was it possible? No. He had a gun. The bullet would pierce her heart or lungs before she finished sounding the alarm, and Gino could dash out the window, climb down the tree, and be off before the police could give him any chase. Maybe they'd catch him, but with all the lights out in the neighborhood and the time it would take them to realize what happened ...

Kennedy held her breath.

"That's right." His voice was gruff.

She trembled a little in his grasp, and he tightened his arm around her neck.

"You run, you die."

Kennedy had no trouble believing each word. She nodded to communicate her understanding.

Her self-defense class had taught her some fancy moves to get out of a bear hold. Her instructors never said what to do if the attacker's got a gun pressed up to your back. She was so weak from fear she doubted she could have fought him off even if he had been unarmed.

How had he gotten in? For a moment, answering that one question seemed even more important than escape. How did he manage to get in here while the police were outside watching? There had to be some explanation, right? Otherwise she was dealing with something demonic and supernatural. But that couldn't be. Those kinds of things were only in paranormal novels, which Kennedy avoided as a rule. He had to be human, which meant he had to have entered the house by human means, which meant he wasn't all-powerful.

Which meant that if she was very lucky, she might get out of this alive.

A sudden urge to chuckle welled up from somewhere deep within her belly. She swallowed down the impulse but wondered where it came from. She thought of the campus doctor in his white lab coat scrawling notes about PTSD on his little pad of paper, and somehow it seemed so comical.

You think I had issues back then? You should see what I'm going through now.

The desire to laugh made its way to her chest cavity, bringing a lightness completely foreign to her.

Who needs a psychoanalyst? Just get me some laughing gas.

No. That was fear talking. Hysteria, maybe. Something was trying to take over her brain. It must be some defense mechanism or other, some primitive instinct designed to shield her from the horrors of death. She wondered how evolutionists would explain it. How in the name of natural selection could people evolve to actually laugh in their final moments before their murder? Sure, it might make their death seem less frightening, but it certainly wasn't a trait they could pass on to their offspring from the grave.

Her body was shaking in silent heaves. If she had been brave enough to actually make noise, she wasn't certain if it would sound more like laughter or sobbing.

Gino kept his iron grip around her neck. "We're going to the garage now. No sudden moves. No noise, or I kill you and your friends here. Got it?"

Kennedy nodded. Hadn't she read dozens of scenarios just like this in all the mysteries and thrillers she used to devour in her free time? In not a single one of them had the hero or heroine fallen prey to a laughing fit.

Yet another reason to cross those books off her Christmas reading list.

"Now open that door real slow." His breath was hot on her ear, and her body went rigid. The shaking fit eased up, and for a moment her mind was clear.

He was going to take her to the garage.

And then he was going to murder her.

She didn't think her limbs would respond, and she observed herself with a somewhat detached curiosity as her hand reached for the bedroom doorknob, turning it slightly. She winced, hoping it wouldn't squeak.

"Down the hall." Gino's voice had an almost hypnotic quality, as if Kennedy were a sleep-walker. No, maybe someone already half-dead. Something out of those zombie movies Willow liked. She could carry out simple commands but had no real will. No real volition.

She put one foot in front of the other and could feel Gino's tense body behind her as he pushed her down the dark hall. She prayed Carl and Sandy wouldn't hear. She prayed they wouldn't come out. One false move, one scare, and they might all end up dead.

Was she ready for heaven? No, not really. There was so much more she had expected out of life. Studying with Reuben. Graduating college. Going on to medical school. Falling in love. Starting a family.

Dizziness seized her, and she reached her hand out to steady herself along the wall. She couldn't see them, but her fingers caressed the frames of so many pictures. Pictures of children and grandchildren. Foster babies. Grandbabies. Each one so precious. Each one so beautiful.

God, I want to live.

She thought about the North Korean refugees her parents took in, Christians with courage to risk their lives to carry the gospel back home. They each expressed their willingness — even their desire — to die doing the work of the Lord.

Kennedy sometimes figured by the time she was old and gray, she might feel the same way.

But not now. Not like this. Would her parents fly her body for burial in Yanji? How would you even transport a corpse overseas?

Her lungs seized up, and she gasped for air. Gino tightened his arm around her neck and pushed her forward.

Her thoughts turned toward Reuben. What would he say? Would he cry?

Reuben.

She had to see him again. She couldn't just die.

They turned the corner to the kitchen. A few more feet, and they'd be in the garage. Her self-defense instructor's voice echoed in her mind. "If he gets you in a car, your chances of survival drop dramatically."

No. She wasn't a statistic. She wasn't a victim. She would survive.

She tucked in her chin, ready to fling her head back. She paused only for a second. He might shoot her right then, but how would dying now be any different than dying in ten minutes or twenty minutes or whenever he took her to her final destination? She thought of the poem *The Highwayman* she had memorized in high school. Bess, the landlord's daughter, fires a rifle that is jammed up against her breast in order to warn her lover, sacrificing her own life to sound the alarm. It had to be now. Either she would surprise him enough to make her escape, or she would die, but at least her death might alert Carl and Sandy and the policemen outside.

Justice would be served.

She sucked in her breath and prepared to give him a head butt he would remember for weeks, even if it was her last act on this earth.

"Not so fast, buddy."

Kennedy's body froze, and her eyes squeezed shut in the blinding light of a flashlight. Gino rammed the gun even harder into her back. "What do you think you're doing?" he snarled.

Kennedy blinked one eye open to see Carl in the kitchen. In one hand was a flashlight. In the other was a gun pointed right at her.

CHAPTER 24

"How 'bout you put that gun down, boy." Carl's voice was threatening, like the neighbor's pit bull that had terrorized Kennedy when she was growing up.

She was so startled, for a moment she forgot her fear entirely and only wondered if Sandy knew how mean her husband could sound if he really wanted to.

"What're you gonna do if I don't?" Gino crouched to hide most of his body behind Kennedy.

Carl kept his gun poised at them both. "I'll give you one guess."

Gino shifted from one foot to another but stayed planted behind her. "You can't do that. What's gonna stop you from shooting the chick?"

"First of all, she's not a *chick*. She's a young woman, and a very bright and capable one. Second of all, I assume you plan to kill her anyway." He squinted one eye and took aim.

"Yeah, but ..." Gino's voice was infused with an infective nervousness. "You take me out, you take her out, too."

Carl shrugged. "Probably. But I know her soul is saved. And I seriously doubt yours is. So she dies and goes straight to heaven, and you ... Well, I'd be willing to bet my retirement savings that you wouldn't join her there."

"This is crazy, man."

Kennedy had to agree with Gino's assessment. Something was wrong. This wasn't Carl. This wasn't the pastor she grew up with. What happened to him?

"Crazy or not, you let her go, or you're a dead man, Gino."

"Dude, you're insane."

Carl cocked his head to the side. "Might be. But I won't even need to plead criminal insanity in this case. You're in my house. My house is my castle. And I'll do anything and everything within my power to protect my castle and the people in it."

Kennedy wondered how heroines in her mom's historical fiction novels could faint at the slightest sign of trauma or fear. If she could pass out on cue, she definitely would have by now.

"It's up to you, Gino." Carl talked as smoothly and as easily as if he were practicing for a Sunday sermon. Kennedy's mind couldn't take in the rest of the words. It was too real to be a dream. Maybe she really had lost her mind. She could hear Carl's voice in her head, could understand the individual words he spoke, but they didn't make any sense when she strung them together.

Maybe he's as insane as I am.

Then she had a thought. What if Carl wasn't really talking to Gino? What if he was talking to her? What if his words contained some secret code? Didn't people do that in spy movies sometimes? Kennedy could swear she saw something like that once with her dad. What was it? Morse code with the eyelids, maybe? She had to focus.

"You see, what Kennedy and I know is that none of us are worthy to go to heaven. We're all sinners. None of us worse than any other, at least in God's eyes."

Was Carl preaching to him now?

Pay attention, she ordered herself. *There has to be something in his words. Some hidden message. Think.*

"And that's why Jesus came, to be the perfect sacrifice, to take away the penalty for all our sins."

No. They were all insane. Carl. Gino. Kennedy. That's all there was to it. They had all gone mad, and somebody was going to die.

"So now's a good time to ask yourself, Gino," Carl went on, "who do you really serve? Are you willing to bow your knees to the God of the heavens, the one who made the earth and the sky and the sea and all that is in them? Or are you going to keep on worshipping the devil, the father of lies?"

He was inching his way to the side, and for the first time Kennedy guessed what he might be doing. He was distracting Gino, or at least trying to. Maybe he thought Gino wouldn't notice his movements and let him sneak around from the side to get a clearer shot. She stood with her body tense, her ears already ringing in anticipation of gunfire.

"Freeze! Police!"

Kennedy must have closed her eyes because she didn't see anything. She heard the forceful shouts, felt the vibrations of heavy boots on the floor. A scream. Someone plowed into Kennedy, knocking out her breath, tackling her and crashing to the floor.

After that, it was like she was hearing everything from underwater — a strange, high-pitched squeal humming above the muffled noise.

"You have the right to remain silent."

Was that the policeman? He wasn't arresting Carl, was he? He had only been trying to help.

She glanced over to see Gino on the floor while one of the cops cuffed his hands behind his back.

Sandy rushed up and knelt on the floor. Carl was doubled over beside Kennedy, and she realized he had been the one who threw her to the ground.

"He's been hit." Sandy's voice rose higher in pitch with each word. "Someone help. My husband's been shot."

CHAPTER 25

Kennedy had never experienced a tornado, but she imagined it must be like this, only she was in the middle, sitting right in the eye of the storm while the chaos swarmed and spiraled around her. One of the policeman led Gino outside in his cuffs while his partner knelt down by Carl and radioed the ambulance. Kennedy didn't want to look at Carl. Didn't want to face him. The bullet had been meant for her. If something happened to him ...

Sandy put a hand on Kennedy's shoulder. "You okay, hon? You didn't get hurt, did you?"

Kennedy clinched her throat shut and shook her head. No, she hadn't been hit. Only Carl.

Dear God, you can't let him die.

It wasn't fair. How could someone like Carl lie there bleeding on the floor while Gino just walked away in cuffs? Silent sobs shook her body. The world was even more topsy-turvy than she had previously imagined.

Sandy wrapped her up in a warm embrace, but it only made Kennedy feel even more wretched. She wasn't the one bleeding. She wasn't the one who had taken a bullet to save someone else. What had she done to deserve Sandy's love and comfort?

A hand reached out and grasped hers. It was tough. Calloused.

Pastor Carl.

"I'm sorry," he whispered. "I shouldn't have ..."

Sandy tried to shush him, encouraged him to save his energy, but Carl wouldn't be dissuaded.

"I never meant to scare you. You know I never would've done anything to hurt you." His voice sounded so pained. Kennedy started shaking even more uncontrollably.

"Ambulance will be here in about two minutes." It was the policeman talking. Kennedy tried to hold onto his words, but it sounded like his voice was receding and then rushing ahead at full speed. "Are you going to want to ride with your husband, ma'am?"

Sandy didn't answer.

"You can't leave Kennedy here alone," Carl breathed.

Kennedy wished the earth would just open up its mouth and swallow her up, forever burying her and her mortification. Even as he lay bleeding to death next to her, Carl was still thinking of her comfort, her safety.

Sandy took in a deep breath. "I think Kennedy and I will take the Honda and meet you there at Providence."

The policeman cleared his throat. "Beg your pardon, but the car's taped off right now."

"The car?" Sandy repeated. "Why?"

"We're pretty sure that's how Gino got in the house in the first place. In the trunk."

The trunk? So he had been inside the car while Carl and Kennedy were driving? But when would he have found the time to hide in there? While they were at the hospital, maybe? Kennedy remembered Carl talking to the policeman before he opened up the garage door and parked, safe and secure, locked up in his little castle. Only Gino had been in here the whole night. Just waiting. Just biding his time.

"I can stay here with Kennedy," Sandy suggested.

No. No, they couldn't do that. Carl and Sandy needed to be together. They needed ...

Sirens wailed outside and came to a stop. Their lights flashed through the window. Kennedy forced her eyes to focus on Carl. The top of his back was bloody, but there weren't huge puddles on the floor as she had feared.

"Is he going to be ok?" she whispered faintly as the policeman got up to show the paramedics in.

Sandy kept her arms wrapped around Kennedy shoulders. "Of course, darling."

"What's that you two yakking about over there?" Carl's voice regained some of its usual jocularity.

"Kennedy was just worried about you, that's all. I told her they'd need a whole lot more than a bullet to take my husband down."

"You got that right." Carl's laugh sounded weak, but it still made Kennedy's whole body fill with a delicious warmth. "Nobody better start planning my funeral yet. When my time comes, everyone here's gonna know it, and there's not going to be any doctors or nurses or policeman who are going to try to hold me back, I'm telling you that much. When God opens those gates for me, you bet your life I'll be speeding on my way. I might look back once, but that would just be to say good-bye to my sweetheart."

Carl and Sandy exchanged a glance that was more radiant, more loving, more passionate than any kiss from those romance movies Kennedy's mom liked to watch.

"Let's get out of these folks' way and let them do their work." Sandy helped Kennedy to her feet. "I should have asked you first if you wanted to go with us to the hospital. I just didn't feel right about leaving you here all by yourself after everything. But then again, you're so tired ..."

"No," Kennedy interrupted. The idea of staying here alone was nearly paralyzing, but she wasn't about to get in the way of Sandy riding with Carl in the ambulance. Besides, she was exhausted. "No, I don't mind staying here."

Her voice must not have sounded very convincing, because Sandy cocked her head to the side and raised an eyebrow. "We could ask the policemen. They might be able to drop you off at the ER."

Kennedy and Sandy made way for the paramedics, who were getting ready to transfer Carl onto the stretcher.

"That's ok," Kennedy replied. "I'm really tired." She didn't have to make that part up. In fact, once she got to sleep, she'd probably be able to snooze right through the apocalypse.

"Besides," Kennedy added, "I know you probably want to be with Carl. Just to make sure everything ... Just to see that ..."

"What? Him?" Sandy waved her hand in the air. "God knows his work here is far from finished. He's gonna be just fine."

"Amen!" boomed Carl's loud voice from the stretcher. "So what's the plan? You two ladies riding in style with us?"

"Actually ..." began one of the paramedics.

"I know, I know." Carl gave Kennedy a wink. "Immediate family members only."

She really hoped he wasn't going to tell them she was his daughter.

"Kennedy's going to stay here and get some rest," Sandy answered for her. "As long as you're sure she's safe," she added with a nod to the police officer.

"We'll call someone to stay in the house just to cover all our bases."

"I'd appreciate that." Sandy looked down and brushed off her floral nightgown. "I guess I better go get dressed."

A few minutes later, a silence settled into the woodwork and paneling of the Lindgrens' guest room, the eerie, almost ghostly quiet after a storm. If Kennedy had the energy to worry, she might have felt afraid. If she had the mental capacity, she might have stayed up praying for Carl's healing, but the paramedics had seemed so calm. They joked with Carl as they wheeled him out the front door. Sandy followed them wearing a quiet, beautiful peace around her like a shawl. Or maybe a crown.

Kennedy's mind spun in small, lazy spirals, the same sensation she got after staying up way too late with her dad to watch a movie. She couldn't string the whole plot together, but some of the chase scenes and more intense moments floated through her mind, letting her recapture the emotions she experienced even if she couldn't remember the details.

Her body was heavy, but her mind was surprisingly light. Maybe it was the exhaustion. Maybe it was the security that came from knowing her attackers were all in custody and there was an armed officer sitting on the Lindgrens' couch. She shut her eyes and inhaled deeply.

Never before had she been more grateful for a pillow and blankets.

Never before had she been more ready to sleep.

CHAPTER 26

The sun was streaming in through the bedroom window when the doorbell woke Kennedy up the next morning.

Her heart leaped up to her trachea for just a moment as all the memories from the previous night crashed and collided into her thoughts at once. She stood up. Who could it be?

She held her breath as she tiptoed down the hall. There was a different policeman in the living room now, and he stood and nodded at the window. "You know that guy?"

She glanced and saw the painted youth group van parked in the Lindgrens' driveway, the winter sun reflecting off its bright tie-dye swirls. She peeked through the window near the front door. The first thing she saw was the blond dreadlocks.

"Yeah, I know him." She ran her fingers through her hair as the officer fidgeted with the deadbolt on the Lindgrens' front door.

"Nick!" She smiled at the St. Margaret's youth pastor, trying to remember how long it had been since the last time she saw him.

"Sandy called me. Said you might want a ride over to Providence." His hair reached nearly down to his waist. It was always a temptation for Kennedy to reach out and give it a good, strong tug. "I tried calling your cell, but it kept going right to voicemail."

"Yeah, that's the dumb battery. Sorry about that."

Nick turned his head from one side to the other to stretch. "Hey, it's no problem. I was gonna stop and see if they needed anything anyway. It's not even out of my way to swing by here first. I can take you now, or wait in the van if you need time to get ready."

Kennedy had slept in her clothes. Her bag was in Carl's car, but she wasn't sure if the police still had everything roped off.

"I just need to use the bathroom. What time is it?"

Nick stuck his hands in his pockets. "Almost one. Did I wake you up?"

It must have been pretty obvious by the way she looked.

"Hey, don't worry," Nick added. "I would have slept in, too. Sounds like you had a crazy night."

"Something like that. If you don't mind waiting, I can be out in just a minute or two."

He jingled the keys in his hand. They were attached to a lanyard with patterns of Jesus fish and surfboards in all the colors of the rainbow. "Sure thing. I'll be in the van. I just got a new Christmas album, so take your time."

"If you're headed out, I'll check everything one last time and be on my way," the policeman replied.

Kennedy thanked him and headed to the bathroom. A few minutes later, she was in the old VW bus with Nick, headed toward the hospital. "How's Carl doing?" Kennedy was almost too afraid to ask, but the uncertainty would have eventually erupted into hundreds of worry pimples all over her body if she didn't find out soon. Had he made it through the night ok? Had he lost too much blood?

"From what Sandy said on the phone, sounds like he's doing great. You know Carl. Already invited one of the nurses to Christmas Eve service. Got another one interested in doing ultrasounds once the new pregnancy center ever gets its own machine."

Kennedy's shoulders relaxed. So he couldn't be that bad.

"What about you?" Nick asked. "You holding up all right?"

Kennedy hadn't bothered to ask herself that question yet today. She knew it would take a while to process everything she had gone through. Logically, it all sounded like great news, all except for the part about Carl getting shot and his car so banged up. But Vinny and Gino were both behind bars, and as far as she knew, there was no one else around who had any reason to harm her.

"I'm just glad it's finally over."

It was over, wasn't it? She already felt more relaxed than she had in weeks. How long had it been since she slept in so late?

Nick strummed the steering wheel as if he were playing an imaginary guitar along with his acoustic Christmas CD. Kennedy had never heard of the band, but she liked the simple, folksy sound. The bobble-head set of Peter, James, and John on the dashboard jiggled when he slowed down to turn toward Providence.

"What about ... I don't know ... all the stuff you went through earlier? Was it hard for you yesterday, reliving that all over again?"

The unseen fist that had taken residence in her gut for the past half a semester seized her insides and wrenched them in its iron grasp. So much for that sense of tranquility.

"It wasn't easy." She forced a little laugh that was far too high pitched for her vocal range. "Just pray you never have to face Carl while he's waving around a gun."

Nick slowed to a stop at a red light. "What?"

Kennedy told him how Carl had been in the kitchen, blocking the way before Gino could get her into the garage.

"He's really still got that thing?" Nick asked. "After all these years?"

"What thing?" Kennedy stared at the van's paint job through the side mirror. The kaleidoscope of colors almost made her dizzy. On her door was a scene of Moses parting a sea full of tropical fish, with surfing flamingos riding the waves.

"Oh, he never told you the story behind that gun?" Nick turned down the music. "Well, he and Sandy had their share of issues when they first got married. Stupid people would give them a hard time — bunch of racist bigots, really."

Kennedy nodded.

"Well, it got so bad in one instance, Carl got himself a license and a gun and took a firearms safety class."

"I never realized it got that bad," Kennedy admitted, trying to figure out who could have made the Lindgrens feel so unsafe Carl would have resorted to such measures.

"I know, right?" Nick asked. "I mean, when he tells these stories, it's like I'm living back in the dark ages. But they were in the south back then. And you know Carl. He'd do just about anything to protect his family."

Kennedy thought about last night, how he had dived at her to get her out of the way. How would she have felt if he really had died for her? How could she ever have looked Sandy in the eye again?

"Well, so he had this gun, and as time went on people became more and more accepting of others, so he never really needed it. Then one winter — I think it was my first Christmas at St. Margaret's — someone breaks in to the Lindgrens' home. Just a kid, really. Seventeen or eighteen, I don't remember all the details, but not a hardened crook or anything. He was just looking for a few quick things he could sell for easy money around Christmastime. I don't think he realized the Lindgrens were home. Probably thought they were on vacation or something. Anyway, Carl hears the noise in the living room, comes out with his gun, and sees this kid poking around under the Christmas tree. And the boy stands up and recognizes Carl and says, 'Aren't you that guy from that big church off the Red Line? My grandma makes me go there every Christmas.' So of course Carl puts the gun away, and then he and Sandy sit him down and he ends up accepting Christ, they invite him and his mom and his grandma over for Christmas dinner, and it's all one big happy ending. But after that, at least as Carl explains it, he decided he just couldn't be a pastor and keep a gun at the same time. He got rid of all the ammo, but he joked about holding onto the pistol just for show if he ever needed to scare someone away. I guess he was serious, though, if he still had it last night."

Kennedy was trembling again. Would she ever be able to talk about the things she had gone through without her muscles all spasming at once? It made more sense now, at least logically, how Carl could have stood there with his gun pointed at her. Part of her had known the whole time he was bluffing, but that wasn't enough to stop her insides from quivering with the memories.

"What about you?" Nick asked as he pulled the van into the Providence parking garage. "You have big plans for Christmas or anything?"

Kennedy hadn't thought that far ahead but was glad to change the subject and talk about something more mundane. "I'm supposed to fly to Baltimore to visit my aunt for a few weeks, but now I'm not sure what's going on."

She'd have to get her phone charged and get in touch with Aunt Lilian. Her parents, too. And she could only guess how many phone calls she had missed from Detective Drisklay by now. With so many meetings and deadlines and demands on her time, it almost felt as if she was still in the middle of her semester at Harvard.

The chances of her getting to the airport in time for her four o'clock flight today were pretty slim. She didn't want to leave until she was convinced Carl was better, and she had enough experience with the police department to know she'd have to answer a lot of questions over the next few days. Maybe she would stay at the Lindgrens' and help take care of Carl while he healed. There had to be some way to repay him for his courage.

Nick maneuvered the VW bus in between a flower delivery van and a pickup. Peter, James, and John kept bobbling even after he parked.

"You ready?"

She nodded. Twenty-four hours ago, she had been preparing to take her last final of the semester. Now she was about to go visit the man who had saved her life from a dangerous criminal. Out of the dozens or maybe even hundreds of thrillers she had read over the years, none of them had prepared her for the relief, the almost euphoric release that came from knowing her captors were in custody. But the joy was tarnished, polluted by the guilt that had glared her in the face ever since she saw Carl's bloody shirt. That bullet had been meant for her. How could she be happy, how could she be relieved when her pastor was in the hospital recovering from a bullet wound — a bullet wound he would have never suffered if it hadn't been for her?

"You ok?" Nick asked. "You look pretty serious."

Kennedy forced a smile. "I'm fine." She followed him toward the hospital entrance, each of her footsteps shouting hostile accusations in her ear.

The wind from last night had died down, and the sky was gray and overcast.

"I'm glad you were able to come with me." Nick let Kennedy go first through the hospital entrance.

Providence's interior was decorated with blue and silver tinsel, with large red Christmas ornaments hanging from the ceiling.

He unbuttoned his coat. "I'm sure Carl and Sandy will be excited to see you."

Kennedy wasn't that certain, but she kept the thought to herself.

CHAPTER 27

"Nick! Kennedy!" Sandy rushed toward them with open arms. After hugging Kennedy, she turned to Nick and put both hands on his shoulders. "What's the deal with this shirt? You relearning your ABCs?"

Nick grinned and pointed to the two sets of alphabets. "The first one's missing the L. Get it? The first ... *No el*. Like the carol."

Sandy rolled her eyes and tucked her arm around Kennedy's waist. "Well, at least you guys are here. Carl's been worrying about you."

"I have not," came the gruff voice from the hospital bed.

Kennedy was used to seeing Carl in button-down shirts and slacks. She was almost embarrassed to witness him lying there in the blue and white floral hospital gown.

"Come on, I don't look that bad, do I?" He stretched one arm out to give Kennedy a hug and turned to Nick. "Gonna shake you left-handed today, if you don't mind."

"How you doing, Pastor Carl?"

It was weird to hear Nick call him *Pastor*, but Kennedy couldn't figure out why. Maybe because Nick was older than she was, and she had dropped the *pastor* title almost immediately after reconnecting with him here in the States.

"I'm all right." Carl's voice was strong. Booming. That in itself sent waves of relief coursing through her veins. "Doctor said I've got a fractured shoulder blade, but I'm just thankful to be alive and kicking."

"Daddy?"

Kennedy didn't recognize the woman standing in the doorway. Her heels made her look at least three inches taller than she really was. She rushed past Kennedy and Nick to Carl's bedside.

"I got Mom's text this morning, but I'm out of sick days, so I had to wait for my lunch break." She glanced at the clock on the wall. "The T took forever. I've only got ten minutes before I have to head back."

"You didn't have to come all this way, sweetie." Sandy gave the woman a loving pat on the back. "You could have just called to talk to him."

She sniffed. "I wanted to come by in person. Make sure ... You know, make sure ..."

"Your old man's not about to croak?" Carl laughed. "Not anytime soon, babe. You're just gonna have to wait three or four more decades to get that massive inheritance check."

"Dad!" Her tone made her sound like an exasperated teenager.

Sandy took a deep breath. "Well, sweetie, now you're here. You can see your father's fine." She smiled at Kennedy and Nick. "This is our daughter, Blessing. And you remember our youth pastor, right?"

Blessing gave a little smirk and crossed her arms. "Yeah, I remember you."

Nick replied with something of a half-smile of his own and didn't say anything.

"And this," Sandy went on, "is the Sterns' daughter. You remember Roger and Juliette Stern from the church back in the city?"

"No." Blessing shrugged at Kennedy. "But I remember hearing all about you on the news."

"Well now," Sandy inserted before her daughter could say anything else, "where's Tyson today?"

"With his other grandma." Blessing glanced again at the clock above Carl's head.

Sandy frowned. "I'm sorry I couldn't watch him."

"Of course you can't. You're here with Daddy, right where you're supposed to be."

"And she won't leave me alone," Carl complained. "Keeps threatening to beat up the nurses who come in here to take care of me." He winked.

Kennedy glanced at Nick, who looked about as out of place as she felt.

"You gonna be home by Christmas?" Blessing asked.

Carl adjusted his bed so he was sitting up a little more. "You kidding me? I'm not settling for hospital food when I can have your mother's cooking."

Sandy smiled and patted his hand. "We're hoping so, at least. Doctor says they may have to do surgery."

"Pshaw." Carl waved his left hand in the air. "They're just trying to get more insurance money out of us. That's the way these bureaucracies work. Money, money, money." He fixed his eyes on his daughter. "So the answer to your question, sweetie, is yes, I'll be home for Christmas. You're coming over for dinner, right? You and Tyson and ... oh, why do I keep forgetting his name? That guy ... one with all the hieroglyphs tatted on his arms ..."

Blessing did not look amused. "It's calligraphy."

Carl frowned. "Really? I could have sworn I saw something just like it in the National Geographic special on mummies. Oh, well. Is old what's-his-name coming with you for Christmas?"

"Damion, Dad. His name's Damion."

Carl kept a good-natured tone in spite of the way his daughter glared at him. "That's the one. Keep wanting to call him Dalmatian for some reason. *Here, boy. Here Dalmatian.*"

Sandy put her hand on Blessing's shoulder. "What your father means is we'd love to have you over for Christmas dinner, of course. All *three* of you." She shot Carl a look laced with warning.

"That's right." He nodded. "All three of you."

"Good." Sandy frowned at the clock and turned to Blessing. "Now you should get yourself back to work so you don't get in trouble with your supervisor, and I'll call you to let you know if I can watch Tyson on Friday."

"All right." Blessing gave her dad a quick peck on the cheek before heading out.

Kennedy watched the way Nick's whole body relaxed when she left. Sandy let out a loud sigh. "Well, Kennedy, did you sleep all right last night?"

Kennedy felt guilty when she admitted that she had. "What about you?" she added. "Did either of you get to sleep?"

Sandy smiled. "Oh, Carl was knocked out like a baby. Whatever they pumped through that IV must've been some miracle maker. I haven't seen him sleep that soundly in ten years or more."

Carl snorted. "I told you we should have gone to Hawaii last summer, didn't I? Didn't I say we were due for a vacation?"

Sandy smiled but didn't respond.

"So we can't afford three thousand dollars for a week in Hawaii, so we'll spend our five thousand dollar deductible instead for a staycation at Providence. Food's not as good, but boy, do you sleep like a rock."

"Well, one of us does." The corners of Sandy's eyes wrinkled up when she spoke. "I was lucky to get that half hour snooze between the x-rays and the doctor consult. They wanted him to have surgery last night," she explained to Kennedy and Nick. "Make sure everything looked all right. But he said ..."

Carl waved his good hand in the air. "I said of course it wouldn't look all right if they went in there with a scalpel and started moving things around that have no business moving."

Sandy shrugged her shoulders. "So the doctor decided we could wait a few days and see."

"I still don't know what all the fuss is about," Carl insisted. "I feel fine as long as they keep that IV bag filled. I'm not dead. My ticker's as healthy as a teenager's — doctor said so himself. But the longer they keep me here, the more they can rack up the medical bills. Probably give all themselves a nice Christmas bonus, too." He reached for his wife's hand. "Remind me, hon, to wait until summer or spring next time I jump in front of a bullet, will ya?"

Sandy cast a furtive glance at Kennedy, who tried to maintain a neutral expression. "Well, sweetie." Sandy's voice sounded far too chipper for the moment. "Have you called your parents or your mom's sister in Maryland?"

Kennedy was a little ashamed to admit she had slept all the way until Nick came knocking at the door, especially after hearing how Sandy had passed her night by Carl's side.

Sandy frowned at the clock. "I guess if Nick was willing to drive, you could make it to the airport in time to catch that flight."

"Absolutely out of the question," someone interrupted from the doorway. Kennedy knew she disliked the voice even before she turned to see who was there behind her.

Detective Drisklay.

He frowned. "You, young lady, have a very bad habit of leaving your phone off when people need to get in touch with you." He had his notebook in one hand, his Styrofoam cup of black coffee in the other. "But since you're all here, we may as well get comfortable." He swept past Nick and sat down on a swivel stool. "All right. Who's gonna start and tell me what happened?"

CHAPTER 28

It was nearly dinnertime before Detective Drisklay was done grilling Kennedy and the Lindgrens. Nick excused himself shortly after the interview started, but Sandy made him promise to take Kennedy home for the evening when everything was done. Sometimes Sandy's sense of protectiveness was smothering, but tonight Kennedy was glad to stay far away from the subway stations.

"So I guess you're not gonna make the flight to your aunt's, huh?" Nick asked as they pulled out of the Providence parking garage that evening.

"No. The detective said I shouldn't go anywhere for a few weeks. There's gonna be tons of questions. Legal stuff. I guess I'm supposed to talk with someone from the district attorney's office tomorrow." She sighed. Being the victim of a high-profile crime was about as time-consuming as her premed studies.

"You hungry?"

Kennedy looked at the clock and tried to remember what she had eaten that day. Just a cold sandwich and fruit salad from the hospital cafeteria. "A little."

"Yeah? 'Cause if you are, I could take you out." Nick's dreadlocks whipped across his face as he turned to look at her and then straightened out to focus again on the road. "I mean, not *out* out, just, you know. Food."

Kennedy was exhausted, but she had to eat something before calling it a night. "Food is good."

Twenty minutes later, they were sitting at a booth in Harvard Square eating soup out of sourdough bread bowls.

"I have to admit, clam chowder is something Boston does way better than New York."

"Oh, yeah?" Nick wiped his face with his napkin. "Because I was just thinking it doesn't quite measure up to Seattle's."

"Are you from Washington?" Kennedy asked.

"Oregon, actually, but I spent a lot of time up and down the West Coast. That was back in my quasi-homeless, semi-nomadic, living-out-of-my-van days."

She raised her eyebrows. "Sounds ... interesting."

He stared past her shoulder. "It was magical."

Something about hearing an adult with dread-locks down to his waist using words like *magical* made Kennedy chuckle. "I'll take your word for it."

"Guess they don't have much surfing in China, do they?"

"Not where we were," she answered.

"Yeah, it's no good here, either, but I knew that when I moved. Just one of the costs of discipleship, right?"

She couldn't tell if he was serious or not. "Why did you end up coming out here?"

"Short answer is God got a hold of me. I was always pretty churchy, but that was just one little part of my life, you know? Like, I took math in high school because that's what my guidance counselor told me I had to do to graduate. It didn't mean anything to me outside the classroom walls. That's kinda how church was to me. After college, I sort of burned out on school. My sister, well she had been going through a lot, too. Pretty taxing stuff. So I decided to take a year or two and just see what was real. Got a beat-up van, but it took me down all the way from the Oregon coast to San Diego, then all the way back up to Seattle before I finally came back home."

He dipped a piece of sourdough into his chowder and went on talking with his mouth full.

"Well, something out there just changed me. The ocean. The waves. I don't know. God talks to everyone in different ways, right? Sometimes he uses angels, sometimes he uses a donkey. For me, it was the coast. And I knew I wanted to spend my life helping others. Kids like me, kids who were pretty decent people but who didn't really know Jesus.

"My friend was working at a home for troubled teens out in Vermont. Asked me to join on a Friday. By Sunday after church, I was on the road in my clunker. It got me just over the Rockies before dying. I stuck around there for a couple weeks, volunteered for a few churches, met some great people, and they helped me get fixed up and back on my way."

Nick took a sip of his veggie juice before continuing. "So I worked at the boys home for a few years, then I met Carl. St. Margaret's was growing faster than anyone could have guessed, and he needed help with the youth and children's ministry there, so I settled down and became a Cambridge boy."

Kennedy was trying to guess Nick's age when he asked, "What about you?"

The question caught her off guard. "Me what?"

He adjusted one of his dreadlocks that had fallen in front of his eye. "I don't know. What makes you tick? Why Harvard? Why pre-med?"

Kennedy wasn't sure where to begin. She fidgeted with a piece of sourdough. "Well, I guess I like helping people. And Harvard had their early-admissions program, so I sort of applied on a whim, and when I got in, well ... It's one of those offers you don't really turn down."

Nick didn't say anything right away, which gave Kennedy plenty of time to think of how ignorant her answer had sounded.

"I've thought a little about medical missions." Why had she added that part? Did she just want to sound more mature? Was she trying to prove that she was ministry-minded like he was?

"These bread bowls are delicious."

Kennedy nodded, grateful Nick was changing the subject.

A few minutes later, he scooted back his chair. "Hey, thanks for joining me. That was a lot of fun." He glanced at the time. "I still have twenty minutes in the parking meter. I could drive you back to Carl and Sandy's now, or we could go for a little walk."

There was something endearing and almost awkward in his expression. Was he asking her out? Or was he just being nice? A year ago, even a month ago, she probably would have been flattered. She glanced outside. The night was already dark. The howling of wind echoed in her memory. What was wrong with her? Wasn't college supposed to be all about living in the moment, being spontaneous, enjoying new people, gaining new experiences?

And she didn't want to spend an extra twenty minutes with Nick because the dark made her nervous?

Or was there more to it than that? Reuben's face flitted through her mind, the kind expression in his eyes as he looked at her with so much concern.

Nick frowned. "You know what? I forgot how tired you must be. What do you say we just head back to the van and I'll take you to the Lindgrens' now. We're not too far."

Kennedy tried to sigh away the heaviness in her chest. "No, it's not that, it's just ..." She stopped short. "It's just, I've got a friend back on campus, and I really want to call and let them know I'm safe."

"They're probably pretty worried, right?" Nick's voice was gentle. Subdued.

"Yeah." Kennedy sighed, glad Nick had picked up on her use of the gender-neutral pronoun. "Yeah, if you don't mind, I think I'm ready to head home."

CHAPTER 29

"Thanks so much for dinner." Kennedy couldn't articulate why she felt like apologizing to Nick during the ride back to Carl and Sandy's. "It was great."

Nick pulled the bus into the Lindgrens' driveway. "They make good chowder there, don't they?" For a minute, he looked like he was about to get out of the car too, but then he just gave a little wave. "Well, I'll see you around, I'm sure."

She opened the passenger door. "Yeah. Sandy said you're coming over for dinner Christmas Eve."

He smiled. "I'll be there."

"All right. Thanks again." She failed to infuse as much enthusiasm into her voice as she had intended, but she hoped she at least didn't sound rude.

"Have a good night."

"You, too."

She walked up to the Lindgrens' porch, aware of his eyes following her. It wasn't until her hand was on the knob that she realized she didn't have a key or any way to get in. She was about to wave Nick down to ask to borrow his phone when the door opened.

"Well, there you are!"

Kennedy was so relieved to see Sandy in the doorway she didn't mind the exaggerated wink. "I was *wondering* where you two went. I left Providence at least half an hour after you did." She leaned forward and waved to Nick, who was pulling the bus out of the driveway. "So you got something to eat, did you?" Sandy wrapped an arm around Kennedy's waist and pulled her in. "That was awful thoughtful of Nick. I knew he had it in him to be a romantic when the right woman caught his eye."

"We were both hungry, that's all. It's been a long day."

Sandy insisted on making Kennedy some tea, and once or twice she gave Kennedy a sly smile while she bustled around the kitchen, but she graciously didn't say anything else about Nick.

"The doctor says now Carl might be home by Saturday." Sandy sat down at the table across from Kennedy. "You know that's Carl's first thought. He hasn't missed a Sunday preaching in years."

"That's good." Kennedy's mind was elsewhere, on getting in touch with Reuben, on the Christmas she wasn't going to spend with her parents or her aunt, on the dozens of meetings and legal proceedings ahead of her. She wished she could dump all her memories onto someone else who would testify as her proxy.

"Oh, I almost forgot to tell you. That newspaper reporter stopped by the hospital looking for you." Sandy spoke as casually as if she had been mentioning a missed phone call from the friend next door. "You know which one I mean? The red-haired boy?"

Kennedy had been forced to deal with all kinds of nameless members of the press over the past few months, but one face stuck out in her memory. "Yeah, I know who you're talking about."

"Nice kid." Sandy looked at Kennedy out the corner of her eyes. "Of course, I don't know if he's a Christian like Nick. Do you?"

Kennedy buried her face in her teacup and didn't respond.

"Well, Carl insisted I spent tonight here at home and try to get some rest." Sandy lowered her voice. "Between you and me, I think he just wants the room to himself so he can watch those silly Westerns he likes so much."

"I'm probably going to go to bed soon, too." Kennedy had emailed her aunt, who had probably called her mom, who had probably left fifteen or more voicemails by now. She needed to remember to plug her phone in tonight. She almost envied Carl. People in hospitals could choose not to return phone calls and blame it on the meds or the nurses or any number of convenient excuses.

Kennedy helped Sandy clean the table, tried twice to help with the dishes, and was finally shoved off to bed with a hug and a good-night prayer that left her feeling like she was five years old again. Kennedy fell asleep right away, thoughts of final exams and detective interviews, car chases and failed assassination attempts retreating before the heaviness and exhaustion that had clung to her the whole semester.

CHAPTER 30

The next few days were a blur of meetings. With all those detectives, lawyers, and media gurus vying for her attention, Kennedy wished she could hire a personal assistant just to juggle her schedule.

Sandy was even busier gophering Carl's books and effects to and from his room in Providence. He still insisted on preparing for his Sunday sermon. The doctors weren't giving him a firm release date yet, but the chances of surgery decreased each day.

When he was finally let out Saturday evening, Kennedy rode with Sandy to bring him back home.

"I told you they wouldn't keep me from the pulpit." Carl had lost a few pounds at Providence. His chipmunk cheeks weren't quite as full when he smiled, and he seemed to boast a few more wrinkles than Kennedy remembered. Still, besides having his arm in a sling, he walked and talked and acted like the boisterous, bustling pastor she had known as a little girl in Manhattan.

Sandy stopped by the store on the way home from Providence to pick up Carl's prescription. "I'll just be a minute or two."

"Don't listen to a word she says," Carl whispered when she left. "She'll be in there half an hour if she's in there a second."

Sure enough, when Sandy got back to the car, she was pushing a cart full of grocery bags and several rolls of wrapping paper.

"Sorry it took me so long."

"What were you doing in there?" Carl asked after she had loaded the trunk. "Making plans to feed an army?"

Sandy turned the key in the ignition. "They had ham on sale."

"So you got a whole cart full?"

"No. But I had to get sides to go with it."

Kennedy loved the way Carl and Sandy always bantered back and forth. Her parents had never really been playful like that, at least not in Kennedy's memory.

"Well, it's just Kennedy staying with us. I don't think you needed to break the bank. The skinny thing eats like a bird."

Sandy waved away his remark. "It's for Christmas Eve, silly."

"You know Christmas is a week and a half away, right?" Carl asked.

She pulled out of the parking lot and patted her husband's leg. "You got to plan these things ahead, you know."

Over the next few days, Kennedy grew to understand exactly what kind of planning ahead was required for a Lindgren-style Christmas Eve dinner. She and Sandy started by making ten dozen cookies to serve the grandkids when they came to help decorate the tree. It took a day and a half to reclaim the house and vacuum up all the colored tinsel, cookie crumbs, and popcorn kernels they left behind.

When Christmas week came, Sandy and Kennedy were in the kitchen for at least six hours a day, slicing, cubing, mixing, and chopping. On the days when Sandy babysat her grandson, Kennedy stayed busy with meal prep even while Sandy helped Tyson make his mom, dad, and paternal grandmother hand-made gifts. From looking inside the fridge, you would have assumed their guest count was in the twenties or thirties, and maybe it was. Sandy was extending new invitations and modifying the guest list at least once or twice a day. She had insisted that Kennedy invite Reuben when she learned he had no other place to go, and Kennedy was happy when he accepted.

On the morning of the 24th, Sandy sent Carl out twice to the store for items she forgot but was convinced no Christmas dinner spread could exist without. She and Kennedy had already scrubbed the house spotless over the past few days, but she went over everything two or three more times in the final hours before the guests arrived. Kennedy was glad to know she'd be one of many seated around the Lindgrens' dinner table. She would have hated the thought of Sandy going through so much trouble just for her. She was a little anxious that Reuben would feel out of place, but then she remembered his hundred cousins, aunts, and uncles, and figured he'd probably be more at home than she was.

Carl had spent the past week and a half alternately teasing Sandy for her perfectionistic tendencies and trying in vain to convince her to rest or relax. Tonight, he placed his left hand on her shoulder, smiled into her work-flushed face, and declared, "Everything looks perfect, dear." He kissed her cheek. "You work harder than any other woman I know."

She paused long enough to give him a small peck on the lips and then scurried to the freezer.

"What are you doing?" Carl asked.

"I need to make sure we have enough ice."

"Leave it."

"I just want to ..."

"Leave it."

Sandy turned and gave Carl a small, tired smile. He came up and gave her a slow hug. "I love you, babe," he whispered, and Kennedy wondered if they even remembered she was there.

"I love you, too." Sandy nuzzled her cheek against his. "And you know what I could use a strong, hunky man for right about now?"

"What's that?" A playful smirk spread across his face, and Kennedy wondered if she should retreat to the guest room.

Sandy returned his smoldering grin. "You could reach up and pull that extra pack of napkins down for me."

Carl took her hand and kissed it. "Anything for my princess."

The doorbell rang.

"Oh! They're here!" Sandy sounded as excited as a little girl on Christmas morning. "I'll get that," she told Kennedy. "You just sit down and make yourself comfortable."

It would probably be a late night, and a loud one too, judging by the laughter of the two grandsons who burst through the dining room waving toy airplanes through the air and occasionally crashing them into each other.

A third boy ran in to join the ruckus, and Kennedy recognized Blessing's son, Tyson.

A few minutes later, another round of greetings heralded the arrival of more guests. By the end of the night, Kennedy would be lucky to remember half of their names. The sounds were so different from the typical Harvard din. Had she really only been in college for one semester? She was an entirely different person with what felt like a lifetime of experiences — experiences that strengthened and sharpened her, as well as some that left ugly, gaping scars.

"Kennedy!" Sandy's voice was playful and teasing. "There's someone here to see you."

Kennedy jumped up, chiding herself for feeling so nervous. It was just Reuben. It's not like they hadn't seen each other every day in class all semester long.

"Hey." There was his same smile, his same care-free demeanor.

"Hey." She was surprised when he wrapped his arms around her for a hug.

"I'm glad you're safe." He was still wearing his parka, the same one he loaned her during their ride on the T.

She gave Reuben a smile and led him to the appetizer table. Nick was in the corner and gave a quick nod. Kennedy tried not to feel embarrassed. She hadn't done anything wrong.

The Lindgrens' house was a blaze of jumbled colors. Christmas decorations hung on nearly every square foot of wall without any common theme other than cheer. Many of them were homemade and looked like they had survived a few decades in and out of storage boxes. It was all so different from what Kennedy remembered of childhood holidays at her grandma's in New York, where she was the only child amongst somber, formal faces.

It was hard to imagine how recently she and Carl had been driving for their lives, ducking while bullets shattered the window of his car. She would probably still worry when she was out at night. She probably couldn't ride the T for a while without a bad case of the shakes. She'd definitely have her fair share of nightmares with Gino's hardened face glaring at her. But for right now, she could focus on the sound of Carl and Sandy bantering playfully while wave after wave of grandkids took over the dining room, living room, and den. She could forget the smell of subway smoke and burned tire rubber and antiseptic hospitals and fix her mind on the scent of savory ham and fresh coffee.

For now, with the happy shouts and greetings quickly drowning out the sound of the Christmas carols on the stereo, Kennedy could finally relax.

She and Reuben sat down with their plates full of candies, veggies, quiches, and mini-sandwiches. Reuben took a bite before announcing, "I got you something for Christmas." He reached into his pocket and pulled out a small box.

She laughed as soon as she opened the present. "You know me too well." It was a new cellphone battery. She hoped it hadn't cost too much money.

"So you'll always have a back-up," Reuben declared with a smile.

"Well, I have something for you, too." She put her plate down and ran to the guest room. She came back with an envelope. "It's not ... I mean, I had a hard time ... Well, just open it."

Reuben tore open the envelope and pulled out the two gift cards. "Common Treasures and Angelo's Pizza?"

"It's the rain check I promised you."

He slipped the cards into his coat. "Thank you."

Sandy bustled over. "Have you two eaten yet? There's lots, so help yourselves."

Kennedy and Reuben looked at their full plates and broke into giggles. Kennedy took a deep breath, thankful that the Lindgrens had opened their home to her once more, thankful that God had kept her safe through yet another fiery ordeal.

CHAPTER 31

If Carl had teased Kennedy for her small appetite before, he'd have no excuse to do so in the future after seeing how much Christmas dinner she packed away. Only halfway into the main course, she already regretted wearing her tight black skirt. Now she understood Sandy's preference for loose-fitting dresses that didn't hug you anywhere around the waist.

Sandy had pulled out three tables, and even then there were a few guests sitting on the couches eating off TV trays. The overfull, bursting feeling Kennedy felt in her gut grew in proportion to the pressure building up in her brain from all the noise. She couldn't remember the last time she had been around so many children. Had she ever? She and Reuben remained in the corner, laughing about Professor Adell and her atrocious penmanship, giving their best impressions of their calculus TA's Korean accent. They already had plans to check out the bookstore and grab some pizza the day after Christmas.

In the middle of the meal, Carl stood up and clinked his cider glass with his knife. His arm was still in a sling, but he was dressed handsomely in a forest green suit with a striking red tie Sandy had adjusted for him two or three times over the course of the evening.

"Can I have your attention?" His booming voice carried over the dozens of smaller conversations, but it still took half a minute before he could continue.

"Two weeks ago, God took something that could have been tragedy. He took something that I know for a fact the devil would have loved to use for evil, and he brought about good. *What good?* you might be wondering." He raised his glass toward Kennedy. "All those who might have reason to harm our friend here are being brought to justice." He nodded to Blessing. "Our family's closer than ever before." He gave his wife a charming smile.

"And I've been reminded every day of my recovery how lucky and blessed I am to have this amazing woman by my side. You mean more than the world to me, babe, and I don't say that lightly."

He kissed the top of Sandy's head, and everyone raised their glasses.

"To the one who does immeasurably more than all we ask or imagine."

Kennedy hadn't heard many toasts before, but this felt more real and more genuine than anything she could have put into words even if she had weeks to prepare. Everyone drank, and several of the grandkids splashed sparkling cider on the kiddie table when they tried to clink their plastic cups together.

"And now I have something to say, too." Blessing's boyfriend stood up. Kennedy hadn't met him officially, but she knew who he was from the way Blessing had draped herself over his lap all evening.

Carl's eyes widened, but he made a broad gesture and sat down. "All right. Here's Dominic now, apparently with something to say to us all this Christmas Eve."

"Damion," Sandy whispered. "His name is Damion."

"Sorry. Go on, Damion."

Kennedy couldn't tell if that was sarcasm creeping into Carl's tone, but she did catch the way he didn't look right at his daughter's boyfriend but instead stared past his shoulder.

Damion took a deep breath and took Blessing's hand.

"I'm not standing up," she hissed.

"Yes, you are."

There was a little tug-of-war, and finally Blessing reclaimed her hand and crossed her arms, slouching back in her chair.

Damion frowned and then cleared his throat. "Well, with this being Christmas and all, and Christmas being a time for, you know, *family,* and all ..." He looked around from guest to guest, but his imploring eyes didn't land on one person for any length of time. "And with Christmas being about the *birth* of baby Jesus, and his mama being pregnant for the holidays and everything ..."

"What are you doing?" Blessing sizzled under her breath.

"Just hear me out, baby. Let me do this."

"We said we were gonna wait." She was talking through her teeth, but Kennedy could hear every word. Apparently, Carl and Sandy could, too. Carl was leaning back in his seat, his eyes wider than silver dollars. Sandy swayed slightly back and forth at the table, her face strained with a mixture of excitement and anxiety.

Damion cleared his throat again and wiped his hand on his forehead. "Wow. This is a lot harder than it looks. Ok, well, um, Carl ... Sandy ... Mr. and Mrs. Lindgren, I mean ..."

"Spit it out, man!" Carl finally blurted.

"Well, we're gonna have a baby."

Squeals of delight and a subdued applause sounded around the table. Sandy clasped her hands to her chest, but she glanced at Carl's serious face, and then she hid her smile behind her cider goblet. Damion and Blessing were arguing at each other in subdued tones, with Blessing's *I told you so* the only words Kennedy could make out.

Damion looked at Carl and wiped his forehead again, only this time with his napkin. "Um, so, Mr. Lindgren ... Carl ... I, uh, wanted to tell you that I know your daughter's really special to you, and she's really special to me, too, and I know that you being a pastor and all probably doesn't mean you want to have ... What I'm trying to say, sir, is I really want to do right by your daughter, by Blessing here."

"I know her name." Carl's tone was so flat you could have chopped veggies on it. Kennedy and Reuben raised their eyebrows at each other and stifled their giggles.

Damion dropped his napkin and glanced around the table imploringly. His gaze finally landed on Sandy. He gulped once before continuing. "And, so, to get to the point, sir ..."

"I wish you would."

Sandy hit Carl's uninjured arm with her napkin. "Hush, now, and let's hear what the poor boy has to say."

Kennedy could tell she was trying not to laugh, too.

Damion shifted his weight. "So, what I really want is I want to ask Blessing to marry me."

Nobody spoke for several seconds. Kennedy was painfully aware of Reuben's presence next to her but didn't take her eyes off Blessing's boyfriend.

"I know it's maybe not the best time, but I thought, you know, Christmas being all about family and stuff ..."

"Yes." Carl spoke so quietly he had to repeat himself. "Yes."

Damion balked. "You mean ... you're saying it's ok?"

Carl took a sip of cider. "It's fine by me, man, but I'm not the one you need to ask."

Damion blinked at Carl a few times before his face lit up brighter than the lights on the Lindgrens' tree. He fumbled in his pockets and beamed down at Blessing. "Now you understand why I told you to get up?"

Still pouting but now blushing like a schoolgirl, Blessing stood and self-consciously tugged her miniskirt. Several women *awwed* when Damion dropped to his knee and opened the small black case he was holding. "Blessing Lindgren, will you marry me?"

She stole a quick glance at Sandy, who nodded encouragingly. Blessing wrapped one arm around her son and gave him a squeeze. "Well, squirt, what do you think? Should we say yes?"

Tyson jumped to his feet and wrapped both arms around Damion's neck. "Heck yeah!"

While Blessing chastised her son for his choice of words, Damion slipped the ring on her finger, and everyone clapped. A few started clinking their glasses demanding a kiss, and when Blessing and Damion complied, the table erupted in hoots and hollers, as well as quite a few snickers and one very loud *"Ew!"* from the kiddie table.

Kennedy shot a quick glance at Reuben, who was smiling along with everyone else. She couldn't remember a Christmas ever feeling quite so full, and it wasn't because of the piles of food she had heaped on her plate. After the holidays, she'd be right back where she started that week. There would be police reports. Long meetings with Drisklay and his cold cups of stale coffee. Interviews with men in drab suits and somber-toned ties from the district attorney's office.

But right now, none of that mattered. Right now, Kennedy was safe.

Right now, she was home.

Policed

"The Lord works righteousness
and justice for all the oppressed."
Psalm 103:6

Dedicated to the selfless police officers who courageously serve and protect.
May the Lord bless you and keep you safe.

The views of the characters in this novel do not necessarily reflect the views of the author.

Policed

First Printing May, 2016
Cover design by Damonza.

www.alanaterry.com

CHAPTER 1

Kennedy rolled down the car window. "How about next time we don't wait until halfway into the semester to go out. Deal?" When Reuben didn't respond, she glanced over at him in the passenger seat. "What are you thinking about?"

His face lit up with his usual bright smile. "Nothing. Just next year."

"Almost sophomores. Can you believe it? And we haven't gone insane yet. Well, at least you haven't." She had to laugh. It was embarrassing enough that she went to meet with a campus psychologist once a week. If she couldn't find at least some humor in her situation, she was in big trouble. In fact, it was Reuben who had encouraged her to take her mental health more seriously, and she was forced to begrudgingly admit something she was doing must be helping. She'd only had two panic attacks all semester. Not too bad considering everything she'd gone through this school year.

But she didn't want to think about any of that. Not tonight. It was only Thursday, not even the weekend yet, but she and Reuben had just finished their chemistry midterm and were on their way to the Opera House to see the Elton John musical *Aida*. They'd been planning for weeks on this date.

Ok, so maybe not a date. Not a real one. Then again, Reuben had texted her yesterday, said he had something important he wanted to tell her tonight. Said she couldn't let him back out. Couldn't let him change his mind and stay silent. She'd lost several hours of sleep trying to figure out what he was about to divulge.

Maybe that's why he was quiet this evening. Beneath his cheerful personality, Reuben could be almost as serious as Kennedy. Her roommate Willow was always teasing both of them for being so studious. Always asking when Kennedy would start dating Reuben for real, but of course, Kennedy never had a good enough answer.

"He's either stuck in the Victorian era, or he's gay," Willow would quip. Kennedy had gotten used to her roommate's teasing, though. And tonight she wasn't going to spoil the atmosphere with negativity from anyone or anything. Wasn't that what her counselor always said? Only let positive energy in, or some psychobabble like that. She figured if seeing the campus quack helped her sit through a calculus lecture without turning into a wheezing, sobbing mess, it was worth the hassle and the time. Besides, as soon as Kennedy mentioned the words *post-traumatic stress disorder* to her missionary parents, they threatened to fly all the way to Massachusetts from China to help her get connected with the services she needed.

Or the services everyone else thought she needed.

It was funny how she was the one who survived a kidnapping and two separate attempts on her life, and everyone assumed she was a big, blaring psychological mess. What about her roommate? What about Willow, who had slept with every single boy in the theater department by now? Who was going to shrink-analyze this karma-fearing, yoga-practicing, granola-crunching pothead roommate from Alaska and tell her all her deviant behavior was the result of early childhood trauma or rubbish like that?

And what about Reuben? There wasn't much Kennedy wouldn't give to gain unbridled access to his psyche, to figure out what caused those quiet, moody spells that sometimes came over him. He hardly talked about his family or upbringing in Kenya unless it was to boast about the birth of his most recent niece or nephew back home. Of course, there were other things she'd want to know too, but they would have to wait until he was ready to tell her.

Like tonight?

The two of them had been through so much together since they met at their freshman orientation last fall. Two kids who grew up on different continents, both living oceans away from their families, doing their best to stay afloat in Harvard's rigorous pre-med program.

She didn't know when it happened. Maybe one night when they stayed up late working on calculus at the library. Maybe one day in the student union as they scurried to finish a write-up for chem lab. Maybe during one of Kennedy's panic attacks, when Reuben's calm assurance brought her back to reality, helped her recover from the scars and wounds of last semester.

She didn't know when it happened, but Kennedy knew she'd found true friendship. Closer than she'd ever experienced before. Nobody could make her laugh like Reuben. Nobody else would argue literature with her like he did. After spending their first semester at Harvard studying calculus and chemistry side by side, they decided to both enroll in a children's literature course during their spring semester. Together, they had discussed the stereotypic gender roles of the Alden children as they raised themselves in an abandoned boxcar and analyzed *The Giver* until there wasn't a single phrase in Lois Lowry's weirdly dystopian novel that they hadn't dissected. One day Kennedy realized she'd found more than a best friend.

She'd found a soul mate.

She only hoped that whatever secret he was planning to tell her tonight was the same secret she'd kept hidden, even from herself, until recently. A giddy, nervous energy zinged up her leg. She really should pay more attention to the road. After growing up on the mission field in Yanji, China, Kennedy hadn't learned to drive until her pastor taught her over Christmas break. She had just gotten her license and still wasn't used to Cambridge driving, with all its funny rotaries and ridiculously congested streets. That was another reason she and Reuben had chosen to go out on a weeknight. Traffic wouldn't be so bad. Besides, they were borrowing Willow's car, and the chances of Kennedy's roommate staying in on a weekend were about as high as Matilda from the Roald Dahl book getting detention for failing a math test.

"So, did you finish reading *My Side of the Mountain* yet?" Reuben asked.

Kennedy was grateful to hear the usual conversational tone in his voice. "We weren't going to talk about school, remember."

"I thought that only applied to math and science," he replied. "By the way, how's your sociology class going?"

Kennedy didn't know why she'd done it, but she let her roommate talk her into taking one of Professor Hill's courses on the American racial divide to fulfill a humanities requirement. On the one hand, it was nice getting to know Willow and a few of her friends better, but the course itself wasn't at all what she'd been hoping for. After reading the catalog description, she assumed the class would be about Martin Luther King, Jr. and the Million Man March. She quickly found out Professor Hill was far more interested in citing every single instance of perceived discrimination that had occurred across the nation in the past three months than delving into America's segregated history.

Kennedy shrugged. "It's all right. I've gotten A's on most of my papers, but I think that's just because I've learned how to write the way she wants and skew everything from the right angle. Actually, the left angle."

The pun was lost on Reuben, who spoke English as his second language, but Kennedy didn't mind. She'd spent the past ten years in southeast China and didn't understand a decent amount of slang or the majority of pop culture references either, so she could empathize with him. She often felt that she had more in common with Reuben, an exchange student from Kenya, than she did with her American peers. On more than one occasion, she wondered if she would have ever made it through her first year at Harvard if it weren't for his friendship.

"What kind of papers do you write for that class?" he asked as Kennedy merged onto Soldier's Field Road.

"A lot of fluff, really. Every week, we have to take something that happened to us personally and explain the racism implicit in the event. Like once, do you remember when you forgot your meal card at the student union and you didn't have any other ID? I wrote that up about how since you're black, the cashier automatically assumed you weren't trustworthy and wouldn't let you give her your student number, blah, blah, blah. Three pages of drivel about the racial injustices implicit in our interactions with the gray-haired lunch lady who knits socks for her grandkids on her breaks."

Reuben laughed. "You really said that?"

She shrugged. "It was for the grade."

"Do you believe it?" he asked.

"No. But it's what Hill wants to hear, and it's a pretty easy class, so I won't complain too much. It's kind of a joke though. I mean, they take all these cases where people just run into bad luck or something, and they turn every single one of them into an example of racism."

"Like the meal card?"

Kennedy nodded. "Yeah. I mean, if I forget my card and she says I can't give her my number, I figure she's having a bad day. Or maybe her boss is telling her to stop doing that anymore. Either way, I don't assume it's racism. But if she refuses to let a black student give her the number, all of a sudden she's a bigot."

"So do you think America still has a problem with racism?" he asked.

Kennedy had asked herself that same question several times in Professor Hill's class. "Maybe sometimes, but not like it used to. Take Pastor Carl. He and Sandy got married in the South back when blacks and whites hardly ever even dated. They've shared some of their stories with me. It wasn't pretty. But this is a different era. I mean, you look at Carl and all he does, and he's the last person to point fingers and say some big, burly white man is keeping him down."

Kennedy frowned. Had she offended Reuben? Before taking Hill's class, she wouldn't have even asked herself that question, but now all the guilt she'd absorbed from being told how anyone with her complexion had inherited an incurably racist constitution, she wasn't so sure. "I know it can be harder for black people to have some of the same opportunities, especially when we're talking about kids from inner cities. But my guess is most of that's related to poverty and education and things like that. It's a socioeconomic issue, not a racial one."

Had she expressed herself correctly? Why did she feel so nervous? If anything, Hill's class made her feel more uncomfortable talking about race with a black man. Or what was she supposed to call Reuben? She couldn't say *African-American*, since he wasn't a US citizen. Why did it have to be so complicated? She decided to steer the conversation in a new direction. "What about in Kenya? Is there much racism there? Or reverse racism against whites or anything?"

"Not really. The white people who travel to Kenya are either tourists who come with lots of spending money or missionaries who start up schools or hospitals, so white and black relations are pretty good. There's still a lot of prejudice between different tribes though."

Kennedy kept her mouth shut so she wouldn't say something ignorant. Up until now, she hadn't thought about how Kenya's tribal past would still have implications on its society today. She glanced at the clock on Willow's dashboard and then saw blue and red flashing lights in her rearview mirror. Some cop was trying to pass. She merged over to the right.

"What's he doing?" she mumbled when she saw the police car switch lanes with her. She checked her speedometer. She couldn't have been speeding. Traffic was too congested. "Is he blinking at me?"

A familiar, unsettling quiver started in the base of her abdomen. No, she couldn't give in to anxiety right now. She had made so much progress moving on from the trauma of last semester. She was healthy. Whole. She could see a policeman without giving in to flashbacks of her abduction. She could get pulled over without her mind convincing her she was back in a car chase, fleeing for her life while bullets shattered the windows around her.

Couldn't she?

She slowed Willow's car down to a stop. The police pulled up directly behind her.

Great.

"I wonder what I was doing."

Maybe Willow's registration had expired. It sounded like something her roommate would let happen.

"What's taking so long?" Kennedy glanced in the rearview mirror. The policeman still hadn't gotten out of his car. She turned to Reuben. "I'm really sorry. We might be late. Maybe I should hop out and explain to him we're in a hurry."

Reuben raised his eyebrows. "I think we better stay here."

She sighed. This was supposed to be a fun night out together. Well, at least it would be memorable. She wondered what Willow would say when she heard they'd gotten pulled over in her car. She didn't know anything about traffic laws and write-up procedures. Would the ticket go to her or Willow? Kennedy would find a way to pay it regardless, but she didn't want it to count against Willow's record in any way.

Finally, the policeman sauntered over to them. He had that typical side-to-side gait Kennedy always associated with cops in movies. Mr. Bow Legs. She tried to remember from the police shows she watched with her dad what she was supposed to do now. Keep her hands on the wheel? No, that was only for suspects and criminals. This was just a traffic stop. Kennedy had replayed every move she'd made since she turned onto Arlington. Not a single mistake. It had to be something to do with Willow's car. She held her eyes shut for a moment. That was so like her roommate. Why couldn't Willow learn a little personal responsibility?

Officer Bow Legs rapped on her window. His hands were massive. Another tremor blasted through Kennedy's abdomen. She forced herself to take a breath from deep within her belly. While her psychologist was busy probing Kennedy's past — certain that her missionary-kid upbringing overseas was the real culprit for her PTSD and not the fact that two different men had tried to kill her last semester — Kennedy had found a few websites with practical advice to ward off panic attacks.

Inhale through the nose. Expand your belly.

Her three-hundred-buck-a-session shrink would be shocked to learn it could all come down to a few simple breathing techniques.

Kennedy rolled down the window. Her first inclination was to apologize to the officer, but somewhere in the back of her head, she remembered her dad warning her about assuming culpability. Or was that only if you'd been in an accident?

The policeman was glaring at her. She did her best to keep her face neutral, reminding herself she had nothing to be scared of. She hadn't done anything wrong. It wasn't dark yet, but the cop held up his flashlight and shined it into the cabin of the car. Reuben shielded his eyes.

"Hands behind your head!" Mr. Bow Legs shouted at him.

"He was just keeping the light ..."

"You shut up," the policeman snapped.

Kennedy glanced over to Reuben who had interlaced his hands behind his head.

"Where's your driver's license?"

Kennedy reached for her purse in the center console.

"Get your hands on the wheel!" Bow Legs barked. How far behind were Willow's car tags?

Kennedy hoped he couldn't see her exasperation. Or was that fear? "I was going to show you my license."

"All I asked was where it was."

She peeked at the time. She and Reuben had to find a parking spot right next to the Opera House and be at will call in fifteen minutes if they wanted to catch the show. It would be best to comply. Cops had hard jobs. She had seen them risk their lives for her on more than one occasion. Bow Legs was probably extra tense after a long day at work. The least she could do is make this stop as easy as possible.

"My driver's license is in my purse." She nodded toward it and noted the cop's whole body tense when she moved.

"Where's the registration?" he demanded.

"I don't know. This is my roommate's car." She didn't bother to tell him she wasn't sure what exactly a registration looked like or how she'd recognize one if she saw it.

"Does she know you're driving it?"

Kennedy thought he was trying to make a joke until she saw his deep-set scowl. She answered with a simple, "Yes."

"But you don't know where her registration is?"

"No," Kennedy answered. "Is that why you pulled us over?"

He jerked his head toward Reuben without answering. "Who's that?"

Kennedy glanced at Reuben to see if he would answer for himself.

He didn't.

"This is my friend from school."

The officer glared. "And what's the name of your *friend*?" He made the word sound filthy. Impure.

Reuben lifted his head. "I am Reuben Murunga. I'm a student from Kenya."

"I didn't ask what boat you got off." The cop jerked his head. "All right. Get out of the car."

Kennedy tried to catch Reuben's eye, but he was staring at his lap as he unbuckled his seatbelt. All of Kennedy's questions, all her protests froze in her throat. Her mind taunted her with memories of a trip she took when she was a little girl visiting her grandmother in upstate New York. Someone had burgled the house across the street, and the police were knocking on doors warning the residents to be extra vigilant locking up. Kennedy's dad had called her downstairs, footie pajamas and all, and forced her to shake the officer's hand. "Police are our friends," he told her. "They're here to help us."

Her dad's words replayed in her mind. *Here to help us.* Well, if she had done something wrong, she would have to accept whatever citation he wrote up for her. That's all there was to it. Her dad would chide her for being careless, but he'd take care of the ticket and that would be that. She just wished she knew what she'd done. Had she forgotten to signal before switching lanes? Is that what this was about?

Here to help us. So why were her insides reeling as fast as a centrifuge machine?

She reached for the car handle when Bow Legs barked, "Just him. You stay put."

She wished Reuben would look at her. What was he thinking? Was he scared? If he was, he was doing a good job hiding it. He opened his door and got out slowly. Methodically. Bow Legs warned him to keep his hands visible, and Reuben held them up by his shoulders the entire time.

Once Reuben was out of the car, the police officer planted one foot behind him. Kennedy recognized the stance from her self-defense course. What did he think, that Reuben was about to attack him?

"All right," he ordered. "Now lace your fingers behind your head. Keep your back to me and take slow steps around the front of the car."

Kennedy kept her fingers on the door handle. "Listen, he wasn't the one driving. I was. If I did something wrong, just let me know so I don't do it again. I already told you, this is my roommate's car, and ..."

"Shut up." The words weren't even a snarl, more like an afterthought. All of Bow Legs' attention was on Reuben. Kennedy probably could have confessed to planting a bomb in Logan Airport and he wouldn't pay any attention.

When Reuben reached the driver's side headlight, the officer planted his hand on his holster. "Stop right there. Don't move."

"Wait, do you really think ..."

Bow Legs wasn't listening to her. He left his post at Kennedy's window and stepped forward. Kennedy tried to pass Reuben some encouraging thought or positive message by sheer will power as the officer lowered Reuben's hands and cuffed them behind his back.

She jumped out of the car. "What are you doing?" Commuter vehicles whizzed up and down Arlington, never slowing down. Didn't anybody see what was happening? Didn't anybody care?

The officer snapped his head around toward Kennedy. "Miss, you need to get back in that car right now."

"No." For once, she was thankful her dad had forced her to role play through so many ridiculous and embarrassing situations. Of course, he hadn't thought to include a scenario in which Kennedy and her best friend get pulled over and handcuffed without any explanation, but if her dad had taught her anything, it was how to stand up for herself. "You can't just pull someone out of their car like this. He hasn't done anything wrong." She struggled to keep the invasive tinge of hysteria out of her voice but wasn't sure she pulled it off successfully.

"I told you to get back in." Bow Legs' hand was still on his holster. It was enough to dim Kennedy's newfound courage. She shot a desperate glance at the stream of traffic, the blissfully ignorant drivers who didn't even see her. Those who did notice probably assumed she was a drug dealer or some other sort of criminal. The entire situation might be humorous if it weren't so terrifyingly real.

She inched her way backward. "He hasn't done anything wrong." She hadn't tried to sound so whiny. She was thankful her body hadn't given in to a panic attack. Maybe she really had made some progress since last semester. But if she wasn't careful, she was going to start to cry. She refused to be associated with those girls who got out of tickets by summoning the fake tears. Except her tears wouldn't be fake. Fear and confusion coalesced in her gut, washed down by copious volumes of scorching humiliation. She touched the door handle but didn't open it. "What are you going to do?"

Bow Legs' icy scowl could have frozen mercury. He ignored the question and slammed Reuben down against the hood of the car.

"Stop!" Kennedy couldn't even guess what Reuben was feeling right now. His cheek was pressed against Willow's car, his face blocked from view. The only thing that stopped Kennedy from charging the officer was the way one hand still hovered over his holster as he patted Reuben down with his other.

Maybe Professor Hill's course hadn't been as big of a waste of time as Kennedy initially assumed. How many times had the class watched those videos of police officers who overstepped their bounds? Of course, Kennedy had never been able to shake the nagging suspicion that somewhere off the screen, the victims must have done something to aggravate the situation, but what about Reuben? What could he have possibly done to antagonize Bow Legs or deserve any of this?

With a renewed surge of confidence, Kennedy knew what she had to do. She got into the car just like Bow Legs had ordered and pulled out her phone. She would record the whole encounter. That should get the cop to lay off. She started the camera up and set the phone in the pocket of her blouse, hoping it would get the entire scene without the cop noticing.

When she was sure it was recording, she leaned out the window, reminding herself how the people in those police videos had stood up for their rights. "Hey, don't you need some kind of warrant to search somebody?" She wasn't sure if that was true or not, but she remembered her dad saying something about it while they were watching an action movie together.

"Listen, I've heard about enough from you little —." Here the officer let out a string of epithets that insulted both Kennedy and Reuben as well as their ancestry. If this whole incident were racially motivated, at least Bow Legs had offended them both with equal opportunity.

Kennedy licked her lips. Things like this didn't happen to people like her. She had always been at the top of her class. Even after everything she went through last fall, she finished her first semester at Harvard with straight A's except for a single A minus. Bow Legs had no idea what he was doing. This was all some terrible mistake. She stretched her spine as tall as she could manage. "He hasn't done anything wrong, and you need to let us go. Now." Her voice only shook once. "You have no business bothering us like this. We're students at Harvard."

Bow Legs turned to her for the first time. "Yeah, right." He spat out another string of profanities.

"We're going to a show." Kennedy didn't know why she was telling him that. What would he care?

"You're not going to any show, girlie. As soon as I finish searching your car, you and your baboon buddy are coming with me."

"Search us for what?" she demanded. The cars were slowing down now when they passed, and she saw several commuters straining their necks to get a better look. How in the world could anyone mistake people like her and Reuben for criminals?

Bow Legs took a step toward her. "Any more lip out of you, and you'll end up in cuffs too. Got that?" He eyed her up and down. "And just so we're clear, I have no problem giving you a full body search right here on the side of the road if you don't shut up and let me do my job."

Kennedy shot an imploring look at Reuben through the dashboard. Other than a slight twitch in his jaw, he kept himself bent over the hood of the car and didn't move.

The cop opened the door and yanked her out of her seat. She was too surprised to try to free herself from his hold. She bit her lip. The sooner they got this over with, the sooner he'd take those cuffs off Reuben. Right?

He started rummaging under the seats and in the crannies of Willow's car. Kennedy's stomach sank faster than a lead ball. What if he found something Willow or one of her partying friends left behind? What if they thought it belonged to Kennedy and Reuben? More than anything, she wanted to call her dad. He would know what to do.

"There's nothing in there." She knew her voice sounded scared. It probably made her appear even guiltier.

Bow Legs straightened up and slammed the door shut. Good. He hadn't found anything. Her phone was still in her blouse pocket. How much of this encounter would the camera pick up? He stomped to the other side of the car, giving Reuben a harsh nudge when he passed. Kennedy opened her mouth to protest, but Reuben shot her an imploring look that silenced her complaint.

She thought through the similar events she had heard about in Professor Hill's class. Young men getting pulled over and arrested for no reason other than being black. Kennedy had read the accounts, felt sorry for some of the victims, but in the back of her mind had always wondered if they were reading too much into it. Sometimes police pulled people over. They had their reasons. Just because the victim was black didn't mean it was racially motivated. But this ... What had either of them done?

Bow Legs jerked open the passenger door so hard the entire car shook. Seconds later, he let out a self-satisfied grunt and pulled out a Ziploc bag from the glove compartment. "Not hiding anything, huh?" He was glaring over the top of the car at Kennedy.

"That's my roommate's. It's her loose-leaf tea."

"Nice try." Bow Legs pocketed the baggie and pulled out another pair of cuffs. "Come on. You better hope your eggplant friend has more brains than he looks. You're both in a world of hurt right about now."

A dozen fears and protests charged through Kennedy's mind. Were they under arrest? Did they need a lawyer? What would happen to Reuben? Did he even have the same rights as an American citizen, or were laws different for international students? She had gone through enough in the past year to recognize the surge of adrenaline flooding her nervous system, but she wasn't sure if it was time for a fight or flight. Or should she let the cop take them in and trust the justice system to sort everything out in the end? She was innocent. Both of them were innocent. So why did it feel like going with the policeman was tantamount to admitting guilt? She was even more scared than she'd been when the Chinese police stopped by her parents' house to question her father about his printing business, his legal front for staying in Yanji as a missionary.

The officer swaggered over to Kennedy. "Come on, Barbie doll. Time to take a little ride."

There's nothing to be scared of, she reminded herself, but she knew it was a lie. There was plenty to be scared of.

"You better start thinking how you're gonna explain that weed."

"It's tea," she insisted again. Kennedy watched Willow prepare it every single morning and had never questioned what was in it. Willow took more supplements than a hypochondriac chiropractor. There was no way Kennedy could keep track of which ingredients were in what concoction. She eyed the bag. Maybe there really was some illegal substance in there. Then what would happen to her? What would happen to Reuben?

Police are our friends. Kennedy could hear her father's voice mentally coaxing her. She wondered if this was the adult equivalent to finding out

Santa Claus was a lie your parents perpetuated in a spirit of fun and holiday cheer.

Bow Legs stepped behind Kennedy and waved the bag in her face. "What do you say? Is this worth a night behind bars?" He leaned into her, pressing her body against the car. She clenched her jaw shut to keep from screaming. Tears of humiliation and hatred stung the corners of her eyes. She held her breath, trying to make her body as small as possible, but the farther she pressed into the car, the more heavily he dug into her.

"Looks like I've got a right to pat you down, don't I?" His breath was hot. Acrid. Kennedy could almost taste it. She fought her gag reflex.

Police are our friends. It was still her father's voice she heard, but now it was taunting. Mocking.

His hands started at her shoulders and lingered as they slid down to her hips. He felt in each of her pants pockets, his pace painstakingly methodical. His hands traveled back up her body slowly, his fingers probing each rib as he worked his way toward her chest. "Nice girl like you wouldn't be hiding anything in here, would you?" he hissed in her ear.

She froze. What did he think he was doing? And how much angrier would he grow when he saw the phone in her pocket? Kennedy recalled a similar simulation from her self-defense course. She could head butt him if she wanted or bring up her heel for a swift kick to his groin. She clenched her eyes shut, unsure which reflex his touch would trigger. But before his groping hands could complete their circuit, Reuben barged between them.

"Leave her alone."

Without warning, the officer punched Reuben in the gut. Reuben doubled over as Bow Legs brought his knee up to his face. Reuben staggered.

"You dirty n—." Without warning, the cop whipped out his pistol and smashed its butt against Reuben's head. He crumpled to the ground, where the officer's boots were ready to meet him with several well-placed kicks.

Throwing all rational thoughts aside, Kennedy jumped on his back. Anything to get him to stop beating Reuben. The officer swore and swatted at her. Kennedy heard herself screaming but had no idea what she was saying. Her brain zoned in on Bow Legs, the object of all her hatred and disdain. She couldn't see anything else, nor could she understand how it was that when her normal vision returned, she was lying on her back staring at a vaguely familiar face, but the officer and Reuben were nowhere to be seen.

CHAPTER 2

"Just hold steady."

She recognized the man. She knew if it weren't for her splitting headache, she would be able to place him.

"We've met before. It's Ian McAlister." The Good Samaritan held out a bottle of water. "Are you thirsty? I don't want to move your head right now, not until the ambulance gets here, but I could try to get you a small sip."

Ian? Pulses of pain shot through Kennedy's gray matter as she tried to connect his face to the name. She squinted up at his head of red hair, which she recognized from their few encounters last semester. "You're a journalist, right?"

He nodded. "Yeah. You feel ok? Any dizziness? How's your head?"

"It hurts."

"I'm not surprised. Try not to move too much before the paramedics get here. I'm sure they'll want to check you out."

"Where's Reuben?" She struggled to sit up, but Ian and a wave of dizziness both prevented her.

"Someone's with him right now."

Kennedy wished she could see what was happening.

"Don't touch me." It was Reuben's voice. She'd never heard him sound so angry. They weren't arresting him, were they?

"What's going on?" she asked.

Ian frowned. "He's pretty agitated. There's some nurse who pulled over, but he won't let her near him."

"Leave me alone!" Reuben yelled.

Kennedy had to get to him. Had to see what the problem was.

"Sir, I'm trying to help. The back of your head is bleeding. I just want to ..."

"Stay back. All of you." Reuben's voice was tense, almost as if he were trying not to cry.

"Is he ok?" Kennedy asked.

"I don't know." Ian glanced at his watch. "The ambulance will be here soon. You'll both get all the attention you need."

"There was a cop," she tried to explain. "He was ..."

Ian frowned.

"Did you see anything?" she asked.

"Just you and your friend lying on the asphalt."

It didn't make sense. Where had Bow Legs gone? She shut her eyes and did what she could to assess her injuries. She could breathe normally. None of her limbs hurt. Aside from the headache and a general achy feel all over, nothing deviated too far from baseline. She took a deep breath and worked through the dizziness until she could sit up. Ian held out his hands as if he wanted to catch her if she fell. "Are you sure you want to be doing that?" he asked.

Kennedy was too focused on keeping her balance to answer. She gritted her teeth and reminded herself she had been through worse pain than this.

Much worse.

She didn't shrug off the journalist, who wrapped his arm around her while she attempted to stand. She let him support her as she worked out her tight muscles and made her way over to Reuben. He was lying on the rocky pavement, no longer cuffed, his head resting in a small puddle of blood. Kennedy untangled herself from Ian's hold.

"Get away from me," Reuben snapped when he saw her.

Kennedy nearly lost her balance. "I just want to ..."

He clenched his teeth. "Get back."

She didn't argue, and she didn't resist when Ian tucked an arm around her waist and led her to his car. "You can rest here until the paramedics come."

Kennedy winced as he eased her down into the driver's seat. "What's wrong with him?" She hadn't been asking about Reuben's injuries so much as his attitude.

Before Ian could answer, a whining ambulance sped toward them and parked. The onlookers dispersed, and three paramedics jumped out the back. Ian pointed at Reuben. "Check him out first."

Kennedy let out her breath and allowed her body to relax a little. Reuben would get the medical attention he needed. Everything would be fine now.

Or would it?

She recalled the cop's roaming hands on her body. She had never felt so violated. Her ears rang with the echoes of his curses and slurs. If she didn't have the entire encounter recorded, she wouldn't believe half of it.

The recording. She reached for her phone in her blouse pocket. The screen blinked with a message. *Memory full. Video failed to record.*

"Everything ok?" Ian asked.

No, it wasn't. After everything they had endured, all the indignity, all the shame, now there wasn't any proof. Memory full? She wasn't sure if she wanted to cry or throw her phone in front of the oncoming traffic.

But maybe it wasn't that bad. Arlington was as crowded as the courtyards of Willie Wonka's chocolate factory the day he reopened his doors. Somebody would have seen. Several somebodies. They could corroborate Kennedy's story.

The cop was long gone. He must had driven off like a coward, leaving Kennedy and Reuben to heal from their injuries. She didn't know his name, but with enough witnesses and police logs, they'd find him.

Right?

She stared at the phone in her lap. Betrayed by a stupid piece of technology. It wasn't fair. None of this was fair. She should have never been pulled over in the first place. And now Reuben ...

"You sure he's going to be all right?" she asked.

Ian's eyes were soft. Like Charlotte's after Wilbur the pig discovered why the farmer was fattening him up. "I'm sure the paramedics will fill you in soon, but I wouldn't worry if I were you."

Kennedy glanced over. The ambulance crew was lifting Reuben onto a gurney.

"I should see if he's ok."

Ian extended his hand. "Want help?"

"No." She winced as she stood up and decided she'd take some Tylenol if the paramedics had any to offer, but otherwise she'd rather have them focus on helping Reuben. She kept her eyes off the puddle of his blood on the cement.

She walked to the side of Reuben's stretcher and took his hand. "Are you ok?"

He pulled away. What was wrong? Did he think this whole thing was her fault? Did he blame her for taking him out in her roommate's car? She had done what she could to stand up for him. His silent treatment bored holes into her chest the size of test tube stoppers.

She stepped aside to let a member of the ambulance crew by. "Is everything all right?" she asked.

The paramedic didn't pause to look at her. "He'll be fine. We're taking him in to Providence now." He hoisted himself into the ambulance.

"Are you the girl who was with him?" his co-worker asked. "You really should let us check you out before you start walking around."

"I'm fine," Kennedy insisted. "I just want to make sure he's ok."

"We're taking him in right now. You're welcome to follow and meet us at Providence if you'd like."

Reuben shook his head. "Just go home. Don't worry about me."

Did he know what he was saying? Was this the kind of brain injury that could alter personalities? Why was he acting this way?

"I'd like to stick around." She wanted to find a discreet way to tell him her dad would probably pay for his medical bills if he was worried about money. All Kennedy had to do was ask.

Reuben jerked his shoulder away when she touched him. "Go home. I'll text you when I get back to campus."

A lump the size of the BFG's big toe had settled at the top of her larynx. "You sure? I don't mind ..."

He scowled. "Just leave me alone."

One of the paramedics shot Kennedy a sympathetic glance. Kennedy stepped aside so they could lift the stretcher into the back of the ambulance. She crossed her arms and watched, expecting any moment for Reuben to change his mind and call her to him. Apologize for his behavior.

All she heard was the chatter of the crew as they prepared him for transport.

She was still standing in the same spot when they pulled away. They didn't put on their sirens, which was a good sign. Reuben's injuries couldn't be that serious. So why had he acted so strangely?

It was cold. The wind always seemed fiercest around this part of town anyway.

"Hey, you need a lift or anything?"

Surprised by the voice, Kennedy turned to face Ian. She had forgotten the journalist was there. He was the only one left. Everyone else had gone. All those potential witnesses ...

"Can I drive you someplace?"

She cringed when he touched her shoulder. She shook her head. All she wanted now was to be alone.

"No, thanks." She tried to force a smile to compensate for the shortness in her voice.

"You sure?"

She gave him one more quick glance and nodded. "Yeah. I'm sure."

He followed her to Willow's car and leaned down once she was in the driver's seat. "Is there anything else I can do for you?"

Kennedy buckled her seatbelt and stared at the empty pavement.

Ian sighed. "I've had experience with this sort of thing. It can get complicated. So just let me know if you need me."

Kennedy turned the key in the ignition. "As a member of the press?"

He shrugged. "Or as a listening ear. It's up to you." He passed her a business card. Until then, she hadn't realized anyone younger than her dad still carried those things around.

"Thanks." Kennedy hoped he didn't take her brusque departure too personally. She shut the door and managed to drive about a mile and a half before she pulled over into a gas station, where she tried to wash away her fears and frustrations with a series of choking, heaving sobs.

CHAPTER 3

"No, he never told us his name." Kennedy was still parked in front of the gas station where she had finally decided to call her parents in Yanji.

"Well, I'm sorry," she replied to her dad's reprimand. "It's not like I wake up every day and tell myself to ask for the name of every single cop who pulls me over and starts kicking my friend on the side of the road."

She could hear her mom sigh on the other end of the line. "You know you're going to have to report this, don't you?"

Kennedy's stomach was twisting and twirling like a double helix. "How can I do that if I don't even know the guy's name?"

"They have records of their traffic stops, sweetie. All you have to do is tell the police department where you were and what time it was when you got pulled over."

Kennedy didn't try to keep the sarcastic barbs out of her tone. "And then he can say it wasn't him and make me and Reuben out to be liars." In spite of all her arguments, she knew her mom was right. She'd have to file a report, but she didn't even know how to begin. Was she just supposed to waltz into the station and ask to speak to the cop in charge of complaints?

"But his superiors will have the record of him pulling you over," Kennedy's mom insisted, "and you'll have the paramedic workers there to verify that's where your friend was injured. That's evidence enough in anybody's book."

Her father cleared his throat. "Not if the officer failed to call in before he stopped. That would explain why there wasn't any backup. Cops do it all the time, pull someone over and unless they write a ticket, there's no paper trail, no proof whatsoever."

"But she can't just go on as if none of this ever happened …" Her parents went back and forth, but their voices were too low for Kennedy to hear most of their bickering.

"All right," her dad finally said, "here's what we're going to do. I'm going to call my friend's son Taylor. He's a state trooper out somewhere in Alaska, but before that he was on the police force in Waltham. I'll get in touch with Taylor, run everything by him, ask what he thinks you should do. Sometimes these cops, they got this unwritten code. Work together to keep each other out of trouble, make a big mess for anyone who challenges the status quo."

So much for his *policemen are our friends* mantra.

"But what about Reuben?" Kennedy noticed the whine in her voice but couldn't control it. "He hurt him really bad. By the time I realized what was going on, the cop was already gone, and Reuben was on the ground, and …"

"You said he's at the hospital, right?" her dad asked. "I'm sure they'll have the police meet him there so he can give his story. And the paramedics said he was going to be fine. You'll just have to take their word for it."

But he didn't even want to talk to me. Kennedy kept the thought to herself. Some things were too painful to speak out loud. Why did her parents have to live so far away?

"Listen," Kennedy's mom inserted, "are you busy tonight? Do you have any homework you need to get done by tomorrow?"

"No. Reuben and I were going to see *Aida*. We got the tickets two months ago …" She cut herself off before her voice betrayed her.

"Ok then," said her mom. "Here's what I want you to do. I want you to drive yourself over to Carl and Sandy's. I was emailing Sandy just a second ago while you were talking with your father. She's already expecting you. I want you to go to Sandy's, take a nice hot shower, do something to relax. Then tomorrow, after your father talks with this trooper guy and gets his opinion, we'll call you back and make some decisions. For now, you just get the rest you need and try not to worry."

Oh yeah. Not worry. That was so like her mom. *Here dear, eat a cookie and all your troubles will vanish.*

"You ok, Kensie girl?" her dad asked.

Kennedy shut her eyes and let out her breath. "Yeah," she lied.

"Oh," her mom piped, "I just heard back from Sandy. She wants to know do you want her to come pick you up?"

"I don't know. I need to get Willow her car back."

"Are you well enough to drive safely?" her dad asked.

"Yeah."

"Then go over to Carl and Sandy's now and take the car back with you to campus later on. Ok?"

When she lived at home, she hated the way her dad had so many rules, so many protocols for everything, but now it was nice to have a simple plan to follow. Why had she spent so much energy in high school complaining about her family?

She spent a few extra minutes convincing her mother she was really ok before telling her parents good night and hanging up. She thought about sending Reuben a text but decided against it.

Get herself to Carl and Sandy's. If there was anyone in the Boston-Cambridge area who knew how to pamper her, it was her pastor's family. A night sipping tea with Sandy or listening to Carl's booming preacher's voice impart some wisdom or inspiration was just what she needed.

She took a deep breath and reminded herself that after everything she'd been through tonight, she should be proud she hadn't had a single panic attack. She sped up before merging onto the freeway on her way to the Lindgrens'.

CHAPTER 4

Every time Kennedy glanced at the car's clock, she regretted she wasn't at *Aida* with Reuben. Would they be into the second act by now? She didn't know a whole lot about the Elton John show. She just knew she liked the music samples she'd heard online and it boasted rave reviews and several Tony awards.

Tonight was supposed to be something special, something she and Reuben could look back on and remember for years to come.

What had happened?

She'd dissected every second, from the moment they got into Willow's car until the ambulance drove him away. What had gone wrong?

He had wanted to tell her something, and in her childishness, she'd dared to hope it had to do with their relationship. Had to do with his feelings for her. Part of her would be happy keeping things as they were. She and Reuben worked so well together, and if they started to actually date, there was always the chance of ruining a perfect friendship. But then again, what if they could go even deeper, enjoy each other's company even more fully? It was worth the risk, wasn't it? She thought about the line in *The Last Battle* by C. S. Lewis. "Further up and further in." The representation of exponential improvement. An eternity of ever-increasing joys that carried you closer and closer to infinity, just like an asymptote.

All of her musings were pointless, however. Whatever it was, something had turned Reuben against her. He had done so much for her last semester, helped her through so many trying ordeals. Why would he shut her out now?

She wasn't paying attention to where she was driving and realized she had missed her turn. If she kept going this way, she'd end up at Providence Hospital.

Providence Hospital.

She weighed her options. She could drown her sorrow and confusion over tea and Sandy's homemade desserts, or she could actually talk to Reuben.

She stayed on the freeway.

When she pulled up at the hospital, her muscles were as tight and wound up as a spring scale. She texted the Lindgrens to cancel their plans and practiced a few of her deep breaths before getting out of the car. She could do this. If she could handle twenty-two Harvard credits and maintain a 3.9 GPA, she could walk into a hospital and offer her friend the emotional support he needed.

The wind had picked up. She clutched her light coat against her chest as her hair whipped across her face. Sometime during her scuffle with the cop, she had lost her barrette. She sighed and tried to envision herself exhaling all her disappointment and anger like those breathing gurus suggested.

It didn't work.

As soon as she stepped inside Providence, she realized she had no idea how to find Reuben. She walked up to the information desk. "Hi, I'm looking for my friend. He came here by ambulance about half an hour ago."

The man behind the booth didn't smile. "Name?"

"Reuben Murunga." She spelled it for him as he typed on his keyboard.

"Looks like they have him in the ER. Do you know the way?"

She didn't answer. Her steps grew slower the closer she got to the emergency room. What was she doing here? Weren't there all kinds of patient privacy laws that would keep her from seeing Reuben, or was that just in movies and TV shows?

When she reached the ER, she wasn't sure who she should talk to, so she rooted herself in line behind a harried mother bouncing a crying baby and a middle-aged man with his arm in a sling. When it was Kennedy's turn, she walked up to the glass partition and explained into the microphone why she had come.

"Let me ask if he's accepting visitors. What's your name?"

"Kennedy Stern."

The triage nurse picked up the phone, but Kennedy couldn't hear the conversation through the partition. The woman hung up and pointed to some empty chairs. "Have a seat. Someone will be out to talk with you shortly."

Kennedy stared for just a moment in hopes of reading the woman's expression. Why would they send someone to talk to her? It seemed like they would either let Kennedy see Reuben or not. Why all the extra meetings and waiting? Did she have to prove she knew him or something?

She sat in a chair and glanced at a young man whose arm was draped around his wife or girlfriend. Kennedy couldn't see her face but could read the sorrow in her posture. The man kept his whole body hunched over as if he wanted to shield her from the world. Fear and grief were written on his face as clearly as the colored pigments on chromatography paper. After a perfectly still moment, he took his finger and lifted some stray hair off the woman's forehead.

Kennedy pried her eyes away from the private scene and glanced at the other faces, the others here waiting. Sometimes it was hard to tell who was here for medical treatment and who had come to offer support. She was one of the only people there by herself.

"Miss Stern." The title sounded foreign. Kennedy glanced up, half expecting to see a nurse ready to escort someone much older into the back rooms. But the man looking directly at her wasn't a nurse.

She stared at the uniformed police officer and wasn't sure if she should stand and go with him or try to run away. Was this what her dad warned her about? Was the cop going to accuse her of drug possession and drag her off to jail?

She glanced around. Several eyes were on her. What did these people think she'd done? There wasn't anywhere she could go.

"You Kennedy Stern?" he asked, and she wondered why he didn't keep his voice down. What happened to confidentiality laws?

She nodded.

He held a door open. "Will you please come with me?"

The hallway branched off in one direction and then another. Kennedy was lost within her first few turns following him. Each corridor looked the same, each hall so brightly lit she had to squint to keep the light from bouncing off all the bleached white walls and blinding her. Why was she here? What was the cop doing? She'd had enough of policemen for the night.

Maybe for an entire lifetime.

He was silent as he led her down the serpentine corridor, past rows of patient rooms, past vending machines stuffed with high fructose corn syrup, caffeine, and a whole arsenal of artificial ingredients. Her headache had returned with increased fury. Where was Reuben?

The cop opened an unmarked door and held it open. "Right in here, please."

She glanced at his face as she entered the room. Late twenties, maybe, or early thirties. A short, well-kept beard covered his chin, with tinges of copper highlighting the dirty blond. Grayish eyes that were watching her every move. She wanted to hide.

"Have a seat." He gestured to a small couch and then sat in a folding chair across from it. "My name's Dominic."

Strange. She would have expected him to call himself Officer So-and-So. Why the informality? Why the plush seat, the lounge room with a fruit basket and bottled water on an ornate coffee table? Why wasn't he bringing her right to Reuben unless ...

Her whole body stiffened as if someone had frozen each of her muscle fibers with liquid nitrogen. This explained everything. Why the triage nurse wouldn't tell her directly how to get to Reuben. Why the officer was using his first name. She glanced around the room, half expecting to see advertisements for funeral homes and pamphlets lying around on how to deal with the loss of a loved one.

She had to know. Had to ask, but her whole body was numb. Is this how Reuben would have felt right before ...

"I just got back from seeing your friend."

Kennedy held on to his words like a drowning lab rat would clutch at a floating island.

"In case you were worried," Dominic continued, "he's doing fine. Getting a few stitches, and then it's home." He glanced at his notebook. "Well, back to his dorm, I guess. He's from ..." His eyes scanned the page.

"Nairobi," Kennedy answered.

"Nairobi?" Dominic glanced at his pad of paper, but even when he wasn't looking right at her, Kennedy got the feeling he could read her mind. He stared at her with the same intensity her therapist showed when she first mentioned she was the daughter of Christian missionaries. "Right. So." He clasped his hands to his knees and leaned forward. "Do you want to tell me what happened tonight?"

Reuben was fine, but confusion clouded Kennedy's relief. Why was the cop asking her? Did he doubt Reuben's story? Warning signals zinged through Kennedy's cerebrum. Hadn't her dad warned her about cops who make it hard for people who rat out other cops? Is that what this was? Is that why she couldn't visit Reuben, why he brought her all the way down here to some secluded room ...

"I'd really like to check on my friend first, if that's all right with you." Why did she add that last part? Shouldn't she be more assertive? What made this officer think he had the right to isolate her, intimidate her ...

"You're welcome to check with the nurse when we're finished," he said, "but last I heard, he was refusing visitors."

That probably only referred to cops like you. Kennedy knew better than to speak the thought out loud. She ran through the entire encounter on Arlington. She didn't remember the details of the fight itself, but she recalled something about jumping on the officer's back. If she was going to get in trouble for that, why hadn't Bow Legs arrested her himself? Why did he just run away? Probably because he was a coward who knew he was in the wrong.

He's the one who punched Reuben. The one who kicked him when he was down. Kennedy was only trying to help, and Reuben wouldn't have given the officer any trouble if he hadn't tried to grope Kennedy like that. Reuben was defending her. She was defending him. She was sure the public would see it that way, but of course her phone had betrayed her with its stupid memory. Why hadn't she taken the time to erase some of those dumb photos of lab results or lecture notes leftover from last semester?

Kennedy hadn't done anything wrong. The more she replayed the entire encounter, the more firmly she believed in her innocence. But would other policemen see it that way? Somewhere in the back of her mind, she remembered a campy cop movie she'd watched with her dad back in Yanji. A jaded long-time officer was explaining departmental policy to his new rookie partner. "You take a swing at one of us, there's no way you're walking into the police station on your own two feet. Not by the time we get done with you." At the time, she'd just thought the threat was for dramatic effect, but after her dad's warning, she wondered if that same unwritten code persisted even in a city as supposedly progressive as Boston.

She studied Dominic's face, trying to read him. If this was some kind of a good cop/bad cop routine like in TV shows or detective novels, he seemed better suited for the part of the good guy. The friendly one. The one who'll make sure you're comfortable and offer you bottled water and keep his expression open and engaged, like he'd taken hours of departmental training in active listening.

What would happen if she didn't comply? Would he turn into a raging maniac, threaten her with every single punishment he could legally throw at her? Or maybe there was a partner hiding in another room ready to take over if this nice-guy performance failed.

Kennedy fidgeted with her phone in her pocket, wondering what she should do. Could she ask him for a chance to call her dad first, or would that just make her look guilty?

Dominic leaned forward. "So, you ready to talk about it?"

No, she wasn't ready. In fact, there was a decent chance she would never be ready. Not like this. For the briefest second, she wondered if he was even supposed to be asking her questions without a lawyer present.

Please God, she begged, *show me a way out of this.*

Her phone vibrated in her hand and then let out a little beep. She glanced at the screen. It was a text from Reuben. *If the police ask you any questions, I haven't told them anything.*

She slipped her cell back in her pocket.

"Who was that?" the officer asked.

"Just my roommate." Kennedy tried to meet his eyes. Wouldn't most cops be able to tell when someone was lying? "It was her car I was in tonight, and she was just ..."

"Yeah, the car," Dominic interrupted. "Maybe we can start there."

Kennedy stared at her lap as if the answers to all his questions might magically appear on her jeans. Why was this so difficult? Her dad had told her to wait before complaining to the police. He didn't tell her what to do if they stopped and questioned her. Why had she thought it'd be a good idea to come here at all? She could be on her third cup of tea at the Lindgrens' by now.

Dominic let out a loud sigh. "How about this. Let's start with me telling you what I know, and then you can tell me what you know."

Yeah, he was definitely taking the good-cop angle.

He leaned back in his chair. "All I know is I've got a patient back there with injuries consistent with what you'd see in an assault. He gets in the ambulance, refuses to answer any questions, won't tell anyone why or how he got hurt. Let's call that exhibit A." He gestured with his hands. "Then over here, we've got exhibit B. Exhibit B is two calls we got from drivers very concerned when they saw a white police officer kicking a black male on the side of the road." He leveled his eyes. "What's really interesting is the drivers were calling from Arlington, and one of the very next calls our operator got was for an ambulance to pick up an injured black male from that very same stretch of road."

He crossed its arms. "So that's what I know. Would you care to take a turn?"

Kennedy was too busy praying for some sort of deliverance to put her thoughts into any coherent order. She stared at the floor and wondered what kind of baked goodies Sandy would have made tonight. She fidgeted with her hands in her lap. "We got pulled over." She couldn't bring her eyes to his. "The officer made Reuben get out of the car. Put him in cuffs." She willed her body to keep as calm as possible. If the story had to come out, it would do so without the interruptions of tears and dramatics.

Dominic still leaned forward. Did he believe her?

"And then I tried to stop him, said we hadn't done anything wrong, so he made me get out of the car too, and ..." Her throat clenched shut, her mind reeling with the sensation of the officer's hands sliding up and down her hips and sides. The putrid stink of his stale breath. The heat from his whispered words, venomous like a hissing snake.

The trembling that had settled into her core all the way back at Arlington now found its way to her limbs. There was no way to hide this kind of reaction from the cop. He'd believe her or he wouldn't. Either way, he'd know how upset she was by the entire ordeal.

She couldn't bring herself to talk about Bow Legs' groping hands slithering up and down her body. She shook her head as if that might convince her brain the entire thing was fictional, the results of an overactive imagination coupled with the exaggerated stories she'd studied in Professor Hill's class. Tears spilled down her cheeks. It was a good thing she hated the caking feel of mascara and never wore the stuff.

If Dominic was surprised or annoyed by her behavior, he didn't show it. "So he made you both get out of the car, put your friend in cuffs, and then?"

Kennedy wanted to go home. Go back to her dorm, take a hot shower, and change her clothes. Forget how degraded she'd felt. Forget how scared she'd been for Reuben's safety.

"Reuben was trying to help me." She was close to sobbing now, but she'd stopped caring. Someone was here, listening to her story, someone who had the power to free Reuben from any charges and punish the real culprit. "He hadn't done anything wrong. He was just trying to help me."

Dominic's open expression turned downward into the slightest trace of a frown. "Protect you from what?"

In a flash, the memory became suffocating. Bow Legs, with all his offensive slurs and leering looks, loomed larger in her mind than he could have possibly been in real life. She couldn't shake him off. A loud gasp. A desperate attempt to suck in air after her lungs had already decided to clench themselves shut. If she couldn't breathe, she couldn't feel. If she couldn't feel, she'd forget the humiliation. The filthy, slimy shame that seeped through her clothes by osmosis, poisoning her bloodstream.

Dominic had crouched beside her and was holding an open bottle to her lips. Twelve ounces of glacial water would never be enough to wash away the hot searing trauma of tonight's events. The entire Bering Glacier wouldn't be enough.

She took a delicate sip, forcing her lungs to calm down enough that she could swallow the tepid liquid. There was a small fraction of her brain — five, or maybe ten percent if she felt like being generous — that was replaying all the information from those self-help websites, all that mumbo jumbo about cleansing breaths and diaphragm engagement. The rest of her mental energy was focused on projecting an increasingly odious image of Bow Legs throughout her entire consciousness, an image that only grew larger as it fed on her fear.

Dominic was rubbing her back. "Hey, you're safe now. Nobody here wants to hurt you." She was glad he didn't offer the usual barrage of senseless advice: *Don't worry. Just calm down. You're ok.*

She wasn't ok. She was glad he didn't feel the need to convince her otherwise.

Her back and shoulders heaved as her lungs wheezed air in and out. Tears splashed on Kennedy's lap and on Dominic's hand that still held out the bottle of water. She wanted to apologize to him, but what would be the point?

"Are you a person of faith?" It was a strange question to ask in the middle of a conference room behind the ER.

She nodded. "I'm a Christian." She was almost ashamed to admit it. What kind of testimony was she offering while blubbering like this?

Dominic slid beside her on the couch. "Me too. I don't want to make you uncomfortable, but I was wondering if I could pray for you. I can tell you're shaken up."

In different circumstances, she might have laughed at his polite euphemism.

"Would that be ok with you?"

She didn't have much faith that a simple prayer from a stranger would do anything to ease tonight's trauma or cure her anxiety, but at least it would give her a break from this interrogation. It could give her the chance she needed to collect herself before the interview proceeded any further. She nodded her consent and bowed her head.

Dominic didn't jump right into a prayer like she expected. He sat beside her quietly for what felt like several minutes. She wondered if she'd misunderstood him. Maybe he just wanted to pray for her silently. Oh, well. As long as it meant she got a break from answering his questions or feeling like a fool while she blubbered away on the couch, she'd take it.

Apparently, however, he wasn't planning on remaining silent the whole time. He didn't begin with any formal opening, no flowery greeting to make sure everyone in earshot knew who he was talking to. But the words that flowed out of his mouth were almost like Scripture itself.

Powerful. Majestic. Inspiring.

She recognized a few Bible verses woven into his words, but it didn't feel forced or artificial. And the way he prayed made Kennedy wonder if he knew all about her. Had he read about her in the news after the kidnapping last fall? Maybe he went to Carl's church and she just hadn't ever seen him there.

Kennedy had lived her whole life hearing Christians pray for healing. *Lord, help Tyson's hurt tummy. Give the doctors wisdom when Aunt Lilian goes in for her biopsy. God, please help Grandma not die from cancer.* But she'd never experienced a prayer like this. It was as if Dominic were a surgeon, searching out the sickness, zoning in on each individual injured spots. He began broadly, praying for Kennedy's peace of mind, for comfort from whatever had made her feel afraid.

And then it grew more specific. Prayers for her mind. Prayers for wholeness. For healing. Dominic interrupted his petition to ask Kennedy if he could put his hand on her forehead. She surprised herself by agreeing. Something in her was hungry for the faith, the power she experienced in Dominic's prayer. Her body tingled with an inexplicable electric power, and when he rested his palm against her skin, the whole area radiated heat and energy.

He asked God for soundness of mind. Asked God for freedom. At the mention of freedom, a quiver coursed through her being. Dominic must have felt it too. He prayed even more fervently for release. Deliverance. Hope surged up in Kennedy's chest. Swelling. Like the giant ocean breakers crashing into the Hispaniola when Jim Hawkins set sail with Captain Smollett, Long John Silver, and his crew of mutineers in *Treasure Island.*

Dominic spoke against fear. Spoke against anxiety. He prayed against the trauma of Kennedy's past, and for the first time she understood what Christians mean when they call somebody a prayer warrior. Up until that moment, Kennedy assumed it was an honorary title given to people who really liked to talk to God. Tonight, she realized that prayer wasn't just a discipline. It wasn't something like flossing your teeth that you're supposed to do because it's good for you.

Tonight, she understood that prayer was a battle. At first, she had compared Dominic to a doctor. Now, she realized he was also a soldier. And not just an enlisted man who could follow orders and carry a gun. He was a warrior, a warrior who for some reason or other had decided to go to battle for her in a way nobody else in Kennedy's entire life ever had. Growing up in the church, Kennedy had sat under a dozen Sunday school teachers or more. Why hadn't any of them taught her to pray like this? Nobody she'd ever known prayed like this, not even her own parents, faithful missionaries by anyone's definition of the term. Maybe if Kennedy had spent more time in her family's prayer meetings instead of shopping the Yanji clothes stores with her friends she would have heard intercession like this, but she doubted it.

Dominic took his hand off Kennedy's forehead, and she realized the prayer was over. Her skin no longer burned where he had touched her, but a halo of warmth and peace settled around her. She didn't know what she was supposed to say but realized she was breathing evenly again. She couldn't recall when or how the panic attack ended. She stared at Dominic, half expecting him to disappear from sight or transfigure into an angelic being while she sat watching. He looked so ordinary and unassuming.

Who was this man?

He was a cop. He belonged to the same department as the one who had accosted her and Reuben. But she'd never met anyone like him before. She'd never heard anyone pray for her like that. Not even Pastor Carl, the godliest man she knew in the States.

What did Dominic have that every other Christian lacked?

"You feeling a little better now?"

It was strange to hear Dominic asking her a question. His voice, which just minutes ago had transformed itself into a weapon of spiritual warfare, was so normal now. He looked even more average than he had when they first met, a slightly tired expression clinging around his hazel eyes.

Kennedy nodded. "Thanks for praying for me. It helped."

It was a lame thing to say, but how else was she supposed to respond? She still wasn't quite sure what had happened to her. Had she just imagined that heat on her forehead when his hand touched her?

Dominic smiled. Such a straightforward, unassuming smile. Did he know what he'd just done for her? Did he know what sort of power his soul possessed? "Now, about your story ..."

So this was it. This was the part when the good-cop skit ended and he demanded to know why she jumped on the back of a uniformed policeman who was just out doing his job. She inhaled. At least her spirit still maintained a shred of the peace that had wrapped itself around her during his prayer.

She was ready. As ready as she'd ever be.

Dominic scratched at his beard. "So, you said earlier this policeman attacked you after pulling you over and cuffing your friend for no good reason whatsoever?"

She didn't want to meet his eyes. Couldn't stand the thought of seeing the disbelief there. But there was an ounce of hope, too. Would he have prayed over her like that if he thought she was a liar? Thought she was a criminal?

"That's basically what happened," she answered, fully aware of how incredulous the entire tale sounded. If she had the video, she could show him. Prove everything.

He was frowning now. "And when he punched your friend and kicked him while he was down, that was also completely unprovoked?"

Kennedy weighed her words. If she recounted everything, it would mean repeating the horrific slurs the man had thrown at her and Reuben. It would mean reliving the degrading search where he pressed his body against hers before Reuben jumped between them.

What would her dad tell her to do? There wasn't time for him to get in touch with the trooper he knew. She had to make her decision now.

"I guess that's not the entire story," she admitted. The peace, the strength she'd experienced while Dominic prayed vanished like a flame flaring up on a glass cell spreader drenched in ethanol. The welcomed sense of security that had burned so hot just seconds ago disappeared, leaving behind nothing but cold uncertainty.

Was it the right choice? She didn't know. But it was too late to change her mind.

Kennedy told the officer everything.

CHAPTER 5

Dominic's prayer had disarmed her. Put her in a vulnerable position until she divulged the whole story. She still wasn't sure it was the right thing to do, but at least she got through her recitation calmly. No more choking heaves or suffocating sobs.

When she finished, she searched his face for any telltale signs of anger or disbelief. Had she done it? Had she broken the unwritten code of police procedures and exposed a bad cop?

Would he say the whole thing was her fault, that she or Reuben instigated the confrontation? Would he even believe her?

Dominic was tugging at his short beard hairs. "And you say when the fight was all said and done, the cop who attacked you was gone? Just like that?"

"Yeah." Her voice was weak. What time was it? Exhaustion clung to her individual muscle fibers.

"He didn't stay and write you a ticket? Didn't arrest you for assault? Nothing?"

She stared at her empty bottle of water and shook her head, realizing how ridiculous the whole thing sounded now that she'd heard it herself. She sat and waited. Waited for him to tell her how stupid she'd been to antagonize an officer. For Dominic to poke a dozen more holes into her story until even she doubted its veracity.

"There's no way an officer would just drive away from a situation like that. Not unless he knew he was guilty and hoped to pretend it never happened."

Kennedy was too busy imagining the conversation she'd have with her dad from a jail cell to piece together the meaning of Dominic's words.

"If he had just cause, he would have written you up. Hauled you both in. That would be the end of it."

For the slightest moment, a spark of hope flickered in Kennedy's core. Was he saying he believed her?

"But instead, he ran away." Dominic was musing now, apparently speaking more to himself than Kennedy. "Which only goes to show he was the guilty party." He leaned forward. "And you didn't get his name?"

"No."

"Didn't see his badge or anything?"

"No."

Frankly, she had been too busy trying to keep him from murdering her best friend to worry about minute details like that.

"Can you at least remember what he looked like?"

Kennedy sighed. She could picture his face but didn't know how to portray it. She did the best she could, certain by Dominic's expression she wasn't helping.

"That could be half the police force you just described there."

"That's what I thought."

He sat for a moment in silence before leveling his gaze. "You know this isn't going to paint a pretty picture when it all comes out in the wash."

What did he mean? Not a pretty picture for the officer involved? Or not pretty for her and Reuben? Kennedy wasn't sure. She glanced up at the walls. There were no clocks here, but she guessed it had to be at least nine by now. The musical would probably be finishing up in the next half hour or so.

She had hoped tonight would end so differently.

She had been looking forward to her date with Reuben for nearly the whole semester. Finally, she'd stopped kidding around like a little junior high girl and admitted her true feelings to herself. Reuben meant so much to her. So much.

She let out her breath. "What happens now?"

She wished Dominic would smile. There was something comforting about his face when he did. But his features were set in a scowl as he tugged on his beard. "I can't tell you what to do, but I can at least spell out your options. You can write a report. File a complaint. If you go that route, I'll show you the ropes. Tell you the right people to meet with. You don't want to walk into the main department building and talk to the first person you see." He let out a sigh that seemed to hold the heaviness of several lifetimes in its breath. "I need to warn you, though, it might not go very far. You didn't get his name. Think you could identify him if you saw him again?"

"Probably."

"Yeah, well, the chances of the chief ordering a dozen of his men to stand in a line-up isn't looking all that hot."

"So there's nothing we can do?" It was such a relief that they were talking about bringing the unruly officer to justice instead of discussing Kennedy and Reuben's plea bargain for assaulting a cop. Part of her would be happy to just walk away and pretend none of this ever happened. She realized, though, that's exactly what Bow Legs was counting on.

So then what? Make herself into an Atticus Finch, stare injustice in the face and jump into some sort of legal battle that was doomed from its inception? And what kind of legal battle would it be if the police department decided to block justice?

Dominic frowned. "I'm not saying it's impossible. I'm just saying you'll face a lot of obstacles along the way. Cops have this code ..."

Kennedy rolled her eyes. "I know." She was sick of hearing about it.

"I'm not saying it's right," Dominic inserted. "I'm just saying that's the way it is. Most folks in the department will tell you police brutality doesn't exist, that anyone who finds himself on the wrong end of a nightstick must have been asking for it."

His chest expanded visibly as he inhaled. "This isn't going to be easy."

She couldn't fully comprehend what he meant, but she sensed the warning behind his words. "Well, what would happen if we just let it drop?"

Her question must have pulled Dominic out of some sort of daydream. He shot up his gaze. "Let it drop? You mean don't report it?" He shrugged. "Nothing. Nothing at all would happen. And then next time that same cop pulls over someone he doesn't like or who looks a little funny to him, well, who knows what would happen then? All because of a little bit of nothing."

"But you just said we couldn't make any progress on a case like this." She felt like Milo in *The Phantom Tollbooth*, who agreed to move a pile of sand with a pair of tweezers before realizing how many thousands of years it would actually take him.

"No, it might not turn out in your favor," Dominic replied. "But it's a start. There'd be documentation. If enough reports come in with similar complaints, eventually the department would have to take a good, honest look at itself. And I'm guessing the chief wouldn't like what he'd see."

Kennedy squeezed her eyes shut and massaged her throbbing temples.

"I'm sorry." Dominic stood. "I'm throwing a lot at you right off the bat. I know you've had a hard night."

Kennedy didn't bother coming up with a response. All she wanted was to get home.

Dominic held open the door. "Listen, I'm not gonna keep you here any longer. You think about what I said." He glanced up and down the hall and lowered his voice. "Then when you've made up your mind, let me know how you want to proceed. Like I told you, I can get you in touch with the right people. It's not ..." He took a deep breath before continuing. "The department's not perfect. We do a lot of good. A *lot* of good. But you get one bad apple in there and ..." His voice tapered off. "What I'm trying to say is you have a question, you have a problem, you come to me. I'll help walk you through the steps if you decide to file a grievance, ok?"

Kennedy nodded. For some reason, his kindness toward her made her miss her parents more than normal. Pangs of homesickness pulsed between her firing temples. She swallowed. "Thanks for everything. I really appreciate it." She was too tired to elaborate, but she hoped he knew she was thanking him for more than just his practical assistance. "I think I'll go check on Reuben now. Do you know what room he's in?"

"Just down this hall." Dominic pointed. "I'll walk you there."

"Thanks again."

His smile was both comforting and warm. "That's what we're here for. Follow me. I'll show you the way to your friend."

CHAPTER 6

Reuben's room was nothing more than a ten-by-ten square partitioned off with colorfully patterned curtains. A nurse was handing him a piece of paper. Kennedy entered, uncertain how he would react when he saw her there. "Can I come in?" She hated feeling so uneasy. This was Reuben. She'd never been self-conscious around him before.

The nurse glanced up, apparently oblivious to Kennedy's discomfort. Her face broke into a welcoming grin. "Looks like you have a visitor."

Reuben gave Kennedy a faint smile. "Hey."

"Hey."

The nurse handed him a pen. "If you don't have any more questions, I just need you to sign your discharge papers and you're free to go."

"Leaving already?" Kennedy asked. "That's great. I'll drive you home." She held her breath, half expecting Reuben to decline her invitation.

Instead, he offered her that same tired smile and nodded. "That sounds great. Thanks so much for coming."

The anxiety that had clenched its talons into her spine melted away like dross. A few minutes later, they were back in Willow's car and pulling out of the Providence parking lot.

"How does your head feel?" she asked.

"I'm ok. Just tired."

They rolled along without talking. Kennedy wondered if she should tell him about her meeting with Dominic. What would he think? What would he say?

"I'm really sorry about what happened. That officer ..."

"Forget about it." Reuben turned down the radio, which was set to Willow's favorite classic rock station.

Kennedy drove past looming business complexes and darkened side streets. "It's too bad about *Aida*. I really wanted to see it with you." She stole a quick glance at him. Did he remember how this evening started?

"That's life for you." Reuben stared out his window.

Kennedy recognized the song faintly playing on the radio but didn't know it well enough to make out the words. "Did the doctor say anything? Anything about your injuries?"

"I needed a few stitches. That's all. It's hardly worth mentioning."

Kennedy sensed he was talking about more than just the ER. She let her mind drift off. She had to figure out what to do next. Part of her wanted to file a complaint with the police department. Even if they didn't catch the cop this time, maybe it would force them to make improvements in the future. Then again, if Reuben refused to talk about what happened tonight when it was just the two of them, how could she expect him to come forward and make the complaint with her? Would they both have to testify against Bow Legs, or could she proceed without forcing Reuben to get involved?

She had no idea what he was going through. No idea what he had felt while pressed down against the hood of that car with his hands cuffed behind his back. No idea how much fear, how much anger must have built up in his system before he finally stood up to the cop. She had spent so many late nights with him, shared so many meals in the student union, so many hours in the chemistry lab. He wasn't the type to bottle up negative emotions. She'd never seen him lash out. Never heard him yell. Never seen him angry.

Until tonight.

Now, with him so silent beside her, she wondered how well she actually knew him. When they weren't talking about their studies or arguing over a piece of literature, he would ask all kinds of questions about Kennedy's life. Listen to her stories about growing up in Yanji. Find out every detail he could about her parents. He knew so much about her past. What did she know about his? He had seven sisters, a whole gaggle of nieces and nephews, and an extended family that could fill an entire floor of a New York hotel. But how useful was that information? She didn't know what he was afraid of, didn't know what made him mad, didn't know what struggles he'd overcome. He grew up in a Christian family, talked about going to church on Christmas Eve with his relatives, but he hardly ever mentioned God. She'd spent the past semester and a half feeling so close to him, but the more she thought about it, the more she wondered if she knew him at all.

Another song came on the radio. *Rocket Man* by Elton John. It only reminded her how disappointed she was to miss tonight's musical. Only reminded her how you can be half a foot away from someone you care about, maybe even love, yet still find yourself drowning in an ocean of isolation.

The song invited her to wallow in the homesickness and loneliness that had plagued her since she first arrived at Harvard. A lump lodged itself in the back of her throat, but as comforting as it might be to lose herself in tears, she knew she wouldn't. Not now. Not here. Not with Reuben's elbow just a couple inches from hers.

She thought back on her meeting with Dominic, how a perfect stranger had seen and even soothed her tears. And now here she was with Reuben, her best friend, and her eyes were as dry as anhydrous sodium sulfate.

"I'm sorry." Reuben's voice was faint. At first, she wasn't sure if she heard it at all. "With the paramedics. When I yelled at you."

She turned the song off. "It's ok."

"No, I was acting like a jerk. I'm sorry."

"I forgive you," she whispered. Did that mean they could talk now? Did that mean their encounter with Bow Legs was no longer taboo?

"I was ..." He sucked in his breath. "I was really scared."

She nodded, mistrustful of her voice.

"I was afraid he was going to hurt you, and I'd have to stand by and watch."

She bit her lip, wondering how different things might have turned out if Reuben hadn't intervened. Maybe nothing would have happened. Nothing at all. The cop could have sent them away with a warning. Or he might have taken them in until Kennedy could prove the stuff in the Ziploc was tea leaves like she claimed. Wasn't it Aslan in *Prince Caspian* who said you don't get to know the what-ifs?

What if they hadn't been pulled over? What if they'd gone to see *Aida* like they planned? What if Reuben had told her afterwards the secret he'd been meaning to share?

"They talked to you at the hospital, didn't they?" Reuben was always soft-spoken, and this time Kennedy had to strain to make out his words.

"Yeah. I didn't really have much of a choice."

"Well, I'm just glad it's over."

She didn't want to tell him it might not be over like he expected. Didn't want to tell him she was considering filing a complaint.

She tested her voice. "Hey, can I ask you a question?" Even with her eyes focused on the road, she sensed his whole body tense.

"What is it?"

She tried to make her words sound natural. Unassuming. "Why didn't you tell the policeman at the hospital what happened?"

He let out his breath, almost as if he were relieved. "Back home, nothing good ever comes from dealing with the police. They're all corrupt, and they don't even try to hide it. So when we got pulled over, I kept reminding myself things were different in America. But they weren't."

Kennedy could empathize. If it hadn't been for Dominic and his prayer, she probably would feel mistrustful of everyone in a blue uniform at this point, too.

"And I haven't been here long, but I've seen enough to know how it would turn out. Everyone who heard about what happened to us would turn it into a race issue. It wouldn't be about a bad policeman abusing his power. It wouldn't be about a sexist policeman taking advantage of a college girl. It would be about a white policeman pulling over a black man. That's all anybody would see."

Maybe he was right, but Kennedy didn't understand why that would make him reluctant to bring the officer to justice. "So you think a white cop should be able to harass a black man and get away with it?"

"I don't think any cop should be able to harass any person and get away with it."

"You're not making sense."

Reuben shrugged. "It's hard to explain. But I still don't want you to make a big deal about it. Let's just forget it."

Kennedy tried not to show her frustration. "So why else did you refuse to talk to the police?" There had to be more reasons than his counter-intuitive argument.

"I'm not comfortable with it, ok?" He must have sensed he was being more forceful than necessary. "I'm sorry. There are just some things I don't feel like talking about."

She furrowed her brows. "I thought we could talk about everything."

"No." His voice was weighed down with so much heaviness, so much sadness that Kennedy held her tongue.

"No," he repeated. "Not everything."

CHAPTER 7

Kennedy dropped Reuben off near his side of campus after making plans to meet the next morning for a late breakfast. Her legs were heavy as she trudged from the parking lot to her dorm. She wondered why some people tried to cheer up their friends by reminding them of how much worse things could be. Of course things could be worse. She could be in a holding cell while cops ran tests on her roommate's bag of loose-leaf tea. She could be standing outside a morgue waiting to identify Reuben's body. She could be bleeding to death in the back of some deserted alley where the policeman dragged her and raped her. Maybe he didn't work for the police department at all. Maybe he stole a car and a cop uniform and drove around town looking for prey.

Of course things could be worse. But how was that supposed to make her feel better?

The door to her room was slightly ajar as she made her way down the hall. She swung it open, ready to let her brain drop into the sweet bliss of dreamless sleep. Sinking down on her bed, she kicked off her shoes. Willow was staring at her computer screen, probably playing one of those shooter video games she liked so much. For being a pacifist, she really enjoyed virtual violence. Kennedy wasn't even sure her roommate noticed her walk in.

"Thanks for letting me use your car." She took the keys out of her pocket and tossed them on Willow's desk.

She didn't look up.

"What are you doing?" Kennedy asked.

"Oh, nothing much. Just watching this little video of you beating up a cop."

Kennedy sprang out of bed. Hovered behind Willow's shoulder to stare at the monitor. "What are you talking about?"

"I got a visit from the police department. They asked what I knew about this video a commuter took of some altercation between a cop, a black man, and white woman. I told them I had no clue what they were talking about, so they said they identified my car by the plates. The same car you and your little platonic boyfriend took out tonight. How was the musical, by the way? Was it good?"

"We didn't see it." As much as she wanted to, Kennedy couldn't pry her eyes away from the screen. The video was running on some kind of loop. It started when the policeman kicked Reuben and ended with Kennedy jumping on his back.

"Interesting stuff, isn't it?" Willow cocked her head to the side and then punched her monitor off. "I already made you a cup of tea. You gonna tell me what happened?"

Kennedy slunk down on her roommate's jumbo beanbag. Willow swiveled her chair around to face her and passed her an oversized mug.

"We got pulled over on the way to the show." As Kennedy filled in the details, she wondered how many more times she'd have to recount this story before she could move on. Somewhere in the back of her mind was the nagging suspicion that normal pre-med students didn't go through this sort of stuff. Normal pre-med students didn't get harassed by police officers on the side of the road.

Willow was silent while Kennedy talked. As soon as she finished, Kennedy expected her to go on some tirade about police brutality and black oppression and the failed justice system in the United States. Instead, she reached over and squeezed Kennedy's hand. "I'm really sorry you had to go through all that. It must have been awful."

Kennedy sniffed into her mug. "Yeah."

"Well, I've got the name of the policeman who stopped by. He was kind of hot, actually, if you're into the trim, athletic, middle-aged type." She pulled a business card out of her pocket. "Here's his information. I was going to invite him to stay and wait for you, but I wanted to get the juicy details first before I passed on his message."

Kennedy stared at the name on the card. Great. Another cop she'd never heard of. Another officer who might be just as bad as Bow Legs, perhaps worse.

"I didn't give him your name or anything, by the way." Willow ran her fingers through her hair. She had cut it short over Christmas break and dyed it just a few weeks ago, so now it was brunette with purple tips. When she was going out, she wore it spiked and gelled, but tonight it hung loose, framing her face like a heart. "I mean, it's none of my business why a cop was giving you a piggyback ride, but I figured if you didn't want to be named, I wasn't going to narc on you. I just told him I've got several friends I let borrow my car, and I wasn't sure whose turn it was to take it out tonight."

"Thanks," Kennedy muttered. Her mind was reeling. So someone had a video. It was short, but the cop's face was clear. Would that be enough evidence to convict him?

Willow pouted her lips. "So, what are you gonna do? You gonna call up Mr. Mid-Life Crisis and cry the whole story into his hard, chiseled shoulder?"

Kennedy stared at her lap. "Reuben doesn't want me to make a big deal out of it. I think he just wants to pretend it never happened."

Willow gestured to her monitor. "It's already on Channel 2. White cop and black kid? It's not the kind of story that goes away."

The more they talked, the more Kennedy began to understand Reuben's line of reasoning. Everyone, even Willow, was doing the same thing. Turning it into another instance of white versus black. What about Kennedy? What about all the cop's chauvinist remarks? His roaming hands? Was it ok to be a sexist pervert as long as you were abusing women of your own race? She was sick of it all. Maybe Reuben had the right idea. Shut the door and pray it'd all disappear.

"I don't know," Kennedy sighed. She knew what Willow and all the other students in Professor Hill's class would do. March their story in front of every reporter, every news outlet available. Keep shouting until someone listened. Until someone demanded the Boston Police Department make the changes that needed to be made. Until they weeded out Officer Bow Legs and any other corrupt cronies like him.

Kennedy understood the thirst for justice. But there was also a need for healing. For privacy. Every time she watched the four-second video on Willow's computer screen, she relived that humiliating attack all over again.

Did she have the fortitude to let journalists and politicians and civil rights activists prod through her wounds before the blood even had time to coagulate?

Willow propped her feet up on her bed. "Well, it's not gonna take the journalists too long to identify you from that video. And you better be ready, because these police brutality cases are all the same. It's a media frenzy where everyone sees who can be first to crucify the victim. Like that black kid the cop shot in the back. Died instantly. And guess what? While the black folks held vigil for justice, the white police force and their media buddies were digging up all the dirt they could find to prove the boy had it coming. Even though he was unarmed. Even though several witnesses claimed he wasn't resisting arrest. But as soon as the media comes out to show this boy was a 'troubled youth,' everyone forgets about justice and just assumes a black kid with a few petty crimes in his record deserves to be executed point-blank. That's America for you. Land of the stinking free."

Somewhere in the pit of her gut, Kennedy wondered if her roommate might be right. Would the media try to attack Reuben? Is that why he wanted to remain so secretive? Is that why he begged her to keep the story from the police and the press? He was such a mature, responsible young man. Was it possible he had anything to hide? Or was growing up in Kenya with its corrupt police system enough to make him paranoid of anyone in a uniform?

"You want some more tea?" Willow held up her electric kettle.

"No, thanks."

"What are you going to do?"

"I don't know. Right now, I just want to rest."

Willow gave an encouraging half-smile. "I don't blame you. Just let me know if you need anything, ok?"

How about a time machine like what the H. G. Wells inventor made? If she could only start today over. Take the T to the Opera House instead of borrowing Willow's car. Or drive another route, where her path would have never crossed Bow Legs to begin with.

She slipped into bed, clothes and all, and pulled the covers over her head. Things could have turned out worse, she reminded herself. But then again, they could have turned out so much better.

CHAPTER 8

She should have known she'd never be able to fall asleep on a night like this. By eleven o'clock, she'd checked half a dozen times to see if Channel 2 had any breaking news. The story was still running at the top of their website, along with the short clip of Kennedy jumping on the policeman's back while he pummeled Reuben.

Other outlets had picked up the piece, too. The story was trending all over the internet. Black leaders were already calling for the police department to divulge the name and rank of the officer, citing how suspicious it was that he hadn't made any arrests and was entirely unavailable for comment. The police department hadn't released any official statements either, but someone close to the head office hinted that the chief was doing everything in the scope of his authority to figure out the whole truth. The chief also urged anyone to call in with information about the two "suspects," as she and Reuben were called in certain publications, while others referred to them as victims.

She kept reloading one webpage after another before she finally flipped on her lamp. Willow was still awake at her desk, the ear buds and flashing lights from the screen proof she had moved back to her blood and gore video games.

Kennedy still hadn't decided what she should do. Willow was probably right. If she told the police who she was, gave her side of the story, they'd try to find a way to make the public believe this whole mess was her fault. But if she stayed silent, what would stop the same thing from happening to victims all up and down Boston? Could she feel safe knowing that cops like Bow Legs were out on patrol?

And what about the race issue? The journalists all treated this as a black and white incident, nothing more and nothing less. On the one hand, she was glad there were watchdog groups ready to protect the rights of minorities, but she still couldn't shake the feeling that pegging her encounter with Bow Legs as simply a race incident was akin to forcing a triangular stopper into a round lab beaker. Sure, she could cite the slurs Bow Legs spurted out like venom, but he'd called her as many bad names as Reuben. There was more to it than ugly racism — misogyny, bigotry, power hunger for starters.

She had to do something. But what? If she went to the police now, what would that mean for her and Reuben? Would they be forced to relive their inhumane treatment each time they attempted to prove that the wrongs they suffered really happened? Was it worth subjecting themselves to public scrutiny until their past secrets and public records were exposed for all to see? Was she ready to accept that cost? Was she willing to force Reuben to do the same?

But the police must already know about her and Reuben. Wasn't that why they sent Dominic to the hospital? So why did they waste their energy asking the public to help identify them?

Unless Dominic had kept their identities a secret. Could he do that? Would he?

Then there was Ian. Kennedy had run into the redheaded journalist a time or two last semester during the peak of her fifteen minutes in the public eye. She had no reason to doubt him, but that certainly wasn't grounds to trust somebody, either. Didn't most journalists scurry around trying to break their story first? Was he just waiting for the hype to increase a little more before he told the world who Kennedy really was?

Would he do that to her? Or maybe the better question was why wouldn't he?

This was all too much for Kennedy. She didn't know about police proceedings other than the tidbits she'd gleaned here and there from the cop dramas she watched with her dad. Besides that and an occasional suspense or detective novel, Kennedy had no idea what she was getting into. She had always assumed that in America, if you were a conscientious citizen and minded your own business, the police would have no reason to bother you. It was like health insurance, important to have around but as long as you were healthy and took care of yourself, and maybe with a little bit of luck, you didn't expect to need it.

Now here she was, wondering if she turned herself in to the police if they'd hail her as a hero for exposing a bad cop or if they'd arrest her for assaulting an officer. How would she know what would happen until she made the first move? And if she waited for them to find her — which they could do easily if they really wanted to — would she look guiltier than she would have if she came forth voluntarily?

"You awake?" Willow asked, taking off her headset. "Sorry. I was trying to be quiet."

"It wasn't you."

"Just having a hard time sleeping?"

"Yeah."

Willow gave Kennedy an almost maternal smile. "Well, you'll be happy to know that Gordon Clarence has taken an interest in your video."

"Who?" The name sounded familiar, but Kennedy couldn't place it.

"Gordon Clarence. The reverend. Head and founder of the Black Fraternity?"

Kennedy groaned. She had read some of his speeches in Professor Hill's class. The last person she wanted championing her case was someone like him.

Willow clicked her mouse. "Here, listen to this. This is Gordon Clarence in a video address to his congregation about the piggyback attack. That's what they're calling what happened. Cute, huh?" She glanced at Kennedy's face and then ducked back behind her screen. "Anyway, here's part of the speech." She unplugged her ear buds, and a booming, rhythmic voice filled the room. *"And that's why I'm asking you tonight, brothers and sisters, that's why I'm standing here before you wanting to know when will the world see these cops for what they really are — a militarized force intent on occupying the neighborhoods and communities where our brothers and sisters are trying to make a peaceful life for themselves. When will the mayor and people of Boston stand up to defend our brother and sister who were brutalized in full daylight by an officer who clearly sees no value in the lives of black men and women? When will my brothers and sisters of color rise up and declare with one voice, 'Enough. Enough of the victimization of our women and children. Enough of the ...'"*

A knock on the door interrupted the reverend's tirade. Willow paused the recording, and both girls glanced nervously at each other.

"You expecting anyone?" Kennedy asked.

Willow shook her head.

Kennedy wished their doors had little peep holes like in hotel rooms. What if it was the police? What if they'd come to arrest her or bring her in for questioning? It was a good thing she hadn't gotten into her pajamas.

Willow stood up and was arranging her purple-tipped hair. "I'll get it. You just ..." She glanced at Kennedy's bed as if she might find a hiding place. "You just wait there."

She cracked the door open. "Yes?"

"I'm here with the Boston Police Department."

Willow adjusted her position so she blocked the policeman's view into the room. "I already answered a few questions earlier. Is there something else you fellows needed?" Her foot was planted by the door, keeping him from opening it any farther.

Kennedy's heart pounded. Her mouth was dry. If they took her in to the station, would they let her make an international call? She would do anything to be back in Yanji with her parents. Anywhere but here.

"I actually stopped by to check on Kennedy. Is she in?"

There was something familiar about his voice. Kennedy tried to peek around her roommate to get a look at his face.

"Kennedy? She likes to stay out late. She sometimes doesn't come back until ..."

The policeman nudged the door slightly and pointed. "Isn't that her in the bed?"

Willow let out a casual laugh. "Oh, yeah, but you know, she's been asleep. Came home right after her afternoon classes and just crashed ..."

The door was wide open now, but the officer didn't step in. He gave Kennedy an apologetic smile. "Hi, Kennedy."

She let out her breath. "Hi, Dominic."

Willow turned around, raised one of her penciled eyebrows at Kennedy, and then gave a little shrug.

"Can I come in?" he asked. "Or would you rather talk out here?"

Willow was slipping on a colorful shawl. "You know what? I completely spaced out and forgot that our director called a rehearsal tonight. I'm already late, so I better run. Don't wait up for me," she called as she hurried out the door. Dominic and Kennedy watched her leave in a wave of colors and patterns.

"That's your roommate?" he asked.

Kennedy nodded. "That's Willow. You can come in," she told him when she realized he was still standing on the threshold of her room.

"I'm sorry to bother you like this." He looked around awkwardly until Kennedy pointed him to Willow's swivel desk chair. "I'm glad I found you awake. You doing ok?"

She shrugged. "I guess." She couldn't read him. Was he here on official police business? More questions, maybe? Or was this some sort of social call? She wanted to trust him. Desperately wanted to trust him. With her dad so far away, who else was there to help her navigate through this mess of legal proceedings she'd gotten herself dumped into? But just because Dominic was a Christian, did that mean he was safe to talk to? Just because his prayer had covered her with a peace and tranquility she hadn't experienced in years, maybe in her entire life, did that mean he wouldn't betray her?

He scratched his cheek. "So, I guess maybe you heard about the news reports." It came out as half question, half statement.

She nodded.

"And well, the chief, he's doing what he can to save face. Trying to avoid any sort of scandal."

It made sense. That seemed like the sort of thing a chief of police would do after a video leaked of one of his officers kicking an innocent man.

"We know the officer in question. Got that figured out even before we saw the tape based on your interview and the location of the engagement."

Engagement. He was using the same terminology as the characters in Willow's computer games. Another reminder that, as kind as he appeared, he was still one of them. Part of the same force as the man who'd landed Reuben in the hospital. Who'd groped Kennedy along a busy Boston highway.

"And obviously, we had your name right away too, but we're keeping that from the press right now for several reasons." His shoulders rose as he took in a noisy inhale. "I just got back from talking with your friend. With Reuben."

Kennedy tried not to let him see how nervous she was when he said Reuben's name. She clenched her teeth shut to keep from spewing out the dozens of questions streaming through her consciousness.

"And after talking with him, I'm even more convinced about what I'm going to say."

Kennedy squinted slightly. Studying his face. If she were a card player, she'd have a better feel for whether or not he was bluffing.

"I know at the hospital I said some good could come out of making a complaint. Might not happen right away, might not result in immediate progress, but if you were willing to jump through the fire, I told you I'd help you start that ball rolling."

She tested his speech, mulling over each phrase. Like one of Willow's gluten-free, sugar-free, chia seed muffins, his words looked appealing at first glance. Looked like words spoken by a friend. A confidante. But the more she analyzed them, the more mistrustful she grew.

He clasped his hands on his knees. "Now that I've seen the way the department's scurrying to handle this particular PR mess, I'm not convinced that coming forward right now is going to be in your best interest. Or your friend's." He put special emphasis on that last part, so much so that it came out sounding like a threat.

She didn't know what to say. She wished Willow were here. Anyone she knew. Anyone she could trust.

"Listen, I know I'm contradicting everything I told you earlier, and you gotta believe me, it's eating me up inside. But not everyone's called to be a David. And you don't want to make the same mistake as others and underestimate Goliath, either."

Kennedy's headache had eased up when she was resting in bed but now returned with even more cruelty. What *others* was he talking about?

He spread his hands out. "I know I'm being cryptic, and part of that's because I'm in a delicate situation myself."

She didn't care about his delicate situation, about his David and Goliath metaphors or anything else he was talking about. She didn't even care so much about vengeance as she cared about people believing her side of the story. What happened to her was wrong. If the chief of police called her on the phone, told her he believed every word she said, and asked her to accept his apology, Kennedy could live with that.

Almost.

It would sure beat sitting here listening to Dominic pretend to care about her and her feelings while trying at the same time to convince her to shut up and accept tonight's harassment as a normal East Coast occurrence.

She wouldn't. She couldn't.

"So here's what's happened so far," he continued. "The chief has a press release set to deliver first thing Friday morning. He's going to explain how one of our cops pulled two people over for speeding. During their encounter, he had enough evidence to suspect the couple of drug possession."

"That's ridiculous." Kennedy couldn't keep the edge out of her voice. "He didn't even have a reason to pull us over in the first place. It was rush hour. I couldn't have been speeding if I wanted to."

Dominic nodded. "I know that." Kennedy couldn't figure out if that should make her feel relieved or even angrier now that he was telling her to give up any hope for justice.

"At that point the chief is going to admit our man made a mistake."

"Good."

Dominic held up his hand before Kennedy could say anything else. "The mistake was that even though he had suspected you of drug possession, he failed to call for backup. And if you hear the chief's side of the story, he's going to be all over it as an example of how the city needs to put more resources into the police force. The reason our man didn't call for backup, at least as the public is going to hear it tomorrow morning, is because we're short-staffed. Budget cuts, lay-offs, the whole enchilada."

"But he attacked us."

Dominic shrugged. "The chief already got the public believing you two are druggies at this point. And based on that video I saw, he won't have a hard time arguing you assaulted him first. There's a reason it's being called the piggyback attack, you know."

Rage boiled in Kennedy's brain, making it impossible to put any rational thought into a cohesive sentence.

The worst part about this whole encounter was how shaken up Dominic was pretending to be over it all. "That's what I mean when I'm telling you not to underestimate Goliath."

"He grabbed me." Kennedy blinked back tears, no longer of shame or fear but of blind fury. "He had his hands all over me." She shut her eyes so she wouldn't have to watch Dominic shrug another time.

"Cops search suspects. It's what they do." Did Dominic really believe any of this? Did he really believe she and Reuben were drug pushers?

"You can search the baggie. All it had was tea."

Dominic frowned. "Do you have any idea how many drug busts we see a week? How hard do you think it would be for someone in the force to sprinkle your roommate's tea leaves with a little weed, huh?"

"They can't do that." Kennedy hadn't realized how childish her argument sounded until she heard it come out of her mouth.

"But they do. It's not right. I'm not making any excuses. That cop, based on what you told me at Providence, he had no business pulling you over, making you get out of the car, restraining your friend, none of it. But it doesn't matter what I think. What matters is what the chief thinks, and all he's thinking about is how he's gonna protect his own. It's an unwritten code."

Unwritten code. That phrase was like fingernails on a chalkboard. So this was it? This was the Goliath she had dreamed of going up against? What chance did she have?

She would never look at a policeman the same way again.

There had to be some other option. This was America. It wasn't China or Kenya or some other country riddled with corruption.

Things like this didn't happen here.

Did they?

A memory tugged at the back of her brain. Something Pastor Carl said in one of his recent sermons. A Bible verse from Proverbs. Or was it Psalms? A verse about God bringing justice to light like the noonday sun. A verse about Christians waiting patiently for God's truth to prevail.

But why should she have to wait for it? She wanted it now. Everything Dominic said made sense. Of course, that's how the chief would slant the issue — an officer going about his business, risking his life to make the streets of Boston safer, when all of a sudden he's attacked by two suspects, and the force is so overworked and underpaid that he fails to call for backup. It was a flawlessly logical argument, however wrong it was. Like a bilayer of phospholipids surrounding a cell's organelles — perfectly watertight.

How could she stand against a Goliath like this?

The truth was she couldn't.

"Wait a minute." A seed of doubt had germinated in Kennedy's mind. It was taking root now. Sprouting. "If he was so convinced we were criminals, why did he just drive off? Why did he leave Reuben there bleeding on the pavement?"

She had him now. This was her slingshot. This was how she'd defeat the Philistine giant.

Dominic's frown did nothing to bolster her newfound encouragement. "The PR guys already thought of that. Between you and me, the fact that he did run off is the only reason the chief hasn't pulled you both in and arrested you for assaulting an officer. He won't admit it, not even to us, but we can all sniff out a rotten egg. If our man believed half of what the chief's saying — that you were carrying drugs or attacked him unprovoked or anything like that — he would have thrown every citation in the book at you. But he didn't. He ran off, and I'm speaking strictly off the record here, but that's the biggest reason I believed your story to begin with." His expression softened for a moment.

She was too busy formulating her next argument to let his words sink in. "But that means that we can't have really done all those things, or else he wouldn't have just left us there like that. So there must be some way to prove to the public ..."

"You're not understanding something here," Dominic interrupted. "The chief doesn't want the public to know the truth. He doesn't want the protesters, the marchers, the Gordon Clarences all taking to our streets. He'd rather throw the media a bone and bury the truth in the backyard. I'm not saying it's right. I'm just saying it's the way things are done."

"So that's all?" She hadn't meant to sound so accusatory. She just couldn't understand how someone like Dominic, someone with a powerful faith who obviously loved the Lord, could sit there and tell her that lies and gross abuses of justice were normal, just as much a part of Boston life as the swan boats in the Common or a strong nor'easter in the winter. Kennedy refused to believe it. "Can't you do something?"

"I am doing something." He pointed to his badge. "I'm getting up every day, begging God to make me a salt and a light to those other officers. I'm putting on this uniform. I'm not the kind of guy who rolls over and watches corruption. Not usually. So when I say it's time to let it go, I really mean it. If not for your own sake, at least for your friend's."

The mention of Reuben was enough to make Kennedy's whole body tense. "What do you mean?"

"I told you I saw Reuben earlier. He has his reasons — very personal reasons — for keeping this quiet. Let me tell you how the chief sees it. You two stay out of the public eye, don't come forward, we keep your identity secret ..." He held up his hand to stop Kennedy from interrupting. "We keep your identity secret," he repeated, "and we don't charge you with assault or possession."

He leaned forward in Willow's chair as if he were about to stand up. "But if you go to the press, if you start broadcasting your side of the story ..." He shook his head. "The chief is willing to do whatever it takes to keep his own guy covered. I need you to remember that. You shout police brutality, I guarantee you they'll find marijuana in that tea-leaf baggie, no matter what was in it when he took it out of your car. You accuse his guy, the chief accuses you. Not just possession. Not just battery. But your past, too. Any mistake you ever made, any ..."

"I don't have anything to hide." She sounded braver than she felt.

Dominic stood. "Maybe not. But what if Reuben does? Out of respect for him, and because I gave him my word, that's all I'm gonna say. But if he's your friend like you claim, you really should let this case drop."

His shoulders sagged as he opened the door. "I'm sorry." He let himself out. As he pulled the door shut behind him, he looked back once and added, "I really, really wanted tonight to end differently for you."

Kennedy didn't reply. She was feeling the exact same thing.

CHAPTER 9

Kennedy had just finished brushing her teeth when Willow barged into their room. "You decent?" she called out. "I brought a friend with me." She led in a tall student Kennedy recognized from Willow's theater troupe.

She tried not to groan. It was almost midnight. What was Willow thinking?

"I'm really tired." Kennedy reached over to turn her desk lamp off. "Could you two go somewhere else to hang out?"

Willow tossed her bag onto her desk. "Oh, we're not here for that." She put her hand on his shoulder. "I couldn't get Othello to go to bed with me even if I wanted to."

Kennedy was left wondering what was so humorous. "Your name's really Othello?" she asked, but the two of them were too busy chuckling to answer.

"So anyway ..." Willow plopped down in her purple bean bag chair, and Othello sank in beside her. He crossed his leg and draped his arm around her shoulder. All he needed was a beanie cap to look like some sort of African-American beatnik poet.

Willow arched her penciled eyebrows and got that artificial look she adopted whenever she was around her theater friends. "I told Othello about your little encounter tonight, you and your pseudo-boyfriend."

Kennedy was about to ask how much he knew, but as if taking a cue from somewhere offstage, Othello shook his head and muttered, "Now, that's what I'm talking about. It's that sort of warfare, that type of dictatorial oppression that's been plaguing our country since the days of slavery."

He paused for a moment to sigh. It was no wonder he was in the theater department.

"For centuries, my people have been the victims of a coordinated assault, a cultural genocide, not with bombs but with racial profiling. The ghettoization of our homes. The methodical incarceration of our young men. The rape of our women. The abduction of our children by welfare workers backed up by policemen armed with guns who know nothing of our way of life, our culture."

Kennedy didn't know how to answer. It was as if Othello had opened his mouth, and Reverend Clarence came spewing out.

"I just want you to know how grateful we are to you," he told her, meeting her eyes for the first time. "Sometimes it takes a tragedy like this for people to pay attention. Black men are brutalized, terrorized every day, and nobody cares. But you, a white woman who gets harassed — now that's something the hypnotized majority of this nation will pay attention to. And I just want to tell you that I'm honored you're here to stand side by side with us to speak out against the racism that's poisoned our schools, polluted our judiciary system, and plagued our inner cities."

He ended his words with a flourish, and Kennedy wondered if he was expecting applause or something of the sort. She'd heard all those arguments before in Reverend Clarence's speeches and Professor Hill's classroom. But this was the first time it'd come addressed directly to her. She wasn't sure if she should give Othello an ovation or apologize to him on behalf of every single white American, past, present, and future.

It couldn't be that bad, could it? And if it was, how would she know? How could she — a white American who'd lived in China since the third grade — know what it was like for minorities in the inner cities? How would she know if it was as bad as Othello said if she'd never seen it, never experienced it firsthand?

From the beanbag chair where Willow was running her fingers through his short curly hair, Othello nodded sagely. "It's hard to find kindred spirits in our light-skinned counterparts."

Kennedy was too tired to tell if he was giving her a compliment or insulting her, but she knew she had to correct his assumptions. "Actually, I haven't decided whether I'm going to file a complaint or not." All she wanted was to go to sleep. She could make up her mind later.

Othello turned to Willow. "You said she was going to take her story to the news outlets."

Willow fidgeted with her scarf. "I said I thought she was going to. There's a big difference."

"I haven't decided yet." Kennedy's voice came out harsher than she intended, but she didn't care.

Othello scowled. "If you keep quiet, it's just as bad as if you let that cop murder your friend. You know that, don't you?"

Willow put her hand on his shoulder. "Hey, all she said was she needed more time to make up her mind. I think it's only fair ..."

He wasn't paying any attention. "So you're just like everyone else. You don't care what happens to us. You'll leave it up to the Reverend Clarences of the world to plan their protests and marches, and you'll just sit cozy, swimming in your white privilege ..."

Willow nudged him in the ribs. "I told you to leave her alone."

"Sure." He shrugged. "Sure. The cops are out exterminating our race one traffic stop at a time, but hey, I wouldn't want you two pretty porcelains losing sleep over it or anything."

He could say whatever he wanted. He had no idea what he was talking about. He could harp and rail about police brutality and violence against blacks. She was too tired to listen. Willow followed him out of the room, their ensuing argument loud enough to wake up anybody lucky enough to have fallen asleep already. It didn't matter. Kennedy didn't have the energy to think about it, let alone let his words discourage her.

She just needed rest. Without even bothering to turn off the light, she covered her head with her blanket and squeezed her eyes shut. Her brain soaked up the comfort of her bed like parched roots drinking up rainfall.

Sleep. That's all she wanted to do. Everything would be clearer in the morning.

CHAPTER 10

Kennedy woke up Friday with the sun pouring in through her dorm room window. An uneasy feeling sloshed around in her empty gut. Even her sleep had failed to provide the reprieve she'd hoped for. She wasn't any more rested than she'd been last night.

She glanced at Willow's bed. Empty. Her roommate never woke up early. Did that mean she'd stayed out? Had she spent the night at Othello's?

Kennedy scratched her head, grimacing when she felt how slimy and gross her hair was. She hadn't even taken a shower last night. At least the thought of washing off all of Bow Legs' lingering filth was enough motivation to get her out of bed. As she was gathering her toiletries together, her phone beeped. She glanced at the text message from Willow.

Headed to the protest. Want a ride?

Protest?

Did Kennedy even want to know?

She was tempted to ignore the message and take an impossibly long shower until her skin was lobster red and her mind washed of all the defiling memories from yesterday. She wasn't due to meet Reuben for breakfast for another hour, and then their only class was children's literature. After that, the weekend. She couldn't remember if she had anything else scheduled, but she wasn't going to worry about that right now.

One day at a time.

Pastor Carl's wife Sandy had once encouraged Kennedy to meditate on the Sermon on the Mount, let the words sink in and minister to her soul. Kennedy was such a speed reader — the only way she could keep up with her courses and still have time to enjoy a few classics or mystery novels on the side — that it was hard for her to slow down to make her Scripture reading very contemplative. As a countermeasure, Sandy encouraged her to memorize certain passages that stood out the most to her, so Kennedy had started with Jesus's admonition to stop worrying about tomorrow.

So far, she was only a couple verses in, but it was a start. This morning though, Kennedy didn't have time to spend in the Bible. She had to clean herself up. She'd pray while she was in the shower. God wouldn't mind, would he?

She grabbed her towel and had just slipped on her germ-proof flip-flops when her phone beeped once more. Willow again, sending nothing but a series of question marks.

Kennedy huffed as she set the shower caddy down on her desk.

Another beep.

Check the news.

Great. This was not the way Kennedy planned on starting her Friday. She typed Channel 2's web address into her browser and was met with a zoomed-in photo of Boston's chief of police who had recently addressed the public. Kennedy scanned the article. It was exactly what Dominic had warned her it would be. The cop she'd met last night — apparently his name was Lorence Burgess and not Bow Legs after all — had a stellar record. He helped crack a murder investigation a few years ago in North End, two men with Mafia connections who dumped a body into a pier before going after a couple of unlucky witnesses. He traveled around to elementary schools warning kids about the dangers of gangs. Kennedy rolled her eyes. He probably baked chocolate chip cookies for his shut-in mama every weekend, too.

After extoling his officer's flawless record, the chief explained that last night at 6:34 pm, Burgess had pulled over two suspects in a drug-related case, which apparently sounded more convincing than the speeding story Dominic had predicted.

Halfway down the screen was a grainy picture of Kennedy hanging onto Officer Burgess' back. Reuben wasn't in the shot at all. They had cropped that part out, probably because it wouldn't look so good to show Burgess kicking an unarmed black man. At that point, the article quoted the chief regretfully informing the people of Boston that when Burgess was attacked by his two "alleged suspects," there were not enough backup officers on duty. The next several paragraphs dealt with budget cuts on the police force.

The article ended, almost like an afterthought, with the notice of a peaceful protest organized by the Reverend Gordon Clarence, who aimed to let the mayor and police department know that the people of Boston wouldn't stand for the slaughter of innocent African-Americans.

Kennedy had lost her appetite by the time she finished reading. She texted Willow back, saying she had to go to her lit class and wouldn't make the gathering. She looked at the clock. Still enough time to shower and dress and maybe catch up on a little reading before she met Reuben at the student union.

She glanced once more at the news article, hoping her brain had made up the entire story, but there was the picture of her straddling Burgess' back. Her only solace was that she hadn't been named. She and Reuben were still safe. They still had their privacy.

For now.

CHAPTER 11

She arrived at the student union a few minutes early and made her way to a table in the back where she and Reuben could enjoy some seclusion. She avoided making eye contact with anyone. Why were they all staring at her? How many of them had seen the video clip? Did they recognize her? She opened her used copy of *My Side of the Mountain* and wondered what it would feel like to run away into the wilderness like Sam Gribley so she could live on her own. Completely alone.

Things had been going so well lately. The panic attacks were finally under control. She had made it through the first half of the semester without any major drama. She was one of the few first-years on campus lucky enough to get along with her roommate. She and Willow had almost nothing in common besides mutual respect, but apparently that was enough for the mismatched pair.

Classes were going well. Even her parents had stopped hovering over her from ten thousand miles away in Yanji. Her mom didn't cry anymore when they talked on the phone, lamenting that her little girl was so far from home. For a short time, life had been good. Really good. And of course, there was Reuben. Always so kind and encouraging. Such an important part of her first year at Harvard. As excited as she was to go back home to Yanji at the end of the semester, she hated the idea of going all summer without seeing him. She had always imagined romance like what happened to Marius and Cosette in *Les Miserables*, when two people look at each other across the way, their hearts fluttering, and in that moment they both know they were meant for each other. Her relationship with Reuben, by contrast, had grown slowly. Organically. Whatever they had, be it a friendship or something deeper, it had sneaked up on them quietly while neither one was looking. Was it God who'd brought them together? If it was, then why couldn't he have kept them away from Officer Burgess last night? Why couldn't he let them go to *Aida* together, let the music surround them, let the love story enfold them? Who knew what would have happened next?

"To know what would have happened, child?" Kennedy could almost hear Aslan's voice in her head. *"No. Nobody is ever told that."*

She shut her book. No use studying *My Side of the Mountain* when her brain was still stuck in the Narnia world. It was just as well. Reuben was coming toward her wearing a tired smile. His step was slower, too.

"Good morning." She eyed his tray of food.

He slipped into the seat across from her. "Hey. Aren't you eating?"

"I'm not that hungry." Kennedy forced a cheerful tone. "How's your head today?"

He scooped his scrambled eggs up with his fork. She was glad to see him devour his first bite with his usual zeal. "Nothing to worry about." It didn't really answer her question.

She nodded toward her book. "Have you caught up on your reading?"

"I was a little busy last night," he muttered.

Kennedy would have liked to get herself some food, anything to relieve this awkward tension, but she was too nervous to eat. Maybe she should have asked Willow for more information about that protest. What would Dominic think? It wasn't as though she and Reuben had anything to do with it, but would the police suspect they were involved? Would the chief retaliate like Dominic predicted?

There were so many things she wanted to talk to Reuben about. Not just the protest. Not just the visit from Dominic at her dorm where he all but threatened her into silence. There was so much more they needed to discuss. Like Reuben's aloof behavior. Was he angry about what they went through, or was there more to it? What did Dominic mean when he said that Reuben had a secret reason to keep their story from the press? How was Kennedy supposed to react to all this confusion?

"I got a visit from the police last night," Reuben said through a mouthful of sourdough toast.

She lifted her gaze. Tried to read his face. "What did they say?"

"I was so tired, I hardly remember any of it."

Slowly, the tension she had felt between them lifted, like a cloud of condensation slowly dispersing. She eyed the French toast and strawberry sauce on his plate. Maybe she could find her appetite after all. She also found the courage to ask, "Do you think we should tell someone what happened? File a complaint or something?"

Reuben took a sip of his Coke. She was glad that he at least appeared to consider her question. He swirled his straw around in his cup, staring at the ice shavings and the carbonated bubbles floating to the surface. "We have a saying back home. When two elephants fight, it's the grass that suffers."

Kennedy appreciated the proverb but wasn't sure why he would bring it up now. "So are you and I the elephants or the grass?"

Neither of them laughed.

"I love my home." Reuben wiped his mouth with a napkin before attacking his biscuits and gravy. "But we've got some messed up politics. Tribal tensions that go back to colonial times and even earlier. I'm not saying everyone's corrupted by it. We've got our Martin Luther Kings and our Gandhis. But it's not like in America. Here, you go to a protest or a march, and you assume that makes you some hero. You wave the banner, and then you go home without worrying about your house getting burned down or your family getting death threats. But that's not how I grew up. That policeman we met last night would fit right into Nairobi, especially during election times. I look at people here in America, and I just see a bunch of the world's most privileged kids wasting time and chanting in their picket lines." He finished off his cup of Coke before starting on his second one. "Maybe it's harder for you, being an American. Maybe it's harder for you to admit the corruption. But for me, that's just a fact of life."

Kennedy didn't know what to say. This wasn't the conversation she expected to have. Was this what Reuben had told Dominic last night? Was that why Dominic had pressured her so strongly to keep her complaints to herself, for Reuben's sake if nothing else? It still didn't explain what the elephants had to do with anything. Was Reuben saying that regular folks like the two of them were the grass, helpless to stand up against raging elephants? That instead of wasting their energy trying to stop a fight, they should just get themselves out of the way in the name of personal safety or comfort?

"So you want to pretend like last night never happened?" Kennedy stared as Reuben bit into a greasy sausage patty, and her appetite waned just as quickly as it had perked up a few minutes earlier.

"Yes, last night happened. It was wrong." Reuben let out a little chuckle and wiped his mouth with his napkin. "In fact, there was one point that I thought I might actually wet my pants."

It really wasn't all that funny, but Kennedy found herself smiling. This was the Reuben she knew. This was the Reuben she had grown so close to this year.

He smothered his hash browns in ketchup. "Last night's probably going to be something we remember for the rest of our lives. But things happen, and then you move on."

Kennedy eyed his bowl of Froot Loops and tried to surreptitiously gauge his reaction. "Did you know they're staging a protest today? My roommate's on her way over now."

Reuben smiled. His eyes were soft. "Yeah, that sounds like something she'd do."

Another shared laugh.

"So what now?" Kennedy's insides quivered as she asked the question. "We just hope no one identifies us from that tape?"

Reuben slurped the rest of his second cup of Coke. "I guess so."

"And what if they do?"

He wiped his mouth with his napkin. "Let's just pray they don't."

CHAPTER 12

Kennedy's phone rang as soon as Reuben got up to get himself more food.

"Hello?"

Without any sort of greeting, her dad demanded, "Please tell me you don't have anything to do with that protest they're planning this afternoon in front of the court house."

Hi, Dad. It's good to talk to you, too. "No, I've got class soon, and I'm headed over to the Lindgrens' for dinner tonight."

She could perfectly envision her father's frown all the way from Yanji.

"Well, I don't want you anywhere near it. These things always start out as peaceful demonstrations, but you never know what can happen after that. It's like piling up all your old gas cans right outside a match factory and then acting surprised when you get an explosion."

"I wasn't planning to go. I already said I'm too busy." She had been longing for her dad's advice last night, but now his paranoid protection annoyed her more than anything else.

"So, did you think any more about what you're going to do? Are you going to file a complaint?"

Had she made up her mind on anything? Or had everyone else just made the decision for her? At least if she let it go, she'd be returning to some semblance of normalcy. A little while longer, and all this would be a distant and distasteful memory.

"I think I'll just forget about it and move on."

"That's good." Her dad had this irritating habit of smacking his lips when he agreed with something she said, a quirk she'd almost expect from a toothless old grandfather. "I just got off the phone with my college buddy

Jefferson. He's a lawyer now. Got a practice in Worchester. He'd already heard about your encounter when I called."

Kennedy tried not to sigh so loud her dad would hear it on the other line.

"I told Jefferson what you said happened. He believes your story, but honestly, sugar, he said you're lucky the department hasn't charged you both with assaulting an officer. They could have identified you pretty easily by now if they'd wanted to bring you in. The fact that you're still on campus making plans to go to class and visit Carl and Sandy's tonight is proof enough that the department knows their guy messed up. But unless you get evidence, a recording of the confrontation or another witness who watched the whole thing, there's no way your word alone would hold up. It sounds like your best bet is to lay low, let this whole thing blow over, and avoid jumping on any officers' backs in the future."

She knew her father was trying to lighten the situation. Knew that he had probably spent hours out of his day talking with his lawyer friend and researching Massachusetts law. But none of this was funny. None of this would ever be funny. Part of her was so ready to forget last night ever happened, ready to go back to being a regular first-year pre-med student. Ready to talk with Reuben about literature and science and foreign countries, not abusive cops.

But another side of her hated the helplessness she'd experienced when she got pulled over on Arlington. The helplessness she still felt as she listened to every single person she talked to, all the way from an apparently sympathetic policeman to her own father, telling her it was useless to seek retribution. No, not even useless. It was dangerous. If she made a complaint, they'd turn around and lock her up for assaulting a cop. No questions asked. No real justice.

Her dad sighed. "I'm sorry, sugar. I know it's not the answer you wanted to hear. And I told Jefferson, and I told your mother too because she's worrying herself straight off her diet over the whole situation — I told them that if you wanted to seek legal redress, I'd support you. Jefferson's a good lawyer, and he agreed to give us a fair rate. So if you really know what you're getting into and still feel like the right thing to do is bring this officer to justice, we're willing to help you try. We just don't want you to get your hopes up too high, because without any other evidence, well ..." He let his voice trail off. Kennedy was thankful. She'd heard enough threats in the past twelve hours.

"You don't need to let us know what you're going to do right now," her dad went on. "It's probably something you want to think through, and honestly, it might be best to wait until some of the media frenzy dies down. And who knows? Maybe there were other witnesses who will come forward. We can always pray that someone who saw the whole thing will have the guts to stand up and tell people what really happened."

Kennedy watched Reuben walking back toward their table with his second breakfast tray as her dad added, "By the way, how is your friend doing? How's Reuben?"

"He's better now. Couple stitches in his head, and he's walking like he's pretty sore, but the doctors didn't seem too concerned."

"Well, I'm sorry this happened to him. I'm sure he's a great guy, and I know he didn't do anything to deserve to be treated like this."

"Thanks, Daddy." Kennedy felt her throat constricting and wished she had a cup of tea.

"You tell Reuben to get better. Tell him your mom and I are praying for him, and you take care of yourself too, baby girl, ok? I don't want to be seeing your face on Channel 2's webpage for at least another month."

They shared an awkward sort of laugh. Kennedy knew her dad's heart must be just as heavy as hers. After the usual rounds of *I love you* and *I miss you*, they hung up just as Reuben sat back down with his extra tray of food. "You talking to your dad?"

"Yeah, how did you know?

"You just get a certain look on your face. That's all."

Kennedy helped herself to a piece of pineapple from Reuben's fruit salad and glanced at the time. Twenty minutes before they had to be at their lit class. She'd only been awake for a little over an hour and already had the feeling this would be one of those days that would never end.

"What did your dad say?" Reuben asked. "About last night, I mean. Did you tell him?"

"Yeah, but I didn't need to. He's more of a Channel 2 news junkie than anyone on the whole East Coast."

"What did he think about it?" Reuben was studying a piece of cantaloupe as if it might contain all the calculus formulas he'd need for next week's quiz.

Kennedy found herself lowering her voice. Why did it feel as if she were part of some big conspiracy? "He talked to a lawyer friend of his. Says unless someone else comes forward with more concrete evidence, there's really nothing we can do."

"So he wants you to drop the case?" There was a hint of hopefulness in Reuben's voice that Kennedy knew he was trying to hide.

She nodded, and watched a small flicker of relief light up in his eyes. She tested her words carefully, like she might do with a piece of litmus paper she didn't want to get too wet. "Hey, can I ask you something?"

Reuben's body tensed, his fork froze halfway to his mouth.

Kennedy hoped she wouldn't regret her question. Oh, well. Too late to backtrack now. "Is there any particular reason ..." She struggled to find the right words. "About last night. Is there something you've been keeping from me?"

Reuben set his fork by his plate. "Like what?"

Kennedy forced a smile she was sure looked totally unconvincing. "I don't know. Any reason you're scared of the cops finding out who we are?"

He grabbed two grapes and plopped them into his mouth with a shrug. "I've just learned that when the elephants start fighting, it's best to stay as far away as possible."

CHAPTER 13

After a semester and half living in Cambridge, Kennedy thought she should be used to Sandy's hugs by now, but it still caught her off guard when her pastor's wife flung her arms around her as if they hadn't seen each other in years. Once she finally let go, Sandy tossed her long French braid over her shoulder, grabbed Kennedy's hands, and pulled her into their home. "I'm so glad you made it tonight, sweetie. I've been worrying my head off about you since last night." She lowered her voice. "That kind of stuff used to happen to Carl and me pretty regular," she whispered, "back when we were courting in the South. It's a shame to think that people haven't gotten over their differences by now. Heaven knows we've had enough time to change."

Kennedy kept her eyes down and tried not to stiffen when Sandy gave her another hug, this one from the side. "Now maybe you don't want to talk about it, and I don't blame you one bit. If you don't mind, I could sure use an extra set of hands with these pork chops."

Kennedy followed Sandy into the kitchen where the sound of sizzling onions and the smell of homemade bread rolls welcomed her. She washed her hands, grateful for a chance to make herself useful. Anything for some sort of distraction. The afternoon had dragged on just like she expected. She didn't know what it was about the spring that made it even harder to sit in a classroom while the sun streamed in from outside, warming everything up like a giant greenhouse.

"It smells delicious." She wasn't sure what it was about Carl and Sandy's home, but she always felt so peaceful here, as if there was some magnetic field at their front door that stripped away all her stress and anxiety as soon as she entered.

Sandy was bustling over the stove and put Kennedy to work chopping up veggies for a green salad.

"Where's Carl?" Kennedy asked. "Is he still at church?"

Sandy slurped a taste of gravy from a steaming saucepan. "No, he was invited to sit on a panel down at Channel 2. Different community leaders are giving their opinions about the ..." She let out an exaggerated sneeze. "Excuse me. I must have dumped too much pepper in here. Tell me, would you mind tasting this and letting me know what you think? My nose has been a little stuffy all week, and I'm afraid I've over-spiced everything."

Kennedy gingerly sipped from the spoon Sandy held out. "Tastes fine to me."

"Oh, good. Thanks. It must be allergy season or something. Can't smell a thing." Sandy started telling Kennedy a story about her grandson Tyson, who was expecting a brand new sister at the end of May. "You should see the way he loves that baby already. Pulls up his mother's shirt and gives her belly rubs. Says he's playing with his little sister."

Kennedy forced herself to laugh along. She wondered what it would be like to be pregnant, always carrying around a little person you'd never even met. Did it feel like an intrusion, or was it more like snuggling with someone you loved? Did pregnant women always think about their growing uterus, or did they get used to it and go on with life as normal? Motherhood seemed so far away in Kennedy's future. Three and a half more years at Harvard, four years of medical school, then residency ... By the time she was settled enough to even think of having kids, would she be too old? Funny how she never pondered these things except for when she was at the Lindgrens'. What was it about this house that made her long for family? For home?

Sandy prattled on, but Kennedy's thoughts still wandered, her ears ringing with the sound of her own screams as she had tried to protect Reuben. The more she thought about it, the angrier she grew. Maybe she should have gone to that protest after all. After her dad's warning, she had checked the news several times. The only coverage Channel 2 offered was a small article at the bottom of their home screen, but the event itself had been perfectly peaceful. Why was it that strangers were protesting Kennedy and Reuben's mistreatment while the two of them hid like Claudia and

Jaime in *The Mixed Up Files of Mrs. Basil E. Frankweiler*, crouching beneath art displays in the Met?

Sandy took some bread rolls out of the oven and set them on a hot pad. The warm, yeasty smell set Kennedy's stomach growling. Other than a few bites of Reuben's fruit salad and a bowl of Craisins for a snack after her lit class, she hadn't eaten all day.

Sandy went back to whisking the gravy on the stovetop. "There's some melted butter in the microwave, hon. Could you grab that basting brush and spread it on top of the roles?"

At the beginning of the semester in her lab class, Professor Adell had posted a quote from a Julia Child cookbook about multitasking in the kitchen. Adell said those same skills would come in handy in the lab, and Kennedy had done enough chemistry experiments as well as assisted Sandy in the kitchen enough times to realize her professor was absolutely right. It also helped to have a partner who could anticipate your moves and know intuitively where to jump in to be the most useful. That's why she was so grateful to work with Reuben. After a week or two of clumsily stumbling over each other in the lab last fall, they could now look at the same set of instructions and perform the entire procedure without having to talk through each specific task. They worked so smoothly, so gracefully together.

She was nearly done spreading the melted butter when the doorbell rang.

Sandy glanced up but didn't look surprised. "Could you get that for me, dear? My hands are a big mess."

Kennedy glanced out the kitchen window to see a multicolored VW bus parked in the Lindgrens' driveway. Maybe she wouldn't have Carl and Sandy to herself tonight like she thought. She dusted her hands off on her pants legs and opened the front door. Nick, the youth pastor from Carl's church, stood smiling on the porch.

"Hey, Kennedy. Glad to see you."

She tried to hide her disappointment. She hadn't expected to be sharing her time at the Lindgrens' with anyone else. Forcing a smile, she stepped aside to let him in. No matter how often she saw Nick, she was always slightly startled by his appearance. From his dirty blond dreadlocks and grungy fashion sense, you'd think he stepped off of a West Coast beach. Today, his T-shirt sported the verse from Revelation where Jesus says, "Behold, I am coming soon," along with a picture of Jesus typing *BRB* into a text message.

"Hi, Nick!" Sandy called from the kitchen, and Kennedy wondered why nobody had mentioned the additional dinner guest. For an awkward moment, neither Kennedy nor Nick knew which one was supposed to be the first out of the small entryway. After a clumsy exchange and a few more apologies than necessary, Kennedy led the way back to the kitchen. The sound of sizzling pork was just loud enough to cover the rumbling in her belly.

Sandy wiped her hands on her apron before giving Nick a big hug. She was as tall as he was, but whenever they were together, Kennedy got the sense that Sandy towered over him. "I'm so glad you made it." She pointed at the dining room table. "Why don't you both make yourselves comfortable? We're just waiting on Carl now. He should be here any minute."

Kennedy wondered what Sandy meant by *any minute* and wasn't sure their definitions would match. She sat across from Nick, trying to guess if he felt just as uncomfortable with this forced arrangement. It wasn't the first time the Lindgrens had gone out of their way to make sure Kennedy and Nick spent time together. Carl kept mentioning how nice it would be if Kennedy found the time to volunteer with Nick during his weekly visit to Medford Academy for an afterschool Bible club. It's possible the church was just short of volunteers, or maybe Carl thought if Kennedy plugged into some sort of ministry at St. Margaret's, she'd feel that sense of belonging she'd lacked ever since her first Sunday there. But then sometimes she'd catch Sandy winking at her husband or smiling mischievously and wondered if there was more to it than the Lindgrens wanted her to know.

She didn't dislike Nick, but that wasn't a good enough reason to pursue a relationship. Besides, she was pretty sure he was interested in someone back in Oregon. He kept a picture on his office desk of a blond girl in a cute tankini, sporting a model's figure and a dimpled smile Kennedy envied. She wished she could be back in the kitchen helping Sandy with the salad. She didn't have anything against Nick. She just didn't like the thought of Carl and Sandy arranging a match for her out of sympathy. Granted, she hadn't made as many friends in college as she'd had in high school, but she had her roommate.

And of course she had Reuben.

She stared past Nick's cross earring and wondered what Reuben was doing now. Was he still upset about their encounter with the policeman or had he forgotten the entire ordeal already? That sounded like Reuben. Never one to dwell on the past. Never one to hold a grudge or harbor negative emotions.

Solid, stable Reuben.

Across from her, Nick cleared his throat.

"So, how's school?" His voice grated her ears with its artificial cheer.

She glanced at Sandy, hoping to find some reason to excuse herself to the kitchen. When no opportunity presented itself, she shrugged. "Not too bad. I'm glad midterms are over. The next few weeks shouldn't be too busy."

"Good." Nick's dreadlocks bounced when he nodded, reminding Kennedy of the apostle bobble heads he had plastered to the dashboard of his painted bus.

"What about youth group?" she asked when the silence grew oppressive. "How's that going?"

A forced smile. More head bobbing. "Good. Good. You should come check it out sometime. We always need volunteers."

Kennedy mumbled her usual excuses about her course schedule and school obligations. She liked the idea of getting involved in ministry. If anything, it might help her snap out of whatever spiritual funk she'd found herself in since she got to Cambridge. It wasn't that she'd rebelled or run away from God. She didn't hate him or doubt him. She didn't even have as much trouble with temptations as she feared she would when she first arrived at Harvard. Her roommate drank nearly every night of the week, partied with harder stuff every weekend, and slept with more partners than Kennedy could name, but so far Kennedy hadn't felt pressured to get involved in any of that stuff. Maybe if she had at least been tempted, she'd find herself more drawn to God and the strength he could give her to resist sin. Instead, she was just coasting through her first year of college. She had drive and ambition when it came to her classwork, but when it came to matters of faith, she was the spiritual equivalent of her roommate — laid back and irresponsible. The only difference was Kennedy felt guilty for her apathy. She doubted Willow entertained those same kinds of self-doubts. She always told herself once she got into the hang of school, she'd get more involved at St. Margaret's, but even now, with three whole weeks before her next major test or paper due, she was reluctant to add anything to her schedule. She was at Harvard for her education, right? So why did she feel so empty?

The door to the garage burst open, and Carl bustled into the kitchen with arms outstretched. He pecked Sandy noisily on her cheek. "And how's my favorite wife today?" He lifted a lid off one of the simmering pots. "You scrape up that squirrel from the driveway?"

Sandy slapped him playfully with a hot pad.

"You know I'm joking, dear." Carl wrapped his arm around her shoulder. "Everything smells wonderful. And how are you two doing tonight?"

Nick was already standing up to shake Carl's hand even though Kennedy figured they must have spent most of the day together at church. After that, Carl gave her a bone-crushing hug that reminded her of her preschool days and a grandpa who'd died when she was only five.

After he let her go, Carl patted her on the back. "Staying out of the news, I hope?"

A disapproving look flashed from Sandy to her husband, who cleared his throat. "Well, let's take our seats. Who's hungry?"

CHAPTER 14

Dinner was even more delicious than it had smelled. Kennedy, who had unintentionally fallen into a mostly vegetarian diet since arriving at Harvard, had to admit she'd eat a lot more meat in the student union if it were as juicy and savory as this. She wondered how many servings Reuben would devour if he were here. Maybe she should have invited him over. Carl and Sandy wouldn't mind.

For a while, the only sounds in the dining room were the scrapings of silverware on Sandy's floral-patterned dishes and Carl's loud chewing and smacking noises. It was the quietest meal Kennedy could remember sharing with the Lindgrens. Sandy diligently kept all the plates at least half full. Whenever Kennedy took more than three bites of anything, Sandy would pass more her way or simply plop another helping onto her plate. Kennedy had spent so much of her college days munching on nothing but dry Cheerios and Craisins she'd probably be anemic if it weren't for these occasional meals at the Lindgrens'.

But tonight, something was different. Carl hadn't given a single commentary on current events, hadn't shared a single political opinion. Nick spent most of dinner avoiding eye contact with everyone, and Sandy made several failed attempts to start up a conversation. She asked Nick about a few of the youth group kids whose names Kennedy didn't recognize, questioned him about an upcoming concert with some Christian band Kennedy'd never heard of. Nick's answers were polite but never more than a single sentence.

Carl, who had been a loud and messy eater for as long as Kennedy had known him, finally finished his last pork chop. He dropped the bone onto his plate and wiped his stained hands on one of Sandy's dainty, rose-embroidered napkins.

"So, you had any more problems with the cops?" Carl's eyes were fixed on Kennedy, so he couldn't see Sandy's disapproving scowl.

"No." She shook her head and caught Nick passing her an apologetic look.

Carl frowned. "The nerve of some people. I just can't ..."

"Honey." Sandy's word was laced with meaning. With warning.

He threw his napkin over his plate. "Now sweetheart, I know you wanted to give Kennedy a night off from all her troubles, but those same troubles will just be waiting for her as soon as she leaves. We're all friends here. We all love each other. So let's talk. You doing ok after everything you've been through?"

The breath Kennedy had been holding rushed out of her. Relief flooded her entire vascular system. No more pretending. No more avoiding the real issue. This was why she loved the Lindgrens so much. And why she was almost always a little nervous whenever she stopped by for a visit.

"Well, it's been kind of crazy ..." She wasn't sure where to begin. How much did Carl already know?

"Sweetheart, it's ok." Sandy grabbed Kennedy's hand. With all the time Sandy spent in the kitchen scrubbing and washing, Kennedy never knew how she kept her hands so silky and soft. "We can change the subject if you want."

Across the table, Nick nodded enthusiastically.

Kennedy stared at her half-full plate, wondering if she'd regain any semblance of an appetite. "Well, I guess you guys saw the video." She was afraid to raise her eyes, afraid of what expressions she'd find on her friends' faces.

"I'm surprised the reporters haven't come to you to get your side of the story." It was the most Nick had said at once all evening.

Memories buzzed through Kennedy's mind like a swarm of Yanji mosquitoes. Dominic, the praying policeman who'd told her to keep quiet unless she wanted to see Reuben hurt. Her dad's lawyer buddy who told her to give up unless she wanted to get arrested for assault. Willow's friend Othello who treated Kennedy like a KKK conspirator when she didn't blast her story to every media outlet on the East Coast. She felt the onset of a headache and squeezed her eyes shut for a moment. "It's a little more complicated than that."

Carl leaned back in his seat, crossed his arms, and stared at Nick. "Let's say she did give her story to the news. What exactly do you expect would be the benefit of that?"

Nick set his elbows on the table. "Justice. Weeding out a racist cop who has no business wearing a uniform. Making the streets safer for hundreds of other young African-American men so they don't have to face the same humiliation."

Flashbacks of Bow Legs' hands on Kennedy's thighs forced the air out of her lungs. She begged her parasympathetic nervous system to function properly and rehearsed the breathing advice she'd gleaned from all those self-help websites.

Carl raised his eyebrows slightly but didn't respond.

"Think about it," Nick went on. "White cop pulls African-American teenager out of a car. No warrant. No speeding ticket. All this kid's guilty of is driving while black."

"I believe it was Kennedy who was driving." Carl's voice was soft.

Kennedy glanced around the table. Sandy was still holding her hand.

Nick's dreadlocks grew even more animated the faster he talked. "Ok, so she was the driver. It doesn't really matter. What matters is this white officer pulled this black kid out of the car, and then without any reason ..."

Carl jerked his head toward Nick but addressed Kennedy. "How much of the story is he getting right so far?"

She glanced at Nick, her cheeks hot beneath everyone's sympathetic stares.

"Go on," Carl prodded. "Tell him how much of what you went through last night was because Reuben is black."

Kennedy inventoried the faces around her, trying to guess what they expected her to say. "Well," she floundered, "at first I thought that might be some of it. He wanted Reuben to get out of the car, but he told me to stay in my seat."

Carl nodded. "So he told your black friend to step out of the vehicle, and Reuben complied. Peacefully?"

"Yeah." Kennedy remembered how calm he had looked. He wasn't surprised. Wasn't angry. Maybe this story did deserve retelling.

"And then what?" Carl prodded.

Beside her, Sandy strained as if she were about to say something, but instead she just patted Kennedy's hand and stayed quiet.

"He put Reuben in handcuffs. Slammed him against the car."

"So he was rough with him?"

"Yeah."

Carl took a sip of water. "And during this whole time, what was Reuben doing? Was he arguing with him? Threatening him?"

"No. He didn't do anything. I was the one who kept asking why we got pulled over." She was trembling now. She hoped the others wouldn't notice, but she doubted that based on the way Sandy gripped her hand a little tighter.

"See?" Nick banged his fist on the table to accentuate his point. "This is clear-cut racial profiling. The officer didn't have any reason to do what he did. Besides, if it was a regular traffic stop, why would he have the passenger step out of the car? Why the handcuffs? It's what's been going on for decades. White policemen with overinflated egos pulling over young black men just to ..."

"So at that point, you jumped on the officer's back, I assume?" Carl interrupted.

Kennedy furrowed her brow. "No, that was later. I got out of the car because I was worried about Reuben. I was worried the officer might hurt him."

"That's what I'm saying." Nick turned to Carl. "Honestly, I'm surprised you're not even more riled up than I am."

Carl grinned. If Kennedy suspected he had a sarcastic streak, she might have said he smirked. "Even more riled up? Why? Because I'm black?"

Nick's obvious embarrassment would have been amusing if Kennedy's memories of the entire ordeal weren't lying just behind her optic nerve, pulsing pain to the back of her eyes and radiating discomfort all the way to her temples.

He frowned into his cup of water. "That's not what I'm saying."

"Oh yes it is. That's exactly what you're saying." There was no trace of a grin now on Carl's face. "You're saying that because I'm black, I need to be just as angry as you, preferably even more so, whenever it comes to any kind of perceived racism."

"Perceived?" Nick's complexion, which still carried the hint of a tan left over from his West Coast surfing days, was now more red than anything else. "All I'm saying is that I'm surprised that you as an African-American man who's endured more than his fair share of prejudice can be so calm after a cop pulls over a black kid, leaves him bleeding on the sidewalk, and gets away with it."

Kennedy could hear the strain in Nick's voice, could sense the tension in his body and almost see the pulse of his carotid artery. Carl, on the other hand, still leaned back in his chair, and Kennedy got the sense he could just as easily be discussing Paul's introduction to his epistle to the Galatians as anything else. He turned toward her, his eyes calm. She wondered if he worked deliberately to achieve that degree of peace or if it was just some supernatural gift or a fortunate personality quirk, a blessing from genetics. He smiled at her tenderly. "And how did it feel for you, a white woman, when this big bad white policeman beat up your black friend?"

She had a feeling Carl expected a certain reply out of her but couldn't guess what it was. "I didn't think about it in that way while it was happening." She spoke slowly, partly so she had time to plan her response and partly because she was trying to mask the tremor in her voice. "He said some really rude things to Reuben, racial slurs I mean, but he was just as crass to me."

Her throat tightened. She hadn't realized how much she was shaking until Sandy wrapped a strong arm around her and said, "I think maybe we should save this discussion for another time."

Carl smiled sheepishly. "You're right, sweetie. Of course. Kennedy, I'm sorry. I know how upsetting this must be."

Nick cleared his throat. "I'm sorry, too." For once, his dreadlocks fell perfectly still.

Everyone stared at their plates. Nick scraped a few green beans around in his gravy.

"So." Sandy turned to her husband. "Do you have everything ready for Sunday's sermon?"

He shook his head. His usual jocular smile was gone. "I'll be spending most of tomorrow at the office. Still have a ways to go."

More silence.

Kennedy wanted to apologize. As if Carl and Nick's argument was all her fault. As if she should have known better than get into an altercation with a cop that would spoil a perfectly delicious meal.

"I have a meeting tomorrow with one of the teens." Nick's comment seemed to appear out of a vacuum, an infinitely dense black hole. As soon as he spoke, he shoved a bit of bread roll into his mouth. Nobody responded. From the living room, a clock ticked, reminding Kennedy of her mother's grandfather clock back in Yanji.

"Well." Sandy spoke with exaggerated cheer and clasped her hands together. "Carl and I haven't made it official to the church yet, but we're so close to both of you, I wanted to share some good news." She glanced at her husband, who nodded approvingly. She reached for an envelope from the countertop and pulled out a photograph. "We just got word that we were matched for adoption. We're hoping to bring our little boy home from South Korea this summer."

Kennedy reached for the photograph that Sandy proudly showed off. Studied the smiling boy. He appeared so emaciated it was hard to guess his age, maybe eight or ten years old. He had two skinned knees, a dimple in one cheek, and a smile that showed two missing teeth in opposite sides of his mouth. Kennedy didn't know what to say. Were you supposed to congratulate the adoptive parents or was that just for pregnancy announcements?

"He's adorable."

Sandy was beaming. It was a special expression she only wore when she was talking about her children or grandchildren.

Nick reached for the photo and raised his eyebrows. "I didn't know you guys were planning on adopting overseas."

"Neither did we." Sandy chuckled. "There was one point before we started fostering that we thought about it, but we ran into problems."

"Yeah." Carl's booming voice was a striking contrast to Sandy's maternal prattle. "Back in the day when prejudice really was a problem in our country, adoption agencies wouldn't consider interracial couples. They said we ..."

"So," Sandy interrupted, her voice still chipper and cheerful as ever even as she glared at her husband, "we don't know much about him yet. We know his name's Woong, and we know he's had a pretty hard life so far. The orphanage can't tell us his real age. I've just been praying so hard about this adoption, and I knew as soon as I saw his picture he was ours. I can't explain it, really. I took out that photo, saw those little missing teeth, that grin — he looks pretty mischievous, don't he? Well, soon as I saw him, I knew in my heart that God had called me to be his mother." She laughed. "I feel like Sarah. Look at me. Already a grandmother with two more grandbabies on the way, and God's decided to add one more son to our family." Her eyes glistened. "It's just so hard to wait now that I've seen his face."

"That's great." Kennedy wondered what it would be like to love someone you'd never met. What if this Woong boy was even naughtier than his picture hinted? What if he had learning disabilities or medical issues nobody knew about yet? What if he didn't want to leave the orphanage? What if he hated his adoptive parents and gave them nothing but grief for his entire childhood? The Lingrens had agreed to take him in without knowing any of those things. Not only take him in, but love him as their own son. Well, if anyone could do it, Carl and Sandy could.

"How long ago did you start planning another adoption?" she asked.

Sandy let out another giggle. Kennedy was amazed at how she looked ten or fifteen years younger just talking about her newest child. "We've been thinking about it for some time now, but we didn't want to get our hopes up. Like Carl said, we had our troubles with international adoptions in the past."

Nick rolled his eyes. "Yeah, back in the old days when racism still existed."

Kennedy bit her lip, hoping Carl wouldn't be baited into another round of verbal boxing.

Naive of her.

"I'm not saying racism doesn't still exist. I'm just saying it's not the number one problem facing America today like Gordon Clarence and his followers want everyone to believe."

"You surprise me sometimes." Nick frowned. "I would think that someone who's been through what you have — like being told 'back in the old days' you couldn't adopt a child from another country because you were black and your wife was white — I wouldn't think you'd forget everything you've gone through so quickly."

Carl ignored Sandy's pleading eyes. "Nobody's forgotten, son. Nobody except these revisionist historians who make their fortunes keeping racism alive. Tell me, what would happen to Gordon Clarence and his million-dollar book deals if racism weren't an issue anymore?"

"But you ..." Nick tried to interject, but Carl cut him off.

"Yes, you're absolutely right. I've experienced racism firsthand. My whole family did, for generations back. From the plantations to Jim Crow to the bus boycott when my mama walked six miles to work both ways for a year. Did you know my father spent the night in jail after sitting in with Dr. King at a whites-only restaurant? You want to talk racism? You want to tell me how bad it was? I don't need that history lesson, son. I lived it. My daddy lived it. My grandparents and their parents and grandparents lived it. So when you jump online, and you read a story by some college-age journalist who hasn't ever seen the inside of a jail cell or the wrong end of a riot baton, when you read his gut-wrenching story about a white idiot committing a crime against his black brother, you and everyone else out there shouts racism. But you know what? There's no one race that holds the monopoly on murder or drug abuse or gang violence or any other vice you name. So when a white cop assaults a black college student with absolutely no provocation, is it possible he's racist? Sure. But is it also possible that he's just a deplorable human being?"

Kennedy glanced around the table. Nick frowned, occasionally picking at a green bean, and Sandy set down her picture of the South Korean orphan and offered it sad glances from time to time. A few beads of sweat had coalesced on Carl's forehead.

"You asked why I'm not more upset about this police incident. The truth is, I'm livid. Kennedy knows I'd do anything for her. I'll walk her down to the police department and help her file a complaint right now if that's what she wants. But I don't think that's what you're really asking. I think you're asking why I'm not aligning myself with the so-called *Reverend* Clarence and waving picket signs and strong-arming the police department into firing their racist cop. Because I don't have all the information yet. He might be racist, sure. Or maybe he's a bad cop who hates everyone equally. I don't see the feminists out there protesting, do you? I don't see them picketing and riling up the masses because a male cop pulled over a female college student. In fact, what disgusts me the most about this entire ordeal is that everybody seems to forget the fact that there were two victims of this crime. You're so ready to call this a case of white-on-black police brutality. Then where does that leave Kennedy? Are you going to tell her that her skin's not dark enough so she didn't actually suffer? Who's rallying for her, I'd like to know? Who's waving signs and demanding justice on her behalf?"

Kennedy felt the flush creep up her face when everyone fixed their eyes on her. Sandy held her in a protective half hug.

Nick fidgeted with one of his dreadlocks. "I can see what you're saying, and I certainly didn't mean to imply that what Kennedy went through wasn't bad. But then there are other cases that are even more clear-cut, cases where white cops harass black teens who aren't doing anything other than driving or walking down the street in the wrong color skin. What about that? Don't you think there needs to be some kind of oversight? Some sort of accountability?"

Carl crossed his arms. "Tell me something. If you're a cop and I told you to track down a dangerous suspect, five-foot-eight, close-shaved haircut, no facial hair, and that suspect happens to be black, is it possible that you might mistakenly pull over one or two innocent citizens for questioning?"

"Yeah. And that's the whole problem with racial profiling."

"So you're suggesting that instead of telling you to be on the lookout for a close shaved, five-foot-eight black man, I should just tell you to be on the lookout for a five-foot-eight man? Wouldn't that become gender discrimination? Should I just say a five-foot-eight person? Would that solve the problem of profiling?"

"I'm not saying that. What I'm saying is a lot of black men are scared of the police. They're scared of walking down the street and getting stopped by cops and searched and harassed."

"And why are they harassed?" Carl asked. "Is it because ninety-nine percent of cops are out to get blacks? Is that what it is? An occupied war zone, as Mister Reverend Clarence likes to call it? Or is it possible that these black men are harassed because they're conditioned from birth to despise the police, to disrespect the police, to take every instance of a white cop talking to a black man as a clear case of oppression? Are there bad cops? Sure. Are there racist cops? Absolutely. Should those problems be dealt with? Yes. But are Clarence's protests going to make the streets safer for our black brothers and sisters? No. And I'll tell you why.

"Let's say Gordon Clarence has his way. Let's say he turns Reuben into a martyr for the black civil liberties movement. Let's say a more comprehensive video comes out showing that Officer What's-His-Name was clearly out of line. Everybody's going to call it prejudice, a case of white oppression. So the police force makes all their officers go through cultural sensitivity training. Tells them they can't pull someone over based on their skin color. Reminds them they could get sued or lose their jobs if they show any sort of prejudice. What happens the next time two white cops are chasing down a black drug dealer or a black rapist? What happens when everyone's hunting for a black suspect who's accused of murdering his girlfriend? What white cop with half a mind is going to pull a black man over because he matches the suspect's profile? What white cop who values his job is going to use that Taser on a black criminal who's resisting arrest? All the sensitivity training's going to do is teach cops — the majority of whom I'm going to say are decent, moral human beings — it's going to teach them that their hands are tied when it comes to dealing with black suspects or black criminals. Now, how is that going to make our streets safer?"

Carl paused for breath, and Sandy took advantage of that moment to scoot her chair back noisily. "Well, it looks like everyone's finished with dinner. Who's ready for some dessert?"

CHAPTER 15

They made it through Sandy's pineapple upside-down cake without any more arguing. Sandy told them about the progression of their adoption journey, starting from the time last summer when the Lord had put it on their hearts to open their home to one more child. She was always boisterous, but tonight, she was even more animated than normal as she spoke about little Woong.

"The hardest part now is waiting. I don't remember praying for patience, but I guess that's what God must be giving us."

Kennedy couldn't understand everything adoptive parents go through, but she got the part about patience. For so long, her life had felt like one big waiting room. Waiting for high school to end so she could leave Yanji and return to the States. Then, once college started, it was waiting for midterms or finals to be over so she could finally rest. Waiting to see her parents again after a whole year at school. Waiting to return to Yanji for the summer, even though she'd been in such a hurry to leave last fall.

There was more to it, though. More difficult experiences that tried her patience. Waiting for reprieve from her anxiety. Waiting for whatever improvements those stupid counseling sessions were supposed to bring. And Reuben. First waiting for her mind to catch up with her heart so she could admit she had real feelings for him. Feelings beyond a simple crush. And then waiting to find out if he felt the same way.

Would she ever know?

She glanced surreptitiously at the Lindgrens' clock.

"I'm sorry," Sandy apologized. "It's getting late. I shouldn't have kept you so long. It's the adoption. Gets me babbling."

"It's ok." Kennedy forced a smile even though thinking about Reuben turned her overstuffed stomach slightly sour. What was he doing now?

How long would it take before things could go back to the way they were before?

Carl pushed his seat back from the table. "I'll give you a lift back to campus."

"You don't have to do that," Kennedy replied. "It's not dark out yet. I can just take the bus and catch the T."

"You'll do no such thing, young lady." Carl turned his pockets inside out. "Now where did I put my keys?"

Nick scooped up his dirty dishes. "Actually, I need to hit the road, too. Some of the youth group boys and me planned a late-night X-Box tournament at my place." He reached over for Kennedy's dirty plate. "I'll drop you off at your dorm. No problem."

Sandy smiled and joined Nick clearing off the table. "So I guess that settles it. Thank you both for coming over and sharing our good news with us. I'm sorry if I talked your ears off."

"Don't believe a word she says," Carl quipped. "At least not the part about her being sorry. If I had known this would happen once we decided to adopt again, I might have asked her to wait another ten years until I had hearing aids I could turn down on command." He leaned over and pecked Sandy's cheek. "Thanks for dinner, babe. It was delicious."

Kennedy and Nick both expressed similar sentiments. Once they got the table cleared and endured a drawn-out goodbye on the porch, they finally made their way to Nick's VW bus parked in the Lindgrens' driveway.

"Is that a new paint job?" Kennedy asked, pointing to a cross made out of colorful handprints on the side door.

Nick let himself in. "Yeah, I guess you could call this an ongoing project. Every few months, one of the youth group kids comes up with an embellishment. I try to be as accommodating as I can. Gives the teens a sense of ownership in the ministry, I guess. Although you might have heard how Carl had to veto the picture of John the Baptist's head on a platter."

Kennedy chuckled and fastened her seatbelt. "Thanks for the ride. You sure it's not too much out of your way?" She didn't even know where Nick lived.

"I don't mind. Gives us an excuse to be together. I mean, without Pastor Carl and Sandy breathing down our backs. You ever get the feeling they're trying to play chaperone?"

Kennedy forced a laugh, even though she felt her face heating up like a beaker on top of a Bunsen burner. "I'm sure they mean well."

"Yeah." Another chuckle, just as forced as hers. "They certainly do."

The pause that followed reminded Kennedy of those moments in class waiting for the teacher to hand you back a test you were afraid you'd failed.

"What are you listening to?" she finally asked when she couldn't think of anything else to say.

"Oh, that? It's my uncle and some of his buddies. They've got this folk, grunge, worship band mix going on in Oregon. Call themselves the Babylon Eunuchs. You know, because Shadrach, Meshach, and Abednego were probably ... Well, never mind. Do you like it?"

He turned the volume up, which made the slightly off-key singing even more discordant. "It's not bad," Kennedy lied. At least it gave her an excuse to not have to hold a conversation. Unfortunately, as soon as the first song ended, Nick turned off the CD. "You know, now that we're alone, I've been wanting to ask you something."

Kennedy felt her body tense and fought her muscles to relax. Her mind raced back to all her previous encounters with Nick, including a pseudo-date over Christmas break when they went out together for clam chowder.

"What is it?" She held her breath.

"Do you think it's wise for Pastor Carl to be so political?"

Kennedy blinked, more confused than relieved. "What?"

The Peter, James, and John bobble heads nodded sagely while he spoke. "Like tonight, for example. It just seems to me like the leader of a racially diverse megachurch in Cambridge would understand how polarizing some of his views can be."

Kennedy had to admit she didn't know as much about American politics as either Carl or Nick. She could only guess what he was hinting at. "So you're upset about the racism thing?"

Nick shrugged. "Partly. But not just that. Don't get me wrong, he's a great pastor, and I couldn't hope for a better boss. He's a good friend too, which is why I don't want to call him out on it. But the American church is on its deathbed, at least when it comes to conservative evangelical Christianity. These folks like Carl, they're not taken seriously anymore. People don't come to church to hear arguments against gay marriage or abortion. They want to see grace. Where's the grace in berating women for something they did to their child years or decades in the past?"

Kennedy frowned. "So does that mean you're for or against abortion?"

"Against. Naturally. But really, is abortion the issue, or is poverty the issue? Did you know that eighty percent of women who get abortions do it because they don't feel like they can afford to raise another child? So what should we do, should we focus on banning abortions, or should we spend that same energy and resources on lifting women out of poverty so they don't seek out the procedure in the first place? Do I like abortion? No. But are we really doing any good when all we talk about is which pro-life candidates to elect?"

Kennedy frowned. She wasn't following Nick's reasoning, and she had the feeling that she was too uninformed to ever catch up with his logic.

"Around the country," he went on, "Christians are seen as judgmental hypocrites doing what they can to strong-arm the government into agreeing with everything they preach. I mean, I'm all for the Bible, but seriously, does it really matter if a courtroom hangs up a copy of the Ten Commandments or not? When Jesus tells us to feed the hungry and free the oppressed, was he really talking about whether or not school kids say *under God* in the pledge of the allegiance?"

Sensing he was waiting for a response, Kennedy muttered that she hadn't thought through those issues lately. And by lately, she meant at all, but she didn't mention that part.

"So then there's Pastor Carl, and I already said he's one of my favorite men in the world. He's totally out of touch with the times, but people keep coming to his church. St. Margaret keeps growing, and I don't know why."

For once, Kennedy felt like she could contribute intelligently to the conversation. "It's probably because people see how much he and Sandy love others. Isn't that what church is supposed to be about?"

"You're probably right." Nick turned his uncle's dissonant blend of banjo, guitar, and inept vocals back on and glanced at her long enough to crack a grin. "You're a smart girl. I guess that's why they let you into Harvard."

The second half of the drive back to school wasn't nearly as awkward as it started out. Nick dropped her off as close to her dorm as he could without needing to park, and Kennedy smiled to herself when she pictured what the other students would think of the pimped out Christian bus. As she made her way to her dorm, she realized she was more relaxed than she'd been in weeks. When she got to her floor and heard Willow and some guy talking, she wasn't even that upset. It was a Friday night, after all. If Willow really wanted the room to herself, Kennedy could text Reuben to see if he wanted to meet her at the library to go over some calculus.

She pushed the door open, but her smile faded when she saw Dominic in his uniform standing by Willow's desk.

"Oh, there you are." He didn't smile.

Neither did her roommate.

Willow took in a noisy breath. "I was just talking with Officer ..." Her voice trailed off.

Dominic shuffled his feet. "I'm afraid I have some bad news."

Kennedy's abdomen felt as if it were crashing to the ground like a poorly executed inertia experiment.

Dominic glanced once at Willow and then cleared his throat. "I'm here about your friend, Reuben. He's just been arrested."

CHAPTER 16

Kennedy's lungs seized up like the bulb on the tip of a Pasteur pipette. She didn't know who to look at. It felt as if both Dominic and Willow had betrayed her.

Her roommate frowned sympathetically. "You want some tea?"

Tea? At a time like this?

Arrested. Had she heard that right? Was it possible they were wrong? She turned to Dominic. "Were you the one who brought him in?" Her tone dripped with anger and accusation, but she didn't care.

He shook his head. "No. This is all out of my hands here. I just wanted to let you know. It'll be on the news soon, and I didn't like the thought of you finding out that way."

"Why?" Kennedy demanded. "You said the department wouldn't bother us. You said they'd be scared of the real story coming out."

Dominic offered the slightest hint of a shrug. "That's what a lot of us are wondering, too. Best guess is the chief was getting too much pressure. The media wasn't buying the whole 'I forgot to call for backup' story. And then came Gordon Clarence and his followers with their protests, turning this whole thing into some kind of a witch hunt. The chief had to do something. Take some kind of action to save face."

Kennedy couldn't believe she'd let this man pray with her. She couldn't believe another Christian could stand by and tell her these things while still wearing his police uniform. Why had he stopped by at all? Was he just here to gloat? Here to warn Kennedy not to get involved? Or ...

"What about me?" She wanted to sound forceful, but her voice betrayed her fears.

Dominic offered a small smile, which looked out of place on his sheepish face. "You're fine. The chief looked into your background and apparently decided you weren't worth messing with."

"Because I'm white?" All Carl's platitudes about racism being a sin of the past now sounded as nonsensical as the Dodo's ramblings in *Alice in Wonderland.*

Dominic's expression grew stern. "No. Because of your background. The chief knows a good lawyer will rip his guy to shreds if this case goes to court. He doesn't want to touch you with a ten-foot pole."

His words took time to settle, like droplets of oil slowly coalescing in an aqueous mixture. "So it's because my parents can afford a good attorney?" she finally asked.

Dominic didn't answer her question. "I'm really sorry. I came by to tell you if there's anything I can do ..."

"Yeah, there is," Willow interrupted. Kennedy had forgotten for the moment her roommate was listening in to their conversation. "You can get her friend out of jail."

"I wish I could." Dominic sighed. "Unfortunately, my hands are completely tied."

Willow scrunched up her violet-tipped hair. "Yeah, that's not good enough." She pointed her finger toward his chest. "You know what's even more dangerous than a corrupt cop? A halfway decent cop who sits in his patrol car full of self-righteousness and smugness and says he wishes he could do something about the bad ones but he can't."

Kennedy wasn't sure if she should try defending Dominic or not.

"It makes me sick to think of how many of you there must be," Willow went on, "going home to your nice little nuclear families, shaking your heads because one of your colleagues just acted like history's biggest jerk, feeling smug because you're one of the good ones and at least you're 'doing everything you can.' You make me nauseous."

Part of Kennedy was ashamed her roommate was subjecting Dominic to this verbal bashing, and part of her was glad Willow had the courage to express what she couldn't yet articulate.

Dominic adjusted his uniform. "I better go."

"Yeah, you better," Willow spat.

He looked at Kennedy. "Is there anything else I can do for you?"

She wanted to ignore him, throw him out of the room with Willow's insults echoing in his ears, but instead she asked, "What's going to happen to Reuben?"

Dominic frowned again. Kennedy realized he could be handsome if it weren't for the strained, worried look in his eyes.

"It's hard to say. He's from Kenya, so they're going to get the embassy involved. Nobody wants this to escalate further than it needs to. They'll have an arraignment, probably charge him with assaulting an officer. If he's convicted, my guess is they'll move for deporting him. By then everyone will have forgotten about the whole incident, so the chief won't have any reason to make him serve more time."

"Do you think they have enough evidence to convict him?" Kennedy asked.

Dominic shrugged. "Depends on what kind of jury he gets."

Kennedy tried to cling to some sense of hope. "But you said if another witness came forward ..."

A sad, heavy sigh. "It's been all over the news. If any more witnesses are out there, we would have heard from them by now."

"But it's possible?" Kennedy wasn't sure if she was making a statement or asking him a question.

"It's possible." He met her eyes. "But I wouldn't bank on it."

What about prayer? she wanted to ask him. Didn't he believe in prayer anymore? Maybe if they all start asking God for a new witness to materialize ...

"He's got school. We haven't finished our lab report. He can't miss that."

"I think right now, your friend has more urgent matters to worry about than his classwork."

"So there's nothing we can do?" It wasn't right. It wasn't fair. This was America, where everyone was promised an equal chance, where justice was supposed to be a non-negotiable guarantee.

Dominic stepped toward the door. "We can pray. And hope another witness comes forward with the full story."

CHAPTER 17

As soon as Dominic left, Kennedy plopped into her roommate's beanbag chair with a groan.

Willow filled up an *Alaska Chicks Rock* mug. "Have some tea." She passed it to Kennedy. "Man, I thought he'd never go. He's got a lot of nerve just showing up like that."

"How long was he here before I came?"

Willow sat down at her desk and kicked her feet up on the bed. "Not long. At first, I thought he might be coming to arrest you. Othello said something like this would probably happen, you know."

"He did?"

Willow nodded and poured herself some tea. "Yeah. I guess he's been following this police brutality stuff for quite a while now. Says that once they get pressured, the department does what it can to vilify the victims. It's one thing for a cop to shoot an unarmed black kid. But if the kid has a criminal record, or if drug tests show he was high when he was murdered, most people go back to their day-to-day lives and assume he must have deserved it."

"This is a little different than a shooting, don't you think?" Kennedy took a sip of Willow's bitter medicinal tea.

"Not really. The only difference was Reuben wasn't killed. You're lucky that way. It could have been a lot worse."

Kennedy couldn't believe she was just sitting here sipping tea while Reuben was probably paralyzed with fear in some jail cell. What would happen to him there? Kennedy didn't even know what happened to American citizens who got arrested. What about an international student? Would they extradite him? Her mind was spinning like a pulsar star. Would she even see him again?

Willow let out a dramatic sigh. "Listen, I'm really sorry you're going through this. It sucks no matter how you look at it." She stood up and grabbed her hand-painted fashion scarf.

"Where are you going?" Kennedy didn't want to admit how much she hated the thought of being left alone.

"I'm gonna go talk to Othello. He'll want to know about this. Maybe he'll find a way to help Reuben."

"The only way to help Reuben is if another witness comes forward." She hated the resignation she recognized in her own voice. Was it really that hopeless?

Willow passed her an almost empty container of raw honey. "Here, take as much as you want with your tea. I can always get more."

Kennedy accepted the Mason jar, trying to find a way to ask Willow to stay with her without having to beg. For the first time, she wondered where she put her therapist's business card with his after-hours phone number. She couldn't just stay here like this. For a minute, she considered tagging along with Willow but remembered how uncomfortable she felt during the arguments around the Lindgrens' dinner table. She couldn't bring herself to get up from the oversized beanbag chair.

"You all right?" Willow put in her long, feathered earrings and stared at Kennedy's reflection in her small desk mirror.

Kennedy lowered her face into the steaming mug. "I'll be fine." She hoped it wasn't a lie.

Once Willow left, Kennedy dissolved two big spoonfuls of honey into the herbal concoction and thought about Reuben. It wasn't fair. She almost wished Dominic had come and arrested her, too. Then at least she'd know her dad would do everything in his power to free her. If Kennedy was arrested, her dad would hire the best defense lawyers in the greater Boston area. The officer that assaulted them would be lucky if he could ever show his face in Massachusetts again. Who did Reuben have to advocate for him? Who would speak up for him?

She glanced at the time. It was already morning in Yanji. She grabbed her phone, grateful to see it still had plenty of charge. She was breathing faster than normal as the call connected. Would he be there?

"Hello?"

"Daddy?" Her voice squeaked. She swallowed down a little more tea. She couldn't cry. Tears wouldn't solve anything. They were just as useless and nearly as paralyzing as her anxiety. She had to get through this conversation. For Reuben.

"What is it, princess? What's the matter?"

She had hoped the news would have already made it onto Channel 2's website, which her dad kept up with more religiously than any locals Kennedy knew. She bit her lip, trying to form the words, afraid of the way they would confront her with their hideous reality once she gave them voice.

"They arrested Reuben."

If she had been talking with her mom, she would have been blubbering by now, but with her dad it was different. He didn't waste time asking about how Kennedy felt or worrying about her emotions. He bypassed all those fluffy preliminaries and jumped right into his formal, businesslike interview. "What did they charge him with?"

"I don't know. Something about assaulting an officer, I think." She took another scalding sip of tea, thankful to find her vocal chords weren't too strained.

"Where are they holding him?"

"I'm not sure."

"Have you talked to anyone else? Do you have any reason to believe you'll be arrested next?"

"No. There was a policeman here just a minute ago. He's the one who told me about Reuben." She wanted to tell her dad more, but he was firing questions at her as fast as a proton slinging its way through a particle accelerator.

"Have you talked to anyone from the press?"

"No."

"Good girl. You keep it that way, all right? I'm on Channel 2's page. They've got the story right here. Looks like they still haven't mentioned your name. That's good. By the sound of it, if they wanted you too, they would have gotten you by now. I don't think you need to worry, princess."

Couldn't he understand? How calloused did he think she was? "I'm not worried about me." Her larynx tightened. She took a gulp of tea and focused on the feel of the honey sliding down her throat. "I need to know how to help Reuben."

For the first time since he picked up the phone, her dad was quiet. She could picture his scowl as he stared at his computer screen.

"He's an international student, right?" he finally asked.

"Yeah."

"Well, there's gonna be red tape. Bureaucracy. The good news is that means it will give him and his lawyer time to ..."

"He doesn't have a lawyer." Kennedy wanted to scream. For being such a business genius, her dad could be completely daft at times.

"He doesn't have a lawyer," Kennedy repeated with a little more restraint.

"Then the courts will assign him one ..." Her dad's voice trailed off. Kennedy hoped he was finally grasping the seriousness of Reuben's situation. She pictured him in his Yanji office, his desk strewn with paperwork, his urgent-message file cluttered to overflowing. He probably had a dozen pressing matters that needed his immediate attention, and she was asking him to ignore all that and help her find a way to get Reuben out of jail. Should she tell him everything? Should she tell him about the drowning, suffocating weight in her chest when she imagined him getting deported back to Kenya? All thoughts of romance aside, how could she make it through the rest of her semester without him? Reuben was the only good thing that had happened to her this entire school year. Everything else had been an anxiety-riddled headache at best, traumatizing torture at worst. Through it all, through kidnappings and murder attempts, through lab reports and research papers, Reuben had encouraged her. Supported her. How could she step foot into the chem lab Monday knowing that she had abandoned him?

She knew her dad. Knew he was probably getting ready to lecture her on the American justice system, how if you were patient enough, the truth would rise its way to the top like the most soluble substances on a paper chromatogram. After what she had seen, after talking to Dominic who had first-hand experience with the police force, she wouldn't believe a single word of it.

How could she make her dad understand? How could she tell him how important this was to her? She felt like a petulant toddler, ready to stomp her foot and throw a fit until she got her way. But what else could she do to save Reuben? How else could she help him? Dominic had mentioned prayer, but what good was that when the entire justice system was willing to sacrifice an innocent student to protect the reputation of a corrupt cop? Back in Yanji, when the Chinese police came into her parents' home to question them about their business, their visa paperwork, or any hint of missionary activities, Kennedy had hidden upstairs in her room wishing to be back home in the States, imagining life in a country where the police were there to protect you, not harass you. Had she really been that naïve? Had she really been that foolish?

She heard her dad let out his breath. "Give me a few minutes, sugar. I'll call Jefferson and see if there's anything he can do."

Kennedy bit her lip, wondering if she should say what she was thinking. Would it make things worse, or would it be better for her dad to know the complete truth at the beginning? She took a choppy breath. "I don't think his family has a lot of extra money for lawyers and things."

Another sigh. Heavier this time and slightly more dejected. "He won't have to worry about that, princess. Just hold on, and I'll call you back in a few minutes."

The small stream of relief that washed over Kennedy reminded her of a bright ray of sunshine in the middle of winter — enough to give you hope without warming you up at all. Still, it was a start. "Thanks, Daddy."

"You're welcome." If they had been face-to-face, he would probably make some sort of joke about how Kennedy was responsible for his growing bald spot or his rapidly diminishing bank account. But there were no jokes this time, just the small clicking sound of her dad hanging up his office phone. Kennedy stared at her screen after the call ended. Her dad would try to help. There was nothing to do now but wait.

For the next several minutes, all Kennedy could think about was a video series for prospective medical students her dad had made her watch when she decided to apply to Harvard's pre-med program. In one of the lectures, a doctor who survived cancer talked about medical testing from the patient's perspective, how hard it is to wait for results that could spell life or death for yourself or your family member. His words hadn't impacted Kennedy much at the time — she had been more interested in the immunologist's speech on AIDS and other disorders that impacted the immune system — but it was all she could think about now while she waited for her dad to get hold of Jefferson. She tried not to think of how hard it would be to contact a lawyer at 8:30 on a Friday night. What if he didn't return her dad's call until Monday? What would that mean for Reuben? She didn't know anything about jails or prisons. She didn't know if they had visiting hours or any way for the inmates to interact with the public. Part of her worried that if she went to the jail to check on Reuben, someone there would recognize her from the infamous piggyback attack video and book her for the night as well.

Well, if that's what it'd take to get the attention of her dad's lawyer friend ...

She should probably be doing her own research, too. Wasn't that what the internet was for? But she knew if she turned on her computer, she'd never get past all the news articles of Reuben's arrest. It was too heinous to have a hundred different reminders bombard her from a hundred different websites. She remembered the way Othello had explained it. If the police wanted to keep their own reputation untarnished, it made sense they'd try to ruin Reuben's. What would they say about him? Did he have his cell phone with him? Could she text him to see how he was doing?

All we can do is pray. Dominic's words rang through her mind like the taunts of a playground bully. *All we can do is pray.* Wasn't that the spiritual equivalent of a doctor telling her dying patient there was nothing left to do but discuss palliative care and make hospice arrangements?

All we can do is pray. Was that the Christian way of saying there was no hope whatsoever?

She bowed her head over Willow's half empty mug. Even the sight of the tea leaves reminded her of Bow Legs, how he had made such a big deal of that stupid Ziploc bag in the glove compartment. She stared at her phone. If it had just taken the video like she'd told it to, none of this would be happening. Bow Legs would be the one behind bars, and she and Reuben would be at the library studying calculus or at the student union finishing up their lab report.

Why had God allowed her phone to fail her? Had he stopped paying attention for those few seconds? Was he too busy helping believers on the other side of the world? But it didn't work like that, did it? Kennedy knew there were people suffering more than she was, but still, did that mean God thought her problems weren't significant enough to waste his energy on? Had he simply forgotten to intervene?

She thought about Carl and Sandy, about all the injustices they suffered in the past. How did they remain so loving and hopeful? What was the secret and the source of their joy? What did Kennedy have to do to discover that same sense of peace she always felt with them?

Her heart leapt like an electron jumping up an energy level when her phone rang. Her dad. Was it a bad sign that he was calling back so soon? He couldn't have gotten a hold of the lawyer, explained everything to him, and come up with a plan to save Reuben in five minutes, could he?

"Hi, Daddy."

"I just got off the phone with Jefferson." No greeting, no *Hi, princess.* What did that mean? Was her dad calling with bad news? Had the lawyer already looked into the case and agreed that the only thing left to do was pray?

Thankfully, her dad didn't waste words. "He said the same thing as yesterday. Without more evidence or some key witness coming forward, there's not much to do. I know it's too late for it now, but if you ever find yourself in that sort of situation again, it'd be a good idea to turn on your phone's video camera and ..."

Kennedy fought the urge to throw her cell across the room. "I did take a video." She wasn't trying to yell, but she couldn't help it. "I started recording at the very beginning when he handcuffed Reuben. It's the stupid phone. There wasn't enough memory ..."

She choked back tears of frustration. Why had she ever left Yanji? Why had she ever gone to Harvard? She could have gotten her college degree online without ever having to leave her parents'. What had she been thinking?

"Calm down, sweetie." It was just like her dad to say something like that. He didn't even bother telling her to pray. He knew how hopeless the situation was. So that was it. Reuben would spend a few weeks or months in jail, go to trial, and get deported back to Kenya in disgrace. Never complete his studies. Never tell Kennedy the secret he'd planned on sharing Thursday night. In a way, this was all her fault. Why had she suggested they go see *Aida*? Why couldn't they have just spent the evening in the library like normal?

"I'm sorry about the phone, princess. I'll do some research. Maybe there's someone in your area who can retrieve the memory for you. You say that you got the entire confrontation recorded?"

"Everything. It was in my pocket, so you can't see it all, but you can hear what was going on."

"And you think the recording would be enough to prove Reuben's innocent?" There was a hint of doubt in her father's voice.

"Of course he's innocent. I already explained to you, that officer ..."

"I remember what you told me last night," her dad interrupted. "I'm just saying that sometimes people remember certain events in different ways ..."

Kennedy had heard enough. "I told you already, he didn't do anything wrong. Neither of us did." She was starting to understand why Dominic had warned her to drop the entire case in the first place. If the media could skew events until her own dad doubted her, how could she expect the general public to take her side?

"All right," he conceded. "If you think the video will help, I'll see if there's somewhere you can take your phone to try to get the memory retrieved. It's probably a long shot, but without more evidence, Jefferson says there's not much of a case."

"So he's just going to let Reuben get deported?" She couldn't believe this was happening. She couldn't believe the country that boasted such liberty and freedom could arrest someone as kind and considerate as Reuben to keep a corrupt officer out of trouble.

"I didn't say that." She sensed the tension in her dad's voice and remembered why she had been so eager as a high-school student to leave home. "All I said was he didn't think there was much of a case. I hired him to look into it for us anyway, and if you have evidence on your phone that might make a difference, we need to pursue it."

Kennedy was ashamed of her outburst. She injected what she hoped was enough humility into her voice and said, "Thanks, Daddy."

"Don't thank me yet. I'm no Atticus Finch."

Kennedy smiled at her dad's reference to one of her favorite novels. "I'm really glad you're at least trying."

"Well, I know a certain young lady who can be pretty persuasive when she wants to be. And I figure it must be a special boy to have caught her heart like that."

Kennedy felt the warmth radiating up to her cheeks. "It's not like that, you know."

"Well, whatever it is, I'm glad I'm able to help. Let me jump online and see what I can find about your phone. I'll call or text you when I have more information."

Kennedy was used to sudden waves of homesickness crashing over her without warning. She choked down a large sip of tea and thanked her dad one more time.

"Yeah well, I just hope this Reuben fellow understands how lucky he is that you care so much about him."

CHAPTER 18

Kennedy's head was throbbing by the time her dad sent her a link with information on retrieving lost photos. The procedure required a certain app, so while she waited for it to download, she got herself ready for bed. It wasn't even nine yet, but her mind was heavy with exhaustion. Sandy's fatty pork chop sat in her gut like a chunk of cement. It was the most meat she'd eaten since Christmas Eve at the Lindgrens'. Things had felt so normal back then. Reuben came with her, and they had spent the evening laughing over every single mistake they'd made in the chemistry lab during their first semester of school.

Life had been so simple. Tests and homework and lab write-ups. Kennedy could handle that. What she couldn't handle was the horrid uncertainty, the fear of Reuben's fate, the sense that God must have abandoned her or else he wouldn't have thrown her into the midst of such a convoluted mess.

Was God angry about her feelings toward Reuben? She'd heard Carl say from the pulpit that the Lord was a jealous God. Did that mean he was mad not to be in the center of Kennedy's attention, so he was going to punish the person she cared about most? Was God really that possessive? Would he really act so petty?

After the app downloaded, she followed the directions to retrieve her lost photos. She wasn't sure what good it would do. The video she needed wasn't lost. It hadn't recorded at all. Still, there was always the small shred of hope. Maybe God was looking out for her after all. Maybe this would be his way to prove it.

As soon as the program finished loading, Kennedy scrolled through the recovered files. Most of them were pictures of lab results she hadn't needed in her write-ups. There were also two photos she and Reuben had taken at the *Nutcracker* ballet when they went last Christmas. The images were blurry, which was probably why she'd deleted them, but she stared for several minutes at the smiles on her and Reuben's faces. Had she ever felt that happy before she met him?

She told the app to save the photos back into her regular gallery. She wasn't ready to get rid of them yet. They might be the last pictures she'd ever have with him. She wished she could have talked to her dad's attorney friend. She needed to know what would happen to Reuben. Would he be deported if they found him guilty, or would they keep him in prison here? She wasn't sure which option was worse. What would his family think? What would his parents say?

As expected, the recovered photos didn't include anything from her traffic stop. She should have known it was foolish to hope. Should have known God wouldn't come through for her. What did he care? He was probably too concerned with the world's missionaries and pastors to fret much over a nineteen-year-old college freshman and her best friend.

She blinked her dry eyes. There had been a time when her faith had come so easily. Mom and Dad loved Jesus, so she did too. Mom and Dad said he died on a cross and came back to life, so who was she to argue? She didn't doubt any of it even now, but what did it matter whether or not Jesus was alive if he just let injustice run rampant? Was the hope of a distant future spent in the heavenly clouds supposed to compensate for a lifetime of sorrow here on earth?

And what about those people who were even more oppressed, the child laborers and sex slaves suffering throughout the globe? Did God see them? Did he care? And if he did care, why wouldn't he do something to free them?

It didn't make sense, and Kennedy was too tired to try to figure it out. This line of reasoning would just make her more depressed anyway. She may as well go to bed. Maybe things would look brighter in the morning.

She doubted it.

She let out a small groan as she laid her head down on her pillow. She hadn't realized how tight her muscles were. Willow had been trying to talk her into joining some co-ed yoga group all semester. Said it'd be great for Kennedy's anxiety, but she was too busy. Besides, why would she want to wear spandex and sweat on a germ-infested mat alongside two dozen other strangers?

She glanced at her phone one more time as if the missing recording might magically appear on the photo retrieval app. No such luck.

Of course.

Her phone buzzed in her hand, startling her. She didn't recognize the number, but whoever it was could wait. She didn't want to talk to anybody, not unless it was ...

Her hand shook when she answered the call. "Hello?"

"Kennedy? Is that you?"

In an instant, her pituitary gland flooded her entire brain with endorphins. Relief collided with nervous excitement. Joy coursed through every single vein in her body. "Reuben?"

"It's me."

"Where are you? Are you ok? Did you get hurt?" She couldn't decide which question she wanted answered first.

"I'm ok." She heard the strain in his voice, recognized his attempt to stay positive. "They said I could make a phone call, and I didn't ... I wasn't ... Well, I called you."

"I'm so glad. I've been worrying all night about you. What are they saying? What's going to happen now?"

"I have some court appearance on Monday. That's about all I know so far."

She tried to imagine what her dad would say in a similar situation. What advice would he give? What would he tell Reuben to do? "You don't have to answer any questions, you know. You should demand to have a lawyer present if they need to talk to you." Wait, was that right? Or was it different for international students? Did he have the same rights as everyone else, or would it work some other way?

"It's ok. I've already talked with someone from the embassy. It looks like if I plead guilty, I'll most likely just get deported. They probably won't give me an actual jail sentence."

He was talking like a crazy man. "You can't do that. You were acting in self-defense. We both were. You have to let the guy know that ..."

"I already made up my mind. I'm showing up in court Monday, I'm pleading guilty, and I'm hoping they'll just send me home instead of making me serve time here."

He wasn't thinking clearly. He was scared. Confused. Who wouldn't be at a time like this? "Listen, my dad's already hired a guy for you. A really good lawyer he knows. He thinks you have a good chance." She hoped he wouldn't hear the doubt in her own voice.

"That's nice of you to say, but I don't want you worrying about me."

She squeezed her eyes shut. "You can't just give up. What about your studies? What about all you've worked so hard for?"

Betrayal. That's what it felt like. Betrayal. Did Reuben seriously believe he'd be better off taking the blame for Bow Legs' crimes? He had worked too hard his first year at Harvard. He and Kennedy both had worked too hard. What about those countless hours studying together? What about their friendship?

She plugged in her phone, determined to keep it from losing charge. "Listen, I'm going to try to figure out how three-way calling works. I want you to talk to my dad. He knows a lot about these things. He'll tell you himself..."

"It's not that simple." Reuben's voice was so quiet, Kennedy could hardly make out the words. She bit her lip and forced herself to listen. When inmates get to make one phone call, what does that mean? One phone call a week? A year? Total? Would this be the last time they'd ever talk to each other?

"Listen, the thing I was going to tell you last night, I ..."

No, it couldn't happen like this. He was acting as if he'd never see her again. He was scared. She couldn't let him say something they would both regret later.

"Don't worry about that right now." She wished her dad were here. He would know what to do. He would have the right words to say. She had to give Reuben some kind of hope. "Listen, I think there's a way my dad knows to get a recording of the attack off my phone." The more she talked, the more she forced herself to believe it was true. Any other alternative was too horrific to fathom. "Once we get that video, everyone's going to see you're innocent. The court, the police department, everyone. So don't do anything right now. Wait until my dad's friend gets in touch with you. He'll know what to do."

"You shouldn't be so worried about me." Where was this fatalistic attitude coming from? Did he want Kennedy to be the first to say the thing they'd both skirted around?

She clenched her jaw and resolved to be like her dad. Unemotional. Detached. Reuben didn't need tears or sentimentality. Not right now. He needed the kind of friend who would knock on every judge's door and pester every single member of the police force until he was free.

"Listen, we've been through a lot together." Now she was the one who sounded like she was saying goodbye. Was she? And if so, would she live the rest of her life in regret if she didn't tell him everything? Her heart was racing in her chest, pulses of fear paralyzing her vocal chords. She took a deep breath. She could do this. She remembered her dad. Meticulous. Professional.

"Just hang on until Monday. By then, I'm sure your lawyer will have come up with your defense. It's going to be ok. Don't think about jail sentences or going back home or any of that. Just think of this as a short break from school. You'll show up to court Monday, the judge will see there's absolutely no case against you, and the only thing you have to worry about is whether or not I do a good job on our lab report to get us both a good grade. Ok?"

There was so much more she wanted to say. Like how scared she was at the thought that she might be wrong. She might not get that video. She probably wouldn't. And even though the lawyer had agreed to represent Reuben, he was far from optimistic. But none of that information would help Reuben right now. All he needed to know was Kennedy was advocating for him. Because she couldn't stand the thought of a single day in class without him. Because she had already allowed her mind to wonder what might happen if the two of them both found the courage to admit how much they meant to each other. Because they shared something deeper than friendship.

Those were the things she wanted him to know, but she couldn't find the words to tell him. Not like this. Not with him stuck in some jail.

"Let's just make it to Monday," she said as much to herself as to him. "Things are going to work out. I promise."

CHAPTER 19

As soon as Kennedy ended her call with Reuben, before she even got the chance to let her tears fall freely, the door flew open. She glanced up at Willow and for a second felt the embarrassment her roommate must have experienced a dozen times whenever Kennedy walked in on her making out with one of her boyfriends.

"Everything ok?" Willow asked, slipping on a few dangly bracelets and grabbing her bohemian cardigan.

Kennedy forbade her voice from betraying her. "Yeah. I just got off the phone with Reuben."

"Really? Did he say anything? Are they treating him ok? I hear cops can be kind of jerks in cases like his."

It wasn't what Kennedy wanted to hear. "Yeah, he sounded all right." Was that true? She knew Reuben so well, but how could she begin to assume what he was feeling, what he was experiencing right now?

"Well, I'm not staying long." Willow threw her lip balm and a few organic throat lozenges into her braided handbag. "I just came back to grab a few things before Othello and I take off." She stood and took Kennedy by the arm. "And by a few things, I'm talking mostly about you." She raised Kennedy to her feet. "Come on. There's a protest outside the courthouse. You should see how many people are already there to support your little Kenyan buddy." She frowned when Kennedy hesitated. "Don't worry. It's gonna be peaceful. There's gonna be some ecumenical prayer time even, leaders from different faiths. Come on. You do believe in prayer, don't you?"

It'd be heretical to deny it. She glanced at her clock. She probably couldn't fall asleep yet. At least this way she wouldn't feel like she was sitting around doing nothing. But still, that kind of crowd ...

Willow draped an arm around her shoulder. "Come on. I think this will be good for you. If it gets to be too much, I'll drive you home. Deal?"

Whenever Kennedy thought about the people who'd helped her most in Cambridge, Reuben and the Lindgrens always came to mind. She realized now she had overlooked someone else just as important. Her roommate.

"Ok. Thanks."

Kennedy grabbed her coat. Attending a peaceful protest wasn't talking to a lawyer or researching immigration laws online, but it was better than doing nothing.

CHAPTER 20

The closest parking spot Willow could find was four blocks away, so she, Kennedy, and Othello got out of the car and started to walk. Kennedy was glad for her new trench coat, a cute birthday present from her dad last February. A spring chill had settled in the air as soon as the sun set. She could hear the crowds several streets away. She strained her ears, searching for any hint of anger or potential violence. Her abs were already quivering. Another reason she was thankful for her coat.

Willow sided up next to her. "Still doing ok?"

Kennedy nodded even though she already regretted letting Willow talk her into coming here. How big of a crowd was there going to be, and how many of them would be sick and contagious? How long would Willow and Othello want to stay? What did anyone hope this mass undulation of human bodies would accomplish?

The crowd spilled off the sidewalks and onto the side streets. At first, Kennedy thought someone must have brought in searchlights, but then she realized the glow was coming from the hundreds of lit candles the people were holding as they stood in front of the courthouse steps. Someone was praying into a loudspeaker system. There was something familiar about his cadence even though Kennedy couldn't place the voice. "Father God, gracious Savior, we come before you as a humbled people. We come before you as a society that is broken, that is riddled with injustice and oppression. We come before you as individuals who are sick, sinful, enslaved to all kinds of depravity. We confess that we don't deserve your mercy. We confess that we don't deserve your kindness towards us. But you are a God who delights in his people. You are a God who delights to extend forgiveness. So forgive us, Father. Forgive us our trespasses, our prejudices, our bigotry, our chauvinism, our selfish ambitions. Forgive us our hatred, merciful Lord. Show us once again had to love one another. Heal our society."

Kennedy frowned. The crowd of candleholders was far too thick for her to hope to see the speaker. She didn't just know his voice. She recognized the way her soul burned while he prayed. Where had she heard prayer like that before?

Dominic?

She was so upset over everything Reuben was going through, she had almost forgotten how Dominic prayed with her that first night they met. He was an enigma. How could a Christian with such passion for God serve in the same police force that had imprisoned her friend? Was he just here to assuage his guilty conscience?

The prayer continued, and the crowd grew quieter with each refrain. "Calm our spirits, Lord. Where there is fear, grant us your peace. Where there is anger, grant us your mercy. Where there is hurt, grant us your healing. Heal our relationships. Heal our justice system. Heal our broken families. Heal our society. We have no hope other than you, Father."

At first, Kennedy found it strange that he hadn't even mentioned Reuben. But on the other hand, he had addressed more in those few minutes than she could have ever hoped to cover if she'd spent an hour in prayer by herself. It was the difference between a nurse wrapping up a gushing wound and a surgeon going in and cauterizing the source of the bleed. Dominic was a powerful man of prayer, but that still didn't explain what he was doing on the speakers' platform. There were far too many people for this to be an open mic night at the prayer vigil. Was he here as a member of the police force? What would his superiors think?

"Thank you very much, Reverend," announced an unknown voice. "That was Pastor Dominic, Protestant chaplain for the Boston Police Department."

Chaplain?

The noise increased exponentially. Whatever sense of peace had rested on the crowd during Dominic's prayer, it was gone now. There was no shouting or anything Kennedy might have expected from a protest like this, only the rustlings from several hundred fidgeting people. Coughs and murmurs threatened to drown out the soft-spoken Episcopalian minister who was the next to offer up her prayer.

"Come on." Willow tugged on the belt of Kennedy's trench coat. "Othello went up ahead. Said he saw some of his friends up there."

Before Kennedy could respond, Willow began her complicated weave through the crowd of candleholders. Kennedy wondered what the fire chief would say at the sight. She pictured the sidewalks covered in candle drippings tomorrow morning. Is that all that would come from this prayer vigil — dried wax and litter? Was any of this doing any good at all?

All we can do is pray. Sure, this was better than the rioting and looting that had accompanied other accounts of police hostility across the nation, but would it help Reuben in the end? If God wanted Reuben saved, shouldn't he have done it already? And what about all the people praying who weren't even Christian? This was an ecumenical event. What if a Muslim went up front and lifted up a prayer to Allah, or a Universalist prayed to some great cosmic being that sounded more like the Force in *Star Wars* than the God of the Bible? What would the Lord think of all this? Was he offended to have his name plastered alongside so many other religious deities, or was he just happy that people came out to pray at all?

It was only a few seconds into the Episcopalian's prayer that Kennedy lost sight of Willow. Oh, well. She'd catch up with her and Othello later. It wasn't worth coming into bodily contact with a hundred different strangers carrying who knew how many billions of germ cells just to keep up with her roommate. She was surprised Willow had come to a prayer vigil at all. Willow claimed to be agnostic, and she usually took every chance she could get to blast the evils of organized religion, convinced as she was that the vast majority of the world's problems throughout history could be blamed on Christians.

For the most part, Kennedy and Willow had gotten along so well because they avoided arguments. Sometimes Kennedy wondered if God wanted her to be more confrontational, if he was upset with her for letting her roommate speak so badly about the church, but she hadn't studied well enough to come up with counters to Willow's unyielding stance. Besides, her dad had always taught her you couldn't argue someone into the kingdom of heaven. Was Kennedy doing the right thing by keeping the peace, or was that just a fancy way of saying she was too ashamed of the gospel to stand up for it? She really didn't know.

She stretched her spine and strained her neck for one last chance to catch a glimpse of Willow. At least they both had cell phones. They could always connect with each other later. Kennedy wasn't very comfortable around Othello and was glad for a chance to avoid his crowd anyway. As the quiet woman up front finished her prayer, Kennedy froze. What if Othello told his friends about her? What if he told them that she was the mystery woman from the video? So far, Kennedy had avoided all that media attention and drama. She knew Willow would respect her privacy, but what about her friend?

She should have never come tonight. Every single person here knew about the piggyback attack. Most of them had probably seen her face in the video. She didn't have the most unique features in the world, but what if someone recognized her? The candlelight was as bright as a hundred streetlamps. How had she let Willow talk her into coming? And why had she allowed herself to get separated from her roommate?

A tap on her shoulder. Kennedy whipped her head around. This was it. The end of her privacy. Her false sense of security.

"Excuse me, Miss." A middle-aged man was frowning at her. "Do you have the time?"

Kennedy let out her breath, wondering if it was possible to get drunk on relief. She reached into her pocket. Where was her phone? "I'm sorry ..." She tried her coat as well as her jeans. Had she really been that stupid? Had she left it in her dorm? "I can't seem to find my cell," she muttered only to find that the man had moved on and was asking someone else.

No phone. How would she get a hold of Willow when it was time to go? She hadn't even paid attention to where they parked.

Why had she ever come here?

"... And Lord, we come humbly to ask that you would bless our brother Reuben. Give him peace. Let him rest well tonight in comfort and safety. May you free his heart from all fear." Kennedy wished she could shut her ears. While Dominic had prayed earlier, she found it odd he didn't mention Reuben once. But this was even worse, this woman who had never met him, asking God to grant him a good night's sleep in his jail cell. This stranger didn't know anything about Reuben, didn't know how many sisters he had, how he doted on his nephews and nieces back home, how steady he could keep his hands when it came time to do a titration procedure in the lab. Kennedy bit her lip. When had it gotten so cold? She needed her heavy winter jacket, not her trendy fashion coat. She clenched her jaw to keep her teeth from chattering. Why would anybody ever want to be in a place so crowded?

"And Lord, we also pray for the young lady involved. Wherever she is, we pray for her protection tonight."

Tightening in her lungs. The hint of a diaphragm spasm.

"We pray that you would bless her."

One gasping breath that did nothing to draw in air. A second attempt, and then a third before the oxygen wheezed in.

"We pray that you would keep her in your perfect peace."

Her heart racing. Her brain's limbic system in complete chaos.

"We pray that you would keep her safe."

She had to get out. So many people. So many bodies. A middle-aged woman coughed right next to her. Was it influenza? Tuberculosis? Who would willingly expose themselves to so many people's contagions?

"Thank you for the love you show us."

Get away. There was no other option. She'd go find Willow's car and wait for her there. But what if she got lost? What if she ran into a cop? Were the police out looking for her? Dominic had said she wasn't in any danger of getting arrested, but hadn't he said the same thing about Reuben just last night? Besides, Dominic was nothing more than the chaplain. What would he know?

The chaplain? Why hadn't he told her that sooner?

"Thank you for your mercy and grace."

Kennedy's heart was about to burst its way out of her pericardial sac. There was no way her body could maintain this level of adrenaline. Could a nineteen-year-old have a heart attack? Would anyone notice her dying in this sea of strange faces?

Another gasping breath. Wheezing. Begging for life. For safety. For refuge.

She couldn't support her weight. Her blood CO2 must have skyrocketed. Soon, acidosis would ravage her body systems. There was no way she could expect her muscles to work properly. She just had to get away from the crowd, otherwise she'd fall and just as likely get trampled as die from heart failure.

Choking on something that was half a sob and half a cry for help. There were hundreds of people here. Couldn't one of them see she was about to pass out? Her head felt as if it would float off her shoulders. She would collapse any second. Her only hope was that her body would wait until she was on the fringe of this mass of humans before it gave out on her completely.

"Are you ok?"

She didn't stop to address the young mother carrying a baby in a front sling. She couldn't slow down. She had to get out.

"Can I help you?"

She became vaguely aware of multiple pairs of staring eyes. She was so focused on getting away from the people, so intent on forcing air into her lungs that she hadn't realized she was crying, if that's what you could call the sobbing, gasping, wheezing noises that came out of her mouth. She stumbled blindly ahead.

"Hey, can I help you?" When did people grow so nice? When did society ever care so much for one individual? And if Boston was really filled with such conscientious citizens, why was Reuben spending the night in jail?

Someone grabbed her arm. Someone she didn't know. She wasn't strong enough to shake him off. "Leave me alone." Her voice was so garbled she hardly understood the words herself.

There it was. She recognized the bank across the street. Willow's car was somewhere over there. The crowd had thinned out, too. She had made it.

Almost.

With the faint sound of the minister's *amen* dying in her ears, Kennedy tripped and barely managed to throw her hands down to the pavement to break her fall. Someone knelt beside her. "Can I do something for you? Is there someone I can call to help you?"

It was hard to focus on his words. She knew you couldn't die from a panic attack — she had looked it up once — but what if this was something else? What if her heart really was giving out because of all the stress she'd been under? Maybe she should have taken those yoga classes with Willow after all. She wasn't ready to die. There were so many plans she had for her life.

Tears streamed down her cheeks. From a distance, someone called her name.

"Kennedy!"

Something in his voice, still so far off, beckoned to her. She could hardly focus on the Good Samaritan who knelt on the sidewalk beside her.

"Kennedy?"

Air rushed back into her lungs. She drank it in like a marooned Ben Gunn dying of thirst. She could almost feel her brain swelling with the welcomed influx of oxygen.

"You know her?" the stranger asked.

"Yeah. Kennedy, can you hear me?"

Relief and humiliation both clashed in her chest. "Pastor Carl?" Her voice broke. A second later, she was sobbing into his shoulder, oblivious to the crowd, the kindly stranger, and the prayer vigil for Reuben that persisted just a block away.

CHAPTER 21

Kennedy could only guess how long she and Carl sat on that cold pavement. He didn't say anything, didn't offer any false reassurances or tell her to calm down. Didn't accuse her of overreacting or offer any pastoral guilt trip that if she only prayed or read her Bible more she wouldn't be such a mess.

Once her sobbing quieted down and she could breathe somewhat normally again, he checked her limbs for any injuries, asked if she had hit her head when she fell. And then he held her longer, as if his only reason for being near the Boston courthouse tonight was to make sure she felt safe.

"I'm glad I saw you," he finally said. "They invited me here to give a prayer, but I was running late. Couldn't find my keys. Must be providence, because otherwise I probably wouldn't have seen you ..." He didn't finish his thought, and Kennedy was thankful to avoid hearing the eye-witness account of her own embarrassing meltdown.

"I don't know what happened," she said. "I was fine one minute, then all of a sudden ..."

"Shh. Don't you worry about it." Carl glanced at his wristwatch. "Listen, I'm already late, and there's no way I'm leaving you here alone." He leveled his gaze to look at her as sternly as he could pull off. "You didn't take the T alone, not this late at night, did you?"

"No, I came with my roommate, but we got separated."

"Well, let me call my friend and tell him I can't make it. He's the one who arranged all this. I'm sure he'll understand." Carl held his old-fashioned flip-phone to his ear.

"I don't want you to miss out." Kennedy took in a deep breath to prove to both herself and Carl that she could. "I don't mind ..."

"Stuff and nonsense," he interrupted and then held up his finger. "Hello, Dominic? Can you hear me?"

Kennedy still couldn't understand why he always needed to shout when he talked to someone on his cell.

"Yeah, it's Carl. Something came up, and I'm not gonna make it." He yelled for a minute longer about how sorry he was for missing the vigil and then ended the call.

"That's a good man," he said as he put his phone in his back pocket. "Most godly saint this police force has ever seen."

"Was that the chaplain?"

"That's right, Dominic. You know him?"

"A little. We met at the ... He was at the hospital last night. He didn't tell me he was the chaplain. I just thought he was an officer."

Carl let out a little laugh. "That's Dominic for you. Most humble, unassuming man I know." He groaned as he stood up and then reached down to help Kennedy to her feet. "You up for a little walk? I had to park behind the bank."

She nodded. "I'm better now." Part of her wanted to leave Carl and go find Willow, pretend none of this had ever happened. But then she saw the ocean of bodies and heard the sound of an acoustic guitar strumming over the loudspeaker. She would never make it back in that crowd. "You sure you don't want to stay? I could wait here while you go pray."

Carl jerked his head toward the courthouse, where some folk singers with only slightly more talent than the Babylon Eunuchs were singing an over-embellished version of *Imagine*. "I'm not that big of a Beatles fan these days, truth be told." He grinned and extended his arm. "Want a little extra support?"

Kennedy was pretty sure she could walk on her own, but she took Carl's elbow and allowed him to lead her slowly down the street until the sounds of the crowd and mediocre singing faded into the darkness.

CHAPTER 22

Carl insisted that Kennedy spend the night with him and Sandy in their Medford home. She didn't have a way to let Willow know where she was, but Carl volunteered to drive all the way to her dorm to get her cell phone while she and Sandy had tea. Of course, by tea he meant cookies, cinnamon rolls, and any number of Sandy's baked goods, but Kennedy wouldn't turn that down. Not tonight.

Sandy was pulling a tray of banana nut muffins out of the oven when Carl dropped her off at his house. Sandy set the muffin tin on the stovetop and wrapped Kennedy up in a 360-degree hug. "Carl told me you'd be coming. I'm so sorry about Reuben."

It had only been a few hours since Kennedy was here eating pork chops, but the first whiff of cinnamon and vanilla set her stomach grumbling.

"You had such a hard night, sweetheart." Sandy led Kennedy into the dining room and sat her down at the table. "You just get comfortable. I have tea heating up right now, and you can keep me company from there while I finish up my baking." She glanced at the door that led to her garage. "Where's Carl?"

Kennedy explained how he went to get her phone so she could call Willow and let her know she wouldn't need a ride home.

"And how is your roommate, sweetie? Are you two still getting along well?"

Kennedy accepted a cup of tea and added a spoonful of honey. "Yeah. I'm kind of surprised by it all, but we're getting along great. We're going to room together again next year.

"That's fabulous, darling. It's so nice when God brings friends like that into our lives."

"I don't know that God had much to do with it in this case. I mean, Willow is about as far from Christianity as you can be."

Sandy threw some cream cheese into an old-fashioned electric mixing machine. "Sometimes those are the ones who fall for God the hardest when their time comes."

Kennedy allowed herself to chuckle at the thought of Willow turning her life around that drastically. Sandy whipped up some frosting in her mixer, and Kennedy wondered what life would be like if she hadn't known the Lindgrens, if she arrived at Harvard without any kind of support system, like Willow who flew here all the way from Alaska. How did people endure the loneliness? The Lindgrens' home wasn't just a place to satisfy her sweet tooth or keep her from becoming anemic. It was a place where Kennedy found love, unconditional acceptance, a sense of peace she'd never been able to fully experience in the dorms.

More than anything, this was home.

Sandy pulled a tray of fresh-cut fruit from her fridge and set it on the table. "I thought we'd start with this while the muffins cool." She winked. "That way, we can at least pretend that we're eating healthy."

Kennedy took a pineapple chunk and remembered her conversation with Reuben in the student union. He had wanted more than anything to avoid a confrontation with the police. Why? Was it because he didn't want to get arrested? Did he have some sort of premonition about what would happen to him? Or was there more to it? She replayed her conversation with him on the phone. What was it he'd wanted to tell her?

Sandy took a dainty bite from an oversized strawberry. "So tell me, darling, how are you doing with all this?"

Kennedy had no idea what Carl said to her when he'd texted Sandy from his car. Did she know about the panic attack? The last thing she wanted to do was to relive those few awful minutes at the vigil, recall how scared she'd been, certain her heart would give out from adrenaline overdose, certain she would die quite literally from fright.

How was she doing? How was she supposed to know? How could she take the time to assess her emotional well-being right now while Reuben was locked away in some cell? Would he be alone or with others? Was he safe? The first day of the semester, her children's lit class had discussed a book depicting a gang rape while the main character was wrongfully imprisoned. At the time, she wondered how the story could have found its way through any juvenile fiction press's editorial process.

Sandy patted her hand. "It's all right if you don't know how to answer. Sometimes our brains know it's time to switch to survival mode, get us through the crisis. We don't always get a chance to deal with the emotional side of things until later on."

It made sense, but in another way, wasn't Kennedy here at the Lindgrens' home because of an overdose of unruly emotions? If there was something she could take to deaden her senses just a little, she could handle it all. She was used to stress. She was used to pushing herself out of her comfort zone. What she wasn't used to, what she would never get used to, were these debilitating panic attacks that could swell up in her, overwhelm her at the slightest provocation and the most inopportune times. Her anxiety had already cost her so much. Sleep. Energy. Her grades would start to suffer if she didn't get things under control soon. She could only guess what all this trauma was doing to her health, but she'd be surprised if she made it through another year at Harvard without her gastrointestinal tract breaking out into a dozen ulcers.

Kennedy stared at the plate of fruit and wondered what they would feed Reuben in jail. She wouldn't blame him if he hated her after this. Wasn't she the one who suggested they go see *Aida* in the first place? Wasn't she the one he was trying to protect before Bow Legs knocked him to the ground? And what had she done to help him? Whined to Daddy like a spoiled brat, but what had that accomplished? Would her dad's lawyer friend even get to Reuben's case before the weekend was over? Even when she tried to get the evidence she'd need to prove Reuben's innocence, she had already filled up her phone's memory with too many stupid pictures from chem lab. Why hadn't she kept better track of her storage space? Why hadn't she deleted all those useless photos once she didn't need them? It wasn't as though she'd ever have to pass pictures of her synthesized salicylic acid on to her descendants.

"What are you thinking about, sweetie?"

At first, Kennedy couldn't splice any words together.

"What's on your mind?"

Sandy's question was as strong as capillary action, slowly defying gravity and drawing a response out of Kennedy's mouth.

"He called me today. Reuben did. He got one phone call, and I couldn't even help him." She shook her head. Tears spilled down her cheeks like tiny drops of rain on oily asphalt. "There's nothing I can do."

Sandy nodded. "That's one of the hardest things to go through when you're unable to help someone you love. I know it's not easy, little lamb, but God gives us the strength we need ..."

"But he hasn't," Kennedy protested. "That's just the thing. I've prayed for strength. I've prayed for patience to get through all these things. I've prayed to be a good example to Willow, but I'm such a mess." She looked down at her torso as if Sandy might see how filthy and defiled she really was. "It doesn't make sense. I've done all the right things. I'm setting aside time each day to read my Bible. I'm praying all the time." She let out a mirthless laugh. "And I'm a bigger nutcase now than I was a year ago."

Sandy didn't speak right away. Didn't chide Kennedy for her blasphemous accusations. Didn't remind her that all things work together for good or offer any of the other platitudes Kennedy was expecting. Instead, she took a long sip of tea and sighed. "I wish I had the answers for you."

So that was it? That was the best Sandy could do — Sandy, who was married to the pastor of one of Cambridge's most prominent churches? Sandy, who volunteered twenty or thirty hours a week at the pregnancy center and ran the children's ministry and babysat her grandson three days a week and still found time to bake cookies for lonely college students? She was saying there was nothing that Kennedy could do, no way to make all the pain and trauma disappear. Then what was Kennedy even doing here? Why was she searching for answers to impossible questions if it was just a big waste of time? She imagined God up in heaven, shaking his head, telling her that her quest was as hopeless as Atticus Finch taking on the Tom Robinson case.

Kennedy stared into her mug. "Yeah, I guess it was pretty silly for me to expect the impossible."

Sandy shook her head. "We never stop expecting the impossible, sweetie, but we have to temper that faith and that hope with the reality that this world is a fallen place. Sometimes evil prevails, but only for a time and only if it somehow works into God's master plan. Now, I don't pretend to understand how it fits together, or how God uses bad events to bring about good, or why he allows evil to persist when Jesus has already conquered. My soul yearns more every day for heaven when I think about how much God's children are suffering in this world. I think about our son, our little Woong so far away in South Korea. Carl and I are his parents, but we can't hold him. We can't comfort him. We can't snatch him out of whatever horror he's had to live through. We can only wait. Do you know how that tears a mother's heart up? But what can we do? We can claim that God is evil for allowing so much pain and injustice. We can lose all hope and turn our backs on him like Elijah was tempted to do in the wilderness. Or we can stick our heads in a hole, ignore the hurt and the suffering around us because it's too much for our narrow view of God to handle. Or we can accept the fact that this world is full of misery, and we can do what we can — limited though our efforts may be — to be the love of Christ to those who are hurting. To be hope to those who are discouraged. To be family to those who've been abandoned. To be healing for the brokenhearted. Balm for the suffering."

Sandy smiled softly. "That's the third option, my dear. It means waking up every day and asking God how you can shed his light into the darkness around you. It means opening your heart to the feeble, the downtrodden, the afflicted. It means speaking up for the oppressed, loosening their chains. The real saints, the ones who are taking God's message of love seriously, are the ones who can see the pain around them, feel the impact of sin, and instead of losing heart or giving into despair, they covenant with God that they are going to push back that darkness. Reclaim the lost for Christ. Resist the decay and pollution and oppression that's brought the world to where it is today. That's the power we have in us, precious. It's a big responsibility."

Kennedy had to chuckle.

Sandy laughed back. "What is it, dear?"

"You went from motivational speaker to Spiderman's uncle without stopping for air."

Joy lines crinkled around Sandy's eyes, even though Kennedy wasn't sure she understood the reference.

"You see what I mean, don't you, darling?"

Kennedy nodded. "Yeah. It's just hard."

Sandy refilled her mug. "No, it's just life."

Kennedy reached for some cantaloupe. "I guess what I mean is I worry about what kind of witness I'm being for Christ. I mean, I don't know if Carl told you, but I was a big sobbing mess before he brought me here. So I love what you're saying about bringing hope to the lost and all that, but when I try to be strong I end up falling flat on my face more often than not."

"Who said you have to be strong?" Sandy asked the question so pointedly Kennedy had to run through their entire conversation to see if there was something she had missed.

"I never claimed you were supposed to be strong to accomplish all those things." Sandy brought the muffins over to the table and started to frost them.

"But I can't even make it through a simple prayer meeting without hyperventilating and sobbing in front of complete strangers. How is that supposed to show God's victory?"

Sandy set two muffins on Kennedy's plate. "It's during those times that we're the weakest when God can show himself the most dramatically. And I'm not talking about just taking away your panic attacks, pumpkin, although if he wanted to do that, he certainly could. What I'm talking about is you having the freedom and courage to live out your life — stress, anxiety, and all — in front of others with a vulnerability and grace that can only come from above. Think about your roommate for a minute. What are her biggest reasons for hating Christianity?"

"She says the church is full of judgmental hypocrites."

"So, she thinks that all Christians put on a mask and act phony to cover up their struggles. But you can show her how that's not the case, how God can take someone at her weakest, at her most anxious, at her most traumatized, and how he can give her the faith to say, 'I know that my Redeemer lives.' That's the message people like your roommate are hungry to hear. It's like Carl and me when the kids were younger. When we had our fights and disagreements, don't you think we wanted to shut the door and keep our kids from seeing us at our ugliest? But we made it a point not to do that. We didn't want them to grow up believing the lie that marriage is easy. No, we fought in front of the kids, and things could get pretty heated at times.

But we did that to teach our children that a godly couple can have their disagreements and afterwards still show love to each other, still respect one another. It's the same thing when we're witnessing. If our goal is to make people think that Christians never struggle, we're just setting them up for failure. What would your roommate think if she became a Christian because she believed you had a perfect, struggle-free life and wanted that for herself? Then, when she faces trials of her own, she'd feel like God abandoned her. So instead, you show her what it means to suffer and still have hope, to go through the valley of the shadow of death but know that the good Shepherd is right there, comforting you with his rod, guiding you with his staff. That's the kind of witness people today need to see."

She reached out and tucked a strand of loose hair behind Kennedy's ear. "We should never try to do God a favor by hiding our weaknesses. Don't hide your struggles. Just ask God to use them to show others his glory. Does that make sense?"

Kennedy nodded, and Sandy placed some more fruit on her plate as the door to the garage flung open.

"Did you miss me?" Carl brandished a smile and waved Kennedy's cell phone in one hand. He sat down at the head of the table. "This smells delicious. Pass me that fruit plate. I'm famished."

CHAPTER 23

Half an hour and two more banana muffins later, Kennedy's body reminded her how exhausted she was from the events of the past twenty-four hours. She hadn't thought until now about any of the toiletries she'd need, but Sandy always kept extra nightclothes and toothbrushes ready for occasions just like this.

"You sure you don't want some help cleaning up the dishes?" Kennedy asked.

"Just leave them," Sandy answered. "I'll get to them in the morning."

If she knew anything about Sandy, she was certain those dishes would be clean and dry in the dishwasher well before sunrise.

Sandy got up from the table. "I think I saved your toothbrush from last time. Let me go have a look." She started to bustle down the hall and stopped. "Oh, I almost forgot! Carl, do you have your note ready? We can ask Kennedy to do the picture tonight."

He scooted his chair back. "I've got it in the den. I'll go grab it."

Kennedy watched him hurry out of the dining room. "What note?"

"It's something we started last week when we first got matched with Woong from the South Korean orphanage. Carl and I made the decision that we'd write him a note each day until he comes home and take a picture of us holding it. It might not be much, but we wanted him to understand how much we loved him even before we met him face to face."

Kennedy figured that any orphan lucky enough to get paired up with the Lindgrens was one of the most blessed kids alive. "That's a really sweet idea."

"So, Carl's gonna grab his camera, and do you mind taking the picture for us? Otherwise, he'll have to fiddle with the timer, and half the time it goes off too early. I swear we could make a collection of all the pictures of Carl's backside to give to Woong."

Carl scurried in carrying a dry-erase board. "It's my night to do the message, right, babe?"

"Yeah. I thought you said you already wrote it." Sandy was repositioning photographs and homemade crafts on the mantle. "Come stand right here, Kennedy. We haven't gotten a shot by the fireplace in a little while." She frowned at Carl. "Weren't you wearing that last night?"

He glanced down at himself. "No, that was my other red shirt. This one's different."

"You sure?"

"Yeah." He reached into his pocket. "Now here you go. This camera ... Wait, where is it?"

Sandy rolled her eyes. "You lost it again?" She turned to Kennedy. "I swear, if Woong knew how much hassle we go through just to get him ..."

"I'm the one who said a ten-year-old boy ain't gonna care if he gets a picture every day," Carl countered. "It's not like he's going to pull out a magnifying glass and read each single date ..."

"It's the principle of the thing. We want him to know ..."

Kennedy grabbed her cell. "How about I take it on my phone and I'll just send it as an attachment to your email or something? Would that work?"

Carl lifted his eyebrows. "You can do that?"

"Yeah." She opened her camera app. "Are you guys ready?"

"I think so."

Sandy nudged Carl again. "You forgot the whiteboard."

"Oh, yeah."

Once everything was in place, Kennedy tried to take the shot.

"What was that beep?" Sandy asked. "Was that the picture? Do you want to take another one just to be sure?"

Kennedy frowned at her screen. "No, it's this phone. It's gotten low on memory. Hold on. I have to delete a few pictures, and then I'll try again." She sighed as she went into her gallery. For five minutes, maybe more, she had gone without thinking about Reuben, about the way her stupid phone's lousy memory was the reason he was spending the night in jail. She really should take those old lab photos and delete them all. It's not like ...

She froze.

"What is it, dear?" Sandy asked.

"Just give the girl a minute to do what she's gotta do."

Kennedy felt the blood rush from her head down to the finger that stood poised over her screen. Could it really be ...?

"Hold on."

Sandy hurried and stared over her shoulder. "What's the matter, sweetie? Is your battery dying?"

"No, it's not that. It's ..."

She wouldn't allow herself to hope. She couldn't. Her phone had said the memory was full. Why hadn't she thought to go into her photo album in the first place? Was it right there?

"Precious, is everything all right?"

"Give the girl some space, woman," Carl boomed without losing his good-natured tone.

Kennedy's finger was surprisingly calm as she selected the recording. It started to play. She glanced up at the Lindgrens. "I think I found the video that will get Reuben out of jail."

CHAPTER 24

Kennedy lost track of how many times she and the Lindgrens watched the video. It wasn't the full encounter, but it was enough. The phone's memory reached its max right after the cop knocked Reuben to the ground. It was enough to show Reuben hadn't instigated anything. Enough to exonerate him. Kennedy couldn't decide if she was more relieved to finally have the proof or mad at herself for not discovering it sooner.

Well, there was no way they would hold Reuben in jail for long, not with information like this. Now, the only question was who she should give it to. She tried calling her dad, but no one picked up either at the office or at home. She sent him an email and asked for the full name of his lawyer friend after a Google search showed at least tweny-seven attorneys in the greater Boston area called Jefferson.

"You know it's late, don't you?" Carl asked as she stared at her phone. "Even if the right people got a hold of this, Reuben won't be getting out tonight."

"Carl's right, hon." Sandy rubbed Kennedy's shoulders. "You can always wake up first thing tomorrow and then decide what to do. These things always seem to make more sense once you've had a good night's sleep."

A good night's sleep? Didn't they know, couldn't they understand that she had been begging God for the chance to get her hands on something like this, verifiable proof that Reuben was innocent? And now they were telling her to go to sleep and wait for morning?

"I'm not an expert in these things," Carl said, "but I know your dad pretty well, and I'm guessing he'd advise you to talk with Reuben's lawyer before you do anything else."

Carl was right, at least the part about that being what her dad would say.

Sandy took her by the arm. "If you come with me by the bathroom, sweetheart, I'll get you your toothbrush and some pajamas."

"We still need to take that picture for Woong," Carl reminded her.

"We don't need to keep Kennedy up for that. We can use the timer on your camera like usual."

Carl stood up with a groan. "Guess that means I better find it." He tousled Kennedy's hair affectionately. "Good night, kiddo. I hope you sleep well."

Kennedy thanked him again for letting her stay over and followed Sandy toward the bathroom. Once she was washed and dressed and alone in the Lindgrens' familiar guestroom, she turned on her phone and watched the video one more time. All her muscles were quivering, but now it was from excitement and not from fear. Reuben would be released. He would be just fine. Life could go on as normal. Hopefully, even better than normal, because Kennedy had already decided that once he got out, she wasn't going to take his friendship for granted anymore. She wasn't going to bide her time, wait to see what the future might bring, and spend her life wondering if things could have been different if she'd had the courage to confess her feelings. Maybe by this time tomorrow, she'd be with Reuben. Maybe by this time tomorrow, he'd know. She thought about the Bible verse that God works all things together for good for those who love him. Maybe that was what this was all about. Maybe God allowed Reuben to get arrested, knowing that this one night with him in jail would be enough to make Kennedy realize that she'd be the biggest fool in Massachusetts if she didn't tell him the truth.

The whole truth.

It would be scary, but hadn't her therapist told her it was time to take baby steps out of her comfort zone? Hadn't Sandy just spent half an hour assuring Kennedy it was ok to feel inadequate, it was ok to feel weak? A cross-stitched verse that hung in the Lindgrens' dining room flitted through her mind: *Weeping may remain for a night, but rejoicing comes in the morning.* Maybe Carl and Sandy were right. Maybe she should try to sleep, get a hold of her dad first thing in the morning, find a way to get the video to Reuben's attorney. Weren't there verses in Proverbs that talked about patience being the wisest course of action? That's what her mom had told her growing up, at least. You regretted rushing into things more often than you'd ever regret waiting.

She lay down, relishing how much more comfortable the Lindgrens' bed was compared to her dorm mattress. If she didn't need access to the college library at all hours of the day and night, she might even be tempted to offer to pay Carl and Sandy room and board to stay here. At the very least, it was the perfect reprieve for a Friday night, a night that had started out disastrous but left Kennedy filled with hope. She wished she could catch this blissful feeling in a lab flask, close it up with a rubber stopper, and let it diffuse into her system whenever she needed.

Hope. One of God's most precious gifts for his children. She was ashamed at how she doubted him earlier, ashamed of how quickly she threw away her faith, when all this time, he knew that the video she needed and the proof she'd been begging for were right there on her phone. Maybe this was all God's way of bringing her and Reuben together.

Together. Another beautiful word, just like hope. Together ...

She had just allowed her mind to drift off into that first stage of drowsy sleep with its long, alpha brain waves when her phone rang.

Willow.

Was she still at the protest? How could Kennedy have forgotten to call her?

"Hello?" She tried to talk quietly in case Carl and Sandy were already in bed.

"Hey, sorry we lost you. Othello and I are going to stay out for a while, but do you want me to take you back to campus first?"

"No, that's ok. I forgot to text you earlier. I ran into my pastor and got a ride with him. I'll be staying at his place tonight."

"Nothing kinky, right?" Willow teased.

Kennedy ignored the remark. "How was the rest of the vigil?"

She had to strain to hear over all the background noise. "It's still going on, actually. They're on the third band doing a Beatles cover, so I'm out of here."

"Glad I didn't miss much, then. But hey, really good news. I found the video I thought I'd lost on my phone. It didn't get everything, but it was recording for over two minutes before the memory ran out. I'm gonna find a way to get it to Reuben's lawyer in the morning."

"What's that?" Willow was shouting now. "I didn't hear that last part. You said something about your phone?"

"I'll just text you." She didn't want to raise her voice and bother Carl and Sandy.

"Ok, I can't hear you too good, so just call or text me if you need something. Otherwise I'll see you back on campus."

Kennedy said goodbye even though she couldn't be certain Willow heard it. She opened up her text messages and sent a quick note about the video.

I want to see it! Willow immediately responded.

The video file was too large to text, so she sent it as an email attachment, grateful to have someone else to share the good news with.

Yes, things had taken a positive turn. A very positive turn.

Kennedy figured she was about to get the best sleep she'd had in weeks.

CHAPTER 25

"Do you think we should wake her up?"

"I'm not sure. We could wait."

Carl and Sandy's words slipped through the fog of Kennedy's heavy sleep.

"She's gonna find out eventually. It might be best if she hears it from us."

"I know, I just wish the little lamb could have a few more minutes to rest. She was so tired last night."

Kennedy rubbed her eyes. She always felt so disoriented when she woke up at the Lindgrens', as if her body wasn't accustomed to a real mattress and was looking for the hard, cardboard-like substitute from her dorm room.

"I think we should tell her ourselves. Otherwise she might see the news on her phone or something."

"You're probably right. I just wish ..." Sandy didn't finish her thought. Kennedy's brain was only half awake, like her computer after she turned it on but had to wait for all her programs to load. What were they talking about? What news did they have for her?

Something about Reuben?

A small knock on the guest room door. Timid. Almost apologetic.

"Come in."

Sandy with her long brown hair out of its normal French brain. A frown on her usually cheerful face. Dark lines under her eyes. Had she slept at all?

Carl muttering something as he passed down the hall. Apparently, this was women's business. So it was Reuben, then. Had something happened to him? Had he been attacked in jail?

Please, God. No.

That giant swell of hope she'd experienced last night, that first taste of true joy she'd felt in weeks, came crashing down around her. Something was wrong. Sandy's face was pale. Kennedy knew her psyche wasn't strong enough for another crisis. Her lungs pulled tight in her chest.

Sandy sat down gingerly on the edge of the bed and placed her hand on Kennedy's knee. "Something happened last night."

Time distorted itself. How could the theory of relativity explain this kind of phenomenon? How could Einstein, brilliant as he was, rationalize the way Kennedy found herself pulled out of normal temporal reality until everything was slow? Viscous. Even her body's autonomic functions, the pounding of her pulse in her ears, decelerated inexplicably.

Sandy took in a deep breath. It was the same look a nurse would give her patient before turning her over for a spinal tap.

Where was that hope? Where was that peace now?

"It's about that video," Sandy began. Even her voice sounded lower, warped somehow. Was Kennedy ill? Was her brain sick? Had she fallen victim to some sort of bizarre sensory disorder that left her feeling so detached? Disoriented?

Sandy stared at her lap. Her hair was beautiful. Silky. Light brown with respectable hints of long, gray streaks. Why didn't she wear it down more?

"I need to ask you something," Sandy began. Kennedy made a note that when she was a doctor delivering a fatal prognosis, she would offer the bad news in a single sentence. No lengthy prefaces. No chitchat to decrease the shock. It was easier that way. Easier to know the truth and confront it than deal with the dreadful uncertainty.

Sandy made an apologetic sound in the back of her throat. "Did you send the video to anyone last night before you went to bed?"

"I showed it to Willow. My roommate. I was excited that we ... I wanted her to see ..." Kennedy stopped fumbling over her words and asked simply, "What happened?"

"We don't know how, but the media got hold of it. Last night before Carl and I went to sleep. There was a ..."

Kennedy watched Sandy's throat muscles constrict.

"Once the video got out, people were even more upset, more angry about what happened to your friend. There was an incident last night at the vigil." She avoided Kennedy's eyes.

An incident? What did that mean? What was Sandy saying?

"Is Reuben ok?" Did Sandy know how Kennedy felt? Did she guess how important Reuben was to her? If this was a little schoolgirl crush, she imagined Sandy would want to talk about it for hours over tea and homemade biscotti, but so far that particular subject had never been broached.

"Reuben's fine, dear." For the first time that morning, Sandy smiled.

Kennedy let her muscles relax. The iron sheath that had encased her rib cage loosened itself, and she could breathe easier.

As quickly as it came, however, Sandy's smile faded. "There was a problem at the courthouse, though." She winced as though the words were painful to speak. "A riot."

Kennedy felt guilty for feeling more relief than horror. Relief that Reuben was still safe. Relief that the public was on her side. The police would have to let Reuben free now.

Sandy let out a small choking sound, and Kennedy was startled to see tears streak down her cheeks. Her pulse quickened. How bad of a riot could it have been?

"Was anyone injured?" she asked and suddenly remembered Willow. Had she been there? Had she shared the video with Othello's crowd at the courthouse and stayed to watch the drama unfold? Kennedy was selfish to only worry about Reuben at a time like this. What about her roommate?

Sandy was shaking her head. "Only one injury." Her voice tightened. "A little baby."

Kennedy was certain she had misheard. What kind of a parent would bring a baby to an event like that? And what kind of criminals ...

She froze, remembering the young mother who had asked if she needed help. The baby in the sling. Maybe it wasn't so impossible, after all. Why shouldn't a parent attend a prayer vigil with a small child? It's something Kennedy's parents might have done when she was little.

Kennedy didn't trust her voice to get out the next question. Wasn't sure she wanted to know the answer. "Did the baby ..." No, that's not what she wanted to say. "Was it very serious?"

Sandy sniffed. "We don't know yet. She's at the Children's Hospital at Providence now."

"What happened?"

"It sounds like the mom was running to get away when the violence broke out and tripped. The baby was in a front pack, and ..."

"Is she going to be ok?" Kennedy wished she could hold audience with God if only for a few minutes. Ask him why he would allow something so horrible to happen. Why he would harm such a young and innocent life for no apparent reason.

Sandy shook her head. "I don't know. I just don't know." She was gripping Kennedy's hand.

"I'm sorry," Kennedy whispered.

Sandy's head shot up. "Whatever for, sweetheart?"

"I shouldn't have sent the video. Should have told Willow to keep it private."

Horror, the full realization of what she had done, sank into Kennedy's being little by little, like droplets of groundwater percolating down through layers of soil and gravel.

Sandy stretched out her arms and wrapped her in a hug. "It's not your fault, honey. Nobody would ever wish something like that to happen to a little baby. It's not your fault," she repeated, but Kennedy had a hard time listening through her tears.

CHAPTER 26

Kennedy texted Willow as soon as Sandy left. She doubted her roommate would be awake at nine on a Saturday morning, but she had to make sure her friend was safe. Willow replied right away, apologizing for the video leak.

I only shared it with Othello so he could see what was happening. I didn't know he was going to pass it on.

Kennedy was just glad to know Willow was safe. According to her text, Willow had sensed the tensions rising and left before the real violence erupted. Othello had stuck around with his friends, and Willow hadn't heard from him yet.

I'm sure he's fine, Kennedy assured her. After all, the only reported injury was that little baby.

The Lindgrens spent the morning keeping Kennedy distracted. As soon as Kennedy got out of bed, Sandy put her to work making a hearty brunch. Saturday morning brunch had been a regular custom in Kennedy's family for as long as she could remember, and she wondered if Sandy knew about their tradition. It took over an hour and a half to get everything baked and cooked. Then while Sandy set the table, Kennedy taught Carl how to use the timer on his camera properly so they could take their pictures for Woong more easily.

Breakfast at the Lindgrens' involved more than just sitting around the table, sipping fresh coffee, and stuffing yourself into a gluttonous stupor. Carl started each day with morning devotions, which he read from a Charles Spurgeon book Kennedy had never heard of before meeting the Lindgrens. Then, Sandy pulled out her prayer box, a cutely painted recipe holder with index cards arranged by category. Kennedy still hadn't figured the system out entirely, but there were certain people the Lindgrens prayed for every day, and others they prayed for on a weekly or monthly basis. After prayers, Carl passed Kennedy his old Bible so she could participate in the reading for the day. He and Sandy made their way through the Bible once a year, and Kennedy read a chapter from Joshua before passing it back to Carl to finish.

After Sandy refilled the coffee mugs and set another round of blueberry pancakes on the table, she took out a journal with a bright tulip pattern on the front.

"So last year at this time," she said, slipping on her pair of reading glasses, "we were praying for Blessing to have favor in her job situation at the bank, and we were asking God for a better daycare situation for Tyson that would be closer to her work." She took a pencil and drew two lines across the page. "God certainly took care of both of those worries, didn't he?"

Carl nodded back with a smile.

Sandy read through the rest of that page, striking out the requests that had already been answered and stopping to pray for those that hadn't yet come to pass. She flowed ceaselessly from her conversation with Carl and Kennedy into prayer and back again, so Kennedy half expected to see Jesus sitting in one of the empty chairs around the table. When she was finished, Sandy flipped ahead in her journal and wrote the day's date in her flowing cursive handwriting. "So of course, we're praying for Reuben's release and that poor little baby who was hurt. What else?"

By the time they finished breakfast devotions, Carl excused himself to get some work done at the church office. "Do you want me to give you a ride back to your dorm?" he asked Kennedy.

"If you don't mind." As restful as her time at the Lindgrens' had been, she knew she had to go back. If Reuben wasn't released over the weekend, he would definitely be freed after his arraignment Monday morning. Until then, Kennedy had to work on their lab report on her own. She also needed to start some research for a Roald Dahl paper for her children's literature class.

Sandy packed the brunch leftovers into various sized Tupperware and set them in a canvas bag for Kennedy to take back to campus. Sandy was clearing the table and Carl was hunting for his missing sermon notes when Kennedy's phone rang. She didn't recognize the number but wasn't about to miss a chance to talk to Reuben. Did he even know about the video? Did he know he was going to be released? Had he heard about the riots and the price paid for justice?

"Hello?" Kennedy made her way into the Lindgrens' guest bedroom for privacy.

"I'm looking for a Miss Kennedy Stern."

Kennedy shut the door behind her. "This is she. What can I do for you?"

"So where is this interview you're going to?" Carl asked as he drove Kennedy back to Harvard.

"Somewhere off the Orange Line." Kennedy fidgeted with her seatbelt and glanced at the dashboard clock. If she got back to her dorm in fifteen minutes, she'd have a little less than half an hour to change her clothes and get ready before she had to catch the T to Tufts.

"And who is this woman who called you?"

"Her name's Diane Fil-something. She's got a show on Channel 2."

Carl frowned. "Have you researched her background or anything?"

Kennedy wasn't surprised that her dad and Carl had been such good friends in college. In many ways, they were exactly like each other.

"She just said she wanted to talk to me about the video, get my side of the story."

"Yeah, I'm sure that's what she said," Carl muttered as he exited off the freeway. "I just want you to be careful. These news anchors, they don't care about you. In most cases, they don't even care about victims or civil liberties. You know what they care about? Ratings. So the more they can shock the audience, the better."

"This should be pretty straightforward." Kennedy didn't know why she should have to defend herself or her choices all of a sudden. "She said they'll play the video clip, I'll answer a few questions about when we got pulled over, and they'll cut to a commercial or something. I don't think it will be too hard."

"That's because you're a decent kid with nothing to hide," Carl explained. "But you better believe me, if you had a skeleton in your closet, it's people like this Diane What's-Her-Name who'd gamble away their grandmother's soul to be the first to break the story." He patted her knee. "I'm sorry. I shouldn't be so negative. I hope you have a really good interview. Just be careful, ok?"

"Thanks."

They drove a while in silence. Carl tuned his car radio to some conservative talk show but punched it off as soon as the host mentioned the riot at the courthouse. So far, Kennedy had resisted the morbid urge to look up footage from the event. She didn't know how much damage had been done, but the streets seemed relatively calm for the middle of a Saturday. Were people staying home? Did the police think the riots would get worse?

Carl pulled his Honda up to a curb near Harvard Square. "See you at church tomorrow?"

"If I get this lab report done by then," Kennedy answered. She slung her new canvas bag laden with leftovers on her shoulder, waved goodbye, and shut the door. She pulled her phone out of her pocket to glance at the time as Carl pulled away. If she hurried, she might even have time to wash her hair before she went on TV.

CHAPTER 27

Kennedy would have never guessed how much work went into preparing for a television interview. She arrived at the Channel 2 building ten minutes late and was immediately whisked into a makeup chair. While two different attendants muttered and frowned and fawned over her, Diane Fiddlestein's assistant barraged Kennedy with questions on every topic, from her time in China to her parents' missionary work, which Kennedy had to explain was a taboo subject due to her parents' sensitive relationship with the Chinese government. He asked her about her abduction last fall, and Kennedy's cheeks burned when she explained to him she still had flashbacks from the event and would prefer not to discuss it on live television. He assured her he would pass the message on to Miss Fiddlestein and then interrogated her about Reuben, the nature of their relationship, what part of Kenya he was from, what kind of grades he got.

"Is she really going to ask all this during the interview?" Kennedy had lost track of the time but was pretty sure they'd been talking for over half an hour when the interview was only scheduled to last about five minutes.

The assistant explained that this was common procedure. While a hair designer slathered Kennedy with hairspray, the assistant told her where to find bottled water or tea while she waited for the interview.

Apparently, she hadn't needed to be so preoccupied with being late, since she ended up with about forty-five minutes to wait behind the set for her turn. She was glad she had brought a book with her and found that *The Trumpet of the Swan*, which was on the suggested reading list for her children's literature course, was the perfect way to calm her nerves. Carl's warning about television anchors buzzed in the back of her head like an annoying mosquito, so she focused instead on the world of Louis, a swan who longed to share his voice with the world.

During a commercial break, while Diane Fiddlestein yelled at the teleprompter operator for some error he insisted he had no control over, her assistant led Kennedy to a beige loveseat.

"Your interview starts in two minutes. Can I get you one last drink of water?"

Kennedy shook her head, and he went on to summarize all the rules he'd already gone over before: speak clearly, ignore the camera, maintain eye contact with Diane, and stay completely on topic. Kennedy figured if she could multitask the procedure for a spectrophotometric determination experiment in the lab, she could make it through a five-minute interview.

"All right," someone in a headset called out. "We're up."

Kennedy found it a little strange that this would actually be her first conversation with Diane, but she was more concerned about proving Reuben's innocence than about how forced and contrived their meeting felt.

The man in the headphones held up his fingers and yelled out the countdown. They were on live TV.

The segment started with a few short snippets from Kennedy's encounter with Bow Legs. She was glad they showed it off-screen so she didn't have to watch it herself. She rubbed her clammy hands on her fitted wool slacks and tried to focus on long, controlled breathing. Five minutes. That's all this was. Five minutes for Reuben. She could do this.

She was so focused on stuffing her anxiety into one small enclosed place in the center of her gut that she wasn't paying attention to Diane Fiddlestein's smiley introduction. Fortunately, after Diane thanked her for being on the show, Kennedy's brain automatically kicked in with the expected exchange of pleasantries.

"So, Kennedy." Diane folded her hands in her lap. Kennedy wondered if there was a metal rod surgically plastered against her spine that allowed her to sit up so tall. Diane's smile was dazzlingly pretty, the dark red of her lips accentuating the perfect whiteness of her enamel, but there was a snake-like quality to her look that reminded Kennedy of the serpent witch in *The Silver Chair*. "Tell me," Diane began, "how did you feel when you learned that Reuben had been arrested last night?"

Kennedy was glad she hadn't asked about her encounter with the police. This was all about Reuben, after all. That's why she was here.

"I was upset, obviously. I knew Reuben hadn't done anything wrong, so I felt it was unfair when they took him away."

Took him away? Maybe she'd been spending too much time reading children's literature. It sounded like she had the vocabulary of a fourth grader.

"So tell us about the video we just watched," Diane went on. "I'm told the camera was hidden in your pocket?"

"Right. I turned it on when it looked like there might be some sort of confrontation. If things escalated, I wanted to have it on tape."

Diane nodded encouragingly, but her next question was far blunter than the previous. "And why did you wait a whole day to bring the truth to light?"

"I thought my camera had malfunctioned. I got a message after the incident that said it was out of memory, so I ..."

"But obviously it wasn't if you had the recording after all."

"I only got the first few minutes," Kennedy explained. "The rest was ..."

Diane didn't let her finish. "And how did you feel when you learned that your video resulted in a riot that injured a seven-month-old baby?"

"I was devastated. I never wanted anything like that to ..."

"So, you'll be happy to learn the baby was released from Providence this afternoon?"

Kennedy felt like she was in one of Professor Adell's lab lectures, unable to keep up with the pace. "That's great."

Diane jumped in as soon as Kennedy paused for breath. "And Reuben, the young man who was arrested, how would you describe him?"

The only reason Kennedy agreed to this interview in the first place was for the chance to clear Reuben's name. She told Diane about how good of a student he was, how encouraging, how he always had kind words, how he loved his family back in Kenya.

The whole time she talked, Diane busied her fingers unfolding a piece of paper that seemed to have materialized from nowhere. She frowned. "It says here that your friend's father was involved in the administration of former Kenyan dictator Daniel arap Moi. What can you tell me about that?"

Kennedy knew hardly anything about Kenya's history or politics. She'd never heard the name Diane mentioned. Reuben's conversation about his family was almost entirely limited to his numerous sisters and their dozens of children. "I really couldn't say," she stammered.

"I also find myself wondering why Reuben was sent overseas for his college education?" Diane's perfect smile chilled Kennedy's spine like the White Witch's winter curse in *The Lion, the Witch, and the Wardrobe.*

"Well, Harvard's a good school with a great international reputation ..."

Diane was frowning at the piece of paper, not listening to Kennedy at all. "Is it possible that Reuben was sent to the States because people with his condition get better medical treatment here than they would in a Nairobi hospital?"

Kennedy wondered if something even as warm as Aslan's breath would be enough to melt the icicles that had attached themselves to her nerve endings. "What medical condition?"

Diane pointed at her piece of paper, even though it was too far away for Kennedy to read. "It says here that your friend was diagnosed as HIV-positive."

Kennedy's throat tightened. She threw a pleading look at Diane, who sat cold and frigid like Empress Jadis on her throne.

"I'm not sure that ... I don't think ..."

"So I guess he didn't tell you before you started dating him." Diane frowned in false sympathy, pouting at the camera. "Well, when you see him again, please wish him the best. You'll be happy to hear I just got word that his arraignment has been rescheduled for this afternoon. If all goes well for his case, you'll be together again tonight. Thanks so much for joining us today, and I wish you both well."

Kennedy was too stunned to leave her chair once they turned the cameras off. Somewhere in a different part of the studio, a weatherman cracked jokes about an early spring heat wave, but his words flowed past Kennedy like time and space zooming past Meg in *A Wrinkle in Time.*

Nobody, not a single one of the dozens of backstage assistants noticed her. She stood herself up, trying to find something to settle her thoughts on, a focal point to pull her out of her daze.

The next commercial break ushered in a cacophony of noise and movement, and Kennedy half expected Diane Fiddlestein to reappear and apologize for making such a heinous joke on live television, but she was already behind her desk, sharing whispers with her co-host. Kennedy was surprised her legs could hold her weight, surprised her brain could still function.

Shouldn't the world have stopped turning? Shouldn't her entire nervous system have shut down?

She let herself out of the backstage area and followed the exit signs until she found the elevators that took her to the main level. She walked out of the lobby and found herself alone on the Boston curbside in a world that in a single instant had lost all sense of beauty, justice, or hope.

CHAPTER 28

By the time Kennedy got off the T and arrived back to campus, she had ignored calls from Carl and Sandy as well as three other numbers she didn't recognize before she turned her phone off.

As she walked to her dorm, she felt the stares of the students around her. Did they know? Could they guess?

It didn't make sense. Reuben with HIV? AIDS was one of those things like malaria — you learned about it, you knew it was bad, but you never expected someone you knew to actually have it.

She thought back to his brooding silences in spite of his otherwise cheerful, steady mood. His reluctance to take their story to the police department or the media. Had he known? Had he guessed the press would dig into his background?

Why hadn't he told her? Or had he tried? Was that the secret? It didn't have anything to do with Kennedy or any sort of romantic feelings at all. It was about his diagnosis.

She realized with irony that she wasn't suffering from even a hint of anxiety. No clammy hands. No racing pulse. No constricting lungs. Just a heaviness, as if someone had replaced her bone marrow with molten lead. Everything seemed to ache, but she wasn't in pain anywhere.

HIV positive? How had he gotten it? How long had he known? Would things change now that the truth was out? Wouldn't they have to?

It wasn't fair. HIV didn't impact people like Reuben. Did it?

She thought back to all her interactions with him in the lab. She couldn't have gotten herself contaminated. It wasn't like catching a cold or anything.

She glanced at her silenced phone, wishing it weren't the middle of the night in Yanji. Who could she talk to about this? Who could she turn to?

She had already spent too much time at the Lindgrens' this weekend. Besides, Carl had tried to warn her before she appeared on that stupid interview in the first place. Why hadn't she listened to him?

And what about Dominic the chaplain? Hadn't he said Reuben had his reasons for wanting to avoid public scrutiny? Had Reuben told him — Dominic, a perfect stranger — before he told his best friend? Had Dominic bewitched him with his powerful prayers as well?

She thought back over every conversation with Reuben, every trip off campus, every late night in the library, every meal together in the student union. Had he ever hinted? Ever come close to telling the truth?

Did she even know him anymore?

She reached her dorm and found her room empty. Good. She didn't have the energy to deal with Willow. She didn't even have the energy to deal with her own chaotic emotions. Why couldn't God have invented a Pensieve like in the J. K. Rowling books, a bowl she could dump her thoughts into and pull them out one by one to examine them until they were organized? Under control.

She slumped onto her bed. Would she ever feel joy again? They had moved Reuben's arraignment to this afternoon. He could be home by tonight. They could spend tomorrow working on their lab and hand it in first thing Monday. But would it ever be the same? Would it ever feel like it had before?

She squeezed silent tears from the corners of her eyes. Why hadn't he told her? And what would happen now?

The door opened slowly, and Kennedy wished she had gotten herself under the blankets. If she had to pretend to be asleep, she'd at least rather be comfortable.

"Hey." Willow's greeting sounded like an apology. "You ok?"

In all the history of the world, had a dumber question ever been asked? Or was it possible Willow didn't know? Possible she hadn't heard.

"I thought you'd be down at the courthouse. Didn't you get my text? The arraignment's in less than an hour."

"I'm not going," Kennedy mumbled.

Willow loosened her scarf and sat on the edge of Kennedy's bed. "Did something happen?"

"Reuben has AIDS." Never in her entire life had Kennedy expected to string those three words together. Why did God create the world to be so full of suffering? So full of horror?

"What?"

"Well, he's got HIV at least."

"How do you know? Did he tell you?"

"It was on the news." She didn't have the heart to tell Willow about the interview. She wished she could wrap herself up like the Very Hungry Caterpillar in its chrysalis and hide out there until she was ready to face the world with wings.

With hope.

With beauty.

Willow rubbed Kennedy's back. "Are you worried? Did you forget to use condoms or anything?"

Kennedy shook her head, no longer surprised at Willow's ingrained belief that it was impossible to be both a college student and a virgin at the same time.

"Well, that's something to be thankful for." She got up. "Want some tea?"

No. She didn't want anything. Except maybe a heavy dose of barbiturates so she could put herself into a medically induced coma until she was thirty and had life figured out.

Willow slipped on some of her hand-designed bangle bracelets. "I'm really sorry. For both of you."

Kennedy clenched her jaw shut. If Willow kept talking, she'd have to scream to drown the sound out.

"I really think you should come to the arraignment." Willow squirted some mousse into her palm and scrunched it through her hair. "He's going to get released, you know."

Kennedy figured that Willow was right. But what if he didn't? What if there was another riot? Another hurt kid? No, a world where God allowed those kinds of tragedies to run rampant wasn't a kind of world Kennedy wanted to live in anymore.

She held her breath, slightly frightened by the intensity of her emotions. Should she call the campus psychologist? Or maybe she was overreacting. It was normal to feel this way. Who wouldn't be a little down after everything Kennedy'd been through?

Willow slipped on her high-heeled black boots. All Kennedy could think of was how hard it would be for Willow to run away if more violence broke out at the courthouse.

"I'm gonna get my car. If you change your mind in the next few minutes, call me and I'll swing by and pick you up."

Kennedy was too exhausted to say thank you and nodded instead.

"It's going to be all right." Willow sounded so convinced. Maybe that's why she was the theater major. "Everything will work itself out in the end."

CHAPTER 29

Ten or fifteen minutes after Willow left, Kennedy still hadn't moved. She knew pretty soon she would jump online to see if the news covered Reuben's arraignment. But what if the judge didn't dismiss the case like everyone was expecting? What if Reuben would have to wait in jail for weeks or months before his trial, or what if the judge decided to deport him right then? She wished her dad had given her the full name of his lawyer friend. She had so many questions for him.

And what would happen if they didn't let Reuben go? People had been upset enough last night. What would they do today? The thought of anyone else getting hurt made her stomach contents curdle. Maybe she should buy herself some Tums.

She avoided her computer for as long as she could. Willow was probably halfway to the courthouse by the time she finally dragged herself out of bed to sit down at her desk. She waited for everything to start up and wondered if she was doing the right thing. Should she just wait? Willow or one of the Lindgrens would let her know once the decision was made, right?

Instead of jumping on the internet right away, she opened the Excel file that had the results from her most recent lab. She still had to manipulate some of the data before she could graph the results. It was a simple task, really, something she could have done in a minute or two on a good day. She botched it up three different times before she gave up.

She moved her cursor to open up the web but paused before clicking. No. She wasn't ready. She hadn't even seen the riot last night, but images of angry protesters clashing with police crept uninvited through her cerebral cortex. She wondered if Dominic had been there when the violence erupted. Did chaplains get involved in things like riots? She didn't even know if he carried a gun.

She stared at the time. The arraignment wouldn't start for a few more minutes. She had no idea how long the whole thing would last. She had no idea when the judge would reach a decision. How long would it take for him to dismiss the case and set Reuben free? How long would Kennedy have to wait in the meantime, wondering, fearful?

She turned her phone back on. Maybe she'd regret her decision. Maybe not. She found the contact she was looking for and waited for the call to go through.

"Hello?"

"Hi, I hate to bother you, but I was wondering if you'd come with me to the courthouse downtown."

"I'm so glad you called, sweetie."

Kennedy had lost track of how many times Sandy had said the exact same thing since she picked her up from Harvard in the Lindgrens' maroon Honda.

"I was just telling Carl I hoped you weren't alone. It can take a lot of courage asking for help. I'm really proud of you."

Kennedy hadn't thought about it in those terms. Honestly, she didn't think courage had much to do with it. She had just been too scared to wait alone to hear the results.

Sandy turned down her praise and worship CD. "I saw your interview, by the way. I was so sorry to hear about Reuben."

Kennedy already hated the way people like Sandy and Willow tiptoed around the subject. They treated it as though it was so private, so painful to mention, yet Diane Fiddlestein had broadcast the horrible, ugly truth to the entire world.

"I assume you didn't know before today?" Sandy said with a hint of a question in her tone.

"No." As soon as she called Sandy to ask her for a ride, she knew this conversation would come up.

"It must have hit you as quite a shock."

Kennedy hated those kinds of clichés. *Quite a shock*. What else was it supposed to be when you found out your best friend had contracted one of history's most horrific viruses?

"I hate to have to ask this, sweetie." Sandy cleared her throat. "But I know how college students these days are, and I know that even good Christian kids make mistakes."

Kennedy rolled her eyes when she realized what was coming next.

"You and Reuben weren't ever ... intimate, were you?"

Kennedy shook her head. Why was that everybody's first concern? And why was everyone so relieved to find out that Kennedy and Reuben hadn't been sleeping together? That still didn't change the fact that one day — whether next month or in five or ten years — he was going to die a hideous, undignified death.

"Well, I'm sorry I had to ask, but you know ..." Her voice died out. "It's not the kind of thing you catch from kissing as far as I understand."

"We don't do any of that," Kennedy replied sullenly.

"Well, I knew you two are close, so I had to ask." Sandy patted her hand, and Kennedy guessed that Sandy was the more uncomfortable of the two right now.

"Do you like him?"

Kennedy didn't want to talk about it. Because if she talked about it, then she had to think about it. The more she thought about it, the more she realized there was no real solution.

"I mean as more than a friend," Sandy pressed. "You like him like that?"

"I've started to," Kennedy confessed.

Neither of them spoke. Kennedy wondered if Sandy had already examined the different options and found each of them just as impossible as Kennedy had. It was stupid to end a friendship over something like HIV. It's not like she could catch it standing next to him for too long in the lab. But to continue on in a perfectly platonic relationship with him, Kennedy would have to deny the growing part of her heart that wanted more. That wanted something deeper. But how deep could it ever go? They could date as long as they kept their physical boundaries, but then what? You don't keep dating someone for the rest of your life. What kind of future did she and Reuben have to look forward to? What kind of ending could their story have besides tragedy and heartache?

"There was a time," Sandy began, "I was seeing two young men at once. Well, sort of. I'd been going steady with a doctor from Virginia for a few years by the time I met Carl. And well, things got more and more confusing from there. So I asked my grandpa about it. He was blind by then. Senile, too. Didn't know what a ruckus I'd caused in the family by even thinking about dating a black man. I just told him there were two men, didn't say anything about their skin color or nothing like that. But I asked him what he thought I should do, and you know what he said? He said the best decision he'd ever made in life was to marry his best friend. So that's what I did, too."

It was a nice story, one that a week ago might have given Kennedy a warm, gushy feeling in her gut. "It's a little different when someone's so sick, you know."

Sandy didn't reply right away, and Kennedy felt guilty. What good was it making Sandy just as depressed as she was?

Sandy hummed along with the worship song for a few bars and then took a deep breath. "We took in a little foster baby once, Carl and I," she began. "Sweetest little thing you'd ever meet. Had a condition. I forget the name, had to do with amniotic something. A lot of birth defects. A lot. Doctors suspected he had some genetic disorders, too, but they weren't able to check for those kind of things as well back then. So this little sweetheart, Spencer his name was, he had a lot of physical deformities. Internal problems, too. When he was born, the doctors thought he'd only last a month or two. It was too much for the birth parents to handle. They're fine people, I'm sure, but it was too heartbreaking for them. That's how we ended up welcoming little Spencer into our family.

"And you know what? It would have been easier for us if we never brought him home, easier emotionally as well as practically. I don't think I got a full night's sleep the entire time he was with us. The doctors told us he was going to die. One doctor even suggested we hold off on some of the medicine that was helping because it was only prolonging the inevitable. But you know what? That precious little child gave us seven months of joy. And when I say joy, I'm not pretending it was perfect and rosy. I'm not saying it was easy. I'm not saying our hearts didn't break, because they did. Every single day, my spirit just ripped in two when I held little Spencer and knew he only had such a short time with us. But you know what? That's what made having him in our home and in our lives so special. We didn't ask to fall in love with a sick little baby with a terminal diagnosis. We didn't ask to go through that valley of grief that stretched on for seven long months and then beyond that after he was gone. But believe me when I tell you that the time I had with Spencer was worth every second of heartache, and if I had the choice, I'd do it all over again."

Kennedy knew that only loosely veiled behind Sandy's words were wisdom and admonitions she could take to heart, but she wasn't ready to think in those terms yet. Sandy seemed to sense she had said enough, because she squeezed Kennedy's hand and turned the music back up.

They were closer to the courthouse now. Kennedy's breath grew shorter with each block they passed. There was some kind of tangible discontent in the air. Fear and anger. Or was that just her imagination?

Police in riot gear had formed perimeters in several locations. Kennedy sat paralyzed in her passenger seat. Sandy held her sweaty hand in hers.

"Don't worry, hon." She pointed. "See those people?" She rolled down her window. "Hear that noise? They're clapping. I think it's good news." She glanced from one side of the road to the other. "Now, I just wonder where I can find a place to park."

At the exact same moment, the victorious roar of the crowd jumped at least twenty or thirty decibels.

"What's going on?" Sandy asked, but Kennedy didn't have the breath to answer. When the Honda pulled up to a stop sign, Kennedy jumped out and started sprinting. Her heart, already overworked from anxiety, swelled to near-bursting capacity.

He was there at the top of the courthouse steps, smiling sheepishly at the thunderous crowd.

She didn't pause as she passed the police line. Hardly slowed down as she maneuvered her way through the congested sidewalks. Raced to the steps of the courthouse and took them two at a time.

She saw the spark in his eyes the moment he recognized her. Saw the joy.

The din on the streets grew even louder when he rushed down the steps to meet her. They hugged. Kennedy was crying, but it wasn't the suffocating sobs like what gripped her in the worst of her panic attacks.

"I'm so glad to see you." Reuben held her close.

Kennedy didn't have the voice to respond. She had spent nearly all semester in agonizing introspection, asking herself if she loved Reuben.

Tonight, she had her answer.

CHAPTER 30

"Ok, so what's the big surprise?" Kennedy asked. "Are we going to shop for books at Common Treasures?"

As hard as he tried, Reuben couldn't hide his smile. "Nope. Well, maybe, but we don't have time for that yet."

Kennedy glanced around at the lazy Sunday afternoon traffic, searching for clues. She and Reuben had always joked about riding the swan boats in Boston Common, but that was expensive. After her dad paid for Reuben's lawyer fees, Kennedy wasn't going to ask for anything extra for at least another month. And Reuben wasn't the type to have extra cash on hand. So where was he taking her?

Last night after his release, they'd been so tired they ate dinner together in the student union and then returned to their dorms where Kennedy slept for eleven hours straight. Today he'd told her to meet him at the library after lunch, but when she showed up with her calculus text and lab notebook, he made her take it back to her room. That's when he said he had a surprise for her off campus.

They still hadn't talked about much else besides school since his release. In some ways, they were like two kids at the end of summer vacation, not willing to acknowledge the obvious signs of autumn in the air.

They would have to talk. Soon. But neither of them was ready yet.

Once she heard about his diagnosis, Kennedy had been so terrified. So worried that even if Reuben was released from jail, things could never be the same between them. There would be long periods of awkwardness. Painful silences.

She had been wrong.

Delightfully wrong.

Reuben held her hand as they sprinted across the street. Would she ever forget the way his fingers felt interlaced with hers? Somewhere in the back of her head, she felt she was growing to understand Sandy's story about the little baby Spencer they cared for. She wasn't willing to admit it, wasn't willing to use terms like *dying* yet, but the story implanted itself to a safe spot in her memory banks, ready for her to pull out and examine when the time was right.

They sped by Common Treasures, the antique bookstore where they could lose themselves for hours wandering through old volumes and early editions of their favorite stories. Kennedy was laughing even though she didn't know what was so funny.

Reuben stopped in front of the Boston Opera House. "Here we are."

"What's this?" she asked.

Reuben slipped in line for call waiting. "Mr. Jefferson said your dad overpaid him. Said the case wasn't as hard as he'd originally planned once you found that video. So he gave me a check, said your dad would want us to do something fun together." He stepped up to the counter. "Two tickets for *Aida*. It's under the name Reuben Murunga."

"Really?" Kennedy squealed but wasn't embarrassed.

Reuben grinned and passed her a ticket. "I have a feeling we've earned this."

Kennedy had grown up seeing musicals in Manhattan — *Phantom, Les Mis, Cats*. Even after her family moved to Yanji, her mom would buy the DVD versions of the most popular shows and watch them with Kennedy on nights when her dad was working late. Kennedy knew musical theater had the power to impact your emotions, take you on a ride of thrills or excitement or joy. But she never knew it could do something like this.

She hadn't known much about *Aida* before the show came to Boston. She knew it was a love story set in ancient Egypt and that was about it. What she hadn't counted on was the sacrificial love shown between the two main characters — Aida, the Nubian princess who was willing to give up her relationship with her Egyptian captor in order to lead her people, and Radames, heir to Pharaoh's throne who forsook his birthright to help his beloved find freedom.

She assumed it would be a story of love fulfilled, but in reality it was the story of impossible relationships. In the final scene, both Aida and Radames were buried alive for their treason against Egypt. Was dying in the arms of your beloved more bearable than facing life without him?

As the curtain closed, she sat beside Reuben, acutely aware of his gentle expression and the tears on her own cheeks. It was stupid to cry. It was just a musical after all. Just a musical ...

She didn't talk on their way out of the theater. She didn't know what to say. She felt like a leaf, floating down a merciless current. The river forked just ahead, but she wouldn't know which route she'd take until it would be too late to ever go back.

CHAPTER 31

"That was a good show, wasn't it?" Reuben asked. They had stopped by Angelo's Pizza to grab a quick dinner before heading back to campus.

A good show? Kennedy wasn't sure that's what she'd call it. She needed more time to think through it all. Process everything she'd seen. Figure out what the musical was trying to say to her. She had this unshakeable sense that somewhere in Aida's tragic romance was a lesson, a warning meant specifically for her. Was she too stupid to discern what it was?

Or too scared?

Reuben ate surprisingly little. He reached across the table and took Kennedy's hand. It felt so natural. So comfortable. Why hadn't they done this sooner?

"There's something I want to tell you," he confessed.

Kennedy tried to look away from the melancholy sadness in his eyes. "You know you can tell me anything."

"I'm sorry I didn't mention everything sooner. I really am. It was ... it was stupid of me." He glanced down at the table.

She gave his hand a squeeze. "Don't worry about it."

"You shouldn't have had to find out the way you did. If I had just told you ..."

"I'm sure it must have been hard. You know you didn't have to keep it a secret."

He shook his head. "I didn't want it to happen like this." A pause. Something in the way he looked at her pierced her spirit. "I really care about you."

She stared at their hands clasped together in the center of the table. "Me, too."

He glanced up at her. Pain shot out from his eyes, lanced her own soul. "I'm going back home when the semester's over."

She already knew that he was spending his summer break back in Kenya. Why was he telling her now? Why did he say it so seriously?

She glanced at his uneaten pizza, and then she knew.

"I won't be coming back next fall." His words were like a concrete ball sinking into an infinite depth.

Did she dare ask? "Why not?"

He stirred the ice in his Coke. "My dad lost his job when the government turned over. I can't afford to stay here."

"I thought you had a full scholarship."

"It doesn't cover flight expenses and things." He didn't look at her. "My family just can't pay for all that right now."

She swallowed past the lump in her throat, unable to picture a single day at Harvard without him. "What about your studies? What about becoming a doctor?"

"I can take classes in Nairobi. It's no big deal."

No big deal? Maybe that was easy for him to say. Maybe he could move away without feeling as if his internal viscera had gotten dropped into a paper shredder.

She certainly couldn't. "Why don't you talk to Carl and Sandy? I'm sure they'll let you spend the summers with them. They won't even charge you rent if you just explain ..."

"That's not all." There was a strain in his voice she'd never heard before. "I'm doing this because it's the best thing for us."

His words were like a punch in the gut.

He let go of her hand and stared at the table. "The longer I stay in Cambridge, the harder it's going to be when I ..." He choked and took a sip of Coke. "I'm sick. I may have another year, I may have twenty. But one day, this disease is going to kill me."

"Everyone dies sometime." It was a stupid thing to say. She realized that as soon as the words passed her lips.

"If I had my way," he began, "if I could choose exactly how this story ends, it would mean you and me graduating, going on to medical school." He cleared his throat. "Together. But I can't drag you through that with me.

I can't risk getting you sick, putting you through ..." He stopped. "I have to go."

Did he mean at the end of the semester, or did he mean right now?

"People with HIV can still be in relationships." She didn't admit she had already done the research, already found websites devoted to helping couples where one partner was living with HIV. It wouldn't be easy, but it couldn't be as impossible as goodbye.

"I can't hurt you like that." He shook his head. "I won't." Tears streaked down his cheeks. She'd never seen him cry before. "Whatever happens, I need you to remember that I'm doing this for you."

Her throat seized up. "What if that's not what I want?"

"You have an amazing future ahead of you. A future helping others, healing others. You are the smartest person I know, the most talented. You're going to graduate from medical school and have your choice of any residency in the country. I'm not ..." He cleared his throat once more. "I'm not going to stop you from achieving that. I care about you too much. I ..." He let out his breath.

Kennedy leaned toward him, ready to catch his words.

"I just don't want to hurt you."

It didn't make sense. Five years from now, ten years from now, Kennedy knew it still wouldn't make sense. She should change his mind. Tell him how she really felt. Tell him all her dreams of medical school and residencies were pointless if he wasn't there by her side, goofing off with her in the lab, joking with her during their late nights in the library cramming for tests. She couldn't do any of that without him. Couldn't even make it through a stupid pizza dinner without crying.

She wiped her face. "You don't have to do this," she whispered.

He passed her a napkin. "I know. But I ..." His voice caught again. "I want you to make me a promise."

She glanced up at his glistening eyes. "Yeah?"

"I want you to promise me that you'll remember this. Remember what we went through. Remember how many other people's lives are torn apart by diseases. You're a brilliant student. You're going to be a brilliant doctor. And I want you to promise me that you'll help them. Help the others so they don't have to go through something like this."

Her throat threatened to clench shut. "And what about you?"

"I'm going back home. I'll still keep up my studies. I don't know how, but I'll manage. I'll read every single journal article on AIDS research. And the day there's a cure, the day doctors tell me this disease isn't a death sentence, the day they tell me I can have a family of my own without having to worry about infecting the people I love, if you haven't moved on, you'll be the first person I call. Deal?"

She sniffed, still unable to believe this conversation was actually happening. She had a better feeling for how Aida felt in that underground vault as the air supply slowly, mercilessly disappeared.

"Deal."

He reached into his backpack. "I got you a present."

Kennedy's hands shook as she unwrapped the small package. "*The Last Battle*?"

"You remember what they always repeat at the end, don't you?" he asked.

Kennedy laughed through her tears.

"Further up and further in," they said at the same time.

"That's the kind of life I want you to have. The kind with new adventures, new discoveries every single semester. Every single day. It's what you deserve, and it's more than I can promise you. I ..." He flipped the front cover open. "I wrote you a note."

Kennedy wondered how she was supposed to make out the words if her vision was so blurry. She wiped her eyes and read his inscription.

To my dearest friend Kennedy. Thank you for giving me the best year of my life. All my love, Reuben.

He had scooted his chair around so he was beside her now. Hugging her. Their tears intermingled on each other's faces.

"I wish you would stay here," she whispered.

He turned his face and kissed the very corner of her mouth. She couldn't tell if it was on her lips or on her cheek. She squeezed her eyes shut, begging God to pause time and let her and Reuben stay here forever.

"You know why I can't do that, don't you?" He kissed her once more.

Kennedy nodded. Some things didn't have to be said.